Whiskey Jelly Blues

9/26/18

Whiskey Jelly Blues

A Novel

Justin J. Murphy

Denny—
Full on mind blower—
+ I really want to listen
to "Althea" right now.
Cheers to being a truly
rad man.

Owl Canyon Press

First Edition, 2018

All Rights Reserved

Library of Congress Cataloging-in-Publication Data

Murphy, Justin J.

Whiskey Jelly Blues —1st ed.

p. cm.

ISBN: 978-0-9985073-4-7

2018939503

Owl Canyon Press

Boulder, Colorado

For Teesha, Queen of California

Bathroom Blues

Four chapters ago, she was on the floor of our bathroom, writhing in pain, blood spilling out from between her legs, the liquid spreading across the pale yellow tile floor. Four chapters ago, we were just married, living in a small cedar cabin near the beach in Los Angeles, chopping wood for heat in the winter, making love on our crimson couch underneath the skylight, underneath the moon, underneath a canyon of eucalyptus, oak. Now, we're gone, traded in the West for the East, and here we are, amid the early morning darkness of a July thunderstorm. 85 degrees outside. Humid. Too early to be sweating. I'm not awake. Not just yet. I sleep late because I go to bed late. Bartending pays the bills, gives me time to write, gives me time alone, gives me time to turn off my brain, space-out while the kooks on the other side of the stick spill guts about their girlfriends, boyfriends, husbands, and wives—mothers.

Phoenix, my wife, is already awake, curled up in a ball next to me. Don't ask how I know she's awake when I'm asleep. If you start asking yourself these questions, we won't get anywhere—we'll be sitting here together running in circles, hours on end with no conclusion, and I'll keep shaking my head because you won't just cool it down and let me get on with it. She's awake because she works in the morning—she's got a stooge job. A nine-to-five, constantly surrounded by bozos and the infinite gray, blue-green stain resistant carpet.

She's awake and she's next to me, curled up in a ball, her high cheekbones and full lips hidden underneath the tent of long brunette hair she's created for herself, kneeling on the mattress, her face buried in the pillow. She suffers from mysterious stomachaches, aches so powerful she can barely breathe, barely move, barely function when they come on, aches so terrifying, tears ball up and explode in her eyes.

When she's curled up in a ball, in the fetal position, crying in misery, I'm immediately transported back to that day in the bathroom. I looked at myself in the mirror with her at my feet, running my sweating hands through my long hair, twisting my mustache until the hairs started falling out, worried, guilty—I knew she was dying. I remember looking in that mirror and thinking, "I look like a Hells Angel." I was wearing tight dark blue Levi's and a denim vest, ripped up black t-shirt and beat-up black leather boots—my tattoos sparkled as if they were made of fresh ink, the letters and images slippery, wet as if drawn by the tongue of a unicorn. My wife was dying in front of me and that's what I was thinking—"I look like a Hells Angel"—a defense mechanism, or a moment of clarity, or the only thing I could think to calm myself down, to suppress the grief of watching her in so much pain. It's better to think of anything else in the world, a typhoon, a tsunami, a falling leaf, *Gilligan's Island*, *Gidget*, a Hell's Angel, than to think of the person you love lost in a tornado of pain in the middle of an abortion.

I've always wanted a motorcycle. I'd look good on a motorcycle. She'd look good on a motorcycle. I'd replace responsibility with pure freedom on a motorcycle. I'd twist myself down the road, flying high, fourth gear with nothing behind me, no past or present, on a motorcycle. When I told my wife I didn't want kids and I wanted a motorcycle three months before our wedding she told me, "Go ahead and get one. But I won't change your diapers when someone crashes into you and crushes your insides and your dick stops working." She didn't mention anything about the kids. I don't think she wanted them back then, or maybe it was just too late to have the discussion, or maybe she thought she had time to convince me otherwise. Or maybe it's because we had already invited everyone and bought the kegs of PBR and made the mix cd's. Or maybe it's because she loved me so much, she didn't care.

I wish instead of bloody bathroom memories and piercing stomachaches this story could begin with an epic blue wave filled with rainbow colored fish, a broken surfboard, a sun-kissed smile, and the remnants of a pina-colada dripping from a mustache. That seems more enjoyable, like a Jimmy Buffet song thrown in a blender and mixed with *Endless Summer*, set to "puree," a cocktail of happiness and irresponsibility, relaxation and coconut suntan lotion. I might be able to come through for you on a pina-colada dripping from a mustache, but the rest, well, I don't surf and there aren't any epic waves where we are now—just some docks in a shady part of town. And the sun—we haven't seen that in days. It rains in the summer over here, thunderstorms with raindrops the size of barn owls, torrential downpours, 99% humidity, hot, wet, mosquitoes and black crawling insects everywhere—some say the spiders can walk on water here—Jesus spiders. And we have to go to work in this rain, rain where the world turns to static, rain where the shapes become blurs, colors take on deep shadows, windshield wipers slap left to right, full speed, all the way, flash flood warnings, pull over on the highway, too difficult to see.

She's a senior copywriter at a PR firm, and she makes decent money, stuck underneath the buzz of electric light all day, writing puns and press-releases. Regardless of the loot she brings in, she hates her job at the PR firm. She hates her cubicle at the PR firm. She hates her co-workers, her bosses, the parking lot, and the security guard at her PR firm. She hates the bathroom stalls at her PR Firm—no toilet seat covers! Can you believe that shit?! "It's an east coast thing," she says. "Fucking east coast." She's an aspiring writer, like me, but she doesn't write because she spends her entire day writing. I tell her to bartend, but she can't—doesn't know what goes in a Vieux Carre—and besides, I don't want her to—I know what goes through the minds of drunk men at bars and I know their hands get a bit fidgety, like airborne darts, around an ass like hers. The truth is, she's good at copy, whether she likes it or not, "the best in the biz," her old boss once told her. It beats the hell out of waiting tables, no doubt about that. Can't put your Masters degree to use waiting tables. She got the job out here when we were still in Los Angeles and she took the job because it was as far away from that bathroom, from that day, from that grotesque start our marriage got off to as we could get. Smiles are hard to come by these days, but when they do happen, it's like sucking on the end of a rainbow.

I wonder how long a human can go without an orgasm. I presume she masturbates in the bath at night, thinking of that Australian actor who plays Thor, or maybe she's just reached a point in her life where orgasms are pretty low down on her list of things to do. There're wars everywhere. Israel, Ukraine, Syria, Afghanistan. Global warming. Drowning Polar Bears. Even the Sharp-Tooth Double Hump Llama is going extinct, no more Blueberry Foxfire to eat. I read an article the other day saying the Gobi desert is growing, and that there's a large sea underneath, ready to swallow up the entire mid-section of China. And no one seems to care.

She's got a deadline looming over her head for Rudy's Candy Tampons, a big press release—I know she's been pretty stressed out about that—how do you market candy tampons? We talk about it incessantly when we have a day off together and I sure as hell can't figure it out—"When your period gives you a lemon, suck on it!" Menstruation and candy don't work too well together—like peanut butter and champagne. It takes a genius to make those two things work, and she's a genius, but even geniuses can't figure everything out. Sometimes geniuses don't feel genius. Her eyes kind of buckle like a bridge when she gets stressed, and no amount of California Cabernet and West Tennessee smoke can unbuckle them, straighten them out, let the good thoughts pass from one eye to the other. She's far off, distant, caught on the other side of the bridge and I'm over here, waving back, wondering when and if she'll get here.

I can feel her shuffling back and forth on her knees next to me, so I let one eye open, take a look, see what's happening. I don't know why I pretend to sleep even after I wake up in the morning. It's a secret, between you and me. We all need secrets to keep our souls intact, to keep something ours, to keep the insignificant things sacred—I bow to my own shrine of insignificance—I pretend to sleep when she's awake in the morning, and I sneak a beer into the shower every now and again, and then I hide the empty beer bottles behind the hundreds of records laying on the ground in my "writing office"—Poco—she hates them— "Without Neil Young, Richie Furay is shit." We don't have to share everything. If we shared everything, we would cease to be ourselves, we would have no mystery. We'd all be an open book, and everyone would be able to dive in and dissect, conjure up and disregard errant hypotheses. How much fun could that possibly be? To sit and look inside of someone's mind, to know everything about them, never have to discover it for yourself, never have to sweat in a dark drunken bedroom, naked, wondering, with half a cigarette dangling from your mouth? My name is Cassidy. I have a 6 ¾ inch penis and every six months I have a flare-up of genital warts—plus I suffer from high blood pressure, even though I'm thin—it's stress. That was too easy. You didn't have to work for anything. Work makes information like that more precious. You should have seen the girl I got genital warts from—now that's a story, another blues story. Hell of a ride.

With that one eye open, I take a look around the bedroom. The walls are colored canary yellow because canary yellow makes you feel positive in the morning. I'm positive this morning sucks. I can feel the edges of my limbs tingling with the overload of alcohol, the sugar crash. Where are my arms? What happened to my legs? I should never drink mai-tais with Bulch—he puts too much coconut rum in 'em.

There is a set of four windows directly in front of our bed, looking out on the covered porch and into the front yard where the roses grow. We've been here almost a year and yet, I've never smelled them. I stick my face into those giant red petals and inhale—nothing. They stand tall out there like a big "fuck you" to beauty, middle fingers outstretched towards the laws of nature. Not all roses smell—what a terrible realization.

I scan the room, check the antique brass clock on my nightstand—6:03. I've been asleep for an hour or so. I can see my wife, moving back and forth, rocking herself like a baby, trying to ease her stomach pain. It's too much. It's sad. It's heart-wrenching. I open both my eyes, roll up onto my elbow, and lay my hand on her spine. "You okay?" I say in a somnambulist half-drunken drawl, accompanied by a yawn and a voracious scratch beneath my scrotum.

"No," she says. She pulls herself up, moves to the bathroom, flicks on the light. She gets frustrated by the stomachaches, doesn't want to talk about them—I need to tell myself it's not me that's causing them, but I know it is. Me and my mouth, my tongue, spitting out stupid things, promises I can't keep.

I like our bathroom. Wooden walls. A clawfoot tub. Turquoise tiles. A portrait of Captain Kirk with his phaser drawn. A three-foot tall statue of Jesus wearing a "Hawaii '83" t-shirt. My generic brand shampoo container is actually filled with vodka—Phoenix would never touch it— her hair is too beautiful, silky, Sicilian for that drugstore bullshit. She stands naked, her small frame ignited by the yellow light. She lights a candle on the edge of the sink, pulls a half-smoked joint from the soap dish, lights it up, pulls the smoke in, holds it deep in her lungs until her eyes start to tear, and lets it all out in a big purple plume, a cloud twice the size of her. She turns the water on for a shower, steps inside. The smoke trails out of the bathroom, hits my nostrils. The scent isn't the smell of California grass, the Northern Lights, the Skywalker, the OG Kush, but at least it's the scent of grass. I used to grow organic OG Kush in my yard in the canyon back home, sell it to a dealer in town for a solid amount of dough, then blow it all on a biannual trip up to Santa Barbara with Phoenix, eating crab sandwiches and sipping beers until it was time to make love, do it all over again, three days at a time, four if we were too hungover to drive home.

Hangovers. It's part of being a bartender, like amphetamines are part of being a trucker. But this hangover this morning isn't totally a result of the bar. Aunika, my childhood best friend, blonde, blue eyes, legs as long as the Golden Gate Bridge, and the face of a Swedish supermodel, had a party at her artisan donut shop last night, out here in the east, celebrating her *Independent Weekly* Newspaper award—"Best Artisan Donut Shop— La Di Donuts." How can a woman knee deep in lard have a body like that? God only knows. Bikram yoga? Is God Shiva?

I worked my shift, cut out a little early because Cherise, the other bartender, wanted the extra loot, got to Aunika's donut shop around 2 am, and found her, alone, sitting on the glass display counter above a pair of candied arugula and turbinado strawberry bear claws, a bottle of bourbon in her hand, a little booze dribbling down her chin, bare feet dangling, one of the straps of her crème colored dress fallen, draped down to her elbow, hair a ratted golden mess, sky-blue eye-shadow smudged and smeared underneath her eyelids. Cesar, her boyfriend, had made an ass of himself, got drunk, and told everyone Aunika had slept with thirty-one men. We talked about Cesar for a few minutes, "The number is actually closer to forty," then reminisced our childhood, the time when we were four and we locked ourselves in a closet and took off our clothes, stuck our fingers in each other's bellybuttons.

Phoenix and Aunika are friends—they've gotten drunk together, they've thrown up together, they've danced ironically to Beyonce together, they've danced completely seriously to Richard Hell and The Voidoids together. It made me happy when they met and hit it off six years ago over sushi and sake bombs in a strip mall in North Hollywood.

They talked about Paris mostly, what they love best about that city—the streetlights—strange women, pure individuals. I've never been to Paris, but I can say with a degree of certainty the streetlights wouldn't be what I'd remember, what I'd internalize. I smiled, sat in silence, let them move forward into friendship while I crushed 22's of Sapporo, and face-fucked salmon and spicy tuna rolls until my stomach pushed up and over my brown leather belt, burping up towards the moon.

I listen to the water drip from Phoenix's body, fall from her hair, slip through her breasts, pound down into the tiny stones beneath her feet. She's my own private waterfall. I watch her scrub, shave her armpits, piss. She turns the water off, dries herself with a towel, moves back into the bedroom giving me a small unassuming smile.

"Feel any better?" I ask.

"A little." Her eyes look tired, yellow underneath. Olive skin has a tendency of turning yellow with exhaustion—I've seen it all too often with her now.

"You sleep?"

"Not really."

She pulls on a gray skirt accented by orange diamonds and a loose pink v-neck t-shirt, ties her hair up into a bun, pushes back some loose tendrils into her scalp, holds them in place with bobby-pins. Although she's horribly mismatched, she's still too beautiful to be wearing such a tight skirt and loose top—she leaves nothing to the imagination. When she bends down to grab a pair of underwear, I can see all of her chest. She slides the underwear up and into her crotch, her hips like jagged rocks, jutting out from her body, dangerous, sharp, a sailor's doom.

"Candy tampons?" I say.

"The Life-Savers of feminine hygiene," she responds. She heads back into the bedroom, lights that j, takes a big toke, jumps on the bed, and blows it right in my face. "Go back to sleep, my love. And write me something good today."

"I'll write," I promise her.

"Write me a best-seller so we can move to Santa Cruz, get ourselves a wooden home in the canyon, stare at the ocean from our Jacuzzi. I want cedar walls and a redwood backyard, and an outdoor shower."

"Gotta sell a shit ton of books for that."

"Then sell a shit ton of books."

"I'm not sure what to write."

"You know what to write." She pulls herself out of bed, sets the joint down on her mid-century vanity, slips on her sandals that give her an extra two inches. I hear her heels pound against the wooden floorboards as she moves into the kitchen, pours herself a cup of coffee.

"Wanna have sex?" I yell to her. "I'll be quick. Like five seconds."

I listen to the coffee pour into the mug, waiting for the response. "Maybe tonight."

I drop my head into my pillow, inhale, exhale. "I love you," I say, but she doesn't hear.

She arrives in the doorjamb, a banana in her hand singing a melodic chantey in French—"Moi j'ai une toute p'tite ligne de chance." She takes a bite, chewing loudly, observing my unmoving body, face buried. "You drink too much last night?"

I keep my face in the pillow, nod my head.

She eyeballs the joint, teetering on the edge. She moves over to it, takes another drag. "You gotta cool it on the booze, babe." She exhales. "You need your brain cells." She drops a hip, lets her eyelids twitch for a moment. "I really want oranges. We need more oranges in our life."

I roll back over. "Hieronymous Bosch." I say. And she smiles. She likes that Henry Miller book.

"Go back to sleep."

I nod my head, roll back over, cover my head with the sheets. I hear her footsteps shuffle towards the door, a pause, a split second of silence, and then she screams, "I hate my job! I hate my job! I hate my job!" at the top of her lungs, curling her hands into fists and punching down at the air towards her knees, whipping her head around the empty space surrounding her. She takes a deep breath, opens the door, and I hear those heels thumping their way onto the porch, down the steps, the door of her '84 BMW open, the engine ignite, and then, she's gone. I close my eyes, fall back asleep, dreaming of two of her doing things to me that would make some of you blush and some of you stand and applaud. But that's for me to write, and for you to read, dive in and dissect, later, maybe.

Turn Your Spaceship Around Blues

Cliff is my best friend. He lives in Los Angeles and sends me text messages that to you, probably don't make any sense. His texts are like an alarm clock for me. He's usually going to bed around the time I'm waking up, on account of the three hour difference between coasts and his drug and alcohol intake.

I'm still asleep, but I hear my phone vibrate on the nightstand, rumble hard, making the bell in my antique alarm clock quietly sing. I throw my hand out from under the pillow, grab the phone. I always check my phone when it vibrates when I'm asleep—what if Phoenix has a flat tire? What if aliens just invaded? What if China has been swallowed whole by the sea underneath the Gobi Desert and they're so upset they've launched a missile strike at The East, and all the Polar Bears are swimming here, and the Ukraine and Afghanistan, Syria and Canada have decided to attack as well?

I grab my iPhone and read, *I want to hand design a pair of diamond shoes for a regular caterpillar.* It's Cliff. No one else could think like this. No one in the world could be thinking of diamond shoes for a caterpillar.

I send a reply. *I want to smear chicken liver on the window of a donut shop, then tell you how much I like foie gras in an email from Istanbul.*

We are masters of non-sequitur, and if you don't believe me, just ask the king of non-sequitur, Reggie DuPont. He told us we were—gave us a certificate and everything.

When Cliff was a boy, he used to dress up like a cowboy and attend a renaissance faire type gathering for people who also liked to dress up as cowboys. He had two six-shooter cap guns in each holster on each hip, and he could twirl them around his trigger finger like the ghost of John Wayne. He shot his caps loud into the air and was pretty good at jumping in and out of a lasso while smiling like a pageant boy. On weekends, his dad used to dress up in a homemade Batman costume and sit at various bus stops around the city as if it was no big deal. He never rode the buses or went anywhere. He just sat there in his Batman outfit, the fat of his gut hanging out over his hand-dyed navy blue Fruit of the Loom briefs. People used to ask to take pictures with him when they got off the bus. Cliff would blow the imaginary smoke from the tip of his pistol as he watched the flicker of cameras pop around him.

Cliff hides forties of malt liquor in strange places, like behind the pillows on his couch, or taped to the exhaust pipe of the car he once owned but is now impounded. He puts vodka in his cans of cola in an effort to be discreet. He takes shortcuts through bars wherever he goes, and drinks whatever unattended beer or cocktail he can find in the twelve seconds it takes him to get from the front door to the back door. As a result, he's been 86'd from a number of bars, holds the "Guinness Book of World Records for 86's," he says. Look no further. He's more interesting than everyone you know.

It's noon and I'm hungover and my eyes feel dry and red, hanging from my face as if red were a heavy emotion or a raw death feeling. I wake up and take off my polka-dot pajama bottoms, stare at myself in the mirror. My penis looks healthy, well rested—hasn't been put to work in awhile. I like the way I look in the morning before I eat. I can suck my gut in if I haven't eaten, all the way in, so that the skin in my abdomen forms to the contours of my ribcage. My love handles disappear. I count calories every day because I drink too much, read too much, write too much, and eat too many pretzels and I'm pretty sure that's what needs to be done if I want to keep living this lifestyle and remain fit. I've decided today I'll eat a few pretzels with organic hummus and a green onion, maybe half a string cheese log. I'm glad to have made that decision. Now I can open up the refrigerator and drink a beer. Two hundred.

I pop the top off and it becomes immediately apparent that I'm still drunk from the night before, my feet kind of shuffling underneath my body, trying to find balance. I pull on a pair of tight black pants and place a Gun Club record on the turntable. As soon as the electric guitar slams into the air around me, I throw myself hard around the room, rocking out to the post-punk country of Jeffrey Lee Pierce, keeping my beer intact as I do so, my hair tumbling around my forehead, tickling my shoulders.

If I ever lie with you again/ I pray I do not sleep
If I ever closed my eyes again/ I'd realize what you are to me

Dancing to the Gun Club is great for hangovers, better than French fries and pancakes, biscuits and gravy, a side of bacon, blueberry-spinach juice, wheat grass. I'm sweating as I look out the window at the driveway. Sometimes the young housewife a few doors down in tight pants, red lipstick, and a Misfits t-shirt will walk past our house, hear the racket, and look inside wondering what kind of anarchy is occurring within the walls. I dance harder when I see her peering in, her eyes opening up at the sight of me—who is this wild man? This rock and roll aborigine? I wonder about her husband. He probably has a real job downtown or works for an independent publishing house, stuck inside a renovated warehouse, staring at the brick walls and exposed heating and air ducts, spitting wit even though no one cares. He eats cream of garlic soup for lunch and sometimes sneaks a single bottle of craft beer down his gullet before getting back to his Aaron Cometbus manuscript. He probably has an ironic mustache and knows a thing or two about Descartes, or at least pretends to. I bet his wife makes jewelry. They probably have a single friend who's pretty and platinum blonde and works at a boutique fashion

21

shop, or bartends at a bowling alley near The Docks, even though she has a Masters in Art History from Columbia.

I've never noticed flowers in the east. If they're here, they're hard to notice. I think I miss most the smell of orange blossoms and jasmine vine. California is made of those two fragrances, the entire 840 mile coastline soaked in it, wrapped up in it, so dense that when you cruise up Highway 1, the old Pacific Coast Highway, you carve right into it like a knife through a piece of apple pie.

My grandmother and grandfather had a home in Tarzana, the San Fernando Valley, Los Angeles, before they died. Their entire backyard was an orange orchard, with jasmine vines winding their way up the backside of the house, into the chimney, crossing the roof, dripping dewy sweetness down my face in the springtime. I miss my grandparents. They were from South Dakota and had no choice but to go West, hunting rifles over their shoulders, pool cues on their arms, goodbye to pheasant and wide open spaces, haystacks and rivers. Los Angeles must have looked like some strange steaming oasis in the middle of a barren desert to them. It probably still does from where they are now.

As I mentioned before, there're some roses outside our front door, beyond the rocking-chair porch, but they have no scent. I've fed them rose food, trimmed the dead stems and leaves. But still, the snow, freezing rain, sleet, heat, mosquitoes and giant flying cockroaches of the east must have sucked the marrow out of them. They are bright red, sticky, and should blast an aroma that can be identified a mile away, but instead, the absence of scent only makes me think of failure and fatigue, sickness, indignation, apathy. I flick the aphids off of the buds every now and again because I like the way they sail through the air to the ground, little green snowflakes of insects. If the day keeps going like it is, I'll probably get nice and drunk and hunt for a ladybug, then take the ladybug and place it on one of the aphid filled buds, and watch the massacre begin. Goddamn roses don't know how much I do for 'em.

I readjust my penis in my tight pants because my junk is getting scrunched-up like the face of a Persian cat. These pants are made for both women and men, they are asexual, or unisex, whatever. I bought them from American Apparel because my wife told me they were adequately priced and made of quality cotton and would make my dick look bold. I personally prefer old Levi 646's with flared bottoms or beat-up 517's with worn knees. Phoenix and I used to wear bell-bottoms in California, running through the avocado groves, comparing Syrah's and Pinots and Cabernets, getting our skin bronze. I rarely wore a shirt out there, out west, in the oasis. Wearing a shirt didn't look right. I could blend in with the dirt and the bark and the sunshine, be a natural child.

I don't wear a shirt today. I open a can of root beer, take a few sips, and replace what I've drunk out of the can with a healthy dose of vodka. I don't know who I'm hiding the vodka from, but, like I said, it feels good to hide something nonetheless. Maybe I'm hiding it from you and doing a terrible job of it. Fuck it.

Cliff was married once to a beautiful girl with sad eyes and strong hands who taught piano and could recite Dylan Thomas upon request. Cliff told me it's a necessity for a man to keep secrets—that's how his marriage lasted as long as it did. He said it's part of our nature to keep secrets, keeps us individualized, gives us something our own, something to live for or laugh at when all else fails. He told me he used to go to the gym to work out, but when he'd get home and his wife would ask where he was, he'd come up with a lie about being at the post office or picking up a loaf of bread. At the time, he couldn't fully comprehend his compulsion to lie to his wife, why he never told her the truth about the gym. She would have been happy for him, glad he was trying to work off his beer gut, attempting to participate in society. But eventually, it got to a point where he couldn't remember all his lies anymore, and she kept catching him with forties behind the pillows and taped to the exhaust pipe. He's divorced now and sends me these text messages that are always three hours too late. I have to remember his words would make more sense drunk at five a.m., than hungover at eight.

Cliff: *The last chance burglar brought home a thick slice of cheese to feed his lamb with.*

Cassidy: *The egg sucker found intelligence underneath the partially weatherbeaten rock. He was somewhat excited, but not enough to mention it.*

Cliff has a handsome, rugged face, a hairy goatee attached to a thin, perpetual beard and uses the inflection of his voice to make it seem as if the entire world and all its inhabitants are a joke. I wish I had his disposition and wherewithal, his ability to not give a fuck, but give a fuck simultaneously. He can stay drunk, and he can live hungover, his body moving in waves of pain and pleasure, mixing pills and drugs and booze all day until achieving the right balance, the sunset blur, the perfect stone. If he were here, he'd be dancing with me to the Gun Club right now. He'd probably take off his shirt and rub his wet beer belly against my sucked-in stomach and nuzzle his hairy face into my neck. We'd sweat profusely together and probably massage each other's shoulders, pushing hard into the tissue with our thumbs. We're not gay. We're more like two Indian men holding hands in Calcutta, or like two plastic army men stuck in the same toy-box, stacked on top of each other.

Cliff: *Lets put a crayon behind our ears and invest in gold stock. Make sure you close the garage door so that the moon can't get out.*

Cassidy: *Let's create a sour cream company, then sell it, then tell everyone we used to own a sour cream company.*

Cliff is covered in tattoos—mostly bunny rabbits—that his brother draws. His brother is somewhat well known, a bit of a celebrity in the artistic community of Los Angeles for his bunny rabbits. He's sold nearly every painting he's ever created, all of which are bunny rabbit themed and feature the creatures in various anthropomorphic activities. For instance, sometimes the bunnies are racking lines of coke, and other times they're slamming H and nodding out, and still, other times, they're at a grocery store piling packages of lamb shanks, one atop the other, onto the checkout counter. Ha! It's funny to think of bunnies eating lamb. That's why Cliff has a tattoo of a sharp-fanged bunny gnawing a fuzzy white lamb on his forearm. That particular painting sold for $750 last March at a gallery in Echo Park. Charlie, Cliff's brother, used some of the money to buy beer and cigarettes and an old brown cowboy hat with a big flat brim. He wears v-neck t-shirts almost daily, so he bought one from H n M on sale for four dollars as well. Charlie has a mustache, but it isn't ironic. He genuinely needs a mustache for his face to look balanced, otherwise it'd look as if his chin were a giant boulder teetering on the edge of his brother's name, like something out of a Wile E. Coyote cartoon.

Cliff: *Turn your spaceship around and let me climb on board your elephant trunk. Lets dance in the firework starlight near a crowded chinese restaurant.*

Cassidy: *use some nailclippers to sing Neil Diamond songs into, then act as if yer going to cut your toenails, but instead, go get an ice cream cone and call your mom. She wants to hear about it.*

The first side of the Gun Club record is over. It's 12:35 p.m. and I feel pretty good.

What Will They Say About Him Blues

My wife is at work and she's miserable and sad, and a bit too stoned—she can't seem to get the wheels turning on this candy tampon copy, lost in a gray haze, barricaded within her cubicle. It's easy to recognize her unhappiness when she's at work because she'll start text bombing me how horrible it is to write copy for candy tampons. My cell phone buzzes. *I fucking hate my job and I hate my fucking job.* Accompanying her text message is a photograph—a box of tissue next to a computer screen, behind a blank white coffee mug—the stark photographic representation of the desolation of office life—a desperate tundra of paper clips and pens, rubber bands and highlighters. She has no pictures on the walls of her cubicle—not of us, not of her, not of me, not of anything. She told herself she wouldn't work as a copywriter for long, so she didn't want to decorate her space as if she had made a permanent career choice and was happy with it, content to sit behind the desk, spew out words for products and people. She never wanted to commit, to move in, to accept public relations, to identify with it—she never wanted to answer the question "What do you do?" with "I'm a senior copywriter at a PR firm." No way. That answer is morose, uninteresting. She wants to be a writer, a novelist like Tom Robbins, a magical realist, a didactic existentialist, an experimental impressionist surrealist. She wishes sometimes she had a mustache and shaggy hair, and that she could build her own home out of found materials, do her own tile work, wood carvings. She's a feminist, and hates when people grin patronizingly when she tells them her dreams of someday building her own yurt, out there on the cliffs of Big Sur, getting up each morning to fish, living off the land, building fire and roasting vegetables from the garden, like something out of *Walden*.

Phoenix: *There's nothing tasteless about Rudy's candy tampons. I hate my fucking job.*

These text messages come from a big black pit in her soul, but, nonetheless, I have to grin every now and again. What our lives have become has some comedic value. I don't respond. I can't engage in the hopelessness of copy right now—too much else on my mind.

I open up a beer and begin dancing to side two, realizing as I take a sip that I poured myself another vodka inside a can of root beer only a few minutes ago and forgot about it. I take a pull from the can of root beer and chase it with the beer, hoping inside my mouth some miracle of gastronomy and mixology will occur, a new cocktail will be born. It doesn't.

Outside the window, I see my neighbor Charlie walking from his car to his house, the sun rays reflecting off the side view mirrors and into my eyes. Charlie is black, with long dreads, and wears glasses with circular lenses, like John Lennon. It's strange he's home this early in the afternoon. He works at an insurance agency somewhere, although I have to say since we moved here I haven't seen a single insurance agency anywhere. On weekdays, Charlie dresses in khaki slacks and dress shirts with ties, and he wears little brown loafers with argyle socks. His pants are hemmed too high, so it's easy to see what kind of socks he's wearing. I think it might be hip to hem your pants like that, but I'm not sure because if it were up to me, it would be 1972 and I'd be dancing through the trees of La Honda, CA with the Bear Republic flag wrapped around my torso in a pair of tight Levi's flares and acting as if I had a Sequoia for a spine and a Redwood for a cock.

On the weekends, in the spring, summer, and early fall, Charlie wears cut-off jean shorts and tank tops with Bob Marley's face on it. When it's cold, he wears old army surplus camouflage cargo pants and giant Rasta colored beanies that he tucks his dreads up inside. His head is three times its size in the winter than in the summer, expanding the height of his frame from 6'1" to 6'5". He has a beard, but keeps it neatly trimmed, perfect lines across the jaw, probably because he's required to uphold some corporate stooge dress code. Sometimes we say hello to each other and he'll offer me a joint, which I always decline politely.

I don't like smoking other people's pot on account of the last time I did, I tried to kill myself with a rather large butcher's knife. And a time before that, when I was single back in L.A., I accidentally smoked weed with speed sprinkled on top. I didn't go home for two days and was locked in a Koreatown loft with a girl who kept cutting her bangs shorter and shorter until she finally shaved her head, stripped naked and cried for seven hours. She spent the rest of the night painting her walls black and dancing recklessly to Roky Erickson and the Aliens records, screaming incoherent ramblings about ancient prophecies. "They drew the anteater on the wall in raspberry juice because they want to farm the gold from our souls!" It was quite a scene.

Black Charlie gets inside his house but leaves the door open. He comes back a few seconds later with an envelope in his hand and gets back into his car. It's probably his rent check. It's that time of the month.

I pick up the pace on my dancing, convulsing around the living room, spilling a little beer on the hardwood floor, and use the skin of my feet to soak it up. I let my hair rattle around my collarbones, tickling the skin, picking up the sweat that's brewing. My cell phone buzzes again. Phoenix: *Babe? Are you there?*

I hate the idea of dancing to such beautiful music made in another era pre-cellular devices while texting. I don't like the idea of mixing the truth of music with the bullshit of technology, which is also to say that today's music is total shit. To go further, I think the world has lost ninety percent of its beauty since the invention of the text message and the smartphone.

I just want to be here, right now, in this moment, alone, just like I would be without a cell phone. No one would know where I was or what I was doing. They wouldn't be expecting a response, or comforting phrases bookended by ellipses about their shit job, or reassuring words followed by a big red emoji heart about the future. I wait for the first song on the second side to finish, before lifting up the needle and picking up my phone—If I'm going to text, I must separate eras. It's the respectful thing to do. Rest in peace, Jeffrey Lee Pierce.

Cassidy: *Don't worry, baby. Everything is gonna be ok...I promise. My new book is gonna be raddddd....*

I drop the needle back down on track two and throw the cell phone into the bedroom, hearing a loud crash. The plastic case explodes off the body, and the phone slides underneath the bed into some profound and unreachable darkness. The phone is dead—for now.

I dance back over to the window. Charlie sits in his car with his head in his hands. I feel sorry for Charlie. He's a corporate stooge, like my wife, but probably would rather be listening to some classic reggae, The Ethiopians or Jacob Miller, in Kingston, drinking strong Jamaican coffee, and smoking sticky green buds the size of cantaloupes. Instead, he's originally from Queens and works at that damn insurance agency. Sunshine doesn't run through his veins, but I can tell his body wishes it did.

Even though I'm dancing, I can't stop worrying about my love and where she is and isn't and what she hopes for. She's alone, and small, and sitting in a horrible gray cubicle praying for an end to something that was supposed to be temporary, because I promised her it would be. I thought great things about myself then, and was confident and happy in my decision to never wear a tie, to never work in a cubicle, to never be something I promised to everyone, including God, I would never be.

Charlie's like the negative image of myself. And he's sitting in his car, crying into his dreads right now. It's possible he could be crying over a death in the family, but I prefer to interpret his tears as tears of failure, of a lost and dead identity, of cheap khaki slacks and number crunching, telephones and customer service, stale office birthday cakes and cheap supermarket coffee.

My wife is just like me, but somehow manages to survive within the bounds of her harsh reality. She knows she must work to afford life, that my bartending will no longer pay the bills when I get older and am not as fun and don't look as cool and the spare tire inevitably arrives around my gut because I can't metabolize the carbohydrates in an IPA or the sugar in an Old Fashioned. I try not to think of those looming dark days, when my arches fall and I need lumbar support and orthotics just to get behind the stick and stir a drink.

I head into the bedroom, flatten myself out on the floor, crawl underneath my bed, retrieve the phone and turn it back on. It immediately buzzes.

Phoenix: *I hate everyone I work with. Here's an actual conversation that just happened between two of my coworkers: "I like your sweater. You should do an Instagram installment of 30 days of sweaters."*

I look down and notice my knuckle is bleeding. I lick the blood from my knuckle unsure of why it's bleeding in the first place. Whatever. That's what happens when you dance hard, when you dance to break loose. For some unknown reason, I'm craving a La Di Donut, the one where they use bacon fat and cayenne pepper in the butterscotch glaze. I have no idea why I'm thinking of this. My wife is remarkably good at her job. If she liked it, committed to it, she would be unstoppable, rich— we'd have California, maybe.

Cliff: *Prance through the Everglades and pretend you are a pretzel. Share this information with a tortoise on your way back to liverwurst country.*

Cliff's words make me smile wide, a smile born of California and the coastline, heaven.

Jesus. My phone won't stop. Can't even dance.

Phoenix: I hate my job.

I love my wife. I wish I could apologize to her for being a writer with no other skills aside from bartending and drinking. A small tear hangs in my eye when I realize this—I'll never be an architect, or an interior designer, a contractor, a painter, a bar owner, a bear tamer, an East Congo expeditionary, a gold hunter. I look again at the sad and vacant photograph of my wife's cubicle. It has the makings of a modern tragedy. Her life and aspirations have been condensed into a box of tissue, an out of focus computer screen, and a blank coffee mug. I'm not even sure what the subject of the photograph is. There's no part of her in the frame—not a lock of hair, not an edge of a fingernail—which makes the mise-en-scene wholly disconnected from humanity, a soulless setting, impossible to identify with. I wonder how hard it would be for her to master pottery, become the next Josiah Wedgwood. I'd much rather receive a picture of her hands sloppy with mud shaping something beautiful, the flames of a brick oven behind her ready to solidify the vision, to make it tangible, to take what is in her mind and make it real and functional. I would roll her pots around my hands, press them to my stomach like a child. I would cradle her within my own hands, shape her, press her into my body, and maybe then I would see a smile and a text that reads *I love my job*. It's all my fault. I promised her great things and instead of greatness, I'm a bartender, a writer without a good idea, a child who impregnated her, then freaked out, lost it, had a panic attack, fell down to his knees and cried into her. "Oh God, no! We can't have a kid now! Oh my God! We're gonna die!"

I dance as hard as I can as I begin to cry, snot and beer dripping down to the wood below, too much for my feet to sop up, though I try. The lyrics hit me, scream at me from Jeffrey Lee Pierce's gut.

What will they say about him?/ What will they say about him?

What happened to my knuckle? It won't stop bleeding. Booze is bad for bleeding. It never stops when you're on the great bender, the bottle replacing whatever blood you lose, an endless cycle, like a storm born over an ocean over a rainforest.

I raise my hands into the air and wonder if God can see me now. If he can, I want him to turn me into a bunny rabbit eating a bacon butterscotch donut that's too big for me, so the scene looks at the same time both precious and heartbreaking, and I want my bunny rabbit wife to live inside of a warm clay pot with me and shyly shrug her shoulders and drag her hind paw in a circle in the dirt in front of her when she sees me struggling to pull the rest of the giant donut inside because she's in love with me and proud I went through all that work to bring home a giant donut for us to share. All we need is each other, but nowadays it seems less and less true, or perhaps, less and less possible. We need a lot more than each other to survive. We need artisan donuts to survive. We need insurance salesmen to survive. We need cell phones and text messages to survive. We need candy tampons and drunks and booze to survive. What will they say about me? What will they say about me? He was never an insurance agent?

Country Time Llama Garage Party Blues

I'm good and buzzed now, so I decide to take a shower, but then just as quickly change my mind and head over to my laptop in my office. When I'm feeling particularly absent from the world, unmotivated, and certain I'll become nothing more than a man whose funeral will be well attended and yet forgotten three days later, I Wikipedia other writers and artists to see how old they were before life started to turn around for them. In particular, I look for authors and musicians and painters who made a name for themselves after the age of thirty. Whenever I hear the number 30, I think of the 1960's "revolutionaries" Abbie Hoffman and Jerry Rubin, how they coined the phrase "Don't trust anyone over thirty," even though they were both over thirty when they coined the phrase. It's a self -reflexive statement, and I understand what they meant by it at the meta level. For example, I no longer trust myself. When I was twenty-four, I knew life was going to work out the way I wanted it to. I would live in California and listen to the Grateful Dead shirtless and dance through my Northern California ranch in the sunshine with a joint the size of a baseball bat hanging out of my mouth and I would be in love with a topless, long haired brunette who smiled with glassy eyes at the free choices she made in her life to get her there with me, twirling away on this ranch. I would internalize and digest her bronzed breasts in the sunshine and the first chapter of my latest novel would read something like, *"I watched her bare and bronze breasts heave to the music in the sunshine of our ranch in August. There was a glow about that day, dandelion pollen, bumblebees, red wine and a little grass as an appetizer to the main course of our life."*

In short, at twenty-four, I trusted I would be happy. Now, I don't trust anything, especially the myth of true happiness. I find I have to search for joy in the smallest minutia of life because the bigger things, like a perfect marriage and sexual bliss, infinity pools on the edge of the Amalfi coast, are just dreams, carrots dangling in front of me. I find happiness in my wife's fuzzy insides when she's on the great stone, how she becomes softer, caring, how she presses herself into me and every now and again wants me to kiss her with my tongue. I find happiness in a bottle of beer, or these moments, at home, alone, when I can be myself and for seventeen minutes my brain loosens its grip, forgets everything, becomes a pale blue sky. I don't have bills to pay or insects to kill in these seventeen minutes. I don't have a wife, responsibility, or rent in these seventeen minutes. The Italian coastline is erased from the globe—there's no need for it.

Abbie Hoffman and Jerry Rubin didn't trust themselves after thirty either. They probably started doubting the possibility of a revolution in America, of capitalism falling to socialism and the people governing themselves. Fuckin a. What a nightmare. They both died as shells of who they once were back in the 1960's, and they probably saw that coming when they hit thirty and the hangovers were ten times worse and their sex drive began to wane and hair started growing out of everywhere. The world is the world and turning it around, reversing its axis, is a pain in the ass—you gotta die trying to do something like that, and then, you're dead.

Chuck Palahniuk was in his 30's when things started to turn around. So was Henri Matisse. My mother continuously tells me "Thirty" is the new "Twenty" for our generation. But our generation is still gonna die around the same age as hers, so all I can gather from her statement is that forty years ago, people had ten extra years of not hating their lives as much as we do now. They could dance in the sunshine shirtless to the Grateful Dead on their Northern California ranches with a joint the size of a baseball bat hanging from their mouths. Today, those ranches are still owned by those ex-hippies and cost 2.5 million dollars even though they were bought for $25,000. And those joints? Shit. Forget about it. You'll never smoke a spliff the size of a baseball bat, so get it out of your head.

I look up Jeffrey Lee Pierce of the Gun Club on the computer and I read about him:

Jeffrey Lee Pierce
b 6/27/58 d 3/31/96 Aged 37 years
Fire of Love, first album, 1981, aged 23 years.
Released 7 albums in 12 years

He was younger than me when people started listening, and he died a little older than I am now. No, I wouldn't trade a successful early life for a premature death. Wait, fuck it, maybe I would.

I open my mouth because I haven't said anything in hours and it feels like my tongue is atrophying, shriveling, disappearing. "Hello, hello" I say to no one in particular. My jaw muscles feel good now that they've moved.

I hear the doorknob rattle at the front of the house—strange—who's trying to get in? "Phoenix?" I yell. I tip-toe out of my office, ducking down below the windows as I pass. I don't want to be caught at home in my tight pants shirtless and drunk by the housewife asking for sugar or a bottle opener—everyone in the neighborhood knows I have plenty of bottle openers—it's my profession.

I peak through the window, notice Charlie's still in his car crying, and find no one out on the front porch. I crack the front door an inch, using one eye to scan the scene, take in a full 180 degrees, and determine it's safe to open it fully.

On the doorknob is a flier for a gala event at La Di Donuts—the entire neighborhood is invited to witness the newest three flavors. Jesus Christ. Who cares about donuts? I don't. Silence. I think I can hear Charlie crying, so I close my eyes and listen. But it's just a combination of a bumblebee and the sound of traffic three blocks away.

"I am a lesbian ghost," I say to myself. I don't know why I say it. Radiant orange feather. Cottonball surprise. I have no idea why anything pops into my head. I run back into my office to write it down.

I open my Moleskine and scribble this: "If you want to follow the lesbian ghost into the donut shop, turn to page 89."

For a while now, I've been working on an erotic series of Choose Your Own Adventure books—Phoenix told me it's a rad idea, groundbreaking. But it wasn't until this very minute I realized how awesome it would be if there was a supernatural element to the books. I could combine the adolescent mysticism of something like the *Twilight* series with a gratifying masturbatory experience! Maybe I could even use their names, recreate the characters, set up an alternate world where Bella and Edward bang constantly. Anais Nin might write a back cover blurb for me, if she's still alive—I'll have to Wikipedia her as well.

Lesbian ghost orgy. It would work for both women and men, if I write it perfectly. The ghosts would have total power and control over the subject. You wouldn't be able to escape their pleasure. If you're a woman, you'd have to accept their advances, or face death. If you're a man, you'd just go along with it, turn to page 89. I don't know any man who would refuse an orgy with hot lesbian ghosts in a donut shop. Chocolate frosting? Vanilla? Sprinkles? Candied arugula? Bear claws everywhere!

I think of donut holes. Donut glory holes.

I realize this book might fail miserably. It's hard to be a feminist when you have a penis, no matter how sensitive I try to be. I decide I must ask my girl what she thinks about a lesbian ghost orgy, if it would turn her on, explain she'd be powerless in the situation but wouldn't be forced to do anything she didn't want to do, and in fact, the lesbian ghosts were there for the sole purpose of pleasing her, and not the other way around.

I have to stop and think for a moment, reverse the situation, put the shoe on the other foot. How would I feel about a group of gay male ghosts roaming around my Choose Your Own Adventure novel, forcing me into sexually satisfying situations? Would that be passable for a heterosexual male? Maybe the demographic for this book is women. I should probably take men out of the equation entirely, as readers. But I have to make sure. I take myself out of my head and meditate on these handsome gay ghosts, who they are, what they're doing. They must be attractive, and definitely older than me. I don't know why they have to be older. I just can't imagine my 24-year-old-self seducing the 30-year-old me. My 24-year-old self would stumble around, say something stupid and endearing, positive, and his body would be too small and eager. I don't want to trust the ghosts, I want them to be dangerous, a bad decision that feels right, so they have to be over thirty. If they were in their mid twenties, they might be full of the truth. If we're all over thirty, maybe we're not really gay because we're no longer accountable for our beliefs, we can't be trusted, we can't trust ourselves, our intuition. We can close our eyes and just let it rise, explode, and fall, like Vesuvius. We can bury our thoughts and the experience like Pompeii and move on to page 90. No one will ever know, unless someone like a therapist digs it up later and discusses latent homosexuality in an incredibly awkward and drawn-out session with each person grinning nervously and hiding sweating palms underneath their thighs.

Too much shit in my head. I need words. I need to hear something and converse with someone. I decide to call Cliff.

I grab my phone, find another beer, look for a bottle opener—where the hell are they? I have about a thousand but can never seem to find one.

Now, here's where you'll start to learn something more about me. This is where everything begins to get personal, where who I am truly shines through like the overlooked bass line at a live Jimi Hendrix and the Band of Gypsys concert.

For example, I've been dancing around the house, half drunk and shirtless all morning, but I'm no longer listening to the Gun Club. Time has passed. We are all older right now, and I'm becoming further and further away from thirty and therefore less trustworthy. I've taken off the Gun Club and replaced it with the Grateful Dead's Europe '72 live record and I've been strutting around in a pair of boots for the entirety of Side 3, which is the first side I put on because sometimes Side 1 is too predictable. I feel a horrible contempt for the East with the Grateful Dead on, this gray concrete bullshit of a place that won't allow me to have goats in my yard, and there aren't even any Redwoods to trip out on.

I've been using the word "dance" as well as it's other related forms because there's really no other word to describe what I've been doing, but I can say without any doubt that "dancing" is pretty far from what I've been doing. I have a terrible rash between my thighs from my jeans rubbing against my skin for nine hours bartending last night. This rash starts around the front of my legs, just underneath the sides of my scrotum, and extends around the back and halfway between my butt cheeks. This rash is literally so painful, that it's at least half of the reason why I decided to get drunk this early in the day. I've been gyrating around the house with my legs spread apart from each other so my thighs won't rub, causing me to look like a convulsing Yosemite Sam, dragging my feet and hunching over as I shimmy across the house. My legs have taken a shape beyond the geometric boundaries of bowlegged, my feet are turned outwards, and I have to sort of drop my hips down to keep my thighs far enough apart to avoid the horrendous pain of them scraping against each other. These tight pants I'm wearing were chosen more for their ability to minimize friction, and to keep the skin that is wet and partially bleeding from becoming completely ripped apart.

And you know what else? I like popping pain pills every now and again. And a little cocaine sometimes too. I keep everything in my secret hiding spot, a book in my office bookshelf next to my collection of Richard Brautigan, titled *Lust for Life*, of which I've glued the pages together, and cut out a hole out in the middle of the book in order to hide all the things that would give my girl a heart attack if she knew about. My first thought this morning was to grab a Norco and pound a beer and let the soft bliss spread down around my crotch, roll around my wrists, let me know I'm here. But I'm out of painkillers, and I've had a hard time enjoying myself on drugs in the East. Everyone seems to be on them, which makes being on them seem normal. And if normal is painkillers and cocaine, then I just want to go back to hacky-sacking on pot and waking up with gold in my eyes and sun in my hair. But still there is this rash. This rash that could end my hacky sacking days permanently if not treated.

This rash is so red and hot that I can feel the heat radiating from underneath my scrotum with my fingers three inches away. The humidity of the East is creeping in and with it, come the rashes. I miss the dry heat of California. I miss my thighs feeling like Dubble Bubble instead of Big Red.

I dial Cliff. I miss pressing the area codes of California. 323, 818, 213, 415. I miss the cliffs of the California coastline. I want to jump off a cliff. I see myself standing on his broad roman nose, one foot dangling, and then bringing the other along with it, out over the ledge and falling...3... 2...1...

.

.

.

Wham.

Cliff answers the phone without saying hello, naturally. That would be too uninteresting. He says instead, "The country time llama garage party," and says this sentence as if it were the name of a business and he were the receptionist.

"Persuasive goat moves from grass to lingerie," I say, and he thinks about a goat eating grass and then women's underwear, and he laughs with one second of laughter because he had a dream about a goat two nights ago—he gave birth to a goat through his dickhole, but it didn't hurt. He just laughed and couldn't believe it was happening. Don't question why I know what goes on in Cliff's mind—I'm warning you. I can easily turn this into a tale about a certified public accountant and his quirky yet predictable breakfast habits if you're not careful.

More about Cliff he doesn't know I know—

Right now, Cliff is shirtless like me. He traces the lines of his bunny rabbit tattoos with a finger dripping with sweet beer. He says certain beers carry an aphrodisiacal scent with them, especially those with lemon, coriander, and also those that are hop heavy—Cascade hops. Those particularly hoppy beers "smell like dank bud," he says. "That beer cologne works good with hippie chicks." His hypothesis has been tested many times, but has never been proven. Most of us have found patchouli and an eighth works just as well with hippie chicks.

Cliff is in a pair of tight Levis, which he loves to wear even though he has a healthy beer gut and plenty of hair crawling up his belly towards his neck. But Cliff isn't fat and I feel I must insist you not think of him as jolly, or round, or chubby. He has the body of a man, a protector, an ass kicker, a Hells Angel. He dresses well, is remarkably sexy, and looks like he could be in that band Turbonegro, with tight jean jackets and one inch buttons of obscure rock and roll bands that are rad and wear all black with tattoos and whiskey and nighttime and switchblades.

He wears a wide flat cowboy hat with a large two-inch button attached that reads "Not in My Pussy!" which has no frame of reference or meaning to him. The real question is, who wouldn't wear a giant two-inch button that reads "Not in My Pussy!"?

"Man, I wish I could just slide you into my gut right now and I could play with your curls and we could just drink so many forties," Cliff says. He pulls a big bottle out from behind a pillow, and I can hear his lips tug at the neck.

"I do too," I say. "You could baby bird the forty into my mouth." I tell him this and I honestly wish he could. I can picture myself with my head on his stomach, sucking down the beer from his mouth into mine. Cliff's body is like my mother's to me. It's firm but squishy and his hands have felt pain in all forms and because of this, they know how to get rid of it. "I went to Aunika's donut shop the other day, and people were talking about how to make toffee, and how toffee is the most incredible topping for a donut. And then this chick told me I look like a friend of Dash's, and I said 'Do you mean Dash Snow?' and she said 'Yeah, how many Dash's do you know?' I'm not even sure that guy is relevant anymore, you know, cuz he's dead and *Vice* never talks about his art anymore."

"Fuck that asshole. I wouldn't have paid anything to see any of his shitty collages. I wouldn't pay to see anything, actually. I'd rather buy an eighteen pack with that money. People would probably want to pay to see me after an eighteen pack. That's something I'd pay to see—me after an eighteen pack. Especially if there was a pile of tight dresses from the nineteen-fifties right in front of me. I'd put 'em on and run around in 'em without underwear in a low breeze and maybe sing Madonna songs but get the words wrong so everyone would get mad at me for not knowing the right lyrics."

Cliff uses the end of a roach clip to pick an apple peel from between his incisors. "I really feel like eating a burrito," he says. "I have an outlandish carne asada craving."

"I haven't had a decent burrito in a year. They don't even have avocados here. I used to climb avocado trees. I had sex on a rooftop draped in the leaves and branches of an avocado tree once. Salvadorans and Puerto Ricans have no idea how to make a burrito, and yet every Salvadoran and Puerto Rican hole in the wall in this shitty city makes em, but throws some weird, Central American or Caribbean flair on it, so I end up eating something that's more like Indian food wrapped in a tortilla."

"You know what would be a good name for an artisan donut shop? Mustard Brothers. No one would want a Mustard Brothers donut. Could you imagine? Every day, the Mustard Brothers would wake up super early and proudly put on their Mustard Brothers aprons and go to work and make their donuts and no one would come in and they'd have to just throw out the donuts at the end of the day. It'd be so sad."

"The Mustard Brothers would probably make a mustard donut. They're world renowned for their mustard donut. They use only fresh organic mustard plants from their rooftop garden for the recipe."

"That goes without saying. I mean, aside from their mustard donut, the Mustard Brothers would make an incredible donut, probably the best donut in all of Mustard County. And they'd make the mustard donut just for fun, you know, like when people order the Three Wise Men shot at bars because they're an asshole. A drunk guy would probably wander into the store one night with like three of his douchebag friends, and he'd get dared to eat a mustard donut, and he'd eat it, and then he'd get a free Mustard Brothers t-shirt for eating it."

"I'm gonna use the 'country time llama garage party' in my next book," I tell him, "Probably as a title of a chapter, or maybe the entire subject of the story. What kind of strange adventures could country time llamas get into inside of a garage?" I shuffle around the house hunched down with my knees spread out and using the broom as a microphone to lip the lyrics to "He's Gone."

Like I told you/ what I said/ Steal your face right off your head

"What are you doing right now? Are you slaving over a Mustard Brothers donut? You're out of breath or something."

"I'm dancing to the Grateful Dead, but I have a really bad chode rash so I'm exerting a ton of energy trying to keep my legs from rubbing together."

"I had a chode rash two weeks ago and I put Desitin on it and it totally went away in, like, three hours."

"I want to open up a Mustard Bros right next door to La Di Donut, but instead of selling lame arugula toffee donuts, I want to infuse my donuts with whiskey jelly."

"Whiskey jelly is genius. Why haven't we done that yet? We need whiskey jelly immediately. I can't live another second without whiskey jelly."

In the background I can hear another voice, and I assume it's Charlie, Cliff's brother. Yes, there can be two Charlie's in one novel, and I'll keep you straight—one Charlie is black and crying in his car outside my house right now, and the other Charlie is white, draws bunny rabbits for a living, has a minor heroin addiction he's been trying to kick for four years, and is currently drinking whiskey in California with his brother Cliff.

"Cassidy wants to make whiskey jelly," Cliff says to Charlie.

"Fuck yeah," Charlie giggles. Charlie giggles at lots of things. He looks just like Cliff, which is to say they are both handsome in the face, like bisexual Roman painters or asexual Turkish warriors, but Charlie is thinner and has longer hair and a beard. Cliff has a goatee, which looks good on him. It doesn't make him look like he plays adult league softball or takes his speedboat to Lake Havasu for spring break, chugging Budweiser cans and getting sunburned with a ham sandwich in his hand. No, he looks like a cross between the poet Gary Snyder and Marlon Brando in *The Wild One*, so if motorcycles were made of tree branches, he'd be riding one. On top, revving that engine, he'd shoot acorns at the forehead of that Lake Havasu douche.

"I want to make pomegranate jelly too," Charlie says, grabbing the phone and talking into it. I like his new dark blue V-neck t-shirt he bought from H and M with the money from his bunny rabbit painting, but I can't tell him that, otherwise it would seem insane. How could I know that? How could I be in control of so much of this world, yet so out of control that a rash between my thighs is absolutely ruining my life? Couldn't I be a rich musician if I wanted to be? Then this story would be about Cliff and Charlie and me in an awesome three piece band that makes Nirvana and Cream and Blue Cheer and all other three piece bands seem stupid because we shred electric garbage-can blues with lyrics about the dirty life of bunny rabbits and Charlie does all the original artwork for our record sleeves and t-shirts and we'd have a magazine dedicated to our political ideology of country time llama garage parties.

"Pomegranate jelly has nothing to do with whiskey jelly—you're missing the point," Cliff says to Charlie. "We're talking about the Mustard Brothers here. We're talking about the Mustard Brothers doing a jelly donut, but the jelly is whiskey jelly. How can anyone live another minute without a whiskey jelly donut in their hands right now? I can't bear even thinking about it. I can't even have this conversation any longer."

Charlie grabs the phone from Cliff and says very clearly and calmly, "I meant pomegranate vodka jelly. I love pomegranate vodka. Bunnies love pomegranate vodka."

He passes the phone back to Cliff, who says, "I don't know about vodka jelly, but whiskey jelly can go with anything. I mean, it'd be great on a fried green tomato sandwich or barbecue pork belly French fries, or a fucking braised short rib taco."

I find myself laughing at most of my conversations with Cliff and Charlie, and I find it's disparagingly difficult to say anything profound when the two of them get going. They are the gurus of nothingness, and out of this nothingness comes everything—an irreverence for the modern world, a "fuck you" to money, a slug of whiskey against doctors orders. I can't remember, but I'm pretty sure both of them have pancreatic issues, but don't care. They aren't in any visible pain, but behind both of their dark eyes lies their father in a Batman costume, and the two of them in their cowboy outfits firing off rounds of caps and wondering what the hell childhood was about and where adulthood is going. And I love them both for it.

"I'm getting Mustard Brothers t-shirts made," Cliff says, "and we're gonna throw out so many donuts."

The next track on the record is a song called Mr. Charlie. There are so many Charlies in my life right now, that it's borderline hysterical to me. I think about last night and the Mai-tais I was crushing and realize there was a Charlie at the bar as well. He was a small Phillipino man with feathered seventies hair that just touched his shoulders and the biggest 80's tortoise shell glasses frames I've ever seen. He looked like a certified public accountant working for a Columbian cocaine cartel in 1983. The Charlie with the glasses tipped me ten dollars on a thirty-four dollar tab, which seemed fair but not outwardly awesome. I couldn't see what kind of shoes Charlie was wearing last night, but I'm pretty sure they were made of Italian Gold Steer leather and make a sound like a waterfall when he slides them off his feet before making love to an imaginary Farrah Fawcett in a bed spilling over with black satin.

White Charlie back in California is wearing a pair of cowboy boots with black Levis 517's, tight around the crotch, boot-cut. He has paint all over the toes of his boots. He likes to paint in cowboy boots because he says art is like a shootout between him and the canvas—someone has to die in the process. It's the Wild West in his mind. And in his fingers. And in his paintbrushes. Always.

"What are you up to tonight," Cliff asks? "If I was you, I would head down to that crappy little donut shop and tell them what's what with the Mustard Brothers. I'd start getting in Aunika's head, but whatever you do, do *not* mention the whiskey jelly, because Charlie and I are getting started on that as soon as possible."

Charlie giggles in the background, "I'm gonna paint a bunny fucking you in the ass, Cliff."

And I know Charlie will do exactly that, because he immediately traces the outline of Cliff's body bent over at the edge of his canvas. He'll probably sell his brother's lovable rodent sodomy for $500.

"I love you, splendid eagle near a semi-circular body of water," Cliff says to me.

"I love you, slender salamander top hat," I reply.

"Stop being east and look out the window at Los Angeles, the west, where the air sucks and it's too expensive but at least there's a Mustard Brothers donut nearby."

I hang up the phone and pull down my pants. I can see a breeze has stirred up outside, so I open the windows, lay on my back on the floor, lift my legs up like a newborn getting a diaper changed, and let the cool air soothe my chafed thighs. I think of a new word I'd like to start using. Upcome. I hope the pashmina wearing, Misfits-t-shirt-loving housewife comes by right now, pops her head in the window and asks my aggravated chode for sugar.

Black Charlie Blues

Phoenix phoned a few minutes ago telling me she'll be home in an hour around 5:30 and also to mention she hates her fucking job. "I'm going to kill myself if I have to work here another year," she told me. "I'm going to hang myself in my stupid cubicle that has no pictures in it, and I'm going to dangle here for everyone to see how horrible this job is. I don't even have a window. I have no idea what today has been like."

"Today is shit," I tell her.

"You're not supposed to say that," she says. "One of us has to be positive."

"Feel like fish tacos?" I ask her. "I'll fire up the grill."

"Sure. And lots of wine. I need a shit ton of wine."

We tell one another we love each other. Her voice softens with those words, like I'm a cat she's coaxing towards her lap.

I've been thinking a lot about whiskey jelly for the past couple of hours and what it would entail. I slide onto the couch and listen to Gram Parsons and Emmylou Harris, daydreaming about a whiskey jelly fortune, where I would live, who I would be, what I would look like, and I have a dream answer for each of these hypothetical questions.

I would live in Northern California, but this Northern California would be the dream of Northern California and not the reality of Northern California. In my Northern California, it would be August always, the real estate would be affordable, my neighbors nestled away in the Redwood forest would all be artists and musicians and stoners with great vegetable gardens and we'd all have an addiction, appreciation, and understanding of Napa Valley wines, which would be reasonably priced, nothing over twenty bucks, of course. We'd grow marijuana that wasn't too strong, just right—enough to put butterflies in our brains—share our fresh fish, read old books of beat poetry, smell like the sea, let our hair grow long and tangled and light from sunshine. The land would be ours, with a river brimming with steelhead trout sliding and jumping between the mossy rocks. We'd eat avocados and oranges straight from the trees. I'd have an old railroad car on the bank of the river to write in, with a full bar cart and a view of the ocean to the west. Dancing shirtless in the grass would be a mainstay of life. The remaining members of the Grateful Dead will play a show on my land once a year. We'd use the river to bathe and splash around in. I'd be a philanthropist to mankind.

In this dream of Northern California, I'd be a writer, a poet, and a visionary. Women and men would strip naked and fuck and love to everything I wrote. I would induce a love filled inebriation within everyone. I would inspire the coming generations to write, to paint, to love, to share, and to rid themselves of the corporate world.

In this dream of Northern California I'd look exactly as I do now, except with better pectorals, slightly straighter hair, and without the zit on the side of my nose and maybe longer fingers, which for some reason I feel inadequate about.

We would feast on Mustard Brothers whiskey jelly donuts every morning. Or, at the very least, in my Northern California, I'd be drunk as hell in an Airstream in tight pants and my bare feet would be covered in grass and everyone else could go on fucking off.

The jasmine we planted seven months ago in our backyard here in the reality of the east has begun to bloom. I have a very keen sense of smell when it comes to sweet things. Even from the living room at the front door where I am now, I can sense the subtle aroma of the jasmine vine. I move to the back of the house and open the glass doors that lead outside from my office. It feels like those little white flowers have opened up like a rain cloud and dumped their sugary moisture onto my face. I immediately lick my lips and swallow—finally, a taste of home—the west inside the east.

I lay on the ground of my office amongst the dust bunnies watching a squirrel split a nut with his teeth and think about everyone else who has ever lied here and what they were thinking when they did. This house was built in 1881, and has most likely held conversations about every U.S. war, nuclear bombs, women's suffrage, black rights, JFK, RFK, MLK and everything else that was both meaningful and tragic in the past century and a half. There were husbands just like me lying on their backs and wondering what to do with their life, asking themselves when they would make love again, where they would end up, whether or not their children would die in a battle somewhere on the planet, whether it was worth it or not to have children, whether or not to quit or keep trying.

I feel a little guilty I've only spoken about donuts and whiskey jelly recently, and nothing else of much substance. There's too much else going on in this world to get tied up with donuts and whiskey jelly. I should be reading the newspaper, learning about the world. Did my grandfather lie on his back and think of donuts and whiskey jelly? Fuck no. He read the paper and headed west for work and joined the army to kick the shit out of the Japs and the Krauts. My generation has learned to be indifferent, not revolutionary towards the system. We need artisan donuts. We need mustache wax and tattoo parlors. We need strong hybrid strains of marijuana that make us see things that aren't really there.

I feel awkward, so I decide to masturbate, get the blood flowing. I close the bathroom door and draw the curtain over the window so it's relatively dark, giving me the illusion of isolation. I think about something I won't ever share and that's perverted but still totally legal and somewhat possible.

Done.

I cruise back to the front of the house, wiping the sweat from my cheeks, and check on Charlie. He's gotten out of his car and has stopped crying, but his face still looks as if it's been turned upside down. He's loosened his tie, unbuttoned the striped vest he was wearing and un-tucked his button-down. His glasses dangle from the neck of his undershirt. He carefully leans against the trunk of his car, slowly tilting backwards, until finally, he's horizontal across it. I think maybe it might be a good idea to walk over and see if he's all right. If I had to guess, I would say something unfavorable has happened to Charlie. Perhaps Jamaica has sunk into the sea along with China and his dreams of renovating a run-down coffee plantation and turning it into an eco-lodge with a two-mile long zip-line have drowned with it.

I grab two beers, twist open the front door, and take a step outside. It's humid and disgusting—my armpits are spitting. The roses have no scent, covered in the soot and shit and chemicals of this place. It smells like tires and then it smells like nothing.

Charlie doesn't move but I can sense he can see me coming. His pants are hemmed too high, and his socks have the faces of wolves on them. When I get to him, I kick the rear tire of his car and put my hand on his knee.

"Everything all right, brother?" I ask him. I feel strange calling him "brother" because he is a "brother." But I call everyone "brother" and if I didn't call him "brother" as well, it would be like admitting he's black and defined by color, and therefore somehow different than me. Although I think Charlie and I are quite similar in a lot of ways, especially in this seemingly awkward mental breakdown he's having, which I myself endure quite frequently on account of my anxiety disorder.

"Hey man," Charlie says. He pulls himself up without using his hands, effortlessly. I know Charlie has some strong core muscles because I've seen him hacky-sacking in his driveway on weekends, and he can get pretty high up in the air on some of his tricks, and he has impeccable control over his body. One time I saw him kick the sack up into the air, do a one handed cartwheel and catch the bag between the arches of his feet.

"Want a beer?" I've already started untwisting the bottles, so he really has no choice in the matter.

"Yeah, that'd be nice."

We take a swig. Charlie's body looks beaten. It hangs on him like chains.

"Got fired today," Charlie says, looking away from me. A tear wells up in his eye and I can tell he's got a lot riding on this job at the insurance agency.

"That sucks man, sorry to hear that."

"I got child support to pay," he says, then looks to me in a way that asks the question, "How about you?" Do you have child support? Are you a man yet? Do you have any responsibilities beyond getting drunk on a day off and dancing all day to obscure bands? Do you have any idea how badly I wish all I had to do was bartend three or four days a week and listen to the Grateful Dead?"

"That's tough," I say in response, shaking my head. "Brutal, man."

Charlie drinks half of his beer in one gulp. "All I ever wanted to do was to just get the fuck out of Queens and get to Manhattan and then when I got to Manhattan, all I wanted to do was get the fuck out of Manhattan. Now I'm here, far from Queens, and I just want to get the fuck out of here. I don't know where to go next, and I don't know if there's a place on this planet I want to be. Things get tighter and tighter the further I try to get away."

"You could cruise down to Jamaica," I tell him. "Eat lobster right from the sea."

"Fuck Jamaica, man. Are you kidding? That place is so screwed up and violent. I don't even want to go there. I hate the beach."

I'm so wrong about Charlie. I suppose when I see the colors of the

Rasta flag on someone, I just assume the gold in it represents sunshine and beaches, the red is an undiscovered sunset, and the green is a wet fruit stuck in your teeth, and that everyone who loves reggae must love all of those things. Jah see and know, right?

"How bout Northern California?" I throw out to him. Charlie hops off the trunk of the car without responding.

"I have a friend named Charlie," I tell Charlie. "He lives out in California, in L.A., and he makes a living drawing bunnies."

Charlie isn't amused by my meaningless anecdote. "I can't draw." He says.

"Ya know what, brother? Don't worry about your job. You'll find another one, and you'll move on, and you'll get out of here. I got a good feeling about you. I know these things, I have a sort of sixth sense."

Charlie pulls a hacky sack from his pocket and tosses it in the air to me. I knock it off my knee and use my shoulder to drop it back down to my foot, where I pop it back over to him. He uses his chest to stop it, lets it roll down his core, and kicks it up in the air.

"You'll be all right," I reiterate. "Plus, I've got a million dollar idea. You can help me out with it."

"What is it?"

"Whiskey jelly."

The hacky sack flies through the air and into my face where it falls to the ground with a beany thud. Charlie looks me in the eye and asks, "Have you taken a shower today?"

"Nope," I tell him. I lift up my arm and stick my nose into my armpit. "Do I smell?"

"No," Charlie says. "I just have a theory about people who don't shower in the morning."

I'm worried about this theory, because to me it sounds like Charlie is theorizing that if I don't shower in the morning, this makes me some kind of psychopathic shitbag. "Ordinarily I shower first thing every morning," I reassure him. "But this morning blended into this afternoon and I was hungover and it just didn't happen."

I see Charlie's eyes shimmer a bit when I tell him this, like he's realizing my entire day has been spent thinking about the playful, yet crazy nuances of life instead of the unjustness of it.

"I wish I was hungover," Charlie says. "Instead of this."

Without anyone knowing, I stashed a third beer in my back pocket before I came over to Charlie, just in case someone had died and Charlie was in need of an emergency beer. I pull the beer out, untwist the top and say, "Now you can work on one. Then tomorrow, you and I will dance and do it all over again."

Charlie smiles for the first time today. He lets his dreads down from the corporate ponytail he has them wrapped up in and lets his head dangle backwards. "I can smell your roses," he says, "all the way over here." He takes a moment to appreciate something, maybe life or the invention of beer. "You may be witnessing a defining moment in my life," he tells me. He drops his chin back to me and nods his head. Before I know what's happening, we're embraced in a heavy hug. "Thank you," Charlie says to me.

I feel good in Charlie's arms. He'll be all right. He'll upcome. I know these things. Trust me?

There Isn't Blues

My wife is hard at work on her press release for Rudy's Candy Tampons, or at least she's pretending to be. When she pretends to work, she just stares into space, doing nothing. As a child, she used to stare out of windows. Her teachers thought she was being indignant, ignoring them when they'd call upon her. The truth is, she's always had more fun inside her head than out in the world. Her cubicle doesn't have a window. Instead she stares into her computer screen, traveling through the empitness as if it leads to another planet.

Her cubicle is right next to the water cooler, so for the entirety of her day, aside from pretending to write copy about candy tampons, she listens to the sound of running water. Both her bladder and her copy are adversely affected by this. Every thirty minutes or so, she has to pee. Right when she gets on a roll, typing up sharp tampon puns and pitches, she has no choice but to unfurl her bladder, cutting off her stream of thought. When she returns, everything seems un-fresh. "Orange you glad you had a Rudy's Candy Tampon?"

The water cooler has been a problem for a long time and she hasn't found the perfect solution to it, partially because there isn't one and partially because the solution, like adding pictures to her cubicle, would be admitting she has grown comfortable and accepting of her job, her role, her destiny that involves thick, gray, indoor air. I bought her a pair of expensive red headphones to block out the sound of the constant water, but the headphones make her ears hot and irritated. She doesn't like pushing the small speakers into her earholes because it uncomfortably stretches out the delicate cartilage. She has very small ears. When the headphones are in, all she can think about is how badly she wants to pull them out and massage her lobes and helixes. Her entire day is consumed by either constantly massaging her ears or continuously urinating. Somewhere between her bladder and her ears, she thinks of a new sales angle for Rudy's Candy Tampons—they're 100% green. No plastic applicator to choke up a dolphin's blowhole and clog up landfills. No, these applicators are made of candy. Totally sustainable—and delicious!

She still can't believe half of her conscious day is spent thinking about Rudy's Candy Tampons. She imagines an eight-hour day of standing topless in the sunshine with watermelon juice running down her chin and neck. She isn't sure if she would want to do anything else besides stand there, free, smoking a long joint and sipping a glass of wine and sucking watermelon. She knows she's supposed to have some drive, some passion for life and accomplishment, but she's not afraid to admit to herself that if she could, she would do absolutely nothing. Maybe she'd write a story about a psychedelic zoo or a fortune telling woodpecker, something unexpectedly fascinating Tom Robbins might write about. And maybe she'd be happy if her friends read her woodpecker story and told their friends about it. But other than that, she would do nothing. Well maybe she'd help the less fortunate, and watch her husband go fishing and chop wood. Oh, and she might plan road trips to unknown waterfalls, and find hiking trails that lead to remote hot springs. Also, she'd make love outdoors, stoned, every day.

Staring into the window of her computer, she thinks about the last time she made love, how much she enjoyed it, how for a half hour while watching Michelangelo Antonioni's *Blow Up*, her husband's hand rested on her clitoris, and every time his fingers moved, her brain shifted away from the film and closer to his body and heart. When he pulled off her clothes and they began, she felt as if her body was on vacation from her mind, each moment lasting forever, yet simultaneously disintegrating. When she was done, her cheeks were rosy and she wanted to eat strawberries and so she did, pulling the little green tops off and pushing the ripe red bodies into her damp cheeks. Everything inside her seemed balanced when she fell asleep that night. Her shoulders felt lighter, and her world had achieved a harmonious equilibrium—but that was a while ago.

She hasn't typed a sentence about Rudy's Candy Tampons in the last twenty minutes, and instead has been massaging her ears while listening to Mozart. She listens to Mozart when she writes because someone told her Mozart's music opens up a door in the brain ordinarily closed to creativity. Most of the time she finds herself tuning Wolfgang out, and then somehow, as if by magic, he is transformed into Neil Young and she has no recollection of changing the music or how "Everybody Knows This is Nowhere" has come on.

She realizes at this moment that Neil Young is playing in her headphones, and she goes through yet another strategic breakdown of the last six hours, wondering when and how she got from Sonata in C to Cowgirl in the Sand—that feeling, she believes, must be like traveling in the afterlife.

She hates her job. Even with Neil's music pouring directly into her ears, she can still hear the water cooler dumping fluid into endless paper cups, one after the other. She can hear the slurping of lips and tongues, the gulping of gullets, and if she really listens—tunes everything out—she can even hear the water gurgling down the anonymous esophagus and dumping with a thundering splash into the belly. Needless to say, it's now time for her to piss.

She gets up out of her cubicle and feels the blood rush down her legs and into her feet. She takes off her heels and stretches her toes then slides them back into her shoes. She says to herself, "From now on, I will make love at least once a day. I have to. It's something I love to do and it makes me feel good and it's good for our relationship."

She nods her head to herself and turns the corner past the water cooler where several of her coworkers have gathered to discuss the Instagram sweater idea that has swept through the office and is gaining momentum. She might be the last hope to stop this exercise in hipster fashion myopia from happening, but she doesn't know this. She keeps her headphones in her ears even though they aren't receiving anything just in case someone attempts to engage her in conversation.

"Hey, Phoenix, what do you think of this sweater idea?" she hears a young intern say. He's twenty years old and hasn't grown facial hair yet, his skin smooth and even, not a wrinkle in sight. His waist is too thin and his arms have little blonde hairs that haven't changed color. He's the obligatory boyfriend in an acne skin-care commercial, running down the beach shirtless in white drawstring pants, smiling, splashing. She drops a lip down, inadvertently scowling, pretending not to hear the question. She sees out of the corner of her eye the young intern throw up his hand to get her attention while simultaneously sliding his petite frame towards her, attempting to cut her off before she can reach the front of the office and escape. She takes three brisk steps, speeding up, but can't make it to the door before he gets in her way. She exhales into the young intern's face and pulls the headphones from her ears.

"Phoenix?" the intern says.

"What?"

"Have you heard about this Instagram idea Taylor and I are working on?"

"No."

"Well, Taylor came in today in this rad sweater," the intern intertwines his arm within Phoenix's, which she finds totally inappropriate even though this intern is gay and is in no remote way romantically interested in her, and drags her towards the water cooler where Taylor is standing and waving and slurping water from his paper cup.

Taylor is another young intern who says someday he wants to be a playwright, or not, maybe a lawyer. When he said this six months ago, everyone knew he would someday be a lawyer. He's handsome and well-built, although to Phoenix he seems small. All young men seem small to her compared to the drunk bear with a chode rash she has at home. Taylor has a crush on my wife and my wife is well aware of it.

Phoenix raises her left hand to her lips, tapping at her mouth with her ring finger, in case Taylor, after six months, still hasn't figured out she's married. Her throat gets choked with contempt when she envisions Taylor's scrawny little body trying to control her own in bed. She'd rather kill a golden retriever puppy, listen to its last dog yelp.

"Do you like his sweater?" the intern asks.

Phoenix looks down at Taylor's sweater, and is appalled by the face of Hulk Hogan embroidered into the navy blue wool. She thinks she's widening her mouth, opening it up like a flower into a smile, but the movement is negligible and therefore unnoticed, the bud forever closed. She looks bored, irritated, unhappy. Taylor picks up on her heavy vibes and says, "Yeah, I don't know if it's a good idea."

"Shut up! You're doing it," the other intern says. He looks back at Phoenix. "Taylor has the most ridiculous collection of ironic sweaters. I think we should do an Instagram installment called 'Thirty days of Sweaters' where Taylor wears a different sweater to work for thirty days and we totally blog the shit out of it. He'll be like a straight sweater fashion guru, which is also ironic."

Phoenix can't get her vocal chords to work. She thinks about her bladder, how badly she wishes she could whip out her vagina and shoot piss all over Hulk Hogan's face, flooding the office with her ripe bladder juice. She lets out a small giggle from the back of her throat thinking of everyone ankle deep, sloshing around in her urine. "Sounds, uh, interesting."

Taylor looks away. "She hates it," he says.

She doesn't disagree with his statement. She detaches herself from the young intern and says, "Excuse me."

Taylor blushes, sheepishly smiles at her. She likes that she has this control over Taylor even though she isn't attracted to him in the slightest. She's the older woman, seven years his senior, which gives her the upper hand she feels she doesn't have in her own marriage.

In the bathroom stall she whispers to herself, "Someday, I'm gonna come in here, light up a j, drink a beer, walk back out, and quit. And I'll buy two plane tickets for us, and we'll fly to an island and stand on the beach with our toes in the sand and just be alone for a while. I want to watch time pass, I want to feel it."

She unwraps a Rudy's Candy Tampon, drops the tampon into the toilet and eats the cherry flavored applicator. There's nothing else to look at aside from her shoes—rattlesnake skin sandals with two-inch heels bought at a thrift store back in California—strange and ghostly underneath the neon light. Her fingers contract into a fist, her face becomes flush—she throws a fist out, landing with a thud against the stall door, the skin breaking at her middle finger, a bit of blood. She takes a deep breath, exhales. "There has to be something more to life!" she screams.

"There isn't," a woman's voice responds, then the sound of toilet paper rolling, the toilet flushing, the door opening and closing, gone.

"There isn't," Phoenix repeats to herself. She's sick of wearing gray skirts all day, sick of Instagram, sick of ironic sweaters. She's sick of this city. But she's afraid to tell her husband this move east now seems miserable and pointless, that the buildings have replaced the trees in her mind, and that the Puerto Ricans and Salvadorans have ruined burritos for her forever. These are sensitive subjects for Californians, and especially to her husband, or so she thinks. She keeps it all to herself. She doesn't want him to get upset on account of his anxiety disorder. His panic attacks are paralyzing, take days to get over. If he wants to leave, he'll let her know. One of them has to be positive.

Palm Frond Blues

Cliff and Charlie don't have a car because when they did have one, they got in a lot of trouble in it. They don't have the sobriety to own a car, and now at 30 and 31 years old, they both realize a car would just bring them more hell in Los Angeles, a city with almost zero public transportation, drunk and heavy stoned drivers everywhere, madness. That's why Cliff and Charlie live on the eastern edge of Echo Park, a little village immersed in carne asada smog, surrounded by burrito stands and dark paisa bars where the bartenders don't speak English and the cocaine dealers play pool all day for free.

They're on their way to one of these bars now, strolling with their loose fingers rattling in the sunshine and their minds absorbing the billboard bullshit and spitting it back out. Charlie wears his wide-brimmed cowboy hat, his cowboy boots, a pair of tight black pants, and his new V-neck t-shirt. He put lotion on his tattoos this morning, so they look more vibrant than usual, shining, deep rubies and sapphires, gold and emeralds.

Cliff is shirtless because it's hot and he's sweating profusely. He carries his t-shirt on his shoulder and is still wearing his cowboy hat with the "Not in My Pussy" button attached. He sucks on a Big Stick, twirling his tongue around the synthetic pineapple and cherry, hop-scotching ahead of Charlie. He turns around and sings a song, the tune of which is reminiscent of something Gwen Stefani or a talentless cheerleader might chant. "Why can't you hop scotch, hop scotch, hop scotch? Why can't you hop scotch all night long?"

A car drives past them and the driver yells "Fags!" Cliff and Charlie raise their middle fingers in unison.

Charlie likes his belt buckle. It's filled with turquoise stones and mother of pearl, silver feathers and a small golden arrowhead. He thinks his belt buckle inhabits the spirit of a Hopi Indian elder that once saved a village from a deadly Fangbug epidemic. He has a reverence for life whenever he looks down at his belt buckle. He does his imitation of an Indian fire dance, slamming his boot heels into the concrete, throwing his chin up to the sky, sucking the tits of the great magic cactus, the eagle feather father, catching up to his brother, eyes wild.

Cliff carries a camera with him wherever he goes, just in case he sees something interesting, out of the ordinary. Often times he and Charlie get so drunk they forget what they've experienced that day. Cliff doesn't want to forget anything. He worries someday he'll die and none of his life will flash before his eyes. He rationalizes that with a camera, he can constantly remind himself of his days, he can actively participate in the reality flashing before him, and he can do it anywhere he chooses, not just on his deathbed.

Charlie karate chops the loose bark of a palm tree barely clinging to its mother trunk. The flimsy frond falls to the ground and he winds his leg up, kicks it into the street. At that exact moment, a police car turns the corner, pulls a U-turn, approaches the brothers and slows down, coming to a full stop about twenty yards ahead. The police officer gets out of the car and walks towards them, his hand resting on the butt of his gun.

Cliff smiles and waves at the police officer, then takes his camera and points it at him, taking a picture.

The police officer puts his hand up and says, "Where you boys headed?"

Cliff looks around, over his shoulder, up at the sky and asks back, "Are you talking to us?"

The police officer isn't amused with Cliff's question, although Cliff is completely sincere in his query. Why would the cop be asking them where they're going? They're two, poor, tattooed man-boys with nothing to do. And they're white.

"Have you two been drinking?"

Charlie says "Yes." Cliff says "No." They look at each other and grin because they know that no matter what happens to them right now, it'll make a humorous anecdote in the future. They also don't give a shit about the cop or handcuffs or a night in jail. They know kicking palm fronds can't possibly be a crime in California. Yet. They've lived in L.A. their entire lives and have kicked thousands of palm fronds into the street, never having been reprimanded for doing so.

The officer gives each of them a sobriety test which they both pass with flying colors, balancing on one leg, counting backwards, following a finger with their eyes, naming the first three Beatles records, and singing a new Gwen Stefani song with a beat-box. Cliff asks the cop if he wants him to do a one handed cartwheel or spell Mississippi backwards without the vowels. The brothers have practiced these sobriety tests since the first night they got drunk together at twelve and eleven years old. They have better coordination when they're drunk than when they're sober and are superior spellers in any state of mind. The alcohol is just blood to them now, and we all need blood to survive.

The cop tells the brothers to "quit kicking palm fronds into the street" and gives them a stern warning. He explains that the "fronds are a road hazard for automobiles." He says that the two of them don't want to be responsible for the death of a toddler or a pregnant woman if they kick palm fronds into the street. The pregnant woman and her toddler and her grandmother and a golden retriever puppy could be driving down the street, mistake the palm frond for a dangerous road block, swerve to avoid collision, and drive directly into an oil tanker. The oil tanker will drag the car underneath, sparks flying, until the entire thing ignites and everyone burns. Then the fire spreads across the city, leaping rooftop to rooftop, and the next thing you know, fourteen million Los Angelenos are dead from a palm frond holocaust. And do you know who would be to blame? Cliff and Charlie. Two-thirds of the Mustard Brothers. Fourteen million counts of wrongful death and arson, murder, and manslaughter. A slew of felonies. Fifty million years in jail.

They try hard not to laugh, but are unsuccessful. "Cool," Charlie says.

And the goon squints his eyes, gives the boys a once-over, polishes his bronze badge with a thumb.

"No problem occifer," Cliff says. "We'll keep the fronds on the trees and keep our knees to the bees, and the seas to the freeze." He adjusts his crotch as the fuzz heads back to his cruiser, rolls away, dust sucked up behind the tires into the halo of sun.

"Why can't you hop scotch, hop scotch, hop scotch? Why can't you hop scotch all night long?"

Cliff takes six more pictures while cruising Sunset Blvd.

One

An discarded mattress leaning against a chain link fence that wraps around an abandoned gas station. The mattress has been tagged by someone called "Pretty Unicorn" in blue spray paint. Underneath the tag, someone has written "Oner" in black sharpie.

Two

A homeless man asleep in a giant wool jacket in a large down sleeping bag. Cliff is surprised the man isn't sweating. He says, "I'm pretty sure he's dead. It's gotta be like a hundred and fifty degrees out."

Three

A teenage Mexican girl kicking another teenage Mexican girl in the teeth after punching her in the face and knocking her down. Cliff and Charlie broke up the fight. Charlie got punched in the chin by another pubescent girl and he laughed as she fell to the sidewalk grabbing her hand and crying. "Kids are nuts these days," he said.

"They have threesomes," Cliff added. "All day long."

Four

An old Mexican woman and a plate of nachos at a burrito stand. She was eating them with only two front teeth, which Cliff considered to be a modern marvel. She seemed indifferent to Cliff pointing his camera at her and her nachos, as if someone is always in her face taking pictures. Cliff thought her manner showed a particular irreverence that he identified with. "Fuck everyone, I'm eating nachos with two teeth," he says.

Five

A dead cat. Charlie said a few words about the cat, how it's black stripes look nice, and that its favorite meal was city rat, then made the sign of the cross and moved on.

Six

A light brown Eames reclining chair in the window of an antique shop. Cliff said, "I have to have this chair. My life isn't complete without this chair. I'll need a pipe to go with it."

"And a house," Charlie added. "And a job, and a wife, and a couple kids, and a necktie…"

At the paisa bar, the brothers order two, tall, cold cervezas and sit down near the cocaine dealer who's playing pool. The cocaine dealer is a young Mexican with a look that defines the term "dope," with medium length black curly hair bouncing above his well-sculpted chin. His eyes are dark, but somehow, capture light. He wears tight black pants, a threadbare black t-shirt, and black zip-up ankle boots, shining with polish.

"He looks like the guy from Mars Volta," Charlie says.

"At the Drive-In," Cliff replies.

"Same thing," Charlie says.

"Not the same," Cliff retorts. "At the Drive-in Cedric Bixler Zavala had shorter hair than Mars Volta Cedric Bixler Zavala."

"Depends on which version of Mars Volta you're talking about."

"Forget it."

The Mars Volta cocaine dealer wears a black bandana folded into his back pocket, with half of it hanging out in a perfect triangle. Inside his back pocket tied to the other end of the bandana is a heavy brass padlock. No one knows what's inside this pocket aside from Mars Volta, and he likes it that way, in case the shit goes down.

Cliff grabs a few cocktail napkins and a black pen from his pocket. He writes Whiskey Jelly in a hungover scrawl at the top of the first napkin and underlines it twice.

"Let's talk whiskey jelly," he says to Charlie. "Lets get Cassidy back out here in the sunshine of the west and lets become whiskey jelly moguls."

"I still think pomegranate vodka jelly is a good idea," Charlie says.

"You don't get it," Cliff says. "We're making whiskey jelly."

"Fine," Charlie says. He finishes his beer and gets up to order two more, and two shots of whiskey. He yells over his shoulder, "I'm getting us whiskey for inspiration."

"It's about time you started thinking straight," Cliff responds. "Don't you dare bring me pomegranate vodka or I'll have you massacred by a palm frond."

Charlie sits back down and the brothers take their shot of whiskey, grinning and rubbing their hot bellies.

"Now, what are the properties of jelly? How do we succeed in creating a gelatinous whiskey product?" Cliff asks rhetorically.

That's as far as the whiskey jelly meeting gets before Cliff and Charlie decide the best thing to do is ask the cocaine dealer for coke, which they purchase in the men's room and snort immediately off an old dirty house key. They head outside to smoke a cigarette and realize the burn of Los Angeles stings a bit more when your heart rate is larger than the U.S. deficit.

"It's too early to be this high," Cliff says.

"Don't think of time," Charlie responds. "It'll just bum you out, man. Time sucks. If we were near the North Pole, it could be light like this at eleven pm. Don't let the drugs dictate your time. You're in control of the drugs."

Cliff loves his brother and you can tell because he hugs him and says, "The carnival is outside today." He takes a deep breath and thinks about how vast the world is, how if he could, he would inhale the breaths of a million people and let it out across the city, blowing the smog, errant palm fronds, and everything else with it out of the planet into space where stars in the shape of a dragon would be created from the waste and Orion would have someone to battle. He wants to touch something wet and soft, a rock inside of a river, smooth and fresh with fish gills. He thinks there must be more to life than this sidewalk, this bar, this blow, this whiskey jelly, but can't be sure. The two brothers remain embraced as they slide down towards the concrete together, lying horizontally and watching the clouds swirl.

"What do you see?" Charlie asks.

"I see myself," Cliff says. "And I'm a shitty little ant."

Fish Taco Blues

The key to a good fish taco is the charcoal. There's a nearby market that sells pure oak lump charcoal from Tennessee, and you can taste the difference between a good oak lump charcoal and the factory made chemical-injected briquettes. There's a relationship between a tree and a river and all animals that live in both. The smokiness of the oak tree brings out the flavor in a grilled piece of fish, just as the water from a nearby river might sweeten the fruits of an apple tree.

The sun is setting as I dump the charcoal into the charcoal tower, stuff the bottom with yesterday's newspaper and light it on fire. The humid breeze kisses the flame, spreading. My fingertips relax momentarily, and the relaxation of fingertips is a hard phenomenon to describe because it's difficult to think of fingertips and how they feel. I think of moist grass bending in the sunshine.

I like waiting for the charcoal to burn. It's a perfect time to put on a record, open a bottle of wine, lie on my back on the redwood bench in the yard, and stare at the clouds, trace their outlines in the air, pretend I can move them. I'm feeling unimaginative after speaking with my neighbor Charlie, so the clouds aren't transforming themselves into anything just right now for me. For some reason, Charlie got to me, opened me up a little bit to the possibility of failure, and failure is like cancer, spreading across the street, into my brain, and tensing up my fingertips.

I shake my head as if trying to whip my brain out of my earhole. I think I see a grasshopper in the clouds, but it quickly morphs itself into the shape of Ireland with a penis wrapped in donuts attached to the western coast of Donegal. I'm glad my creativity is back. This could have been a miserable chapter.

I hear the old Bavarian rumble of my wife's engine as it pulls into the driveway and I immediately jump to my feet and run through the backdoor towards the front door. I like to greet her with a kiss and a smile before she gets inside because I know how much she hates her job, and I feel responsible for her increasing unhappiness, the great emptiness.

I can see her pulling the parking brake, getting up and out of the car, still in that mismatched outfit. I watch her move, the gray skirt hugging her curves and I contemplate how remarkably attractive she is to me even though her fabrics seem to lack any color and suck the blood right out of her face. She could be wearing Antarctica or the surface of the moon as a dress and I would still proclaim her perfect beauty. When I take a moment to ponder her presence, I realize I can't remember her wearing this gray skirt this morning. For some reason, I thought she had been parading around the house naked, sucking on the joint with her butt cheeks out. I can't see it any other way, and rationalize that she must have been naked. She must have slid the skirt on in the driveway as she left. She blew me kisses through the window and they landed across my chest.

"Forget about it," I yell to her in the driveway, preempting the list of complaints she's about to unfold about her job writing for a candy tampon company.

"Thirty days of sweaters," she says and shakes her head. She bends down for a moment to smell the roses in the yard. "There's no smell." She pulls a petal and lets it float up into the air, fall to the ground.

"I love you," I say. "It won't be long til the roses smell again."

"I hope not," she says as she gets to the door. "It saddens me to see them so full yet so empty. What's the point of roses if they don't smell? I'd rather have gardenia."

I look deep into her face and her eyes are like gold coins in need of a shine.

She takes her thumb and rubs it against my bottom lip. "Red wine?" she asks.

I lick my lips, a little embarrassed at my purple mouth. I kiss her and use my hands to push her face hard into mine, as if trying to combine our heads into one unbeatable mass of intellect, an intellect so powerful nothing ill could ever penetrate it.

We get inside and she drops her purse, slides off her heels and lets out a sigh. "I'm so glad to be home," she says.

I run to the backyard and grab the bottle of wine and pour her a glass. She takes a sip with her eyes closed, lost somewhere between the door and myself.

"I've got an idea I want to run by you," I say.

"What is it?" she says, opening a window in the kitchen.

She gets minimally excited these days when I have an idea. I'm usually quite bad at putting my ideas into words, so whatever comes out of my mouth usually sounds unimpressive, uninspired, and unprofessional, and as a result my wife usually shrugs and dismisses my attempt at genius as an accomplishment of stupidity. She has asked me not to run anything by her when it comes to writing, painting, collaging, or cooking unless it has already been completed and is ready to be digested. She likes the element of surprise. She wants her brain to be a blank slate, wide open to interpret my whimsy.

"Lets say a group of lesbian ghosts captured you and made love to you, but, like, in a good way," I start out.

"So they rape me?"

I instantly know I should have kept my mouth shut and just written my Choose Your Own Adventure book without consulting her first.

"No, not rape. More like, they're there for your pleasure, and they wouldn't do anything to you that you wouldn't want done, and it was all very ethereal and romantic."

"I'm not into women," she says.

"I know. I'm not into men. But I think there's a homoerotic side to everyone, whether or not we want to admit it. Somewhere deep down, everyone wants to be pleased by someone else, so I'm just wondering if you as a woman could be remotely turned on by a pack of lesbian ghosts making love to you in a very erotic and sensual and consensual way."

"It'd have to be written pretty damn well, and you'd really have to get inside of a woman's psyche to pull it off. I mean, men just want an orgasm, but for a woman, it's more about the experience, the mentality of it than the end point. I can have a wonderful sexual experience without an orgasm, so you might need to tap into that if you want to convince a reader to allow their imagination to go homosexual. And you better make the room look cool. No one wants to have a new sexual experience in a shitty room. It needs cool wallpaper and lots of candles, incense, and like, a bearskin rug."

I know I'm a sensitive man, although I have to say I've rarely had a gratifying sexual experience without an orgasm. Nonetheless, I can imagine the hands and lips and heat of a woman's body against my own. I take this heat, and I transfer it to myself, transforming if only for a second, into a woman. I nod my head, confident I can write a good piece of women's erotica and decide to add plenty of detail about the underwear. Everyone loves pretty underwear, delicate, like a cathedral. My wife looks at me with a perplexed expression on her face, sucking on her wine which she's just about done with. She takes this time to internalize our home and she's impressed I've kept it clean even though I've been drunkenly sloshing around in it all day with a terrible chode rash.

I meditate on womanhood for a few more moments and I start to feel a familiar crystal tear welling up inside my stomach and sizzling upward. That tear has been there for a while and is the result of the abortion, a small uncomfortable tickle scratching at a part of my body I can neither locate nor place.

"Anything interesting happen today?" she asks me. "Aside from your lesbian ghost epiphany?"

"Charlie got fired from his job at the insurance agency."

Phoenix pours herself another glass of wine and uses her thumbnail to scratch up a bit of dried mayonnaise from our countertop. I can't remember when I could have dropped mayonnaise. I think of what I had for lunch today, and I'm pretty sure it didn't involve mayonnaise. Maybe my wife dropped the mayonnaise.

"Wow," she says. "He's got child support."

A man's greatness is gauged upon how much responsibility he has.

"I think Charlie's more upset about the outcome of his life than his job." I drop a hand down my pants and try my best to waft air at my rash.

"What is that?" Phoenix asks me. "What ya got goin on down there?"

"I got a gnarly rash between my legs from work last night from my thighs rubbing together. It's been killing me all day." I walk out the back door and drop the fish onto the grill along with some sliced jalapenos and take a moment to listen to the leaves rustling.

"Is that why you slept naked last night?" she yells to me.

"Yeah."

"How long til the fish tacos are ready?"

"Fifteen minutes."

My wife takes off her blouse and skirt. I see her smile and drop her head. I know what this expression means. She moves towards the bedroom, unfastening her bra as she does so. I hear a soft howl that could be the breeze or my soul. A chill arrives in my fingertips and rushes in, sliding up my chest. As I enter the bedroom, I see four seductive ghosts hovering above my wife as she slides onto the bed. They're wearing clouds for underwear, their intangibles just barely covered and peaking through like the sun over an ocean where the weather swims and parts. I put my lips together and blow against the clouds, shuddering with an icy sweetness as they float away and reform, raining down upon my wife's warm body. "Come," they all say, luring with their pointer fingers, their tongues braiding between each other and dripping with saliva.

As you move closer, you sense vulnerability in yourself, an inexplicable fear. You look the ghosts in the eyes as they drop their braided tongues down onto the hips of the woman below them and suddenly you can't remember who you are. "Who am I? Where am I?" The door begins to close behind you. The woman on the bed opens her eyes as the spirits spread her legs, moving their tongues slowly down, slowly. She lets out a small sound, her voice resonating, a sound that pierces your stomach with anticipation. Her eyes close and her palms press out. The clouds are coming towards you. The ghosts are waiting for an answer.

I'm tripping. I'm trying to create this magnificent scene in my mind, the lesbian/bi-sexual ghosts hovering in the air above my wife, teasing her with foreplay, waiting for me to join in in some volcanic explosion of mysterious sexuality, but I can't seem to separate my manhood from the experience. It needs to be about the woman, not me, not my balls. Still, it's been weeks since we made love and I want this to be perfect, to replace all the time we've lost, to last a thousand years, to be ingrained in memory. I see her, strewn across the bed, her hands out, her legs open. "What's up?" she says.

I look at her, take it all in, the mole underneath her ribs, those hipbones, my God, those hipbones. Men would kill for those hipbones, die for those hipbones. I won't last long staring at those hipbones. I unzip my pants, pull them off, walk slowly into the bed, drop my head into her neck, and kiss. I move down

down

down

my lips brushing against each inch of skin,

collarbone, armpit, breasts, watching as the goosebumps rise all across the plateaus of her limbs, and when I get to her stomach, I hear a rumble, a crackle, a contraction, a whine.

"Ow," she says.

I lift my head. "What's happening?"

"Ow," she says again. She uses her hands to maneuver me off of her, rolls onto her knees and begins rocking back and forth, back and forth, clutching her stomach.

I place my hand on her spine. "Are you okay?"

"I'm so sick of being in pain," she says. Then silent crying, whimpering.

"It might be time to see a doctor," I say.

"I don't want to see a doctor. I know what it is. I know what it is."

Maybe she does know and maybe she doesn't. It doesn't matter now. I don't want the fish tacos to burn. I get up and tuck my erection into my pants. "I better check on the fish," I say.

She nods her head, keeps rocking, back and forth, back and forth. "Yeah," she says.

I grab the last of the joint from her vanity and place it and the lighter on the nightstand for her. "Maybe this will help." I back myself out of the room, watching as she buries her face into her hands. I grab the spatula from the dining table, head back outside, and flip my two sizzling filets of Mahi Mahi.

Someday It's Gonna Burn Out Blues

Aunika has been my best friend since birth. Our mothers have been best friends since kindergarten and frequently tell us both how we are destined to marry, even though the most we've ever engaged in physically is platonic hugging. Plus, I'm already married and she's in a semi serious-relationship with Cesar, the unemployed actor. Aunika has tried and done more shit than I have, but I've thought more shit than she ever will—who thinks about the flight path of the Mallorcan Jawbreaker Butterfly, how it feeds the flytraps of Zambia, affects the climate and flora of Kiribati more than I do?—No one.

In a span of twelve years since we graduated high school, Aunika received a Bachelor's degree in journalism from Rutgers, wrote a critically and socially praised article on the decline of the western domestic kitchen for the Huffington Post, graduated from a prestigious law school on the Pacific Ocean, modeled for the *Free People* swimsuit catalog at the Canary Islands Teleport Research Center on Tenerife, made love to Jeff Goldblum in an abandoned taxi cab in Sienna, worked at a used books and record store in Burlington, Vermont, experimented with collage art using 1960's Mexican tabloids and Jacqueline Kennedy Onassis as her primary medium, sold tie-dyed wife-beaters at a Cape Town, South Africa psychedelic music festival, lived in Cambria, CA, Portland, OR, Livingston, MT, an air force base in Tel Aviv, on a river in New Hampshire, and now resides in a two-thousand square foot loft featured in *Interiors* magazine and owns, operates, and slays La Di Donuts. Aside from all this, she's deeply passionate about and dedicated to drinking bourbon straight from the bottle and dancing to old Tyrannosaurus Rex records, even though those Marc Bolan/Mickey Finn albums aren't very danceable and would be better put to use at LSD inspired séances. Regardless, she manages to get stoned and shake across her living room with her candles lit and a bowl of cold spaghetti marinara in the Eastern summer's rain. She also played bass for a band called Eastern Summer Rain, but they disbanded a few months ago when the lead singer/guitarist/songwriter, Amanda, started dating Cole from The Black Lips and decided to head out on tour with them as a solo acoustic act in which she disseminates her opposition to genetically modified food products and the captivity and illegal sale of the Southern Madagascar Green Trouble Slug to the masses. All that's left of Eastern Summer Rain is a seven inch EP, framed in Topanga Scrub Oak on one of the brick walls of Aunika's massive loft.

Aunika never knew how to cook anything until she discovered her grandmother's old recipe book and decided to experiment with a donut. She found the ingredients easy to acquire, and the process to be remarkably simple. She had an epiphany one day at a Coldstone Creamery while ordering her favorite treat, Sweet Cream Ice Cream with crushed Butterfinger candy. Since that day, she's been covering her own donuts in homemade candy bars and confections, organic flowers and fruits, orange peels and apple skins, which has literally turned the donut world upside down in recent weeks. Right now, if I wanted to, I could walk the eleven blocks to La Di Donuts and get a donut topped with chocolate jasmine-petal butter, or mint sassafras sprinkles, or Dead Sea Saltwater toffee, the saltwater of which she has imported by a gentleman acquaintance of hers she met during her time in Tel Aviv.

Aunika has long blonde hair, perfect teeth, and as was mentioned before, is both beautiful and captivating. She is so captivating and beautiful in fact that the first bank she sought a business loan at gave her the money at an unnervingly low interest rate with little or no questions asked, except one, by the loan broker—"Would you like to have dinner with me sometime?" Aunika smiled and wrote down her phone number without answering. She got the loan and when the banker called, she didn't answer. She's a loyal girlfriend to her idiot boyfriend, or at least she says she is—she's getting impatient with him—we can all see it. She told me Cesar says he has meetings and auditions all day, but one day she followed him—saw him head to a coffee shop, stare out the window for three hours, drink four Café Bombons, occasionally checking Facebook on his iPhone. She shook her head. Pathetic.

Last night and its stomachaches and fish tacos has come and gone and now it is tomorrow morning. Aunika is at her donut shop, leaning on the glass display counter, filling out several legal documents in an attempt to obtain a beer and wine license from the city. She doesn't want to stop at just donuts, and sees her retail space growing beyond the walls, globally, a brand, a household name. She wants to serve craft brews and small batch wines from the Northwest and California. She thinks donuts and beers go hand in hand and she's correct in her assumption. She has an idea to create the first ever meatball donut—essentially a lavender and rosemary meatball wrapped in donut dough and covered in a sweet marinara glaze with St. Stephen cheese. She's a pioneer of the donut world. She sees the circular pastry as breakfast, lunch, dinner, dessert, art.

I'm personally not a big fan of donuts. I could never eat them because of my hypersensitivity to sugar as a child and especially because, as an adolescent, I was convinced fried foods caused acne flare-ups. Nonetheless, La Di Donuts is directly across my bar, off Love St., and it is I who first told Aunika she should open up a donut shop in the vacant space across the way. It just so happens the owner of my bar, Bulch Rangoon, owned the vacant space across the street and was willing to rent it out. He gave her a sweet deal once he took a look at her sweet face. Now, I'm somewhat jealous of Aunika. She's beautiful, independent, and owns a burgeoning business—on her way to the top. And all she wants to do is have me work for her so we can be close again, like we were in that closet at four years old, naked, pushing our fingers into each other's bellybuttons. She has an idea that my presence and prowess at each business will generate income for both the bar and the donut shop. And I think she might be right. When I get drunk and my shoulders drop, I can charm the pants off of any patron. I have not too shabby a singing voice, and every time a Guns and Roses or Johnny Thunders record plays at the bar, I launch into an all out rock and roll assault, wailing and playing air guitar, ignoring customers until they have nothing left to do but sing along, shake out the stars.

Aunika finishes one of her long forms for the alcohol permits and takes a moment to appreciate what she has. She sees the world outside, the buses and taxis moving past, everything going forward, and takes a look around her space—concrete floors, her own original collage art on the walls, posters of T-Rex, and a California flag draped in the window. In five minutes, at 8 am, the donut shop will open. There are already seven people shuffling around outside, and another couple walking arm in arm towards the window. Everyone knows you have to get there early—most days she sells out. She waves and smiles, raising a finger as if to tell them, "hold on one more moment," and then she reaches for the handset of the old rotary phone behind the counter, and calls me.

I contemplate not answering my phone, but I always have to—it could be Phoenix. Ever since her car got a flat tire on the way home from work on a narrow canyon road back in California and she was stranded alone in the dark coniferous forest for hours, was forced to hike up a mountain in search of cellular service, fight off a family of hungry black bears, and eventually call me to rescue her eleven hours later, I've been paranoid about not answering the phone. Every time that phone rings, I think about Phoenix's small helpless frame and the teeth of a of some wild bear.

I roll around in my bed, listening to the phone vibrate against the wood. I can't remember Phoenix leaving this morning, probably because after we ate fish tacos and she went to bed last night, I got even more drunk and watched reruns of the original Star Trek. I don't even remember falling asleep last night. It's as if the rest of last night doesn't exist, lost somewhere between a stomachache and a spatula, vanished.

Without looking, unable to pull open my eyes, I answer the phone. "Hello?"

"Hi," I hear Aunika say. I know Aunika's voice. I've heard it nearly as much as my own.

"Still sleeping," she laughs.

"I'm a bartender."

"A vampire," she says. Aunika's voice is elegant, made of diamonds. "What are you up to today?" she asks.

"Gotta work tonight, why?"

"Come down to the shop and drink beer with me. I'm getting a liquor license and I want your opinion on a few brews I got over here. I'm not much of a beer drinker, as you know."

"Bourbon."

"Bourbon's always been my vice."

I never need a second invitation to drink free beer. "Sounds rad," I tell her.

"Eleven o'clock?"

"I'll be there."

Aunika and I have a strange relationship, probably because it's always been completely non-sexual. I've often wondered whether or not she's ever dreamed of me in that way, ever thought about it, ever desired to press naked against me in the moonlight. She may have. I know I have. I think it nearly impossible to be conscious of someone for that long a time and never have a sexual dream about them. Still, when that dream finally happened eight or nine years ago, I felt strange the next morning, like I'd done something wrong, and since then, I feel like she looks at me differently, like she knows what we've subconsciously done to each other.

I get up, hunch over, move into the bathroom, turn on the shower, take a pull from the shampoo bottle, get out, dry off, and immediately begin fighting my instinct to pre-party with a beer before meeting her at eleven to drink more beer. I let the water hit my thighs—good news—my chode rash is getting better.

I fix myself a turkey sandwich with raw jalapenos so I'll be full when I get there. I can't stand the thought of devouring a meatball donut or whatever other carnivorous ingredient she might be dreaming up to stuff into her sugary dough. I wonder how Aunika has remained so slender over all her years of donut experimentation—I don't rule out bulimia.

La Di Donuts is packed when I get there. The employees don't wear uniforms, and are dressed as they would be if they were drinking at a dive bar in the Lower East Side. They're young and wear ripped up t-shirts that say "Minor Threat" on them. They have tattoos, piercings, custom jewelry, dreams of making a name in the art world, and they all have three or four jobs to afford living among these dreams.

Aunika spots me from the kitchen and gestures to come back and meet her. I slide past the employees as they pile diabetes inducing portions of toppings on the donuts in a highly effective assembly line, recognizing the soundtrack playing in the background as I do so. "Cat Power?" I ask the girl at the register.

"Yeah," she says.

"A bit depressing for donuts, no?"

"Whatever." She barely looks at me when she speaks. She's focused on the tip jar in front of her and how much is in it—sixty more dollars and she can pay the rent. "It's not like I'm listening."

"Come to me, mon frare," Aunika says. Back in the kitchen, away from the donut madness, we embrace, take a moment to look at each other. She's wearing a loose tank top exposing her side boobs, high wasted jeans, and an apron that reads "Gnarkill." Every time we see each other, it reminds me of that scene in *The Royal Tenenbaums* where Richie and Margot see each other at the docks for the first time in years— everything becomes slow motion, subtle smiles, peace, comfort. We have a brother-sister love that transcends sexuality. It's an appreciation for each other's existence, an acknowledgment of our presence in each other's life. We pick up wherever we left off.

"How's Cesar?" I ask her.

She rarely small talks about her boyfriends with me, unless they do something incredibly stupid. She isn't concerned with love and relationships outside of our own when we're together. "I don't care," she says. "Cesar is Cesar. Still an idiot."

"Any new acting jobs?" I ask. "Any good theater going down at the coffee shop?"

"Shut up," she says and elbows me in the ribs. She rips open the refrigerator door, revealing several six packs of beer from promising craft breweries that would love to get into the hottest donut shop in town. She pulls out two IPA's and asks, "What the hell is an IPA?"

"India Pale Ale," I say. "Hoppy and strong and tastes like weed."

She opens the beers with an opener she has in the pocket of her apron and takes a sip before handing me the beer. "I don't like it," she says. "Don't like swallowing dank either. I'd rather smoke it."

I take the bottle, find a glass next to the sink, pour the beer into it, stick my nose inside, and sip. I use my tongue to press the beer into the roof of my mouth, to inhale it, to swallow, to inherit. "Lots of pine," I say. "I like it. Reminds me of California, Humboldt style."

"Help me grab some more," she says.

We carry as many bottles of beer as our arms can hold and head out the back door to the small garden and sit down at a picnic table wedged between a chain link fence and the exterior wall of the donut shop. The sun is out and Aunika's cheeks are moist with sweat, reflecting the green of the weeds growing along the fence.

"Did you eat lunch?" she asks.

"Yeah, before I came."

"Too bad. I got a foie gras and truffle pate donut I'm working on."

Aunika drinks down her beer and opens two more. She tells me her friend Josephine, whom I slept with fourteen years ago, is getting married to a man who's never had a job and refuses to wear pants—boardshorts only. She tells me Cesar has been depressed lately, acting weird, and she's thinking of leaving him. She twirls the stem of a bright green leaf between her fingers. She opens two more beers, and I soon realize we aren't really taking inventory of the brews or what they taste like, which is what I thought I was doing here in the first place. I immediately realize Aunika is lonely and that the tears she cried at my wedding two years ago were not tears of joy, but tears of terror. She has very little love in her life, and always has.

"How's your writing?" she asks.

"Let me ask you something. Could you get turned on by lesbian ghosts?"

"Yes."

It takes us an hour to get drunk, but we get there, arriving at inebriation like astronauts booming up and out of the stratosphere and crashing down on Mars. I have an urge to stare at the sun. Aunika already is, saying "Someday, it's gonna burn out." I'm pretty sure she's speaking in a first person metaphor. She puts her hand on my hand and squeezes. "Will you come work for me when I open the bar up?"

I hate to say yes, because saying yes is always a commitment no matter what it is the answer to. I don't want to commit to Aunika because I know I will let her down. I want to leave the East, someday, hopefully soon, when Choose Your Own Adventure Erotica becomes the next big literary trend. I want to swim in California again. I want Phoenix to be happy and let her armpit hair grow out in the poppy fields. My cell phone buzzes. *I hate my fucking job. Just saw the first day of sweaters.*

I chug the rest of my beer, an amber ale with a chocolate cake aftertaste. I look into Aunika's blue eyes and they ripple like a backyard pond in a thunderstorm. She's crying inside. "Sure," I tell her.

She doesn't smile. She lets her head fall down and her hair collapse over her eyes. Her fingers loosen their grip around me. "I love you," she says. "Thanks."

I open us up two more beers.

Just Making Sure I'm Still Here Blues

I am a stoned boulder, one thousand feet high, dangling in mid-air and waiting for the water to fall.

I've got to make this good. Or I will die near an artichoke farm on my way to Big Sur.

. This period keeps following me. Watch where it goes, always ending things, always killing everything moving forward.

Periods are in the soil and this tree is turning brown. Periods are finite and definable and they are real, sliding down the rapids, towards the stone boulder, one thousand feet high, dangling in mid-air, waiting for the water to fall...

.

Bearclaw Murphy's Blues

Bulch Rangoon prefers to outfit himself in African safari clothing circa 1935. He buttons one side of his canvas outbacker hat to the crest, and dons an elaborate mustache only a man named Bulch Rangoon could pull off. He wears knee-high olive green wool socks with a stylish pair of oiled brown leather safari boots, laced tight, all the way up. He smokes a long thin pipe and winks at the ends of his sentences before chomping back down on the bit.

All us bartenders are pretty sure Bulch's last name isn't Rangoon, but no one can prove it isn't. He claims his birth certificate was lost at sea somewhere near Palau. Bulch leads a particularly private life, aside from his infamous absinthe after-hours parties we all take part in, biannually. He's got a tattoo of a pirate ship on his stomach and can make it move as if it were on waves. He too has a magnificent core, built like a Hemingway character. We learned this halfway through our last absinthe party when he balanced a bowling ball on his head for thirty minutes, sweating, flexing.

Tonight, Bulch is in the back office of Bearclaw Murphy's Bar working on a crossword puzzle and munching a free foie gras and truffle pate donut, courtesy of Aunika. I arrive two minutes early for work, a little drunk from my "beer tasting," but ready for another drink. Bulch likes us all to be a little drunk all the time. He idolizes Hemingway, and carries himself as if he has both conquered Kilimanjaro and inhaled the last drunken breath of a Basque revolutionary, somewhere near a cave, shoulder strapped with a deerskin canteen filled with wine and a mustache soaked in goat milk.

On my walk across the street to work this evening, I thought briefly about Aunika and what she meant when she told me she loved me. I wonder what is behind her eyes besides foie gras and truffle pate donuts, and I can feel my face constrict, my neck tighten. I love you. We're friends. Friends love each other. But her hand wrapped around my own when she said it felt like it meant more. Perhaps this is why when Bulch sees me walk into the back office and yank at my eyelids in the floor length mirror, he says, "Women."

Bulch's office looks exactly like the headquarters of an expedition deep in the Congo circa 1929—De Brazza for those of you inclined to history—Indiana Jones for those of you who aren't. An old Remington typewriter, ancient and incomplete maps of Sub-Saharan Africa, mosquito nets, ivory tusks, hand painted red cedar Bengal tigers, a worn wooden dartboard, shoe polish kit, a canister of gasoline, binoculars, tin canteen, an elephant rifle, and a stuffed African Guadalupe Bone Condor are strategically placed around the room to take your eyes on a rollercoaster of the visual senses. A pipe stuffed to the brim with vanilla tobacco smolders in front of him.

"It's in your eyes," Bulch says. "Those eyes are the same as the men who have died in the jungle. Lost, but somehow in awe of it all."

"You know about women?" I say to Bulch.

He pours us both a shot of bourbon from a nameless glass bottle. "I know enough to tell you sometimes the jungle is safer."

Bulch pulls at his mustache. When his antique phone rings, it sounds like a train coming down the tracks, an early electric earthquake. He answers it by saying, "Rangoon here."

I take one last look at Bulch on my way out the door as he pulls from his pipe and smiles. "Sounds like a real goatfucker," he says into the phone.

WHISKEY JELLY BLUES

Bearclaw Murphy's isn't unlike Bulch's office. Both spaces harken back to a time before any of us were born, a time when our grandparents were teenagers fascinated by the pages of Encyclopedia Britannica and Edgar Rice Burroughs novels. The only difference between the décor of Bulch's office and the décor of Bearclaw Murphy's is the geographic location. Bearclaw Murphy's is the world of Lewis and Clark, not early-century Congo. Bear traps, fox fur, a seven-foot stuffed grizzly bear, a Girandoni air rifle, snow shoes made of dear antler, dream catchers, stuffed pheasant, duck feet, a two inch thick circular round of a redwood tree, a map of the Oregon Territory, and a ten foot tall painting of Sacajawea are just a few of the ocular stimulants Bearclaw Murphy's has to offer. Behind the bar is a wall of mid to late 1960's records—an anachronism within an anachronism.

As far as booze and beer is concerned, Bulch has an exquisite palate. My favorite spirit at Bearclaw Murphy's is Cosmic Grizzly Bourbon. It tastes like molasses covered cornstalks cooked in an Appalachian forest fire and is best with a Durham cigar.

The clientele of Bearclaw Murphy's is something you might find between the dusty encyclopedias in Rangoon's office—The French Congo and the Lewis and Clark expedition all rolled into one. It's filled with savages, explorers, hunters, gatherers, drunks, foreigners, outlaws, animals, sticks of dynamite, Indians, Poles, Parisians, Africans, Portuguese, and an endless sea of lost travelers.

Most of the patrons blend into the hunter green and brown motif of the establishment, as if they have been camped out there for generations, hunting the last rhinoceros. Their faces wear the look of unwilling determination. Wrinkled and cramped, even the younger portraits look as if they have been hanging on the wall for thousands of years.

In short, Bearclaw Murphy's is the sort of place someone can easily get lost inside.

If you ask me how I feel about my job when I'm out drinking at night,

I'll tell you I hate it, that the customers are drilling black holes into my brain. But when I'm actually here amongst the scent of dust and dead oil, leaning against the bar in the dim yellow light, I don't mind it. There's as much top-notch booze here as I need to numb myself and tickle my eyeballs, enough to get me through another night, to believe one more time in something.

I take my place behind the bar, greet my first customer with an indefinable nod. Gail asks me for a vodka soda with three limes and a kiss on the lips. I embellish her first request, pouring four fingers of potato juice on the rocks. I compromise her second request, giving her a half-hearted hug. She pushes her sloppy wet lips into my cheek anyways. Gail is 57 years old and looks like a cheap Italian snail. She wears turquoise eye shadow and heavy red lipstick that is a far cry from precisely applied, plenty of polyester. She smells like the fragrance section at a bargain department store.

"Your bulge is looking good today," Gail says in her dead lung smoker voice, raising her eyebrows in rapid succession. I look down at the crotch of my pants and shrug.

"I got that goin for me," I say. I am a piece of meat—A piece of meat that just received a five-dollar tip from a turquoise snail. I let my hips push outward, giving Gail a little more of what she wants. She's never been married and has no children. I imagine she's the type of woman who frequents male strip clubs and insists on stuffing the singles down the front of the g-string.

I cut limes, oranges, and lemons, fold a few towels, turn the lights down lower and pop some popcorn in the microwave. I listen to the microwave motor for two minutes, wait for the popping to slow down, four to five seconds between kernels, open the door and drop the popcorn in a few bowls, scatter them down the bar. It's relatively quiet. Usually Bulch plays records in his office over the central PA system, saying strange things into a microphone like "Make sure you've always got a good pair of socks. The Nyangani Tiger Bunny is attracted to podiatric perspiration." Last week we listened to the great speeches of JFK for forty-five minutes until everyone finally left, bored out of their minds. Bulch was none the wiser. I didn't mind everyone leaving. Secretly, deep down in some dark corner of my soul, there's a sliver of selfishness, and this selfishness has me hoping I will lose this job, Phoenix will collapse under the dissatisfaction of her own, and we'll find ourselves poor and knee deep in the needles of California redwood.

A few hipsters with beards and skateboards finish up their beers and roll out of the room, arguing about whether or not Lena Dunham is a genius, or just a lucky rich kid. I pull a Jerry Garcia Band record from the wall behind me and lay it down on the player. Bulch has a soft spot for the JGB and has on many occasions shimmied like a magical eel-footed LSD guru across the barroom to their sounds. When the music reaches his office, he immediately says into the phone "Well Dick, it's your horse, you better feed it the lemon curd," and hangs up. As expected, Bulch appears from behind the office door with a grin on his face and a bead of sweat cutting through his mustache. He lets one brown polyester pant leg dangle slowly out, teasing the appendage like a showgirl.

"You are a savage," he says to me. He twirls around, flailing his thin arms in front of him, letting his neck spin as if it were a ball bearing. "Time is a stripper, doing it just for you," he sings.

Oftentimes, when the off-Love St. foot traffic witnesses Bulch's gyrations, we see an immediate spike in sales. This evening is no different. There's a sweetness in the air, in part because two nights ago I dropped a few orange blossoms in a vase next to the till, but also because this evening is arid and warm, and everywhere beyond the bay window that at this moment Bulch is cranking open allowing the music to spill out into the neighborhood, people are smiling, moving towards something, the unknown.

Upon my suggestion, I find myself making a few of my world famous

Mai-tais for a pair of young women who wear different loose fitting tank tops, one black, one white. They are both Puerto Rican and recent graduates of NYU.

"This is exquisite," one of them says.

"Fuck yeah it is," the other replies.

Bulch winks at me and twirls back to the center of the room where he declares to his audience of eleven, "You are my disciples!"

Bulch is like a tornado, widening in its path. The more he spins, the more people are sucked in, until finally I find I'm working my ass off, sweating, listening to slurred drink orders rattled from unseen tongues, and praying for ten small seconds to take a deep breath and drink as much Cosmic Grizzly as I can swallow. I'm so busy now, in fact, that I didn't even notice Cherise has arrived.

Cherise and I work together every night we bartend. Bulch likes to have a male and female bartender on together during the busy nights, and he believes the relationship between two bartenders should rival that of a married couple. In some ways, Cherise may actually know me better than my wife. She's seen me do things my wife would never guess I would do. It's because of this that Cherise and I have a unique bond, one that binds us together for life. I've lifted her off the toilet when she's passed out with her pants down and piss dribbling down her legs, and she's cut the straw for me in the men's room above a line declaring "You aren't going to die here," after I've declared "I'm going to die here."

I take a moment to relax when I realize Cherise is here. She's a skilled bartender, an accomplished drinker, and a medical school dropout with a photography portfolio based primarily in dendrology, or "trees," in layman's terms. She identifies herself as a "sculptor."

"Chainsaw," she says as she passes me, twirling two bottles in her hand.

I'm not sure what she's referring to until I notice her wave one of her hands at me. There's a bandage with blood leaking through it tied around her thumb. "You're gonna have to wash the glasses tonight," she says.

I nod my head and curse under my breath. Cherise may be the most beautiful woman in the world, with jet black hair and Elvira bangs, a body like a waterpark in August, and a nose that wouldn't look out of place on a bunny in a neon forest, but I wouldn't know at this point. Bulch has successfully bred sexuality out of his coworkers. We are the old married couple that no longer makes love.

"Are you fucking serious?" I say.

She doesn't respond.

I move as far away from her as possible as she passes me again, making sure that neither my body nor my clothing touch any part of her. "You just added fifty percent more work to my night. There's not enough rum in Barbados to make up for that."

She sends me a middle finger with a smile, slides me a shot of Mount Gay rum, then chats up the next patron, a businessman in a suit with a gold tooth and his initials carved into the side of his head, "ASS." "I'm in art," he says.

Cherise grabs his hand and introduces herself. "I do chainsaw sculpture," she replies.

"Ansley Sunbeam Salinger," he says. "Pleasure to meet you."

It's 11:11. Five hours to go. Rangoon's socks are falling down, but his shoes haven't stopped moving. We've just finished side one of The Guess Who's "American Woman" and the bar feels like it's on fire. The flames rip and tear, rise and fall, and rise again, until last call sounds, and the revelers fold themselves up and deliver themselves home. It is the end.

Cherise and I take a seat next to Bulch at the bar and begin counting our tips. Bulch offers us both a joint, which we oblige—I trust Bulch's weed. He steps behind the bar and starts pouring ingredients into a shaker.

"You hear St. Claire's throwing a rainbow party tomorrow night?" Cherise says.

Both Bulch and I raise our eyebrows.

"Rad," I say. "Who's playing?"

"Volcano the Spacemachine," she replies.

Bulch shakes his cocktail, tilts his head back, and says to the ceiling, "The foundation of this world isn't enough." He stomps his boots as hard as he can against the wooden floor. "Someday, it's gonna break." I think he's speaking in a first person metaphor.

I pull Cherise into my ribs and she puts her head to rest on my shoulder. "I wish I had a Jeep. Like one of the ones in M.A.S.H.," I tell her.

"A Willys," Bulch says. "A masterpiece of American automotive engineering." He pours the drinks into three rocks glasses.

I can tell by the black murkiness of the cocktails that we're about to wipeout on a Surfer-on-Acid. I smell the pineapple, the Jagermeister, the coconut rum. We open our throats and swallow.

"I want to drive down Highway One to the Pacific in my Willy and catch a salmon, bring it home to my wooden cabin and roast it over an open oak flame, let my toes dangle in the marine layer," I say.

Cherise looks up at me. "Someday," she says. "And I'll come over and chop down a redwood and sculpt you a bear."

I can feel some anxiety welling up within me, which worries me slightly. After all this booze and pot, I should be completely indifferent to whatever emotions are inside. But there is this feeling of guilt within I can never seem to shake. I am just a bartender. I am only a bartender. And my wife sleeps at home alone without me. And at 4:30 am, I'm counting money with Cherise, and smoking pot with Rangoon, and soon I'll just want to put my head somewhere and it won't matter whose stomach it may be upon. I'm tired of everything.

My cell phone vibrates. *Got a start on the whiskey jelly. The corn is in the goose. From, Saccharine Cowboy.*

"Whiskey jelly," I say to no one in particular.

"Whiskey jelly?" Bulch replies. He pumps his pipe full of tobacco and lights it. "What's this about whiskey jelly?"

Abortion Blues

The abortion happened on a Saturday two years ago, and has been an unpredictable bomb exploding every now and again in the back of our minds ever since. What started inside my wife during our honeymoon, ended less than three months later inside our house. A medium sized white pill was all it took. The amount of blood was staggering. The stain on the carpet was the reason we moved. Her sorrow is incalculable.

Since that day, we've spent less time making love and more time reexamining what we love about our life, taking inventory of everything beautiful against all things horrific. Often, it feels as if we're maniacally grasping for each other as we plummet off the edge of a cliff, looking to each other for rescue, but receiving nothing in return.

Bulch spins his keys around his index finger and rattles his fingernails on the bar in front of me. "Where are you?" he asks.

I pull at my eyelids. "Rangoon."

He winks at me. "Goatfucker."

I get my shit together and cruise out the door and into the night, a wad of twenties stuffed in my sock.

Armpit Blues

It's 5:30 in the morning and I'm standing in the doorjamb of my bedroom examining Phoenix's sleeping face. Her fingers inadvertently twist into each other, tightening and loosening, pink to white, with every unknown breath. On her nightstand, two empty wrappers of Rudy's Candy Tampons glow electric red in the reflection of her alarm clock. In thirty minutes, she'll awaken and make herself coffee and perhaps a turkey sandwich with not enough mayonnaise, and she'll smoke pot and blow it into the world and wonder what our life would be like if we had made different decisions. Forty-five minutes later, I'll hear her heels as they reluctantly depart for another day in a cubicle, which may contain dangerous, health-compromising blue-black mold, according to the last text message I received before she went to bed last night. I wonder about her at work, how she acts, the way her neck moves, the bite of her teeth against her lips, what the inflections of her coworkers voices sound like when they discuss sweaters and awkward intimate encounters. I've never visited her office, and whenever I mention this to Gail the Snail, she says, "You're not a very good husband. One of these days you should surprise her and take her to lunch." In my defense, I would ask this—who would want to visit an environment so unconditionally detested and hated by their wife and attempt to cultivate any happiness from it? It would be like throwing a beach party bonfire at Auschwitz.

Phoenix sleeps snore-free because she rarely drinks, which apparently is the major cause of my own minor sleep apnea. She smokes pot and her lungs puff up and suck in and blow out as naturally as the trade winds pumping the big suck across the globe. I take off my socks as carefully as I can, undo my belt, drop my pants, and rip off my shirt. I crawl in bed next to her and gently maneuver her legs out of my spot. Her chest rises up, then falls back down. Her lips are moist with drool. I rub my thumb across her forehead and she flashes a somnambulist grin like a cat in a gravel heaven made of yellow parakeets.

Outside our bedroom window, I can hear the sound of cheap tin, a light silvery rattle every half-second. I hear a set of keys jangle. Then a trunk pop open, the climax of the cheap tin orchestra, falling perhaps into a pile of itself, and then the trunk closing. A few moments later, I hear the sound of canvas rustling, keys jangling, and once again, a trunk pops open. I quietly slide out of bed, making sure no part of my body touches my wife's, and tiptoe across the room to the window. I fold a two-inch section of our curtains back and pop an eye out. Across the street, Black Charlie is busy packing his car full of backpacks, camp gear, pillows, and six-packs of beer. His dreads dangle down the side of his ribs and flirt with the waistband of his boxers. He's naked aside from his boxers. I wonder if Charlie might be a sleepwalker. I tap lightly against the window with my finger, having read somewhere that sleepwalkers rely on an acute sense of hearing to maneuver and function in their surreal dream state, much like a hungry bat in a midnight cave. Charlie doesn't look over, but my wife wakes up.

"Babe?" she says in a half sleeping voice.

"Go to sleep."

She rolls over and descends down the black tunnel into dream— there's an ice cream cone balancing on a thin aquamarine wall of a bathroom stall. She's naked and sits on the toilet, staring at the ice cream cone. It teeters above her head, one melted drop lands on her bare shoulder. Several faces appear, men and women, peering over the walls and under the door, watching as she urinates. Horrified, she struggles to cover her exposed body—not enough hands. The faces grin and swirl across her eyes, lips moving closer, towards her pussy…

I see my wife's leg shimmy as she rolls back over and lets out a sigh.

Back through the window, Charlie holds a pipe in his hand. He takes a huge rip, high-steps in place and drops his head, allowing his arms and hands to rise up and hold parallel to earth like that famous picture of Jim Morrison. He shakes his head back and forth and I can barely make out a song trailing from his throat.

I walk my hands across the dresser searching for a lighter I thought I saw when I departed earlier today. My pinky nail drags across the plastic cylinder. I raise the lighter to the window and roll the flint wheel with my thumb, sparks igniting, fire. Charlie doesn't seem startled by the orangey reflection rippling across the street. He turns his head towards me and smiles. He gestures with his hand for me to join him and raises up the pipe as an offering. I look back over at Phoenix who's still dreaming, her face turning gray like the mud of Siberia.

I find my jeans in the darkness and leave the bedroom, hopping on one leg across the kitchen as I pull them on. I grab two beers from the refrigerator, and put two more in my back pockets in case Charlie has finally gone off the deep end and we need to celebrate the end of earthly sanity and the beginning of intergalactic psychosis.

Charlie hops on the trunk of his car as I approach him and pats his hand on the metal, asking me to take a seat. I hop up next to him and he wraps a large arm around my neck, grabbing a beer with his free hand.

"What's up, Chuck?" I say, using the lighter to open his brew.

"I have it figured out," he says. He takes a big swallow of his beer and smiles wider, pointing up at the few stars in the sky, then dropping his hands. "You know how many stars there are in our neighborhood?" he asks me.

"Millions," I reply.

"Nope," Charlie says. "I count five. The things you can't see don't count, even if they're there. The key to life is to one day see 'em."

I feel like I've had far too many cryptic, philosophical sentences uttered to me lately, so I say, "Charlie, what the fuck are you doing in the middle of the night, standing in the street in your boxers, smoking dope and slamming your trunk all loud and shit?"

Charlie nods his head at me and takes in the question, just like an actor in a movie, subtly moving his lips and pulling on a dread. "I'm going to California," he says.

California. Shit. Everyone wants to go to California. I'm happy for Charlie, even though I secretly want him to break down somewhere around Kansas, never make it. What California doesn't need is more people moving there and taking jobs and driving up real estate. What California needs is an exodus. It needs the Charlie's of the world to want to stay put, to think where they are is just as cool if not cooler, and there's nothing as rad out west. It needs the Charlie's of the world who haven't found what they're looking for to move to South Dakota, start something beautiful in the blizzards, create color in the flatlands, carve out faces in the Black Hills, and declare everything groundbreaking and up-and-coming to be found in the streets of Watertown.

"Where in California?" I ask him.

"Where the trees meet the ocean. Ital," he says.

"Ital," I say.

"Jah see and know," he says. "I lost this job to gain something else."

Charlie's optimism is a bit off-putting in the middle of the night, but I don't want to bust his bubble. I nod my head in agreement and start drinking my beer a little faster until it's gone. I open up the next one.

"You ever wonder what your life would be like if you were born in North Korea?" Charlie asks me and I immediately hate this question because it's been asked over a zillion times during countless "what does it all mean?" conversations.

"No," I respond. "I'm here, fuck it. And I already know what you're going to say, about how lucky we are to have freedom and knowledge and to be able to love anyone we want and to see the world, but everyone has their misery, no matter where they are or what they have. We're all alike in our suffering. Sadness and happiness are the same anywhere in the world, and we can't even imagine the degrees of those emotions unless we're living them."

Charlie shakes his head. "You have everything already," he says. "You are where I want to get. You have roses in your front yard."

His sentence traps my breath. I can't breathe, so I smile. I feel horrible for Charlie thinking what I have is beautiful. I always thought his incredible core muscles, dreads, and rich black skin were beautiful, that someday we would eat lobster together.

"I thought someday we would eat lobster together," I tell him.

"They used to feed prisoners lobster back in the day," he replies. "Can you imagine that? I bet they were all like 'oh shit, please no more lobster, it's disgusting!' and just laughing their asses off splitting those tails and claws in half."

"I'm pretty sure it wasn't considered a delicacy back then," I tell Charlie. "I think they cooked them dead and dried them in salt—pretty fucking gross."

Charlie doesn't hear me. He's focused on a star in the sky and remembering a time when he was a boy and he believed that each star was a small portion of his dead mother. "California is my lobster. I'm going there to eat it all."

I leave the last beer with Charlie and write down Cliff's number on a napkin for him. "In case you wind up in L.A., my buddy is a pretty solid guy—he'll show you around. L.A. is big, man, big and a bit fucking nuts.

"Thanks, brother." He promises he'll send me an address when he settles down there. He winks with both his eyes and says, "Whiskey jelly. I can taste it."

I think I hear a frog barking at me as I cross the street back home, but attribute the strange sound to my stoniness. Three feet from my front door my cell phone rings, Cliff's name and number glowing at me. "Riverbank," I say into the phone as I twist the front door open.

"Cassidy, you gotta do something right now for us. There is no debate."

"What?"

I can hear Charlie laughing in the background. "Tell him," he says.

"Listen to me, Cass. We need you to go into the kitchen, open the refrigerator door, pull out some cream cheese and some lox, and some capers if you have them, then spread the cream cheese, lox, and capers on your wife's armpit and eat it."

Charlie breaks down laughing in the background. Cliff remains completely serious, waiting for an answer.

"No way," I say. "She's sleeping and she has work early in the morning."

"You have to understand what is happening here. We are recording this conversation, so you should know that forever will know what you did. We are recording, and we want a picture or video of you eating the cream cheese armpit. Do you understand? We need you to record yourself doing it. And we are recording the conversation. And this cream cheese armpit is going to save the world from itself. And the whiskey jelly, and the Mustard Bros…"

There's no doubt in my mind Cliff and Charlie are wasted to the point of no return.

"My wife is definitely not gonna be cool with me eating cream cheese out of her armpit while she's sleeping," I tell Cliff.

"Mischief leads to interesting things. Maybe you'll learn something about her if you do. Did you ever think of that? You're so concerned with the negative that comes from situations, but did you ever stop to think that from the negative, a positive might come? That, although she may be angry at her cream cheese armpit at first, she'll probably tell this story for eternity, and your little idiot grandchildren will pass it along for generations until finally, Cassidy and Phoenix, great great great great grandparents of Cassidy The Sixth are legends of cream cheese lore?"

I can't argue with Cliff. Everything he says is logical through the disproof of illogic. "Hold on." I grab a butter knife, cream cheese, lox, and capers from the fridge and hold the phone in my ear with my shoulder. I crawl on my knees towards the bed in my bedroom, and quietly pull the blankets down from my wife, exposing her arms. Her eyelids are half open and twitching. I lift up one of her arms, hearing Cliff and Charlie giggling in the phone as I do so. I take the knife and dip it into the cream cheese and begin spreading it across her armpit.

"What are you doing?" Cliff whispers.

"I'm spreading the cream cheese," I whisper back. Phoenix shifts a few inches. I pull the salmon from the plastic package and lay it across the cream cheese. I take two capers out of the jar and push them into the spread.

"Are you eating it yet?" Cliff asks.

"Not yet," I say. "I just put the last caper on"

Cliff and Charlie can barely contain themselves on the other line.

"Put the phone next to her armpit so we can hear you munching," Charlie says.

I lay the phone down on the bed, open my mouth, and start eating. Phoenix immediately jumps up out of bed and screams "What the fuck is happening!?" Cliff and Charlie are laughing so loud into the phone it feels as if there are four people in the room.

"What are you doing!?" Phoenix yells, turning on the lamp on her nightstand.

"I'm eating your armpit," I say with the butter knife in my hand. "Jewish style."

She looks at the clock. In one minute, she's supposed to wake up, shower, and drive somewhere to do something she hates.

She looks around the room, drops her arms. "I hate my fucking job," she says. She shoves a finger into the cream cheese, and puts it in her mouth. "Can you pack me a bowl and make me coffee?" she asks, sliding into the bathroom.

I raise the phone back up to my ear.

"I'll see you in Mongolia," Cliff says.

"Tell Cassidy I'm turning him into a bunny rabbit right now," Charlie says into Cliff's face. "With cream cheese all over his stupid bunny face."

"You're a bunny rabbit with a cream cheese face," Cliff tells me.

I hang up the phone with cream cheese on my nose and a bunny toothed smile on my face. I lie on my back and listen to Phoenix's water pound against the porcelain tub. I can hear the roar of Black Charlie's engine as he fires up his car. Light creeps around the edges of the curtains, illuminating the corner of the room. "The abortion happened on a Saturday," I say. "And I'll never forget her face."

Strawberries Mean Love Blues

I hate thinking about Phoenix at work when it's such a beautiful day in California. 82° at the coast, clear skies, 51% humidity. I'd prefer it if I were sitting in a strawberry field in Oxnard CA, listening to the soft rustling of oak leaves in the ocean breeze. But I'm not. And neither is Phoenix. As a matter of fact, Phoenix's office environment might be the exact opposite of a strawberry field in Oxnard, California. The walls of her cubicle are blank and gray. There are no windows to speak of, except those behind the closed-doors of her bosses. There is a dull electric buzz just beneath the surface of all other sounds inside the space—there never is and never will be any pure, natural quiet.

From every cubicle, a different station of Pandora or Spotify plays, a mind-numbing cornucopia of pop and rap, Taylor Swift and Kanye. From outside every cubicle people gather to gossip about interoffice relationships and who could be getting fired next and what sweater Taylor will wear tomorrow. The carpet is gray, the ceiling is gray, the kitchen is gray, and the coffee is gray. Even the water that goes into the coffee is gray. Phoenix is sure the water is gray for the same reason the ocean is blue—it's a reflection of the atmosphere. Phoenix usually takes lunch at her desk so she can leave work an hour early. Today lunch is a turkey sandwich she prepared for herself last night in her pajama bottoms with the television on in the background at 10:11 pm. On two pieces of low carb bread is a decent amount of Duke's mayonnaise and three thin slices of turkey. She takes it out of her plastic sandwich bag and inspects it like an unknown meteor. It looks gray. She takes a bite and swallows, but would rather just throw it out and order a fourteen-dollar salad from the café across the street to be delivered, dropped in her lap with plastic utensils, dressing on the side. But she resists, thinking I would be upset if she did. She knows we don't have much money and knows I haven't bought a new pair of jeans or a new pair of socks in almost two years even though my jeans and socks are farming holes at an accelerated rate. Still, fourteen dollars wouldn't bankrupt us and I wouldn't care if she got herself a salad—it might make her smile. But maybe it's better to eat the turkey sandwich. There are starving children in India and Africa and China and Los Angeles.

Back here, at home, it's 1:11 in the afternoon and I've just woken up. I have the next two days off, so I force myself to get up instead of fall back asleep, and move to the couch where I can lie down and stare out the skylight above. If I stare long enough through the skylight, I can make believe I'm in that strawberry field. If I look straight up in The East, and not straight ahead, I can be anywhere. It's the noise that gets to me, even in a quiet neighborhood like our own. We've got neighbors who scream at each other on their porch. College kids are renting out the house down the street for the summer—kegs arrive, drunk twenty year olds come and go. A garbage truck picks up and dumps out Charlie's trash across the street. A car honks its horn at the garbage truck. The garbage man yells something inaudible yet hostile at the car and the car honks again and peels out with a middle finger.

I think today I'd like to go fishing. I drag myself to the refrigerator pretending the kitchen is a lake. I pull a beer out but don't untwist the top. Instead, I stare at it like a brand new fishing rod and dangle it from my wrists. I know I shouldn't drink first thing in the morning, but there's something romantic about trying to forget everything, pushing it back somewhere, back into the Stone Age, and beer is the perfect beverage for this type of thinking. I twist off the top and wade back over to the couch.

It takes me a few minutes to realize I'm naked. I can't see myself, but I'm sure I don't look very cool with my penis out and a beer in my hand. A bottle of beer is a terrible accessory to the male form. It's phallic, dripping, filled with a pale yellow liquid, redundant. I probably look like some grossly pornographic alien with two dicks pointing outward in a terribly offensive way. On the other hand, the bottle of beer is a perfect accompaniment to the female form, for reasons that must now seem obvious. I wish for a moment I was a woman—I would look cool right now, like a photograph of a famous artist just before the zenith of her career, instead of a deadbeat bartender at the apex of a downward slope.

***

Over in California, windows open, a slight breeze wafting through, Cliff and Charlie have gotten up early and begun phase one of what has become known as "The Whiskey Jelly Experiments."

Cliff has lined up seven shot glasses and half-filled them with seven different jellies, jams, and preserves—Boysenberry, Peach, Marmalade, Raspberry, Strawberry, Apple, and Fig. Charlie sits on the couch with an old blue t-shirt tied around his head, blindfolding his eyes.

"Okay, Here's what's gonna happen. I'm gonna start mixing the whiskey with the jellies, then I'm gonna feed 'em to ya and you're gonna tell me which tastes best," Cliff says.

Charlie giggles. "I'm so hungover," he says. "I really need a shot, like right now."

"Like right now?"

"Yeah, like right now."

"Hmm."

"Just pass me the bottle."

"Wait, I have to take a piss," Cliff says. "Just hang tight for a minute." Cliff likes to torture his younger brother and gets a kick out of his brother's bad habits. He grabs the bottle of whiskey and takes it into the bathroom, locking the door behind him, knowing full well his brother will rip off the makeshift blindfold and attempt to pour himself a drink while he's away.

"Motherfucker!" he hears Charlie yell when he can't find the bottle. "Give me whiskey!"

Cliff settles Charlie down by promising he'll receive a shot after he's reapplied the blindfold and taken a seat on the couch underneath the window overlooking the filthy boulevard palm trees below.

"I don't want your palate to be ruined by a shot of straight whiskey without jelly. This is serious business. This is Mustard Brothers," Cliff shouts through the bathroom door.

Charlie sits down, reties the blindfold, waits. The toilet flushes.

Cliff's steps are taken carefully, one boot in front of the other, grinning. "Is the blindfold back on?" he asks.

"Yeah, dickhead."

"I don't know—looks a little loose."

"I'll punch you in the face."

Cliff laughs, heads into the kitchen and pours the whiskey into the fig preserve, stirring it with one of the three spoons the brothers own. Spoons are scarce around the brother's loft, mainly because Charlie consistently burns and bends them all with his drug sucking.

Cliff pours the fig jelly whiskey into a shot glass and hands it to Charlie, taking a seat across from him on an old piano bench, pulling his small notepad from his back pocket. At the top of the notepad he scribbles the words "The Whiskey Jelly Experiments." He crosses his legs like a headshrinker. "Now I want you to be very specific in your descriptions of each whiskey jelly. I need to know what works best. This is research. This is important stuff, so no fucking around."

Charlie shoots the fig whiskey down his throat and sticks his tongue out. "It tastes like shit," he says.

"Can you expand on that?"

"No. It tastes like shit. Don't do it. Don't fucking mix whiskey with fig jelly, man. What the fuck is a fig anyways?"

"How'd you know it was a fig? Maybe you just don't like figs. I don't want to discriminate against fig lovers."

"I knew it was a fig because it tasted like shit, not shit with a hint of strawberry."

"So are you saying the fig tastes like shit?"

"No, I'm saying the fig jelly and the fucking whiskey together tastes like shit."

Cliff scribbles something down in his notepad and returns to the kitchen. He pours the whiskey into the strawberry jam and stirs.

When he returns to his brother, he's dismayed to find him without the blindfold and with a look of disdain on his face. "None of this shit is gonna taste good with whiskey," Charlie says.

"I beg to differ," Cliff responds. He hands Charlie the strawberry whiskey jelly.

"Why don't you do one of these shots with me if you think it's gonna taste good?"

"Your palate has always been better than mine," Cliff says. "You could always tell when the milk got rotten, even when you were all smacked out on the booboo stone and chasing angels in your dirty shorts."

Charlie nods his head and grins with the compliment. "That's true. I've got a wise old tongue. My tongue has seen the world develop at the tip of it."

Cliff doesn't know what this sentence means, and neither do I. Neither one of us are sure if it's some type of sexual innuendo or just complete nonsense that may or may not sound interesting.

Charlie takes the shot and once again shoots his tongue out of his mouth. "Tastes like shit!" he says.

"Expand Charlie—use your words."

"I *am* using my words, and my words are 'shit.'"

"That's one word."

"It. Tastes. Like. Shit. Literally. I think I'd rather suck on your boot."

Cliff takes off his boot and throws it at Charlie, the heel connecting with a tooth. Charlie grabs the boot and whirls it back at Cliff, distracting his brother just enough to slide past him into the kitchen and rip into the bottle of whiskey with a fist on his hip and his chin pointed towards the sky. He takes three big slugs and wipes his mouth with the back of his hand. "I'm not drinking any more of that shit. If you ask me, it shouldn't be whiskey and jelly mixed together. It needs to be whiskey jelly, just one semi-solid, gelatinous mixture that gets pumped into a donut or however they do it, and fucks you up."

"Yeah, I was pretty sure that's what needed to happen to begin with, but it sounds like a lot of work. It would have been much easier to just mix it with some boysenberry, open up a Mustard Brothers, and call it a day."

Cliff takes a seat and asks Charlie for the bottle by raising his bushy eyebrows twice. The brothers don't have much to do today, except make a few phone calls to a couple galleries and art dealers, paint bunny rabbits, and critique near finished pieces. Charlie lets Cliff handle the business of art for him, and Cliff is a wolverine when it comes to negotiating money.

***

Sometimes I feel a bit lonely out here, alone, with Phoenix at work and me just pretending to be somewhere I'm not. I feel like communicating with someone back home, so I text Cliff something semi-serious and easy to respond to—*I miss California, I can't wait for whiskey jelly.*

What I don't know is I've accidentally sent this text to Phoenix, probably because I've been thinking about her this whole time, wondering how bad it must be for her olive skin to be cooped up all day long in that gray place without light, her cheeks sucked out slowly in the neon burn, her cells and molecules caged and her arms cramped and typing.

Phoenix has taken a couple bites of her sandwich and is now back at work on the "green" press release for Rudy's Candy Tampons. She's surprised by the text from me, and searches her mind for any clue as to what I could be talking about. "I knew he hated it here," she finally says under her breath. "And what the fuck is whiskey jelly?"

The gay intern overhears her as he passes her cubicle on his way to the water cooler. "Whiskey jelly?" he says. "I like it. Lets fucking blog it."

Phoenix is confused by whiskey jelly. She wonders if "whiskey jelly" is some secret sexual term I use with an unknown California mistress. She writes back, *What?*

I'm utterly confused when I receive a text message from Phoenix that reads *what?*

I look around the living room, wondering if I've said something out loud, and maybe Phoenix didn't go to work today and she's outside watching me drink beer naked like some dirty alien. *What what?* I text her back.

Whiskey jelly? she replies.

I can't figure out how she could possibly know about whiskey jelly. I haven't mentioned it to anyone besides Cliff, and I'm pretty sure it's been an inside joke between us since I said it. It takes me the second half of the beer before I realize I've accidentally texted Phoenix instead of Cliff. I instantly want to blame my phone for the mishap, not myself for being sucked into a technology ruled world of communication barriers disguised as thoroughfares. I vow to phone Cliff next time, tell him my thoughts with my mouth and tongue. Or shit, even better, I'll write a two sentence letter and send it in the mail, the envelope creasing at the corners as it travels across the country through rain and weather and dirty hands.

My phone vibrates again. *Who is whiskey jelly? Are you cheating on me?*

Phoenix has never asked me if I've cheated on her, which makes me wonder if she's cheating on me. I can't figure out why anyone would think "whiskey jelly" was a term of endearment used fondly for a mistress. *No. I was texting Cliff. Whiskey jelly's a long story…it's about whiskey jelly donuts.*

Phoenix doesn't respond to my text. Instead, she stops working on her Rudy's Candy Tampons press release and stares at the blank walls until they begin swirling towards a distant dimming black focal point. She doesn't know why, but this text seems to have deeply affected her. Perhaps it's that she had never known I missed California, or had strange ideas about donuts. There's a split second where Phoenix wonders who exactly I am, and what I do during the day. Do I drink beer naked? Do I dance recklessly to Gun Club records? She feels sick. She wants to come home. The door to her boss's office is open. She pulls her high heels back on her feet and walks over to it, dropping a hip when she hits the doorway. "Jerry," she says to her gray-faced boss with a raspberry Danish in his hand. "I don't feel so good today."

Day Off Blues

On my days off, I like to pretend I'm a famous painter. I wear the tightest polyester death-black pants in my closet and trim my facial hair in such a manner that I have a barely distinguishable mustache. Bulch says I look just like one of his friends, an art scene guru who refuses to speak English even though he was born in Kansas. His friend is a fellow named St. Claire. St. Claire believes French is the only language that truly makes words sound as beautiful as they are intended to sound. "Aujourd'hui, est une belle journée," he says whenever he swings by Bearclaw Murphy's and dumps a gin down his throat. He's made a few films over the years, but his movies don't make any money and his actors are down on their luck dreamers with broken attitudes. No matter, St. Claire believes art should always be poor, otherwise no one will ever be able to truly relate to it, to allow art to create an emotion. He makes his money betting on horses and throwing parties he calls "Rainbows."

I select my pants from the closet and slide my legs into them, rolling out the wrinkles at the thighs with my palms. Most of the time on these days, I get a beer down the street at my local bar where no one knows my name and no one asks who I am, and most importantly, no one cares. I drink my beer with a look of magical wonder in my eyes and politely nod and smile each time the bartender brings me a fresh cold brew. I tip her well and she smiles. Sometimes I think she's talking about me whenever I see her texting behind the bar. She'll grin and look up at me, and I'll nod with my chin and continue doing my best impersonation of a famous painter, rattling my pinky against the pint glass. I act as if I'm paying attention to the most minute details of the room, using my eyeballs like typewriter keys to pound notes into my brain. I take inventory of how it smells like a combination of a rainy-day Catholic church and squashed raspberries in Oregon mud. How the roof seems to be collapsing in the center, the wooden beams across the ceiling bending like a rainbow. Almost always, the bartender is listening to The Doors. She looks young and has three freckles that form a triangle underneath her right eye. They are a constellation, and I can see her face floating right up off her body like a balloon out into the sky. She especially loves the song "Light my Fire," and every time it plays she sings along as if no one else is in the room. I've seen her reading Schopenhauer a few times in there, watching as her lips move with every silent word she reads. Her love of Schopenhauer is not surprising to me, as most bartenders are amateur philosophers and must be for a great many reasons, including rationalizing our own decision to be a bartender in the first place. We are like Plato at the symposium, standing before everyone, commanding attention, creating a theory with a Heineken in our neck.

On this morning, breakfast is a bowl of organic corn flakes with Stevia leaf sprinkled on top and unsweetened vanilla almond milk. This sentence sounds like something you would feed a unicorn.

Outside my window, I see the roses, and beyond them, Charlie's mailbox. He probably isn't too far away right now, maybe he hit traffic somewhere south, wherever that is. I wonder if he'll make it to California.

As I turn the doorknob to leave, I hear a car pull into the driveway. When I open the door, I see Aunika getting out of her Subaru Outback, another loose-fitting tank top with the word "California" written in vintage block lettering across it. She's rocking turquoise lipstick, which would look idiotic on the average human, but Aunika isn't the average human. Her jeans have a large hole where the right knee pops out. Her boots look like something Mick Jagger's mistress would wear to his concert in 1975. I want to chop wood into tiny little pieces and throw them up into the air just to see what she would look like walking through it, because I think she would look good walking underneath a storm of small wood chips. I rub my fingers across my lips.

"Hey," she says. She pulls off her sunglasses and walks towards me.

"Whats up?" I say. I have an apple in my hand. I don't remember grabbing an apple, but I look pretty fucking healthy with it between my fingers.

She pulls my head into hers and kisses me hard with her turquoise lips. My eyes are open and hers are closed and seem overworked around the lids and the kiss seems to last slightly longer than is comfortable for two friends, but before I can start to wonder about it, she pulls away and walks past me into the living room.

"I broke up with Cesar this morning," she says. She walks over to the bar and pours herself a few fingers of bourbon, gulping it down, a drop traveling down her chin, which she catches with her free hand and pushes back into her tongue.

"Holy shit—you cool? What happened?"

"He isn't right for me. I think he's gay. I hate that he doesn't work and doesn't have any talent really, and I'm repulsed by him—I saw him spit inside a bar the other night, like on the ground. Like, I'm sleeping with a man who spits indoors on the ground at bars in front of people. I'd rather make out with Phoenix's armpit, and I don't find other women attractive in any way."

I like the thought of Phoenix and Aunika making out with each other's armpits, but realize I'd be extremely jealous if that ever happened—I'd feel like the obtuse corner of a strange triangle.

Those boots are in Mick Jagger's mouth walking across my living room floor. Her toes are the strings of Keith Richard's guitar, twanging like broken summer glass. I don't want her to stop moving, and she doesn't, moving back towards the bourbon. I want to shred green leaves of oak and dress her with it. I want to delay the moon at night and then deliver it to Detroit with a long kiss. She is captivating—a good friend, a beautiful friend, a friend whose presence alone makes me look and feel better.

"Want one?" she asks, raising the whiskey up.

I nod my head, unable to speak because now I'm thinking too much about Aunika's kiss and the residue of her mouth drying tightly against my subtle mustache. I've never felt her lips before. Those lips—they felt like they did in my dream and now I wonder if this too is a dream, if St. Claire is throwing a rainbow party up in the sky and a unicorn is getting pumped full of sweet almond milk corn flakes.

She finishes her drink in one gulp, pours two more and takes the bottle with her to me at the door.

"You gonna shut the door?" she asks me as she shoves a boot into it and closes it with Mick's big lips.

I swallow the bourbon down and love the way my belly feels with a bit of burn in it. Aunika knows what she's started by kissing me and is betting I won't mention it to her because if I do, then it would be a kiss, and if I don't, then it's just her lips touching a friend's lips as she walks in the door, a simple, innocent "hello." This kiss is a friendship loophole. This kiss is something she needed to do because she feels lonely, and if I had to guess, because she's already a bit drunk.

"I've wasted so much time on him. I could have three La Di Donuts by now if I hadn't put up with his struggling actor shit for the past two years. I'm not even sure why I'm here. How did I end up here? I should be in fucking Ibiza."

She lays down on the couch and looks up out the skylight, letting one leg fall open and drop off the couch. She lifts up her tank top, exposing her stomach and scratches it with a turquoise fingernail.

"We could be back in California by now," she says and looks into me. "Me and you, side by side, running La Di Donuts and fucking around, dancing to T. Rex with our knuckles dripping in goose liver."

My silence is starting to make both of us uncomfortable. I can tell because Aunika begins to blush, and because she's thinking to herself "He's not saying anything. What the hell's wrong with him? I shouldn't have pecked him on the lips—he's too American, not enough European in him, unable to accept and commit to other forms of love and sexuality." She thinks, "If I could, and he would, I'd book us two flights to Barcelona, just he and I, and I'd show him the city, open him up, give him something to look forward to, something more than writing and his wife, this house and this town."

How do I know what she's thinking? How could I possibly know? Quit asking yourself why and pretend you're on mushrooms and be confident in eight hours it'll all be over.

I head over to the record player and drop the needle on the Gun Club. I feel the need to touch something, so I run my hands across the wooden countertop in the kitchen and peel a banana which I take a bite of.

"Give me a bite," Aunika says, outstretching her hand. I hesitantly walk the banana over to Aunika and hand it to her. She places it up to her mouth, parts her lips, and takes a totally normal bite out of the banana that is in no way sexual. She shoves the banana back at me.

"What do you think?" she says, chewing with her mouth open.

"I think Cesar wasn't good for you, so I think I'm glad you're free again. I think it's tough to support an artist who isn't very good at whatever art they're into—it takes a toll on everyone. Plus he didn't eat sushi. You can't be with someone who doesn't eat sushi. Anyone who orders a teriyaki chicken bowl at a sushi restaurant can't have anything to do with you."

"Yeah, well, I was trying to redefine Cesar in my mind to have the qualities I desire, but it never worked in reality. If he wasn't such a boring, unattractive, low budget Thespian, it might have worked out better, but even so, it would never be the best—there's no intimacy with him—we don't know each other well enough. And he's never seen me with a skinned knee, or on a merry-go-round, or crying about ice-cream, or naked in a closet, or crying in a bathroom on a thirty-eight foot yacht in the Caribbean. It'll never be the best. It can't be."

"It can be the best. You just have to find the best. The best is out there—go skin your fucking knees for someone, take him on that yacht and sit on his lap while you weep. Closets are everywhere!"

"Ha! Not happening. Trust me. It can never be the best." Aunika lets her eyes linger in mine for a split second too long for friends to remain comfortable. Her eyes dim as they turn back towards the skylight. Something is happening—I know this feeling.

I stare at Aunika for a few moments, watching her fingernails trail up and down her belly until her skin turns a light pink underneath. "I like your boots and your lipstick," I tell her.

"Thanks," she says. "No one else does. Cesar doesn't. Didn't. Whatever."

When I hear the familiar sound of my wife's Bavarian engine, my heart skips a beat. I immediately feel as if I've done something wrong just having Aunika in the house lying on the couch with her belly exposed and legs open, staring out of my skylight and dreaming of California.

"Is that Phoenix?" Aunika asks.

I look out the window at Phoenix's slightly astonished face as she pulls into the driveway, notices a car in her parking space, reverses, and parks on the street a few houses down.

"Should I move my car?" Aunika asks but has no intention of doing so.

"I think she found a space a few doors down," I tell her.

"You sure?" Aunika says, sitting up and shaking out her hair.

"Yeah," I say. I take a look at Aunika sitting upright on the couch and I immediately wish she hadn't sat up. It would look less suspicious if she were lying down, comfortable, not sitting up as if she had been lying down. I open the door for Phoenix who has a bewildered look on her face.

"Who's here?" she asks.

"Aunika," I tell her.

Her face looks immediately relieved and her teeth open up. "Oh. Cool. I was thinking bad things, baby—I'm going crazy. I thought it was 'whiskey jelly.'"

"I can't believe you think I'm cheating on you with someone named 'whiskey jelly.'"

"I just hate my job and I'm paranoid about everything lately, and I feel like I'm under water or something. Like it's hard to breathe. I'm gurgling. I'm gurgling through life." She swims over to me.

I kiss Phoenix on the lips, feeling the difference, wondering for a moment if she can taste Aunika on me, the dried saliva flaking off.

"Why'd you come home early?"

"Couldn't take it."

Phoenix moves past me and into the house where she hurries over to Aunika and tackles her with a hug. "What's up, girl?!" she says.

"Nada," Aunika replies. "Just hangin out."

"Is this your whiskey?"

"Bourbon."

Phoenix slugs the whiskey and pours herself another shot. She wraps her hands behind her back and undoes her bra, pulling it out through the armhole in her blouse and throwing it towards the bedroom where it falls about seven feet short of the door and near the record player.

"I hate my job," Phoenix says. "Why aren't you at the donut shop. It looked crazy busy when I drove past."

"I broke up with Cesar," Aunika tells her.

Phoenix replaces the semi-relaxed look on her face with one of false concern. "Oh my God, what happened? Are you okay?"

Aunika rolls her eyes a bit and uses a toe to jab Phoenix in the ribs.

"Don't act like you give a shit. Neither one of you liked him." She grabs the bottle and pours a little more into her mouth, spilling most of it on her face, her tank top, and the couch.

"Yeah, I didn't like him," Phoenix says, getting up to grab some paper towels. "His hair was too good—and the sushi thing."

There is a moment of silence. I like to think of meteors when there are moments of silence. I see myself riding one from another galaxy, one made up entirely of the evergreen Eel River in Humboldt County, one that winds from wherever to Earth, and I'm on the rapids and the rapids end, and there's a bucket of ice cold cans of beer and redwood trees with bushels of marijuana hanging from the branches. I like to think of myself naked in that river, a river without eels but named the Eel because it darts and shoots its way through California the way I wish my own soul did. I want this meteor to crash through my roof right now. I also like clotheslines, so perhaps I'll think of that next—a long clothesline with patchwork jeans and translucent women's underwear swaying in the breeze. And salmon—I like salmon as well. I can pick one right out of river and hold it up to the sky and breathe in breathe out breathe in breathe in breathe in, breathe out, and I'll raise it higher up above my head until I can no longer get any higher, and I'll come back down with that meteor, a big shower of myself, splashing around and pulling on my patchworks and heading over to the bushels and rolling a joint the size of a lightning bolt.

"St. Claire's throwing a rainbow party tonight," I say. I'm not really in the mood for a St. Claire rainbow party because they demand a large amount of energy. If he doesn't feel like you're providing enough energy, he gets very angry, and when someone's angry at a rainbow party, it can ruin the whole experience. I've seen some pretty bummed out faces at a rainbow party and it isn't pretty.

Aunika's eyes light up. She digs on St. Claire and his rainbow parties, and has never refused an evening with Rangoon. "Is Rangoon gonna be there?" she asks. "I think I had a dream about him last night. He was a lion made of yellow candy, and he was wearing spaceboots, and he told me he would press the button. He had his hand up in the air with his finger pointed down, and he was dropping his arm towards this button, and then I woke up."

"Rangoon'll be there," I assure Aunika. I wonder if she's ever kissed Bulch.

Phoenix wipes the sweat from underneath her armpits with her hands and kisses her finger. "I hate my job. But I love you both."

Phoenix looks me long in the eye, the way two people in love do, and this look makes me feel comfortable, at home, California has been brought to me. Aunika sees this and picks herself up off the couch, one foot in front of the other towards the front door, her fingers dangling in the invisible wake of magic behind her elegant gait. "I'll see you tonight," she says and opens the door. When she walks out, she leaves the door open behind her. "We'll chase rainbows," she says over her shoulder and we can barely make out the words over the breeze. She slides past the roses, yanking one from its stem and brushing the petals against her nose before dropping it in the driveway and running it over with her car.

"She's a strange, but magnificent woman," Phoenix says. She takes off her heels and rubs her toes. "Will you make me a sandwich? I only ate like three bites of mine at work."

I open the refrigerator door, take out a beer and the mayonnaise, and say "Sure." My wife loves mayonnaise. I'll make her a damn good sandwich with a dill pickle and a word written into the bread with mustard. *Love*

Phoenix takes the Gun Club record off the player and replaces it with Joni Mitchell and everything turns a shade of blue. She lets down her hair and stretches out her eyelids. She looks like an ancient Etruscan statue coming to life when she does this, blood surging back into those parts of her body that were dead only a few hours ago. "So seriously. What the hell is whiskey jelly?" In her mind, this is only part one of a two-part question, but she won't ask the second—*Are you unhappy? Do you want to move back to California?*—it's too heavy to deal with right now. We are here. We need to live for today, not for the future.

I take a deep breath and look her in the eye. I'm not a famous painter. "Mustard Brothers," I tell her.

Reality Blues

"Fuck, man, I'm going to die writing this book. And I'm gonna be late for work."

Pennsylvania Pyramid Blues

Somewhere in Pennsylvania, Black Charlie is taking a piss at a gas station and reading a day old newspaper stuck to the wall above the urinal. A new pyramid was discovered buried underneath another pyramid in Ethiopia. Archeologists believe there may be yet another pyramid buried underneath *that* pyramid. Black Charlie wonders about infinity, but the end of his stream brings some closure to that thought.

Pectin Bunny Blues

Aisles and aisles of multicolored condiments line the shelves of the local Hispanic grocer in Echo Park, Eastside L.A., an endless array of colors, chilies, plastics, and canned goods varying in language from Korean, to Chinese, to Spanish. Cliff dances with 5/6ths of a sixpack in his hand to imaginary electric guitar music, sucking from a can of beer while Charlie pushes the shopping cart behind him, using his paint stained thumbs to drum a beat against the red plastic handle. They hum together two different songs that come together as one experiment in auditory chaos, something the other shoppers find borderline unbearable, apparent as they scamper and scatter, parting as the brothers rumble down the center of the aisle with wild-eyed grins.

"Drink up, Chuck," Cliff says, then tosses a beer over his shoulder and into Charlie's hand.

"What's that smell in here?" Charlie asks.

"Carne," Cliff responds. "Blood of the god goat."

The butcher in the rear raises a knife and sinks it down deep into a thick slab of meat, swatting at the hovering flies.

"Pectin pectin pectin," Cliff repeats to himself, snapping his fingers, scouring every inch of aisle in search of the key ingredient to their secret whiskey jelly recipe. He holds his hand up and stops mid stride, spotting something on the shelf. "Candy tampons?" he says. He immediately tears into the box, removing three different flavors of Rudy's finest, shoving the discreet packages into his nostrils. "We got cherry, lemon, I think this one is orange, but it could be tangerine. Not sure if the color of the wrapper is more orange than tangerine—I think tangerine is a little darker." He peels open the cherry tampon, removes the applicator, and takes a bite, throwing the superfluous cotton to the floor. "That's a pretty tasty tampon," he says.

"Hey man, do you think a vagina could have a personality?" Charlie asks his brother.

Cliff doesn't humor his brother with a response, but instead shrugs, as if the question is retarded and the answer is well known.

"Yes?" Charlie says.

"Of course," Cliff responds. "Especially with one of these in there." He takes another bite before putting the box back on the shelf and continuing down the aisle. "I've met a few, and they're all different. One was as hilarious as Charlie Chaplin," he says. "And it had the same mustache."

"I wonder about bunny vaginas," Charlie says.

"There's no personality in a bunny vagina," Cliff responds. "You're gonna have to take artistic license with that, maybe do a vagina within a vagina. A Charlie Chaplin vagina on a bunny would be the way to go. I mean, who isn't gonna love a painting of a Charlie Chaplin vagina on a bunny vagina. Vaginas on vaginas on vaginas."

An old woman smiles at the boys and Cliff tips his hat to her, saying "Hello, my love. How do you do?" The old woman continues crawling through the store without responding.

"She must be deaf," Charlie says, then sneaks up behind her and snaps a finger by her ear. No response. His suspicions are validated. "Being deaf must suck."

"Not if you're around us, it wouldn't."

Cliff, now blossoming into the vast openness of the produce section spins on the toes of his boots and asks a question to the universe—"Who doesn't love a mean mint julep?"

He reaches behind and grabs hold of the grill of the shopping cart, pulling it and Charlie with him to the herbs, whereupon he throws his hands into several bushels of mint. He carefully examines each tied bundle with a rigorous visual and olfactory inspection, testing the leaves for pliability as well as oil content. When he's satisfied, the shopping cart is nearly full of vegetation.

Moving on, he makes a right turn onto aisle eleven where he exclaims, "Holy Moses Golden Toes!" and does a yet another spin, this time with his arm outstretched towards the sky. As Charlie rounds the corner with the shopping cart, eager to see what his brother has discovered, a bright yellow box of pectin falls, as if from the heavens, landing on the soft bed of mint in front of him. "Whiskey jelly," Cliff exclaims before taking off in a full sprint towards the checkout counter, sliding in his boots across the linoleum floor and arriving in front of an attractive Mexican girl with long black hair who can't be more than sixteen years old. "Que pasa?" Cliff says. She blushes like a Baja sunset and blinks her long midnight lashes. Cliff finishes his beer with siete booming gulps, foam and liquid dripping down his cheeks and onto the floor, before cracking another and offering it to the girl.

"No," she says. "Gracias."

Charlie, in his minimalist heroin gait, arrives a few moments later, a smile plastered on his face and his eyes dangling in his sockets like weightless blue meteors. He pulls the yellow box of pectin from the cart and places it on the conveyor belt in front of the young Mexican woman and says "One box of pectin, please. We're making whiskey jelly."

"Shut the fuck up, Charlie!" Cliff says. "That's Mustard Brothers, man." Shaking his head in disappointment at his brother's faux pas, he thinks for a moment about the possibility of finding gold in the Sacramento River. His head falls backwards and he can imagine himself in that river with a mustache, dressed in black and white, pushing his hands into the cold water and finding a fish instead. He'd live in a wood

125

cabin and fry it in a cast iron pan over an open flame.

The young Mexican woman, noticeably confused, asks, "Que onda la cerveza? Y menta?"

Cliff smiles and nods his head, as if he understands the young woman's perplexity and slides his thick hand gently across her delicate fingers, calming her nerves. "We brought the beer from home," he says. "We never go anywhere without a six-pack."

Her eyes widen a bit, then dim like the lights before a small-town opera. "I saw you," she says. "You took."

"Nope," Cliff says. "From me casa." He winks at her, reaches into his jeans pocket and pulls out a small colored pencil drawing of a bunny rabbit smoking a carrot like a joint, with it's paw holding a kite. He passes it to her as if it were a secret note and rattles his fingers across the counter, pushing his tongue into his cheek, waiting for a reaction, which he believes will be one of pure joy. When the expected reaction doesn't arrive, he pulls his eyebrows up, sighs, and after a dramatic pause, says, "Charlie, come here and autograph this drawing."

Charlie giggles and pulls a pen from his jeans.

With an outstretched dirty finger in the air, Cliff motions for the young Mexican girl to move in close to his lips. Twitching at the cheek, she inches cautiously towards his booze stained breath, the heat and whiskers of his face close enough to tickle her pores. "This right here," he says and points, "Is worth plenty more than beer and mint." He pulls three greasy dollar bills from his back pocket and places them down in front of her. She scans the pectin, places it in a plastic bag and reaches for the mint with a grin.

As she enters the produce code for each bushel and passes them down the line, Cliff receives them, stuffing them underneath his shirt, into his pockets, under his armpits, until finally the young Mexican woman looks at him with an affectionate smile and says, "Fourteen dollars."

Cliff bows before her, extends his hand, and says, "Yes, fourteen dollars." He backs himself slowly out of the market, and Charlie leaves the cart behind, moving out onto the street and never looking back. The Mexican girl, pausing only for a moment to rationalize, interpret, and comprehend the occurring theft, removes herself slightly from the register and starts a sprint towards the office in the back.

"It's getting harder and harder to pay for things with art these days," Cliff ruminates as they hit the hot afternoon streets of Echo Parque with a relaxed pace. "She got a three dollar tip and all we got was pectin, beer, and some low-brow mint, and she didn't dig. She's got an original Charlie in her hands right now and should be living like an untorn, unhanging piñata. Unreal!"

To observe Cliff and Charlie walk the ganged-out streets of the Eastside in the outlaw sunset is very much a musical experience. Perhaps because they share the same blood, or perhaps because they have spent most of their lives within a few feet of each other, they move in syncopated rhythm, each hip to heel movement of their bodies like a cosmic psychedelic death dance with bullet belts and tattooery, drunkenness and irresponsibility. Several of the pedestrians passing them on the sidewalk turn their heads and follow, piqued with intrigue, and almost all of them immediately hear a melody, a tune, a chantey they know and love—the brothers have this effect on people.

"I love the color purple," Charlie says and stares at the sky as the orange turns to red, to love, leaning towards the lavender prism of night.

"The fucking movie?" Cliff asks. "With Oprah?"

Back at their loft, Cliff arranges pots, pans, mint, sugar, and several bottles of whiskey across the spearmint and white art deco tile on the small kitchen counter Cliff designed himself. Charlie, on his knees, is hard at work transforming a dirty old pair of Levi's into jean shorts. When he's finished with the scissors, he pulls the shorts on, the sweat and slime of the Los Angeles summer soaking deep into the fibers, and slides on his cowboy boots over his damp heels. "It's officially summer," he says to his brother. "Jean shorts."

Cliff pushes his tongue into his mustache and nods his head in agreement. "Indeed it is. You ready for the Mustard Brothers to become the quintessential donut house in America? Maybe the entire world?"

Charlie smiles and says, "I don't care, as long as I have enough whiskey to get me through my life."

"Well, sir, if all goes well, we'll be eating and drinking whiskey until the day we die." Cliff ignites the stovetop, crushes several bundles of mint in a pot, adds water and covers it with a lid. He pops open a bottle of whiskey, slides a shot glass to his brother, and pours them both a drink. "To Mustard Brothers," he says, "And to bringing our brother Cassidy back home, alive, with stars in his hair like we all remember."

When the water has boiled, Cliff strains the mint, takes the leaves to another pan, adds sugar and a little lemon juice and pauses, knowing full well this could be the crucial moment of the Mustard Brothers Whiskey Jelly Donut franchise. "I shouldn't add the whiskey now, right?" he asks his brother. "We want it to get us fucked up."

"Of course we do, don't add it 'til the very end," Charlie says. "We can't be burning off alcohol. We need the alcohol, man."

He brings the mixture to a boil, adds the pectin, uses his strong wrist to stir, and transfers the mixture to several glass jars, waiting a minute before pouring several different doses of whiskey into each and locking them tightly down with lids, labeling each one as he does so with the words "Batch 1, 1oz, Batch 2, 2oz," and so forth until he reaches the tenth jar. He takes the jars and places them back into the boiling water.

"Pretty sure the alcohol can't burn off once it's already trapped inside a jar, right?" Cliff asks his brother.

"Pretty sure that's how they make whiskey to begin with," his brother responds. "They gotta heat it up somehow, don't they? Are the lids tight? You have pussy hands."

The next two hours are spent scouring the Internet for donut recipes, which until only two hours ago, Charlie and Cliff had completely forgotten about. Cliff had turned to his brother and said, "Now what?" and Charlie had said, "Well, we got the whiskey jelly, but not the donut."

"How hard can it be to make a donut," Cliff had responded, and now two hours later, after wasting most of their time on eBay looking for vintage tiki shirts and old Dead Moon records, they have a rather rudimentary recipe for a jelly donut, which they both agree is nearly impossible for them to accomplish with their limited culinary skills.

"Maybe we take things one step at a time and start with the whiskey jelly," Cliff says.

And so the brothers pop open the first batch of mint julep jelly, dip their spoons inside, and grind. "Not strong enough," Charlie says. Cliff agrees. Instead of opening batch two, they move directly to Batch 10, and although they both wish for Batch 10 to be the best because it tastes almost purely of whiskey, they both agree the general consumer's palette might not be ready for that specific flavor. Regardless, they finish the entire jar in about five minutes and collapse on the couch with sweat and grins, wrapped up in each other and staring at Charlie's latest painting of Voltaire skinning a rabbit. The rabbit smiles as Voltaire rips into its flesh with a large hunting knife. In his paw, he holds a shattered smartphone.

"I like it, but it's missing something," Charlie says.

"Charlie Chaplin vagina."

"Would it be a meta meta concept if I drew myself as Charlie, inside of Charlie Chaplin, inside of a vagina?" asks Charlie.

"Yeah, but only if yer retarded enough to care about a meta meta concept," replies Cliff.

"Man, that's some heavy shit," Charlie says and peels himself from the couch, finding a thin paintbrush, and performing the first stroke of a tender labial eyeball. "I love the whiskey jelly," Charlie says and purses his lips as if waiting for a storm.

"Mustard Brothers," Cliff responds. "Fucking Mustard Brothers."

Rainbow Blues

You can feel the energy emanating from a St. Claire rainbow party all the way down the street. The sidewalks buzz with cool, the buildings shake inside the eye, windows rattle even though an El train isn't passing. This Rainbow is out by the water, in a place the stooges haven't discovered yet—The Docks. This rainbow soiree is only three miles from my house, but closer to planet Mars.

If I were a shoe collector doing a coffee table book on the radness of footwear, the St. Claire rainbow bonanza would be the place to start compiling and photographing material. I walk most places with my head down in this city, because there aren't any trees worth a damn, and buildings are buildings—they're rectangles with glass and sometimes a cool looking gargoyle or bricks or some other shit—so I see a lot of shoes, instead of the architecture of a lost generation. I like thinking about the dead men who built these structures, but it's hard to think of death when you're looking up at the sky. Down here, where the best shoes I've ever seen live, is where the heart should be—it gives it something to aspire to, maybe a tree. My hand slides down my wife's wrist and finds her glass knuckles. I feel strange as my boots bang the streets with a twenty-two of Four Loko in my hand and a tall boy of High Life in my back pocket—back in California, you can't just walk around with booze in your fist. It's the East that enables public drink, or perhaps it's just that I feel like I'm on a permanent death vacation here, like at some point it's going to end, reality will sweep back in and that Eel River

California love bone will be stuck between my teeth.

I suck down the rest of my Four Loko and look up towards the heads, finding Bulch and Cherise arm in arm walking slow, stoned on some narcotic, or drunk on whiskey, or both, their arms and legs twisting and gyrating, two epileptic urban giraffes. I think for a moment how strange and coincidental it is that we should be arriving at the same time, walking down the same street, in such a big city, but then I realize this is my book and I can do whatever the fuck I want.

"Check it out, Bulch and Cherise!" I say to my wife, and she slides her hand into my back pocket, lifts the can, and cracks the High Life.

"Neat," she says, wiping the froth from her lips. I stop to take a look at the night, counting the four stars above, thinking about water and fly-fishing and Montana, because Montana seems like a cool place, with Jim Harrison and frontier promises and whiskey bullshit. My wife yanks at me with the weight of her body, pulling me behind her and at this moment I see my girl as if I'm seeing her for the first time. She's in a dress that's too short, designed in the mid-sixties, with big juicy watermelons wrapped around the hem, and pure white everywhere else. Her shoulders are bronze like summer pie crusts, her tall brown leather boots push at her kneecaps and at this moment I have the inexplicable urge to lick the crease behind her knees, all the way up her thighs into God knows where.

"Do you think birthmarks are an alien thing?" my wife asks.

"Of course they are."

"I mean, they're weird right? Everyone has one. There's got to be a reason."

"It's so your own personal alien can keep track of you—they're out there, watching."

We give a slender man with an impressive beard and a pair of suspenders attached to stiff, rolled-cuff Levi's five dollars each to get inside. My wife says, "Look at how beautiful this building is," and points up at the roof. I take a look up, see the windows glowing and simmering in the moonlight, reflective colors squirting out from the cracks in the brick falling like raindrops of every kind of fruit juice and for once, I dig the architecture here. My wife's cheeks are damp with humidity and sweat and her eyes meet mine in that brief moment where life seems worth living, every second, and then the moment disappears, thrown out to sea with the rest of our trash. She turns her head away and pulls me by the hand into the building, my boots shuffling behind my bones.

Inside is pure psychedelic mayhem. It's dark, with a scent of leather and musk. Incense circles the room in spirals, sucking in and out through the exposed air vents at the top of the ceiling. At the base of each of the four walls, two-man teams of bearded hipsters operate schoolroom projectors, using turkey basters to drop multicolored oils and liquids onto their screens, the space filled with moving color, rotating, dripping across eyelids, so that each human looks as if it were being tie-dyed, their necks and hands twisting with blue, orange, pink, an American flag, a bullfrog in the night. The soundtrack to the festivities is provided by a semi-long-haired disc jockey who pulls records from their sleeves in a mad frenzy, searching for tracks, and dropping needles on the biggest bombs of musical orgasm. Through a corridor, a freight elevator takes people up and down with a great whirling howl, and from what I can see, there seems to be a healthy dose of drug use taking place within each car. I can almost smell the cocaine from where I stand. And let me tell you about the shoes—In all directions, men strut in leather stitched by Mussolini, men shimmy in high heeled sneakers bounding from one person to the next, women in boots and avocado skinned slippers and three-inch python heels twirl and spin with diamonds in their toes, ankle bones sharp and pointed.

"That girl is topless," my wife says. "And her breasts are magnificent."

I turn to find a brunette in a pair of pink and purple paisley bell-bottoms swimming towards me with a large plastic bucket hanging from her arm. She smiles a broad toothed smile, drops her neck, and asks,

"Goo balls?" in a sugary voice, her eyes like waterfalls near a statue of Jesus.

"How much?" I ask.

"I like your face," she says, and pushes her wrist into the bucket, pulling out an ice cream scooper with a perfect ball of sticky granola and dropping it into my hand. "You look like a cat." She runs her fingertips across my lips before she walks away. "Goo balls," she yells into the spinning colors.

The heavy ball coats my palm in oil and smells of heavy cannabis. I take a bite, dangle it before my wife, and she swallows the rest without blinking or asking me if I want more. She may have inadvertently saved my life tonight by acting in such a manner—she's always been more inclined towards the positive in life rather than the negative, and so can handle a big goo-ball trip—I stare at shoes—she, at buildings. Shoes are far less interesting when you're on the great stone than the calculated and worn edges and corners of humanity, the infinite up.

We make our way towards the light at the center of the room and find Bulch and Cherise at the edge of the large stage sucking down cans of cheap beer, hands dancing in the air, waving to us. To our right, geeked-out patrons sink their wrists into several plastic trashcans, pulling out a grab bag of brew and rubbing skin, sweating on each other—St. Claire's rainbows have that effect on people—strange and unexpected intimacy.

"Lets grab some beers," I say to my wife, and the volume of the room rises so it seems as if there is a tangible weight to the sound, a wave of whispers and gasps—scattered, yet enthusiastic applause. Before we can reach the trashcans, it becomes apparent St. Claire has entered the room. Through a spotlight, he moves with ease, across the dark space, towards the stage. His stature is perfect, like a monument, and his fashion sense, impeccable. Tonight, he wears a crème colored suit with a brown shirt made of golden triangles, and his hair slicked back and combed to the side like a villain in a Godard film. A Jurassic sized red rose bursts out from his lapel, his brown leather boots glimmering. He raises his hands, each finger decorated with a different shade of precious stone set inside golden rings. He sparkles like the lights of a discotech dance-floor, and for some reason, this entrance makes me stick my tongue into my wife's mouth where it dances and floats for what seems like two years.

"Wow," she says and smiles. At this moment the weight of sound, the color of life is all that soars through her mind. She has forgotten the gray, the unborn, the sweaters she's haunted by. She pushes her hands into the icy water of the trashcan and pulls us out two beers, wrapping her arm around my waist. "I love you," she says.

"Let's go check out Bulch and Cherise," I say, and we make our way over to the stage, swinging our hips through the heaving crowd. And then, pure darkness. The lights, the colors, the faces disappear and we are left alone in the dark, our bodies pulled and pushed against others, a sea, a wave. The whistles and howls of several hundred souls pick up, vibrating the hairs in our ears, tickling down the limbs. I let my hand slide down my wife's belly and to her crotch, where I rub delicately, and she responds by doing the same to me. The noise of what sounds like a thousand chainsaws startles us, but nonetheless, we continue our grope, this once familiar sensation of arousal rushing through my body.

From the stage, a fire ignites and in the center, St. Claire reappears, flipping the switch on some type of machine, mist fills the air, an entire spectrum of color reflected through it, spreading out in wide, flat rays, falling, dropping, and then continuing forward, curling around and between our heads. He breathes deep into a microphone and says, "Please welcome, Volcano the Spacemachine."

The heavy thud of a kick drum brings us back to earth, and we move slowly, calculated, with our hearts through the color towards Bulch and Cherise at the front of the stage. The first twang of Volcano the Spacemachine's guitars rips my ears to electric glassy shreds. I can feel something heavy on my back, but keep moving forward until finally the weight is so heavy, I can no longer continue, I must find out why gravity is assaulting me. I look over my shoulder to find Aunika has attached her elongated frame to my body and is riding me like a horse. She whispers in my ear with the stink of whiskey, "Take me somewhere." With my wife's hand on my crotch and my best friend on my back, I trudge forward, thankful for the relative darkness that would render my erection a tad embarrassing.

I see Bulch close his eyes, let his eyelashes dangle, and use his mammoth stoner energy to part the crowd for me, each person sliding sideways to each riff and thump, until finally Aunika licks the back of my neck to my earlobe and bites down, jumps off, and reattaches herself to Bulch, who welcomes her into his wiry arms.

Cherise, using her uncanny sexual instincts, stares immediately down at my crotch and raises an eyebrow. She's seen it all before.

The thunder from the stage continues without interruption, Bulch, still with his eyes closed, twirling himself around the four of us. We join arms and sway to the music, watching as the men of The Spacemachine pound their fists into their instruments, topless, donning feathered Indian headdresses, roses between their teeth, and finally, the front man, a wild-haired mass of macho rock and roll panther, materializes from the darkness, butterfly earrings dangling, flying round his head. He grips his microphone, wraps the cord around his neck and wails into the night, "I've got one foot in the grave and I got them whiskey jelly blues!"

"Whiskey jelly!" Bulch howls, and throws his arms up into the air.

I drop my head to the side and find my wife's eyes, astonished, bewildered. "Whiskey jelly?" she says to me.

"Unreal," I reply.

Our eyes meet and inside the pupils there is one of each thing we love.

A Quick Individual Recap of St. Claire's Rainbow Blues

Cassidy Blues

Cassidy continued drinking trashcan beers until the Rainbow no longer existed outside of him, but rather, now took up every molecule of his being, including the twenty-one grams of his soul. He took turns trading gazes between both his wife and Aunika throughout the night, and even made it over to the freight elevator underneath the dragging weight of the great goo-ball stone looking for a way back up, but couldn't wait for the contraption to come back down, so just went to the men's room where he was sure he could score a bump of coke. To his dismay, the only man in the restroom was a fellow more than thirty years his senior sucking on a bottle of Pepsi with a long beard—the man said, "Can I interest you in a blow job?" Cassidy replied, "Absolutely not," and laughed, unzipping, pissing, and missing the toilet by a good foot and a half while looking over his shoulder. Back from his piss and at the front of the stage, Cassidy played with the zippers on Bulch's outfit (Indiana Jones inspired, lots of pockets, safari wear), while waiting for his wife to get back from her own bathroom break, where Aunika had disappeared to as well. Phoenix didn't come back for some time, and when she did, she was blushing, hot, rubbing her lips.

Aunika smiled seven times at Cassidy throughout the night, the kind of smiles that speak Shakespearean sonnets, lips filled with wilted roses and tragic love. Cherise raised her eyebrows seven times, one for each time she caught Aunika looking at Cassidy. Cassidy wondered if Aunika would make love to Bulch that night, but figured she wouldn't, the wounds of her failed relationship too fresh, and Bulch, as far as Cassidy knew, uninterested in American women—only the most exotic, foreign speaking women in the world could turn Bulch's head—or so he thought.

Cassidy, due to an astounding inebriation, nearly fell down eight times on the way back from St. Claire's rainbow. His wife propped him up on her shoulder and brought him back home, where he threw-up for two hours, and spent most of the night on his hands and knees, head in the toilet, exclaiming to his wife he was "sorry he couldn't give her everything she ever wanted in life." Phoenix held his hair back and even used her own finger to gag him, trying to get the alcohol and goo-ball out of his belly, and saying to him each time he professed his failures, "It's okay baby, you'll make it someday. You need to stop drinking so much," to which he repeatedly responded, "I don't drink too much." On his back gazing up at her, he realized he truly had failed—a woman with so much beauty should never be with a man so fucked up. He vowed to love her as much as possible, but halfway through the night, he had forgotten everything he had thought, only remembering Aunika riding on his back and the way the heat from her thighs permeated his clothes and softened his waist, which brought a smile to his face, and even sobered him up enough to make himself some chicken noodle soup and open another beer from the fridge before sitting down on the couch in the living room and watching reruns of Star Trek. Phoenix said good night and slipped between the sheets. Eventually, Cassidy managed to crawl into bed before the sun rose and masturbate to Aunika's warmth while staring at the naked backside of his sleeping wife, which he did so very cautiously and silently, impressed with his stealthy discretion. His eyelids kissed with the closing words of a Choose Your Own Adventure chapter on his mind—

Justin J. Murphy

If you follow your best friend into the freight elevator, turn to page ?? If you politely decline and go home to masturbate, turn to page ??

Phoenix Blues

Phoenix loved every moment of the St. Claire Rainbow, and even managed to slip away from Cassidy on her way to the bathroom to swing by the freight elevator for a pick-me-up. Phoenix had had sex several times with Cassidy on cocaine, but had never told him, keeping a private little stash for those moments where The East seemed unbearable, and the West, unattainable. Charlie across the street used to get the drugs for her. She thought him a good friend for never mentioning it to Cassidy. She smiled over her little secret on the way to the darkened shaft. In the elevator, Phoenix met an attractive young woman who told her she had been "Reborn after dying at Kent State," and was back on earth "To see Christ come again." The young woman then attempted to kiss her, only half of her sloppy bottom lip landing on Phoenix's mouth before Phoenix obliged, and let the woman kiss her. She didn't feel she had been unfaithful to her husband because there was sorrow in the young woman's eyes and, besides, the kiss hadn't felt sexual—instead, it had felt matronly, and this motherly feeling of compassion, in that moment, had replaced the emptiness and guilt of her abortion. She ran her hands through the young woman's hair, took another small bump of cocaine, and went to the bathroom where she rubbed the young woman's lipstick off her lips with a small square of toilet paper. She couldn't help but feel alive at this moment, the blood rushing to her cheeks, an inadvertent adventure, a little freedom, a bit of independence, a small secret. For once, this place, The East, didn't seem like a diversion on a journey somewhere else. With the hearts of everyone around her bouncing, and the heat of the night opening up her pores, she could see what this city was all about, and it wasn't half bad—if it were surrounded by redwoods, it could be truly great—like ancient Rome.

Back at the front of the stage, she witnessed Aunika stare at her husband, lingering a bit too long on him, mystified perhaps by his full lips—her own favorite part of his body. She wondered if Aunika could be in love with Cassidy, but believed in their friendship and trust, and rationalized best friends are intrinsically in love with each other regardless of gender—but that doesn't necessarily mean they would fuck each other. Besides, Cassidy had told her several times he felt Aunika was "like a sister" to him, and there isn't a man on planet earth who wants to screw his sister. Also, it seemed pretty obvious Aunika was going to bang Bulch—her fingers were too close to his waist and her mouth was perpetually wet.

On the way home, she practically carried her husband, still finding the strength under his weight to gaze up at the buildings, taking mental note of their characteristics for a book she might one day write. She thought hard about a good title for a novel. According to her philosophy on writing, she believes all sentences are born from the sentence before it, and so, the title must be the matriarch of the family. "Love a thousand times spits in your face before you can ask it to die," is what she came up with. But she didn't actually feel that way about love. It just seemed like a good title—she wondered if her husband would understand it, how he would feel about it—would it hurt him?

At home, she stuck her fingers down her husband's throat and told him he "Should try not to drink so much all at once, in such a short time," to which her husband continually responded "I don't drink too much," and she felt as though there had been a miscommunication. "I don't mean that," she said, "I mean…" and then she realized having a conversation with this man was futile, that he was still back on Mars with the other rad-shoed Martians. She went to sleep naked, waking only to the bed shaking and her husband unsubtly masturbating next to her and smelling of chicken soup.

Bulch Blues

Bulch is such a secret, such an enigma, that even I can barely tell you what happened to him during the remainder of St. Claire's rainbow. Sometimes he disguises himself as night, filled with a million stars, and that's all there is to tell. But sometimes I can see through his night, can pick up small, radiant starlight that brings glimpses of his movements to me. This much I do know—Before the Rainbow, Bulch and Cherise joined forces, hopped a subway train and strutted down to the Volcano the Spacemachine compound—a bombed-out building once home to a band of heroin addicted squatters who sold stolen Phish merchandise for drug money. Inside, among the eclectic art and darkness, they pre-partied with a new experimental drug, James, the front-man, was hip to—banana oil. The effects—a sideways gait, a belief in time travel, a slowing of the earth's rotation, an icy spine, a smile, a frown, and finally an acceptance of the hard mellow, the incapacitation, the moonbeam as God.

James sang a new tune for Bulch, Cherise, and a naked seventeen-year-old runaway who'd been bunking down with the band for the past three weeks in the stone-walled living room. James hadn't named the song yet and was particularly unsure of what to call it—He knew the music was pure electric blues, the big up—but that's all he knew. Bulch, swirling the bead of banana oil around his tongue and swallowing, responded, "Whiskey Jelly Blues," at the conclusion of James' rendition. He then pulled Cherise up by the arm, lit a cigarette for her, and walked the sideways banana stroll several miles underneath the silver moon towards The Docks and St. Claire's rainbow.

When the banana oil began to wear off midway through the Spacemachine set, Bulch dropped to his knees, closed his eyes, let his head fall back, and raised his palms to the sky. Aunika stood before him and placed her hands within his. When he opened his eyes, she was gone. He rubbed his palms together and headed towards the backstage area where he found his friend St. Claire rolling a marijuana cigarette and rapping in French to a few heads about energy. Here's the translation of what St. Claire was preaching—but forgive me, I'm not very fluent: "It can neither be created, nor destroyed, nor duplicated perfectly. Each of us is unique in a way—and so is each rainbow. No two are ever the same."

The heads nodded. St. Claire and Bulch embraced as if they were long lost brothers, their chins neatly folding into each other's neck.

"Hell of Rainbow tonight, my man," Bulch said.

"Il y a une peu de cette larme d'argent la bas," St. Claire responded. "Ca passe directement par le centre du plateau." He pointed towards The Spacemachine and Bulch took in a strange silver ray glowing up through the center of the stage, an enigma. It could've been the banana oil acting up again—but who knows?

"Fascinating," Bulch said. He lit one end of the joint and inhaled deeply, wondering about this mysterious silver ray and why it had come on this night. He pulled out his small Moleskine notebook from his breast pocket and wrote something down in it. St. Claire attempted to take a peek at the sentences, but could only see a few words over Bulch's lanky arms and broad shoulders. *Beyond the day, in the light of...* Bulch has been known to write spontaneous poetry in the middle of a crowded room, and I suppose that's exactly what he did tonight.

When the Spacemachine finished their set, Bulch said his goodbyes and the band thanked him for the Whiskey Jelly inspiration, presenting him with a plastic cup filled with orange juice and vodka. He drank the cocktail, sucking the pulp from his mustache when he had finished. He said, "Rock and roll can soothe the heart, break the heart, or create a new one." Back out in the sea of heaving stoned bodies, he found Cherise leaning against a trashcan with a thimble-sized key-bump in her hand, barely able to stand.

"Whatcha got there, my love?" he asked.

"A popsicle," she replied, then pushed the key into her mouth and swallowed the powder. Her eyes lit up for a moment, but it seemed within seconds, her light faded back out. He escorted the inebriated Cherise by his arm out the door, onto the subway, and through the streets, dropping her at her doorstep. She laid her head to his shoulder and mumbled something he couldn't understand, something about "a rabbit death hole." He noticed his shoes needed polishing—they had been stepped on by several at the Rainbow, showing wear and tear around his toes. She kissed his neck and ran her fingers through his hair. "It feels so good," she said. "Your hair is like a shower of silk." He opened the door and used the palm of his hand to shove her by her bottom into her building. "Don't get too sweet on the frosting," he said to her and winked.

When he found himself at home seventeen minutes later, he couldn't remember how he had gotten there. It seemed the great stone had taken over his body and the only remedy was a big slug of Cosmic Grizzly Bourbon, which he delighted in over reruns of Hawaii Five-0 on the television. He thought about Aunika, which he thought strange. Ordinarily, she wouldn't have been his type, with her long California beach drawl. But there was something about her hands within his that made his stoic, brave, mysterious heart skip a beat. He rubbed the remnants of her oily palms from his hands into his arms. He liked the couch he was sitting on, and perhaps it was time for a woman to be by his side. He would have liked that right about now. He fell asleep underneath a bearskin blanket staring out of his skylight at the moon above his bed. "Whiskey Jelly," he said under his breath.

Aunika Blues

Aunika's night began with half a bottle of Cosmic Grizzly bourbon, a piggyback ride on her best friend's back, a licking of his neck, and bite of his ear, a subtle sweat between her thighs. She could feel Cassidy's spine between her, touching something in her his body had never touched before. She felt pleasure in his spine, in his strong, athletic gait, but it wasn't enough. She wanted more from him, more from her life, more from this night. If she could have, she would have pulled the shirt off his back and ridden that strong spine until climax, shouting into the night, the electric rock and roll shocking her veins into bits of bluish flame, turning her red, lifting her up off the ground and slamming her back down like an anvil made of angels. But from her position perched atop his back, she could see his hand wrapped around his wife. She felt guilty for her newfound fantasy, and the guilt was something she had not yet considered. It wasn't until she let herself slide down Cassidy's back to the floor that she realized she had created an impossible situation for her heart.

She spent most of the night catching herself staring at Cassidy, wishing that he might use his eyes to deliver a message to her, one that said "Meet me in the electric forest and make love underneath the neon branches of the bourbon tree." She thought it strange in all the years she had known him, she had not fully understood the beauty of those eyes— a dark green with splashes of amber in the center, the whites glassy and reflective, perpetually stoned and drunk. He might have written a thousand love letters in those eyes, sonnets dedicated to her mind or ass or both—but how could she ever know?

She hugged Cherise and toyed with Bulch's palms, shook her hips slightly but not overtly to the sounds of The Spacemachine, letting the thundering bass line move up her legs into her stomach, but nothing could satiate her growing desire for her married best friend. Dejected and somewhat bored with the scene, she led herself to the freight elevator where she rode up and down for an incalculable amount of time, watching the drugs go up and down with her, the lights fading in and out. From her pocket, she pulled a flask of bourbon and drank the entirety of it before putting her hair up in a bun and wiping a bead of sweat from her brow, exhaling her alcoholic breath into the air, thinking it might singe the arm-hairs off her fellow passengers. As the night ventured on, the freight elevator became more and more cramped with the wild heartbeats of the leather jacket drug generation. She slunk herself into the corner, using the walls as both an emotional and physical crutch and was surprised when she saw Phoenix enter. Her surprise turned to disbelief when she witnessed Phoenix snort the great white powder, and her disbelief turned to pure astonishment when she saw her best friend's wife slide her tongue into another woman's mouth. From behind the shoulders of strangers, she let her mind run away with this image, plotting what a small bit of information and manipulation could do for her love life. Her own innocent kiss to Cassidy, just a few hours ago, could come again, naked, in the Pacific, with tongues this time.

She closed her eyes and thought of Cassidy's spine, letting the guilt of his backbone fade away until that sweat brewed up again inside of her. When Phoenix left the elevator, Aunika quietly escaped St. Claire's Rainbow, striding out into the street where she took several deep breaths and asked a man with a martini in his hand for a cigarette.

She felt she was being followed on her way home from the subway station, and so began a light jog, which turned into a full sprint by the time she reached her door. Inside, she pulled off her clothes, started a bath, and spread her legs for the stream of hot water to penetrate. She bit down on her bottom lip a minute later, and exhaled. She lit a few candles, and sang her favorite Smiths song, the subject of which she still was unsure of. "A shoeless child on a swing reminds you of your own again..." she cooed. She used her toes to turn the knobs off and let her body ooze in the warmth. "She took away your troubles, oh, but then again, she left pain," she sang.

Cherise Blues

Cherise accomplished precisely what she set out to do that evening—score drugs and find a hot boy. Little did she know that boy would be Bulch and that Bulch was uninterested. The banana oil had acted as a kind of lubricant for her soul, loosening her up for new chemical adventures. With everyone watching, she swallowed a hit of Molly, snorted, swallowed, and gummed several doses of cocaine, and had even procured another hit of banana oil for late night when the dreaded come-down would inevitably occur.

On the dance floor, she felt the vibrations of The Spacemachine rattling her bones to the core, her ankles like conduits of electric lightning, slamming the rest of her body against the swirling color of the room. Her hair flew wildly in the air, opposed to gravity, her hands grasping for something in front of her that wasn't there. She found herself lost in the crowd, moving backwards it seemed, until she found herself against a trashcan with a key bump of the great white stone in her hand.

The show hadn't ended by the time her night had. The realization of loneliness hit her like a tornado of blenders set to "grind." She had been lonely for an eternity. She had been lonely in her art. She had been lonely when she was surrounded by the world.

Leaning against that trashcan of beers with the great white stone in her hand, there was nothing left to do but look down, all the way down to her shoes. She realized shoes were everywhere, marching against her, onward, moving without arriving anywhere, or arriving somewhere unknown, or arriving somewhere so unknown that the destination became completely meaningless. And then there were his shoes—a perfect leather boot, the toes slightly worn, shuffling towards her, twirling to the music, rocking backwards on the heel, pushing up onto the toe, bending the soul.

She began her ascent upwards to the tightened crotch of brown polyester, the perfectly unbuttoned shirt revealing masculine strands of black hair, onwards towards the bronze and salty neck, and finally found herself sucked into Bulch's red, white, and blue eyes. She saw that perfect mustache, could almost feel the brunette bristles against her upper lip, tickling her breasts, moistening her armpits, scratching against her elbows. She wanted him, or anything perhaps, but anything wouldn't do. Bulch was a man. Bulch was a mystery, perhaps the greatest piece of art she could ever personally experience.

She felt his hands slide around her waist. She mumbled something about a popsicle and swallowed the key bump, wishing it was made of icy water—her throat was parched. The world spun away from her, only a flash of color and light, then night, the scent of the city stinging her nostrils, the sea air, a wind of fish and tar, a subway filled with the insane faces of a world spinning too fast, out of control, the sun burning out. She ran her hands through Bulch's hair, the smoothness of the tendrils licking the webbing of her fingers. It could have been the ecstasy, or perhaps it was love. She could no longer tell her emotions from the drugs, or herself from anything. She could have been a lamppost or the Pacific Ocean. His hand pushed her bottom into her building and when she turned around to find the rest of his body attached to the palm, he was gone. She stumbled up the stairs towards her apartment where she placed her key in the wrong door, awakening a neighbor.

Her neighbor, a small Korean man with a missing finger and an irregular heartbeat, helped her up the last flight of stairs to her door. He found a key covered in white residue in her pocket, just beneath her right hip, opened the door for her, dragged her to bed, and felt her breast brush soft like a goose feather against his elbow as he laid her down. This breast was a touch he had never felt. His heart skipped a beat—dudunk, du...dudunk. He had thoughts about his immediate future, the possibility of death. Perhaps he could unbutton her shirt, just for one last glimpse of beauty, something to live for. Dudunk. He noticed the chainsaw in the corner of her bedroom. He left her alone in her bed, exiting amongst the volume of a thick snore, locking the door behind him, erased. Cherise rolled over onto her shoulder and vomited translucent bile onto the floor beside her, a hand dangling in the stomach acid as she faded out and was left only with her forgotten dreams.

Warren, Ohio Blues

It took Black Charlie seven hours and eleven minutes to arrive in Warren, Ohio, via interstate 80. A minor car wreck outside the city held him up for about thirty-three minutes, but he still managed to make good time. And what was that time again? 7 hrs 11 minutes. He double-checked his watch several times to make sure that indeed it had taken him seven hours and eleven minutes to arrive, and thought this was a fortuitous sign. He's tired now, and a bit hungry, and his bladder needs relief—and this is precisely why he finds himself parked in front of a 7-Eleven convenience store. Switching off the ignition , the mystic eeriness of this current situation begins to sink in—it took seven hours and eleven minutes to arrive at a 7-Eleven in Warren, OH. He smiles and opens his car door, lays a boot to the tar, closes his eyes. "I've got the numbers," he says.

Inside, he moves through the aisles, extending his arms and letting his fingers rustle across the plastic packages of chips, instant ramen, dry roasted peanuts. "Seven eleven. Seven. Eleven." He thinks, if there's a tattoo shop nearby, he might get those numbers ingrained somewhere, perhaps behind his ear where they could soak into his brain—or even better, directly above his heart. It's obvious there's a reason for him to be here, in Warren, Ohio, at, holy shit, 11:07 a.m. He taps the watch on his wrist, the one his deceased father left him seventeen years ago. "Eleven o seven," he says. More than a few customers move away from the dreadlocked man repeating numbers to himself, mostly because Warren,

Ohio isn't a place where natty dreads roam the streets. He pulls at his tri-colored Rasta beanie, adjusting his thick tendrils, massaging his scalp. "Seven eleven, eleven o seven." He heads to the can, pisses, washes his hands, stares at himself in the mirror. He thinks there's a new mole growing underneath his left eye—a stress mole perhaps? Doesn't matter. He wants Funyuns and a beer, a tall 24 oz High Life. "Seven eleven," he says once more on his way up to the counter.

The cashier's seen his fair share of nut jobs in this business, and so isn't afraid of the dreadlocked man with bags under his eyes muttering numbers to himself. He does, however, wish to see identification for the beer.

"Got ID on ya?" the cashier asks.

Charlie likes the cashier's face. Sixty-five years old, the eyes wrinkled and etched, hands shaky from high blood pressure, or alcoholism, or divorce, or arsenic in the water and rice—or perhaps he's a war hero, a veteran of Viet-Nam who risked his life to save his platoon and lost a kidney in the process, saved a village baby, named it Willie, like the Jeep.

"I sure do," Charlie replies, and pulls out his wallet, lifting his driver's license from its pocket.

"From back East?" the cashier says.

"That's right."

"What brings you to Warren?"

"Just passing through on my way to California."

"California? Beautiful country out that way," the cashier says. "Whereabouts?"

"I don't know. Los Angeles maybe?"

"When I was a young man, I was headed for California. But, well, you know how it is."

Charlie thinks he's heard this sentence before but can't place it. His eyes roll into his head, as if trying to pull the memory from somewhere. He rattles his fingernails on the countertop, and says, "I've heard that

149

somewhere before."

If I could transport myself to Warren, Ohio and stand right there behind Charlie I could help him—I'd tell him it's a direct quote from the 1968 film *Easy Rider*. Charlie likes that film and has seen it four times. If I had to guess, the answer will come to him somewhere between Warren, Ohio and the middle of Kansas.

The cashier pulls at his eyelashes and says, "That'll be seven dollars and eleven cents."

Charlie's knees buckle a bit. He has the urge to grab the cashier by the collar and ask him "What the hell is going on here?" throw his hands up into the air, or maybe collapse into a ball, crying. He thinks this particular reaction might be a bit irrational and could get him into trouble in Warren. He is black, after all, and racism and prejudices still exist, even if they aren't expressed outwardly. Maybe he should just explain the past several minutes to the cashier, see what he thinks about it.

"You know, brother," Charlie says, pulling the money from his wallet. "It took me seven hours and eleven minutes to get here, this Seven Eleven, at eleven o seven in the morning, and I'm giving you seven dollars and eleven cents."

"Sounds like a lucky day to me," says the cashier. "I'd purchase a lottery ticket if I was you."

Charlie pauses for a moment. "How much for a ticket?"

"One dollar."

"I'll take one...and a scratcher for the hell of it."

The cashier hands Charlie a lottery ticket, and Charlie fills in the six bubbles, making sure the numbers 7 and 11 are circled in. He says, "What's there to do here in Warren?"

The cashier looks Charlie up and down a bit, handing him the scratcher entitled "Showdown." "Dave Grohl was born here," he says. "Know who he is?"

"Yeah, I know who Dave Grohl is."

"Well we got an alleyway named after him. People like to take pictures of it."

"Huh. I dig. Anyone else famous from here?"

"Casey Anthony, if you can call her famous. More like infamous I guess. You ever watch the Dukes of Hazzard?"

"Of course. I grew up on that show."

"Well, if you're a fan of the Dukes of Hazzard, Catherine Bach was born here. You know, Daisy Duke."

"Wow, man."

"She came in here once." The cashier reaches underneath his register and removes a large centerfold of Catherine Bach in a bikini circa 1983. "She signed this for me. We had it up in the office for some time. Course it wasn't a Seven-Eleven back then." He uses a dirty fingernail to point at the signature, smiling proudly. "She's a knockout, isn't she?"

"Certainly was."

"Legs that went on forever."

Charlie shakes hands with the cashier and says, "Take it easy," sliding the lottery ticket into the back pocket of his jeans. "Seven eleven," he says to himself.

Charlie climbs back into the driver's seat and fires the ignition. His eyes feel heavy and his bones don't seem to want to move forward. He thinks about this Dave Grohl Alley, how it might be nice to take his time getting to California instead of making a beeline for the coast. Besides, he could use a few hours to relax, let his neck loosen, rest his heels and legs from the pressure of the gas pedal. If he could find a park nearby, he might set down a blanket, pull off his socks, enjoy his Funyuns and take a nap underneath an elm tree. The weather is perfect today in Warren, holding steady at 71 degrees with a tickled breeze and no noticeable humidity—ideal for an outdoor afternoon snooze.

He heads west out of the 7-Eleven parking lot and cruising towards the city center. The streets of Warren are lined with brick storefronts and

Victorian style homes, paved walkways and olive green metallic lanterns that harken back to a time of antiquity, simplicity, syphilis. There's a scent in the air, something cinematic and picaresque, the aroma of typewriters, yellowed pages, old pennies. Charlie can almost imagine Bonnie and Clyde running down the road, guns blasting, their two-door Ford sedan screeching away at 50 mph in a cloud of gunsmoke.

It takes Charlie seven minutes to arrive at Dave Grohl Alley. The coincidences, at this point, are making his stomach turn. He feels like he's in the middle of a *Twilight Zone* episode, a dream without an end, a false existence. This town, this place, this life can't be real. He parks his car, reaches into the back seat, and pulls out his beer. Anxiety begins to take hold. It starts with an icy numbness at his fingertips, continues up into his wrists, forearms, and biceps, until finally it lodges itself in his chest, his mind convinced the heart attack is imminent. He can't be sure, but it seems there's an electric twitch in the left side of his face, slicing backwards, spreading to his ear. His jaw tightens. He closes his eyes, takes one large breath in, and sucks down half of his beer in three swallows. "You're not going to die," he tells himself.

He makes a rational decision to remove his watch and place it in the glove compartment. From now on, there will be no time. He won't count anything. He'll only exist. He continues drinking his beer, looking in his rearview and side mirrors as he does so, carefully examining his surroundings. Warren is not a place for public drink, especially in an automobile. The town seems idyllic, suited for families, smiles, a blockbuster movie that comes to town for two weeks in July, a jubilant parade celebrating our independence on The 4th. This is not the town for debauchery.

When he's done with his tall boy, he slides the empty can underneath the passenger seat. His anxiety passes as the booze takes hold of his blood. He looks up outside his windshield and sees the street-sign. "DAVE GROHL ALLEY." Charlie doesn't know it, but from the time he cracked his High Life to the moment he finished it and slid it underneath the passenger seat, seven minutes and eleven seconds passed. If he had known this, he might have been brought to tears.

"With the lights out, it's less dangerous," he says to himself. "Nirvana. Foo Fighters? I don't know any Foo-Fighters songs. Interesting."

He opens the door and lets a leg out, the alcohol rushing through his blood down his thigh, relaxing the muscle.

Dave Grohl alley isn't too exciting. There's peaceful graffiti covering the walls and walkway, a few custom spray-painted portraits of the drummer. Charlie looks around, sees no one, stands underneath the street sign and takes a selfie with his iPhone. He turns the cellular device around to examine the photo and sees he's only captured his forehead, the space of the frame principally held by the street sign. He contorts his body in a way that both his face and DAVE GROHL ALLEY can be seen in the photograph, smiles, and presses the button with his thumb. When he reexamines the photograph, he's irritated to find this time he's captured his entire head, but left out the DAVE GROHL ALLEY street sign. "Fuck," he says to himself.

He contorts his body further, dropping down into a squatting position, letting his arm dangle down to the street, pointing the device upward in yet another attempt to get both his face and the street sign in the frame. He hears a chuckle, a deep yet feminine laugh, and finally the sound of two hands clapping in applause. From a garage, a young woman approaches. She wears an old dress, maybe late 50's in origin, the pattern of which displays dancing avocados wearing sombreros and shaking maracas that aren't attached to their bodies, buttoned all the way up to her neck. The sleeves wrap tight around her biceps, reaching down to her elbows. The hem comes to a halt three inches above her knees. Her hair is jet black, a faux black, an inhuman pigmentation. Her eyes are blue, her fingers are long, her lips are a natural cherry red.

"Want me to take a picture for you?" she asks Charlie.

"That'd be nice, thank you."

Charlie hands his phone to her and she steps back three feet.

"Move to the right," she says.

Then, the sound of a digital "click."

"Fan of Dave, are ya?" the woman asks.

"I wouldn't say I'm a fan, but I'm passing through and someone told me about this spot. Strange."

"It is. Strange indeed. Pretty sure no one thinks an alley dedicated to Dave Grohl is normal."

"Definitely not normal."

"Where you from and where you headed?"

"Back East, heading to California, Los Angeles or San Francisco—not sure yet."

"California. I wish. But I hate traffic, and shit it's expensive out there. I hate earthquakes too."

Earthquakes. Damn. Charlie hadn't thought about earthquakes. What the fuck do you do when an earthquake hits? You probably need to stock up on water and canned food, guns and ammunition, comic books and board games, oil lanterns, candles, grenades—a typewriter for correspondence.

"I like your dress."

"You've got great boots."

"Thanks."

"I got this dress in Kansas. I was passing through here about two years ago myself, on the way out of Santa Fe to New York. Stopped in Kansas, found a pile of dresses that reflected past lives, made it to Warren, my car broke down, found a job right here in DAVE GROHL ALLEY."

Charlie has so many questions to ask her about that sentence he doesn't know where to begin. He wants another beer. Did Cassidy give him one before he left? He can't be sure. Better check the trunk.

"Would you like a beer?" he asks the woman.

"Yeah, sounds good. My name is Evelyn, by the way."

"Charlie. Give me one sec." Charlie starts a casual jog back to his car where he pops open the trunk. He says "Seven eleven, give me a beer." He moves his belongings out of the way to reveal a nice warm brew. He jogs back to Evelyn, opening the bottle with a cigarette lighter. "Here ya go."

She takes a big slug of the beer, the foam racing up and out of the bottle, splashing to the ground. "Shit, sorry. Kinda warm."

"No worries."

She takes another sip and hands it back to Charlie.

"I'm sorry, but a second ago, did you say there was a pile of dresses in Kansas that reflects past lives?"

"I did. This guy Miles Macombe wrote a book about it called *Driving to Kansas for Dresses*. I thought it was fiction, but it turns out it was based on a true story. Got it on Amazon for a couple bucks."

She can tell from Charlie's perplexed expression that he neither understands nor believes what she's saying. "I'm not joking. Go there. If you pick up a dress, this like, projection of the owner's life who wore the dress before starts playing. It's a fucking trip. I left with a few dresses because they were cool, unsure if I was dosed or something. But every now and again, this dress will just shoot a ray of light right out from the heart and I can see her, the woman before me, who wore it. Her name was Joyce. I think she was a secretary at an ad agency, but I can't be sure—the films are silent, like home movies."

Charlie is now positive this woman is a complete lunatic, dropped off the moon, landed here. He distances himself, looks down at the beer with her saliva on it and thinks twice about putting it back in his mouth—her lips are probably covered in LSD, each molecule of her bodily fluid drenched in psychedelics. He hands the bottle back to her and says "Where do you work now?"

"I work over here—I'm a carpenter. I make all kinds of crazy shit. Like right now, I'm converting an old train car into a fully functional eco-friendly house. With a garden on the roof, and a spiral waterslide coming down from the top."

Evelyn moves towards the garage, shuffling in her pair of broke down Converse All Stars and Charlie follows, keeping his distance. His urban instincts kick in, his eyes darting side-to-side waiting for the shakedown. When they reach the edge of the garage, Evelyn points, and before her finger, an old train car sits, half-gutted, with a bed, sink, wallpaper of blue triangles against gold flake, olive green shag carpeting, and a chandelier of upside-down wine bottles. Grass covers the roof of the structure, rosemary and mint growing out from it around the edges. Surrounding the train car is a myriad of soiled tools, Bobby Kennedy banners, old road signs, a broken Standard Oil gas pump, worn and weathered antique furnishings, model airplanes, an ongoing project for both the soul and eyes.

"Pretty cool," Charlie says.

"It pays the bills," she replies.

Charlie begins to rethink his stance on her mental capacity. "Where did you say these dresses are? And do they have men's pants?"

"The middle of Kansas. And yes, they have pants in a different pile."

Evelyn excuses herself and moves into the garage where she pulls out a book from a small library hidden behind a stuffed elephant.

"Here ya go," she says. "Read it and you'll know where to go." She hands the beer back to Charlie and he, without knowing why, responds by throwing everything he has into her in the form of a hug. He smells like sweat and beer.

"You're welcome," she says. She smells like patchouli and jasmine.

She smiles when he waves goodbye. He wonders about asking her for a date, remaining in Warren for some time, and perhaps, down the line, marrying, but instead he gets in his car and flips to page 1. *Thomas Taylor arrives at the Wild Nixon Space Travel amplifier factory...*

He'll find a park and start reading, fall asleep and dream of those lives before him and the life ahead of him. It will be a good day. Thank you, DAVE GROHL ALLEY.

Breaking News Blues

Malaysian Airlines flight 3077 has gone missing en route to Beijing from Kuala Lumpur. 297 people were on board. It's widely believed aliens are involved.

Create Change Blues

The stomachaches started about seven weeks ago. Seven weeks ago, it happened over a bottle of wine and *I Dream of Jeannie* reruns—she could barely breathe, started hyperventilating—seven minutes later, the cramps had passed and we chalked it up to the sulfites in the wine or the shellfish she ate. Today, the pain is excruciating and has been so for nearly an hour. She's on the floor of the bathroom, and at first I tell her it's just a hangover. That she drank too much and needs to get it out—but nothing is coming out. She retches into the toilet bowl, but only spit falls from her bottom lip. I see her on the floor of the bathroom, her bare breasts spreading out against cold tile, her nipples erect from the chill, the goosebumps rising from her legs, open, spread out, nearly naked aside from a pair of hot pink underwear, her least favorite pair, the ones she wears when the others are dirty. She looks sexy to me, even though she's crying and, for a moment, dying. She looks exactly as she did that California morning when the blood fell out of her and the snot of her nose mixed with the tears in a horrifying cocktail of mistake or savior—we're still not sure.

When I see my wife in pain, I have a very strange, yet predictable reaction. I get defensive. I think, "Why can't I solve this problem? Why can't I pick her up, curl her into my arms, blow air into her belly button, rub a strong thumb across her lips and turn this torture into memories of candy canes and Mike and Ike's, Slip-and-Slide and Twister. But I can't. Adult life is void of candy canes and Mike and Ike's, Slip-and-Slide and

Twister. It's made of pain—women on the bathroom floor writhing, too weak to put a hand out for comfort, and men too worried to reach a hand down to ease. If I put my hand down, rub that spine, it means there's something wrong and I'm admitting a problem exists. If I move into my office and find that warm Sierra Nevada bottle hidden underneath the couch, it just means it's a simple stomachache, nothing serious—one simple stomachache that's been happening for seven weeks—seven weeks today.

"Are you ok?" I ask her.

She doesn't respond. It's the fifth time I've asked her in the past few minutes. I drink the warm Sierra Nevada under the couch in my office and watch my hand go from slightly shaking to a nice calm "normal." I can handle anything. Four minutes later, I'm back in the bathroom and her face is halfway down the toilet bowl. "Are you ok?" I ask again.

"No." The echo of her shaky voice rumbles up out of the porcelain.

"Should I call 911?"

An emphatic "No!"

"What can I do?"

"Nothing."

Nothing is what husbands are supposed to do—my mother gave me this advice after my first nuptial argument with my brand new wife two years ago. She said, "Men always want to fix things, but they can't. And sometimes all women want is a man to say 'I'm here for you, you're going to be all right." I trust my mom's advice because she's been married four times to men who wanted to fix her. She's just as broken as she was the day she was born. No one wanted to stick around to be there for her. Nothing was all right. Nothing got fixed. Nothing is worth everything.

"Let me get you some tea? Or I'll draw you a bath. Baths are good for stomachaches."

"Baths don't work," she manages to squeeze through her teeth, through the pain, through the disdain of her body.

She says, "This is punishment," and looks up to me waiting for agreement.

"It's not punishment," I say. "It's a fucking stomachache. You drank too much. What did you eat?"

It's 11:11 a.m. and she's only had an egg to eat this morning, poached, with a little salt. Last night, a spinach salad. Yesterday for lunch, a turkey sandwich on gluten free bread. I know all these things but ask her anyways. "What did you eat?"

She says, "Nothing that would do this."

What I don't know is she did cocaine last night, but if I did know, I'd probably tell her we need to go to the hospital because it was probably stepped on with baby laxatives and arsenic and whatever else it is that makes today's cocaine the worst hangover ever. She pulls her knees into her stomach, forms the fetal position, and starts sobbing. "I'm so sorry," she cries. "We fucked up, we fucked up, I know we fucked up. God is punishing us. We threw it out like trash."

"We didn't fuck up. God isn't punishing us."

She nods her head "yes" in disagreement.

I try to think of the good things in my life while I watch my wife roll around on the ground.

Good Thought #1—My chode rash is completely gone.

Good Thought #2—California still exists. A major earthquake hasn't destroyed the coastline, a tsunami hasn't eliminated Santa Barbara or Santa Cruz or Arcata. The Sierra Nevada mountain range, the tall peak of proud Mt. Whitney, still cut across that blue sky like a Keith Richards guitar solo on acid, ripping right through your brain like an ice-cold orgasm.

Also, I have an idea about this new Choose Your Own Adventure Book. I read the first fifteen pages of Linda Howard's *Cry No More* the other day and realized something about women in romance novels—they need to be stripped of everything, endure the most painful experience, then be built back up with both unconditional compassion and handsome cock. I know now that my Choose Your Own Adventure erotica novel must start with an abortion. There she is, lying on the ground, blood pouring out, a commitment to her husband she didn't want to commit to, knowing the punishment will come, either from God or from her own mind. Either way, that handsome compassionate cock has to get pushed back up in there and recreate something lost.

I drop to my knees and let my hands play along her belly. I close my eyes and meditate, sending white light into her body. This white light comes and untangles the knots of her gut, lets her knees slowly draw away from her chest. This white light will not only cure this stomachache, but all future stomachaches, and all the past seven weeks of stomachaches. It'll also turn my wife into a full-blown sex machine, wanting to suck the clitoris of her best friend while I masturbate. Wait. What am I thinking? Sometimes my life turns into cheap erotica without me wanting it to. Besides, a literary agent once told me women don't want to read about threesomes. Only one-on-one sex with good men, the kind of men that open car doors and throw their capes over muddy puddles so women can walk across the street without dirtying their shoes.

These stomachaches, seven weeks now, are starting to affect my life. Our sex life is nearly non-existent. We used to make love three times a week. We've had sex one time in seven weeks. This carnal numerology hurts my soul. It either says something terrible about our marriage, or says something terrible about my wife's physical state. These stomachaches are making me think of Aunika right now, and that can't be healthy. Aunika is definitely not writhing in pain on the bathroom floor. She's probably shooting guns off a mountain peak with a fifth of whiskey in her hand, or stomping subpar humans into the ground with her Catherine Bach legs that never end. She's probably running a lucrative donut shop and wearing an incredible pair of pants, one made of butterfly wings and rose petals. My god, her thighs felt hot last night. I can almost feel her warm center on my spine, that hot tongue licking up my neck to my ear, the scent of whiskey close enough to inhale all night long.

I start the water for a bath using my fingers to test the warmth and say "I'm gonna start some tea. Mint. It's good for stomachaches." I'm not sure if mint is good for stomachaches, but Indians like it and Indians are pretty good about utilizing healthy herbs and spices. Or is mint more of an Asian thing? Or Lebanese? I don't care—I need an excuse to get out of the bathroom and back into the kitchen where I think I have a bottle of vermouth in the refrigerator. I'm out of beer. Vermouth will have to do. I start the water on the stove and open the fridge, happy to find the cheap green bottle. I take three slugs, making a face as if I've just seen my sister naked, and wipe my mouth.

"Owwww!" I hear my wife moan. "Oh my god Oh my god Oh my god, owwwwww."

She's in the midst of full-blown pain, excruciating spasms. I can no longer deny that. This is serious. I can feel my heart beat, my pulse bouncing around my neck. Stomach cancer. It must be stomach cancer. I wonder if I know anyone our age that's had cancer. Is it possible? At such a young age? I need more vermouth. Iggy Pop once said vermouth is good for the vocal chords, but my vocal chords don't matter, just my fingers and brain.

In my office on my computer I Google "severe stomachaches." Crohn's disease. Peptic ulcer. Stomach cancer. Asteroid poisoning. Snake bite. Yellow Elephant Tumors. Dukes of Hazzard Syndrome. Arsenic glass arthritis. African Meningitis. Indonesian Chicken Pox.

My anxiety builds. Luckily I remember the forty I stashed away two weeks ago in my typewriter case. I unzip the case and swallow a warm twelve oz's of strong malt brew and wipe my mouth. Not enough dialogue. Not enough. I have to speak to her, find out what's wrong, what's happening. Asteroid poisoning doesn't sound good—The victim begins writhing on the floor of the bathroom feeling remorseful for some past event, then retches violently for hours, nothing coming up but viscous spit. Soon, the victim turns into a small, benign alien with tentacles under the chin and large oval eyes, a being without any sense of independence that can never be left alone. It sounds terrifying—like a child.

I fold up my MacBook and head back into the bathroom. I can't make love to an alien, no matter how cute and benign she may be. Maybe I can. No, I can't. I don't know, maybe I can.

"Your bath's almost ready," I tell my wife.

"I can't," she says.

"C'mon," I tell her. "The heat will relax your muscles."

I scoop her up off the floor, cradling her in my arms, and gently immerse her in the hot water. She keeps her knees tucked into her chest at first, not wanting to let go, to rediscover the sharp pain, but eventually, they move slowly outward. Her eyes shut, the tears stop, a breath is inhaled. I take water and cup it in my palms and pour it onto her neck, keeping her body warm, letting the heat roll down her taught body. I kiss her cheek and sing a Crosby Stills and Nash song. "Four and twenty years ago I came into this life, the son of a woman and a man who lived in strife…"

This is our marriage. This is days on the bathroom floor, nights of absence, cubicles and bars, women and men, strangers, sweaters, candied tampons, a lost California redwood shoved through our hearts. We chose our own adventure. Turn the page, make a new ending. "This is not punishment."

Her lips tremble.

I sit on the edge of the tub and dunk a foot in the hot water. "It isn't your fault."

Donut Hole Blues

This is the moment. This is the culmination of Cliffs' life, where everything he's been preparing for in an inebriated haze will pay off. He's without a shirt, without a care, with a mustache and with a glass of bourbon. He takes a look around the loft—his brother's paintings stacked against every wall, seven, eleven deep. His brother's paintings hang from each wall, taking up nearly all of the fifteen-foot vertical space. His brother is everywhere. He thinks to himself, "I am nowhere." "Now here."

The large bay window overlooking Echo Park Lake is stained with hard rain—a rain now five months in the making, a rain that nearly shut down the streets below. This loft smells like cigarettes and sweat, incense and oil paintings, paint thinner, an alcohol gravity, hard drugs, if hard drugs can have a smell, and they do. Hard drugs smell like tile floors at a house party in Silver Lake and brand new condoms at midnight.

Cliff holds Charlie's rig in his hand, the empty barrel of the syringe waiting for the fix. In front of him, steaming on the counter, the first ever Mustard Brothers donut. Light, flaky, doughy, hot—fucking beautiful. It's a perfect golden hue, not bad for his first foray into donut creation. This piping hot circle reminds him of his wedding band, now seven years removed, the one that shined for two years on his finger, now stuck nowhere inside an old Black Sabbath record sleeve.

Cliff has never felt like he's been in competition with his brother. He's proud of his brother's success, and grateful to have a sibling that gives him a livelihood and occasional inspiration. But today, something feels different. Cliff realizes Charlie's success surrounds his entire life—the paintings, the drinking, the drugging, the mundane management of an up-and-coming artist—all of these things occupy his temporal existence. Now here. Mustard Brothers will be his creation, his mark on earth, like crop circles and pyramids made of fried dough and booze. The donut shop, thousands of them, will be what his children, illegitimate or legitimate, will remember him by and thrive from. Mustard Brothers Whiskey Jelly donuts means swimming pools and vacations in Baja, lobster in Puerto Nuevo. Mustard Brothers Whiskey Jelly donuts means cool summer evenings with good drugs and sloppy friends, better tattoos and old audiophile records. Cassidy will be there with him. Together, they'll drink until the sun rises each day, and then again when the sun sets. Their pancreases will be perfect, like pink candy hearts with "Be Mine" written in sugary red across them. They'll chop down eucalyptus trees for the hell of it and build bonfires in each other's eyes. He'll purchase gallons of banana oil—he read about the hip new drug craze in a motorcycle magazine the other day and it sounds like a full blown donkey trip—and they'll glide between each other, lifted towards the great oozing stone, slithering, dangling, naked.

He sets the syringe down on the counter and pulls a jar of whiskey jelly from a cupboard—the four-ounce mint julep. He stares at the jelly, wants the burn in his mouth and in his gut. But Charlie would be upset if Cliff started without him. This is supposed to be a fraternal endeavor, two men piecing together two dreams, and getting drunk and high as shit in the process. But fuck it, Charlie's at the gallery hanging paintings and probably jonesing for a hit, flirting with the gallery girl and drinking a bottle of semi-expensive wine straight from the bottle, saying things like "I'm pretty sure composition, and all that the term entails, is for pussies. Fuck composing. Fuck color. Fuck everything. Fuck whatever anyone ever said about art. These are bunny rabbits. They come from somewhere undiscovered, fervent with light and electricity, cocks, pussies, asses, sweat, drugs, cum covered lips and jellyfish tits." Cliff likes those sentences and wishes his brother would actually say something poignant like that in an interview. Most of the time Charlie just giggles and says, "I don't know, it is what it is," when a journalist asks him about his process. "I wear cowboy boots and pretend I'm in a shootout." Fucking lame. Boring. He sounds like a kook.

Cliff needs to have ill feelings towards his brother in order for him to inject the first whiskey jelly donut without him there. But he has no ill feelings towards his sibling, so he tries his best to search deep down for that competitive spirit he never had, but must create. The truth is, Cliff's life is pretty decent, aside from the wife that left him over his habitual drinking and inability to perform sexually as a result. He still believes she's the prettiest, the most beautiful, the most intellectual woman he's ever met, and is positive those qualities made it easier for her to leave him. A gorgeous and smart woman can't be involved with a drunk who likes to play electric guitar on Tuesday mornings and is perpetually inebriated with his half-junkie brother. She could do better, and maybe she did, marrying that Certified Public Accountant with great tooth brushing habits. But fuck all that shit. He's got a syringe about to be filled with whiskey jelly and a piping hot donut in front of him. Not even a double blow-job from Scarlett Johansson and her clone could top this moment.

He dips the syringe into the jar of 4 oz whiskey jelly, 100 proof, and pulls back on the plunger—nothing—the needle is too thin to suck the gelatinous mixture up into the barrel. Syringes are meant for the thin, hard drugs, not viscous whiskey jelly. This syringe now seems a bit superfluous, weak. A turkey baster is what he needs, or maybe he could just roll the jelly up in the dough before dropping it in the fryer, pray for a miracle. His mind races with what to do next, worried Charlie will bust through the door at any moment with giggles and wild eyes, and this moment, his one true moment of independent success, will vanish. He's got a couple of options—first, Cliff's pretty sure there's a turkey baster somewhere in the house—but here's the rub—Charlie was dating another half-junkie several months ago who, along with her casual use of heroin, was also a full-time alcoholic. But this woman couldn't stand the taste of alcohol. Instead, she used the turkey baster as a rig, pulling straight vodka up into it, then sliding the baster into her ass, squeezing with both fingers, pushing it up into her delicate internal tissue. "It gets you fucked up fast," she explained as she exited their bathroom bowlegged. This turkey baster, most likely, is still there, underneath the sink, a few feet from the toilet, and whether or not it has ever been cleaned and sterilized is a mystery with a pretty obvious answer—No.

The quickest solution Cliff can find to the problem at hand is to take a deep slug of whiskey, get bleary eyed and dangerous, self destructive and reckless, listen to Guns and Roses' "Rocket Queen," scrub the gnarled turkey baster with soap, and get on with it. He does each of these things, aside from listening to G n R—he can't find the Appetite for Destruction record in the mess of vinyl just outside his bedroom door. He settles for Black Sabbath, letting his lonesome wedding ring roll around in his empty palm, carving fate lines leading nowhere. Now here.

He stares down at his fingers, the tips and prints touched with the asshole of a junkie, and drops the baster down into the whiskey jelly. He presses his fingers together, watching the mixture get pulled up. He uses a shaky finger to poke a hole in the center of his donut, raises the baster and says, "This is Mustard Brothers. This is the zing." He pops the tip of the baster into the hole with one swift movement of his wrist, then dumps the whiskey jelly into the center.

The door swings open, the doorknob denting the wall behind it. Charlie is noticeably high, gazing at his paint-spotted cowboy shoes, his body shrugging off the endless worldly detritus, an antibody to society, slunk, loose, unaffected. His lingo is slurred, his mouth moving in half time trying to catch up to a brain moving at quarter time. "W h h a s s s s s u p p p p p?"

Cliff can't help but smile when he sees his brother, even though he knows his brother is killing himself at a quicker pace than he himself is. "Are you fucked up?" he asks.

"Nottt. Realllly," Charlie replies. "Just tired, I guess." Every junkie lies about being high, so Cliff automatically knows Charlie is stoned to the asteroids. If Charlie had replied, "No, just wasted on some Napa wine and Polo vodka—I feel like shit," Cliff would have known Charlie wasn't high—drunkards tell the truth, either in speech or with their eyes—in vino veritas—it's been that way for thousands of years.

Charlie stumbles towards the couch landing perfectly on the cushions, lets his head fall to a shoulder, his eyes dilate with wonder, wandering around the room as if he were seeing this place for the first time. His eyebrows cross as he scans, locking in on the space filled top to bottom with the bunny rabbits of his deranged pop-art psyche performing odd human sins, before becoming fixated on his brother with the turkey baster in his hand. "Couldn't wait, huh?" Charlie says.

"Couldn't wait for what?" Cliff responds.

"To get drunk? You're doing the old asshole trick?" Charlie rubs his left forearm, pushing the bruise back.

"Sure."

"Gross man. I think you have a problem." Charlie closes his eyes and lets his arms loose, an unfolding of tired wings, exhaling. "So fucking tired."

Cliff holds the donut in his hand, inspecting it, saying a small prayer to someone somewhere that this donut will taste unlike any other, the perfect creation, the alcoholics' morning savior—ten times better than a bloody-mary with scrambled eggs and bacon. His fingers burn with the hot fried heat. He unhinges his jaw, feels the steam tickle his gums, belly grumbles...

"Is that a Mustard Brothers!?" Charlie yells from the couch. "Are you fucking kidding me?" Then, as if hit with a shot of burning charcoal to the heart, ice cubes up the ass, Charlie pops up, raises his shoulders defiantly, rips off his shirt, and heads towards his brother with his fists rock hard.

"Chill out, man. You can have a bite."

When Charlie reaches Cliff, he grabs him by his arms. "I wanted to watch the injection! That's the best fucking part!"

"Get your shitty little hands off me!"

"Fuck you!"

Charlie attempts to wrestle the donut from Cliff's hands, unhinging his own jaw while simultaneously moving his face towards the pastry. "Give me the donut!"

"No way, dick! Fuck off!"

Charlie drops a knee into Cliff's groin and Cliff falls to the ground, pulling Charlie down with him, the donut falling a moment later, rolling across the kitchen floor, landing at the foot of their burrito stained trashcan.

"You fucking asshole!" Cliff yells. "This is Mustard Brothers! This is my future!"

"It's Mustard *Brothers*! Not Mustard *Only Child*! It's *our* future!"

On the ground, on top of each other, they both stare at the greasy donut, now partially covered in loose hair, a bit of dust, some dark blue lint from a wash done three weeks prior. They share a deep breath, a sigh of failure.

Charlie gazes down at his brother, their bellies pressed together and smiles, shakes his head. His bones are too goddamn weak for this. "Sorry dude."

"You're such a dick sometimes. You get all fucked up and do stupid shit."

"I'm just tired man. Gotta finish these paintings."

Cliff tries not to look at Charlie's arms. The tiny holes give him a feeling of death on a rollercoaster ride towards hell. Nonetheless, he takes a peek, and spots the fresh bruise. "You gotta quit."

"I know. Tomorrow. I swear."

On his knees, Charlie crawls towards the donut, wipes it off on the inside of his forearm, and takes a bite. His mouth morphs, slowly, in quarter time, into a smile. "Delicious."

You Blues

Phoenix took off work yesterday and laid in bed all day, a heating pad attached to her belly, nursing the perpetual stomachache. I spent most of the day in and out of our bedroom bringing her chicken broth and mint tea, peaking a head in once or twice an hour to see if she'd fallen asleep. I told her, "You need sleep. Sleep cures everything." She's only slept a few hours in the past two nights, and I know this is deeply unhealthy for a woman in her current physical and mental state. Eventually, after nine hours of *I Love Lucy* and *Dick Van Dyke Show* reruns, her eyes closed, and her body slowly let itself go. She purred through the night as I watched her sleep, her eyelids fluttering with dreams, a somnambulist Pacific storm.

In the morning, I hear the alarm go off, her tiny footsteps flutter across the wood, a lighter flicker, the shower turn on, the heavy thuds of sudsy water falling from her thick brunette locks. I take a deep breath, the edges of sunlight peaking around the teakwood blinds in our bedroom. I'm tired, but relieved—"no hangover today," I think to myself. "And her stomachache must be gone." I pretend I'm asleep when she exits the bathroom, frightened she'll tell me it's still there, the pain hasn't quite left, that the Yellow Elephant Tumors have gripped hold of her precious inner tissue, are nesting inside of her, sprouting children, building cities.

I hear her whisper "Fuck." I open one eye, noticing her sort of bent over, a hand just above her pelvis. She takes a deep breath, pulls the towel from her body, and begins dressing, still hunched over. I smell the marijuana smoke as it fills the room, wraps me up in its bluish warmth. I hear her open the cupboard in the kitchen, scoop coffee into the coffee maker—but the coffee maker never turns on. She must have thought twice—caffeine and coffee are hard on the stomach. A few moments later, I hear the front door close, her heels pound the pavement outside, and the rumble of her engine as it disappears down the avenue.

I get up to take a piss, to stare at myself in the mirror and rub the wrinkles forming underneath my eyes. These wrinkles are new. They didn't exist in California. They're accentuated by the gray of the east, the crevices of skin deep with black storm clouds instead of the gold of sunshine waves. I say a prayer to God in the mirror. I say "Please God, make sure these stomachaches are nothing serious. Please heal her, lift the pain from her. She doesn't deserve it. She's beautiful and small—and perfect."

I make the sign of the cross and get back into bed, throwing a leg to the heat where she had been sleeping, close my eyes, and think of a smooth pink pearl wedged between Aunika's legs, before falling asleep once again.

At the office, Phoenix arrives with her usual mixed-bag expression of torture, disdain, and determination. The Rudy's Candy Tampon press release is due by the end of the day. She told her boss she'd have it done yesterday, but she was sick. He gave her an extension, but expects something promising, something the client will rave about. He thinks Phoenix is the best writer he's got—perfect for a candy tampon—plus she's a woman—she most likely knows a thing or two about feminine hygiene.

The first thing Phoenix does at her desk is Google "birthmarks"—they've been on her mind since St. Claire's rainbow party. *The exact cause of birthmarks is unknown.* Wow. A truly stunning realization, considering we've figured out how to send space junk to the outer reaches of the universe and walk on the fucking moon.

She plugs her headphones into her computer, finds Mozart, and begins the daily grind, proofreading and reorganizing words, one in front of the other, until it's noon, Mozart's powdered wig has been replaced with Neil's shaggy hair, the piano and violins now guitars and harmonicas. She pulls a small sandwich from her lunch sack and takes a bite. Her stomach growls when the food hits bottom. She's concerned for a moment—unsure of what will happen next. She allows five minutes to pass before she's satisfied, then takes another bite. She grins a bit, hoping the episode two days ago was the climax of whatever it was that has been happening. Maybe it was a hangover. Maybe it was the cocaine. She'll never do the drug again—there's no point. She only does it to do something Cassidy isn't doing, to have something to herself. Everyone wants a secret no one else knows. That secret is like a small, unbreakable safe inside of yourself, something no one can ever get to, the combination impossible to attain. We need to lock something inside, just one thing, if we want to stay sane.

She pulls the headphones from her ears, listens to the water dump into paper cups, hears an intern say "Day Five!"—the click of an iPhone camera.

This is just about the time I wake up. I stretch out and yawn, thinking about the amount of time we miss in each other's life. When the day is over, we sum everything up in three sentences what it took nine hours to accomplish. We use a paragraph for a month, or a poem for a lifetime. It all seems fascinating to me as I think to myself, "I wonder what Phoenix is doing at work right now?" I look at the clock and it reads 12:11. She's probably eating a sandwich, worried about her stomach, and listening to an idiot intern talk about Day Five of the Thirty Days of Sweaters campaign—this is all just a hunch. It's warm inside the house today, the sun shining through the skylights. How can anyone wear a sweater on a day like today? It seems borderline torturous. This day makes me want to stand naked in the yard, lift up my arms, knock my head back, close my eyes and point west with my brain, let it lift up and fly, drop right down into the Pacific, ride the back of an Ahi Tuna towards Trancas Beach.

These stomachaches are tough to deal with, so tough, it's nearly impossible for me to deal with them. I brush my teeth and move directly to the record player, put The Gun Club back on, open the fridge and pull out a beer. Maybe I'll head to the backyard and just lie in the grass on a blanket, drink my beer, wait for work tonight. I'll write a little, but mostly read that biography on Richard Brautigan I just got in the mail—eight hundred plus pages dissecting the life of the great author, beginning with his gruesome suicide. I'll take breaks every ten pages or so and turn the clouds into something, create a new sky above, inhale and hope for the roses to fill my lungs.

I'm too lazy to get dressed, so I remain naked, listening to the electric guitars roll through the house. I stroll back through the kitchen, past our bedroom, towards the back door, stare out the window at the day, and twist the lock.

"Boo!"

A figure leaps out at me, a whipping tornado of blonde and turquoise, a flash of bronzed skin. I'm so frightened I throw my hands in the air and trip over myself, tumbling backwards, all the while letting out a small high-pitched yelp as if I've just seen a mouse, falling onto my bare ass, but nonetheless, keeping my beer intact, not a drop spilled. When my backwards somersault comes to an end, I refocus my eyes on the hysterical face of my best friend above me. "Holy shit!" Aunika laughs. "I didn't think you'd be naked!"

I am naked. My dick dangles between my legs, the shrunken tip resting on the wood beneath. I'm still too stunned, my heart too thick with blood, to cover myself. I take the can of beer in my hand and jam it into my crotch.

"You scared the shit out me." I am naked. Aunika doesn't turn away, doesn't offer to grab me clothes. She just stares and laughs. In fact, instead of moving away from me, she moves towards me and offers me a hand.

"It's nothing I haven't seen before," she says.

"Maybe," I say. "But you haven't seen mine before."

"I have now."

I extend a hand, keeping the cold beer against my cock, my balls popping out from the can like Dumbo's ears.

"Go put some clothes on," she says. "I'm gonna grab a drink."

As I turn to head back to the bedroom, I feel a firm, long, slender hand smack my ass.

"Yow!" she yells. "You do yoga?"

I look over my shoulder at Aunika and she winks at me. I look down over my shoulder and see the red imprint of her hand.

As I pull on a pair of jeans I think to myself how strange it is to be naked in front of Aunika, how it didn't feel all too embarrassing, felt as if it were the thousandth time it had happened. I'm not ashamed of my body in front of her. It's nothing she hasn't seen before. She's seen it now—it's over with.

I don't bother to put on a shirt, because what's the point? It's warm, we're friends. "What's up?" I yell to her from the bedroom as I slide my brown leather belt through the tight denim loops.

"What's up with what?" She yells back.

I can hear the metallic ceramic collision of plates and silverware, the sucking and thumping of the refrigerator door opening and closing, the cedar squeak and knock of drawers and cupboards swinging and slamming.

"Why aren't you at work?" I appear in the doorjamb pulling on a pair of blue socks patterned with orange marijuana leaves, trading balance back and forth between each unsteady foot before sliding my feet into a pair of old brown ankle boots.

"Nice boots."

"Thanks. Got 'em on eBay for twenty bucks."

She holds up a couple avocados, rolling them through her fingers like emeralds. "I'm making guacamole." She slides a knife into the center of the fruit. "Um, I'm not at work because I have some good news for you."

"What's the good news?" I join her in the kitchen, watching her hips shake as she chops the cilantro.

I casually place my hand on the wooden counter top, run a hand through my hair. I smell my armpit because that's what close friends do in front of each other. My armpit doesn't smell like anything, or if it does, it just smells like sleep, hot bed sheets, strange dreams, leftover patchouli.

"I got approved for the liquor license today."

"That quickly?"

"I know someone."

"You know everyone."

"I guess."

She stirs a glass of bourbon with a finger, twirling an ice cube around in a circle. When she's satisfied with the temperature of the booze, she slides it over to me and raises her own glass. "Cheers," she says.

I know what this toast means. It means I'll be working with Aunika, by her side, our backs to shelves of perfect alcohol, perfect irresponsibility, forty hours a week. This toast means "to temptation," "to drunkenness," "to memories," "to childhood," "to love," "to friendship," "to something in between the two."

I hesitate for only a moment, but the moment lasts five seconds too long. She squints her eyes and presses her glass into mine without my acknowledgment of the agreement to the terms of our cheers. She refocuses her attention on the guacamole. "More cilantro," she says and slams her knife into another handful of leaves and stems. "Can you grab me a jalapeno?"

As I open the refrigerator, I have the feeling I've done this before—and I have. I used to do this with my wife, frequently, weekly. We both love guacamole. We pass each other the peppers and we chop the cilantro. We carve the avocados. We add lime juice, salt, black pepper. We take the guacamole to the sunshine and we dip tortilla chips into it. Sometimes we drink a bottle of Rose, or a buttery California Chardonnay. Sometimes, after that, we make love, a little drunk, faces flush, smiling, blood and hearts pumping, until the sun goes down and there's nothing left to do but talk or watch *Mad Men*, have another drink or two. It's been awhile since we made guacamole together. Lately, I've been making guacamole alone.

"I thought we'd eat outside, have a few drinks, and talk about what's gonna happen with the bar. I wanna have it done and ready to rock within the month, if that's possible. You need to tell me what kind of booze and beers I should order. And put together a kick-ass cocktail list or program, or whatever you bartenders call it. I want it to be fucking spectacular."

I take a long look at her, internalize her, pay attention to her. She's wearing another tank top today—*M.A.S.H 4077th*—vintage, from the TV show, army green, too big as usual, her side boobs exposed all the way out to their tips. She doesn't wear bras when it's warm—I know this because I've known her forever. She says she hates when her boobs sweat. She gets a rash underneath. It's all nothing I haven't seen before—I've just never seen hers.

"Ok," I say. I'm still not sure I want to make this decision. But I know I've already committed to Aunika—I've pressed my glass into hers, I've made guacamole with her in my kitchen, I've passed her the jalapeno. I've felt her warmth against my spine, her tongue up my neck, her lips on mine. She's seen me naked, vulnerable. She's touched my ass. There's very little left to do between us but fuck, fully solidify this lifetime-long relationship. I take a sip from my glass and dip my finger in her guac.

"Needs more salt."

***

In the cubicle, Phoenix finishes her sandwich, pops her earphones back in, presses play on Neil Young, and continues writing about Rudy's Candy Tampons—"This is the cherry you've been waiting to pop." Sometimes when she writes copy, her mind fades into a fourth dimension. She can feel her fingers moving, the ideas arriving on the page without ever being thought up. It's as if there are two sides to her—one dedicated to dreaming, and the other determined to work, pulling the weight of consonants and vowels somewhere they don't want to go, but must arrive at nonetheless. There are two sides to everyone. There are sides that do cocaine and kiss other women, and sides that love their husband and have chronic stomachaches. There are two sides to everything. There are west coast sides and east coast sides, ones with redwoods and summer and ones with cherry trees and winter.

Her fingers pound against the keyboard, but what's really on her mind is the lick that Aunika placed on her husband's neck the other night. She knows the relationship is more than just friendship, at least it is to Aunika—but telling Cassidy how she feels about his best friend might make him think she's jealous, absurd, out of her mind—paranoid, unattractive, nagging. But she knows her feelings are true and can't deny the signals when she sees them. She gets a tingle in her arms when she witnesses other women out for her man. She's been right about every man she's been with that's cheated on her and she's known who with without asking. It's a sixth sense. She reaches for her phone and begins composing a text to Cassidy, reaching out to him, a subtle nudge that will put her back in his mind if she's not already there. At first she punches, I *hate this fucking job*, but soon after, while looking down at the words, realizes everything she texts him is negative. The word "hate" dominates her digital vocabulary. She erases the words and instead types, *I love you. I hope you're having a beautiful day.* She presses send, sliding down in her chair so she can rest her neck on the backrest. She decides to spend a little time on Facebook, creeping on Aunika's profile, analyzing the thousands of pictures her husband's best friend has posted of herself in the midst of every imaginable activity in as little clothing as possible, in an endless amount of far-out locales—islands, mountains, oceans, yachts, fields, hills, flatlands, glaciers, deserts, rivers, seas, lakes, cities, towns, atolls, bumfuck—she can accessorize a bikini with them all—she can zip-line straight across the planet with her apple-shaped butt cheeks popping out. Seemingly, this woman has been everywhere, done everything, and perhaps everyone. In the photographs, she smiles in a way that transcends happiness and verges on wisdom. In this other woman's eyes, Pheonix is entranced. These other woman's eyes move with her. They sense her every emotion. "This isn't jealousy," she tells herself. "This is real. There's something about her. I don't know what it is that changed. But something is different." She realizes she hasn't opened her mouth in several hours, so makes the conscious decision to pull the earphones out and grab a glass of water at the cooler, small talk about sweaters or Instagram photos or the triviality of the latest *Girls* episode. She stands up, checks her face in a pocket mirror, rubs the rouge of her lips with a finger, yanks at her tired eyelids in an attempt to pull back the time lost underneath them, smooth the endless seconds all out, then emerges from the dark box she's been locked within since nine a.m.

She shuffles her bare feet towards the water cooler, but no one is there. No one to talk to or open her mouth for. She pours the water into her paper cup and takes a sip, takes a breath, watches her breasts push outward, then recede. She is a woman. She is somewhere nowhere. Nothing to do, nothing to say. Get back to the cubicle, move the words, move the tampons, move the candy. When she turns around, Taylor is there, young, bashful, watching her swallow the last gulp.

"Hippie water," he says. "Reverse osmosis."

"It's nice," she responds.

"Haven't seen you all day."

"Deadline for Rudy's."

"You okay?"

"Yeah. Why?"

"You look tired."

"You're not supposed to tell women they look tired."

Taylor pulls at his tie, loosening it. "I don't mean it in a bad way. You're still incredibly beautiful. Like a...."

"Haven't been sleeping too well."

"Still sick?"

"A little." A sharp pain pinches her gut. She does everything in her power to keep from grimacing, but her eyes flicker with the sharpness— like a switchblade tumbling through forty-eight stories of intestines.

"What's wrong?"

"Nothing." She puts her hand to her belly and shuffles past Taylor and back into her cubicle where a tear wells up in her eye and drops to the floor. She silently whimpers to herself, the pain now growing, deeper and deeper, tearing her apart, until finally she's doubled over in her chair and Taylor is rubbing her spine up and down. A few people gather outside the cubicle but Taylor silently, invisibly, shoos them away with his free hand.

"Phoenix," he says. "Can I do anything?"

"No."

"I'm worried about you."

"I know what it is."

Taylor's hand slowly moves down, watching as his fingers carefully glide south. He uses his other hand to pull the hair out of her face. "It's gonna be ok," he says. He wipes the sweat from the back of her neck.

She curls further into herself. "No, it's not."

***

I hear my phone vibrate in the other room, but am not interested in dealing with technology at the moment. I find a blanket in a closet and a bottle of Chardonnay in the refrigerator. Aunika and I head out to the backyard, throw the blanket down, open the bottle of wine, drop the guacamole and tortilla chips between us, and sit down. The sun is high, the blades of grass folding up towards the light. A few flowers wilt in the heat, thirsty for water—I'll do that later, when it cools down. I'll attach the hose, spray it up into the air and let it fall on me, cool my skin and mind.

Aunika pours us each a full glass, dips a chip, chews, drops onto her back, rolls her tank top all the way up to the bottoms of her breasts, and slides sunglasses over her eyes. "Beautiful day for a tan."

I take a look at her belly, perfect, her hipbones jutting out like double Cape Horns.

She notices me noticing her through her sunglasses, and her lips widen a bit. She takes a bare foot and drops it on my thigh. "What kind of cocktails do you have in mind?"

"I don't know—we need to start experimenting."

"Bourbon."

"Plenty of bourbon."

"Every hip joint has to have a few craft cocktails these days, right?"

"I think craft cocktails kind of suck."

"What do you mean?"

"I think it's cooler to have forties of High Life, imported shitty lagers from weird countries. Like, when I was in Taiwan on a layover before my trip to Thailand, I had this beer called 'Taiwan Beer.' That's it—it just said 'Taiwan Beer' on the can, in simple white writing, on a light blue body—it looked like those old Diet Pepsi cans from the eighties. And it was a pretty rad beer."

"Hmm"

"Yeah, but I think if you're going to do craft shit it should be unpretentious—or even better, do a tacky nineteen-seventies Tiki menu—rum punch, blue Hawaiians, zombies, painkillers. But we'll take 'em to the next level with fresh squeezed juices, homemade grenadine and falernum."

"Can you do that?"

"Of course. I'm a fucking syrup master."

"Tiki cocktails and donuts sounds like a lot of sugar."

"Yeah well, we can throw some local gin and Cynar in a glass too."

"Hmm. Gin and donuts? Maybe, like, together."

Shit. Gin and donuts. It's just a matter of time before she figures it out. Up until now, the Mustard Brothers just sounded like a joke.

"I'm so glad I have you on my side." She takes her other foot and drops it down on my lap. Her feet are perfectly pedicured. They're delicate yet strong, tan, the tips twinkling with peach polish.

"You have nice feet," I tell her.

She smiles.

These feet shouldn't be on me. Six weeks ago, these feet would have just been a friend's gross feet on my lap, but today, they're different. They are the feet of a woman, not a friend. There's something growing between us, making it hard for me to talk. I want to tell her about Phoenix's stomachaches, how much pain she was in the other day, how much pain I'm in watching her be in pain, but now it feels as if I can't. I wonder if there's any more of Aunika's saliva stuck to my lips. "Phoenix has been having serious stomach problems lately."

"What's wrong with her?"

"I don't know. We can't figure it out. She'll just double over in pain, like an excruciating pain, rolling around on the ground and sobbing."

"That sounds serious."

"Right?"

"How bout going to the doctor."

"She doesn't want to. She literally refuses to go."

"Well, you can't help her if she doesn't want to be helped."

"Yeah, well, it's affecting my life."

"How so."

"We don't have sex anymore."

Aunika raises herself up onto her elbows. "That's unacceptable."

"I feel like I'm gonna go crazy."

"I would too. Seriously, that's fucking crazy."

I shouldn't be talking about sex with her. I shouldn't be talking about sex with her. I shouldn't be talking about sex with my wife with her. "We got into an argument like six months ago because I told her she refuses sex all the time. And she said I was being unfair, that *I've* refused sex before. And I admit, I have—about nine times in seven years."

"Yeah? What'd she say?"

"I told her I've refused sex nine times in seven years, but she probably refuses sex at least a hundred and fifty times a year."

"Holy shit! That's impossible—unless you're insatiable."

"Most men are, I think. Anyways, she got pretty mad and told me I was making her feel bad about herself. She said there was no way she's refused sex that many times. So, I started writing down every time she refused sex with me, you know, to see if I was crazy."

"And?"

"In six months, we're over a hundred denials."

"Damn."

"I've had to, you know, take care of myself a lot lately."

Aunika smiles. "So have I. Cesar wasn't much up for sex. I bet he's refused sex over hundred times in the past six months. I think he's gay, maybe. I mean, shit. C'mon. I'm not bad, and I'm totally down, like, all the time." She laughs and pours us each another glass of wine even though we haven't finished the first one. "What do you think about when you, uh, take care of yourself?"

I blush, noticeably. This conversation cannot keep going forward. I've thought about Aunika, alone—I'm pretty sure every man who's ever met her has, but mostly I think of my wife when I'm pumping myself towards the great release.

"I don't know," I tell her, cramming the wine into my mouth.

She laughs and dips her head back, exposing her neck, her hair reflecting the sunshine.

"How 'bout you?"

She lifts her head back up, looks me straight in the eye, opens her mouth, and says, "I can't tell you," then drops her head back again, laughing.

I know I shouldn't pry, but I want to. I should. It's information about women and I need to relate to women if I'm going to write a hit Choose Your Own Adventure erotica series. No, I shouldn't ask—too personal, I'm crossing a line. What if that fucking intern asked my wife what she thinks about when she masturbates? I'd kill him, pop his little head off. Fuck it, I'll ask. "Seriously, what do you think about?"

She pulls herself back up, readjusts herself so now she's on her belly, her elbows lifting her body up, pushing towards me. She finishes her glass of wine, drops her chin. "I'll be right back."

My heart skips a beat as I watch her move towards the backdoor. The wine is hitting me in the sunshine, making everything around me—the trees, the flowers, the grass—seem as if it was underwater. Am I sinking. This is not a question. I am sunken. How can a friendship change so quickly. This is not a question. It changed. How can a marriage change in the blink of an eye. This is also not a question. I love my wife. I wish she were here. I wish she didn't have stomachaches, that she was happy, that

I was with her, alone, in an Airstream trailer somewhere in California, uncomplicated, with a bottle of bourbon and a little Grateful Dead—a clothesline and a drum kit, an electric guitar and amplifier set up in the tall grass. We could play electric blues together, master our instruments, tour the world as The Cosmic Californians.

Aunika throws open the backdoor, the bottle of bourbon swinging in her hand. She stands above me, blocking the sunlight with her body, her face silhouetted in the eclipse. A breeze blows her blonde hair forward, the tips of her tendrils kissing my lips and cheeks. "You want to know what I think about?"

"Yes."

"You."

Anxious Stomach Blues

Part I

Seven weeks ago when the stomachaches started getting serious our life together perhaps was not as perfect as I'd like to believe. We have secrets. For one, I desperately want to go back to California, but here we are on the East Coast and we came here for a reason—because California was too expensive and there seemed to be more opportunity out here. Although, now that I'm here, I'd be willing to live in an Airstream as long as it was placed near the California Coastline, somewhere around Santa Cruz or anywhere swimming with Pacific Blue for that matter. I don't need much in life—a happy wife, a few beers, my record collection, and my books. Also, my computer. I need my computer to write my Choose Your Own Adventure erotica series, because I know someday this series will be worth a million dollars, will be turned into a board game, will buy us a house away from it all, where we can control the flow of friends and emotions, where the days will slow down because all there is to do is stare at the sea, watch as the sun turns pink and dips into the ocean, wait for the shade to pass over, spot a school of dolphins, open a bottle of wine, let our hair grow, soak ourselves in a passing storm, catch a fish, grow our own vegetables, make love again.

Seven weeks ago when the stomachaches started we had gone out to dinner—a rare date night. She ate grilled duck breast with a sixty-degree duck egg, Anson Mills grits, and oyster mushroom gravy. I ate roasted bone marrow with grilled bread and Italian parsley, a little vinaigrette. We each had a cocktail—she, a bourbon and ginger ale, me, a vodka martini, a little dirty. We toasted to the future. I told her about my idea for the Choose Your Own Adventure Erotica series and she said, "That's fucking brilliant. It's perfect for our generation because we were all obsessed with those books when we were growing up. I can see it at, like, Urban Outfitters, in the front on that table when you walk in."

I said, "Yeah, but what if the books were, like, really good? Like I did some Jonathan Franzen type shit and talked about the economic policies and domestic gross product of each Canary Island that the story takes place on?"

She said, "Don't do that. Franzen and his writing are completely unsexy."

That night, I made us popcorn and we watched Barbet Schroeder's 1969 heroin-sex-psych-rad film *More*. We swore that when the Choose Your Own Adventure Series paid off, we'd take a trip to Spain, travel to Ibiza, maybe never come back, living on a rock up near the sky, staring down at the Mediterranean, smoking dope. She said, "If you sell that book, maybe then we can try to have a kid." I replied, "Uh huh, yeah, maybe. I still want to travel before we have a kid. Can't travel with a kid."

She slunk further down in her sheets, watching the movie with only half her mind, pretending not to care about her biological clock that rings like a church bell every morning.

"You're only twenty-eight," I said. "You have plenty of time." But I know her time already came, and I chose not to allow her time to come.

In the morning, she woke up and said, "My stomach hurts."

That's all it was. Just a small, insignificant stomachache, growing exponentially into what it is today.

Part II

Here's something I know Phoenix doesn't know I know because I know everything and she doesn't know I do. When Phoenix was sixteen years old, she was an uncharacteristically gorgeous teenager with a maturity in her figure and mind that brought much unwanted attention, mostly from her high school peers, but also from men, young and old. Needless to say, the hormone riddled boys of her high school couldn't keep their eyes off of her. With such adoration, (love notes in her locker, love poems slipped into her backpack), she rose to popularity with absolutely no effort. Focused more on experimenting with marijuana than with the politics of high school, Phoenix had no interest in her teenage social status. She didn't know why she was so popular, nor did she care if she was or wasn't. In the mornings before school, she would wake up with only minutes to prepare, throw on a pair of torn up jeans and a vintage t-shirt, roll her hair up into a bun, and slide out the door with an apple in her hand, not a hint of makeup on her near flawless skin. As a result, her style was inadvertently perfect, attractive—she exuded confidence, naturalness. The boys wondered what she'd look like dressed up at a Friday night house party, and the girls worried about the effect such an event might have on their own visibility—if she could look this good without doing anything, imagine if she tried. If it had been up to Phoenix, she would have traded all the unwanted, irrelevant attention for pure peaceful anonymity. She's always been the type to listen to records in a secret room filled with sweet incense, lick a popsicle alone underneath a tree, daydream of The Youngbloods, live on the edge of a coast, toes dipped in the water, naked, independent. She's comfortable amongst herself, in her own skin, self-controlled within the unknown, like the samurai.

Regardless of her ambivalence to the teenage strata surrounding her, she became the focal point of her high school, a focalization perhaps fueled by her nonchalance, which may have been misconstrued as arrogance. When it requires no effort to achieve something others strive tirelessly to gain, resentment develops. And so, jealousy raged through the hearts of her female peers who aimed to equal her position on the social scale. Soon, Phoenix was threatened with physical violence. She became the victim of lurid gossip involving five-man gang-bangs and various roles in pornographic films. It was said she loved giving blow-jobs and frequently partook in lesbian acts. They pushed her in the hallway, spit at her, chased her down in the parking lot with their cars.

The bullying reached a climax, when, one afternoon, a "friend" of hers tore the shirt off her back, exposing her breasts to the hundreds of classmates surrounding her in the hallway. She woke up the next morning, shuffled down the stairs in her sweat pants and told her parents, "I'm done with high school," crawled back up the stairs of her rather affluent home, and laid in bed for three days, crying, smoking pot with the doors locked, appearing only periodically to eat chocolate chip cookies.

On that third day, she had a stomachache. She smoked more pot to get rid of the pain, but the pain grew. She was alone. The world wasn't where she wanted it to be—It was out of her control, moving across a cosmic map to places her finger couldn't point at. The more she thought of the chaos of the entire planet, the innumerable amount of people pushing the globe around and around, the insane economic policies of the Canary Islands, the bombs going off in Parisian subways, the more nauseating it became. Pain only brings up questions that have no answer. And questions without answers only bring more questions without answers. The mind, in such a state, can become like quicksand hovering above a black hole—it will fall, collapse, suffocate, and eventually lose contact with the universe.

After weeks of self medicating with cannabis, not attending school, wandering aimlessly from bed to bath and back again, Phoenix's stomachaches had reached a breaking point. Her mother, worried to death her daughter had come down with an especially aggressive case of Eastern Madagascar Stomach Rhythm Parasites, took her, finally, to a doctor. The doctor took blood, x-rays, pressed against her belly, and sent her home to shit into a plastic cup to bring back for thorough fecal examination the next day. Less than a week later the doctor proclaimed, "There's nothing physically wrong with Phoenix. I suggest seeing a therapist."

Phoenix's first therapy session went much longer than the one hour allotted. In fact, the therapist cancelled her next two clients, rescheduling them for a later date. For three hours Phoenix wept, lamenting her life, her looks, her brains, her disillusionment with the world, how it seemed insane to be spinning in the middle of space, on the surface of a planet with so much suffering. She examined her relationship with her mother, citing several instances where her matron neglected her emotions, telling her to "toughen up," instead of doling out the necessary nurturing she needed as a child. She spoke of the bullying, of boys treating her like a sex object, how she could feel the eyes of her father's friends crawling up her legs into places that as of yet remained untouched. To her, this wretched nature of mankind was enough to stick her head in an oven— just like Sylvia Plath. To her, this blatant and offensive sexism was enough to fill her coat pockets with heavy stones and walk into the Pacific Ocean—just like Virginia Woolf.

Eventually, after several months of treatment, the stomachaches lessened, and finally disappeared. It was decided Phoenix suffered from an anxious stomach. She was told to eat healthy and maintain a stress-free life.

But a stress-free life didn't seem possible for her. After changing majors frequently throughout college, Phoenix decided on pursuing a life as a creative writer. Now, as many know, pursuing a life as a writer is about as stressful a pursuit as one can chase—especially when you fall in love with another writer. When Phoenix and I started dating, the attraction was undeniable. The first kiss was like all poems written about a first kiss, only better, because sparks actually did ignite between our lips—we both saw them, chased them, held them in our palms, and followed them all the way back to my apartment where we made love in the middle of the night, our feet pushing against each other, our tongues braided. The moon came through the window that night and carved out a cave within her eyes that I knew I could push myself into to find inspiration. And so, as a result, we both had a muse, and words began to spill out of us.

Love in Los Angeles is a theory that cannot be dissected without discussing finances. It's expensive to live in Los Angeles. It's expensive to eat in Los Angeles. It's expensive to drink, walk, drive, breathe the air, go to the beach, park, have friends, watch television, turn on the heater, buy firewood—it's even expensive to work in Los Angeles. So with all relationships that bud outward from that city, there's always a strange, sinking weight of coins to carry along with it. When you begin to realize as you exit your apartment every day to sit in twenty miles of traffic in order to toil as a bartender, that you will never own the four bedroom Spanish villa across the street from your shitty one bedroom apartment on Los Feliz Blvd, you begin to realize your life and effort might be better spent somewhere else, where a four bedroom Spanish villa might be affordable. Sure, there are things like winter, republicans, honkies, rednecks, and blue bloods wherever that place might be, but maybe it's possible to avoid them, to live out in the middle of nowhere and be content with the lack of decent tattoo shops and international cuisine. How hard can it be to make your own falafel, order lavash off Amazon?

It's been seven years since that night we made love. We chose to leave Los Angeles eleven months ago, to live in this place in the East, to discover winter, learn to despise it, create our own falafel, order lavash off the internet. I wanted to stay in the Golden State, maybe head north to the Santa Cruz Mountains, stare at the San Lorenzo River. She wanted to be adventurous, move away from bad memories, out of our nest, build a new one, create better memories. Neither one of us has spoken a word about the magnets of the west that pull at our souls, but these magnets exist and yank at our blood, sucking at the iron like a gargantuan prehistoric metallic mosquito. I don't want to upset her, and she doesn't want to upset me. It wasn't until that text message she accidentally received the other day, the one in which I expressed my urge to get back west, that Phoenix had any idea of my unhappiness here. Knowledge of my unhappiness, coupled with her own unhappiness—a result of her constant hours at work and her inability to write as much as she would like—as well as her innate feminine instinct that another woman might be trying to snatch up her husband—and lets not forget the abortion, the guilt of which endlessly bores through her spine like a starving termite—my non-urgency and apathy towards children, which can be construed as "not wanting a child"—the realization that just because you move someplace cheaper doesn't mean it's not a struggle because, holy shit, you get paid less—along with the gray of her cubicle, the gray of her life, the gray of money, the gray of water, the gray surrounding everything since that night we made love, the gray of living a life further away from the life intended—this is when stomachaches happen, three p.m., still bent over in the office, another man's hand running up and down her spine. "I know what it is," she repeats.

Beautiful Day Blues

She stands there above me with the sun behind her, enveloping me in shadow. She's waiting for a response, but there wasn't a question to respond to, only a statement, an honest answer to my question, and there isn't much else to say about it—she thinks of me when she masturbates. We've launched our friendship into an uncharted sea without a map home. There's nowhere for us to return to. Our relationship has undergone a chemical change. The elements that make up this relationship—childhood, memories, secret conversations—are now pumped full of sex, creating perversion out of innocence, carnal alchemy. She's taken this step and I allowed her to take it. I made her feel comfortable enough to say what she said, believing there would be little or no repercussion. I let her kiss my lips, I let her lick my neck, I let her see me naked, I let her feet rest on my thighs. I agreed to work with her, to be by her side, to work towards something together, sweating inches away, our damp skins pressing together as we pass one another. I've told her about my unhappiness and she interpreted my unhappiness to be a direct result of Phoenix's state of mind. She's thinking to herself "Why would he stay with a woman who doesn't want to have sex? Why would he try so hard to be somewhere he doesn't want to be, to struggle financially, and still have nothing to come home to?"

I have a decision to make that will change my life forever. I can feel the love for my wife surging through me, and I can feel the danger of Aunika like a rush of adrenaline knocking my heart around, bullying that love into places it doesn't want to go. My heart skips a beat, comes back with a thundering thump, then repeats itself.

The blood exits my face, and my eyes trail down away from hers, landing somewhere on the grass. I nervously suck on my wine even though there's nothing left. She reaches down, pulls the bottle up, and pours more into my empty cup.

"Have you ever thought of me?" Aunika asks.

I shouldn't say anything. I should never say anything. I should always keep my mouth shut, stuff it into the neck of a bottle, stare off into a vast blankness, disconnect. But I'm already too deep. It doesn't matter if I continue this conversation because the damage has already been done. We're no longer best friends—we are two humans with opposing genitalia waiting to do battle. If I reply "no" to her question, maybe she'll forget this conversation ever happened and we can just ignore whatever is happening between us for the rest of our lives—we'll simply remain "two humans with opposing genitalia," genitalia that will never meet, genitalia that will sign a peace treaty, go their separate ways, gaze over the city walls at each other from time to time.

"Yeah, I've thought about you," I say. There's no reason for me to say this sentence aside from trying my best to confuse things, to make my life and everyone else's life around me more difficult. It is research. We must live in order to write. This is living. This is stirring the pot in front of me, creating a story that hadn't existed before, moving forward or backward, or both simultaneously.

"What kinds of things have you thought about?" she asks me.

I shake my head. "No way."

"I'll tell you what I've thought about you."

"I don't think I want to know."

"Yes, you do."

I do, if only for the excitement of being thought of by another woman. It feels good even though it shouldn't. "Maybe I do. But I still can't know. If I know, then I can visualize it. If I can visualize it, then it might as well just happen. And that's a road I can't travel down—we can't travel down."

"There are many roads to travel down, and most of the time they all lead to the exact same place you're supposed to end up."

"I'm not quite sure if that's true."

"Trust me. It is. I've been everywhere and done everything. I'm here, East, in your backyard, telling you I think about your head between my legs, in the sunshine, somewhere tropical with a pina-colada in my hand."

"Shit."

"I've thought about pulling on your hair, waiting til I'm just about to come, then pulling you up, unzipping your pants, and pushing you into me."

"Fuck."

"And sometimes your wife is there, watching—I don't know why, I'm not attracted to her. Maybe it's just my competitive side."

"Jesus."

She reaches her hand out to me. "Take my hand."

"Take your hand where?"

"Just take it."

I let my hand slide between hers and she leans back, pulling me up off the blanket.

Upright, looking into her eyes, she slides her fingers between the waistband of my jeans, her fingernails tickling my hipbones.

I look her in the eyes. In them, oceans and islands. In them, diamonds and white bikinis. In them, drunkenness and irresponsibility. In them, donuts. In them, some other road leading perhaps to where I'm supposed to be.

I lean in, pushing my forehead to hers. I can smell her breath—whiskey, sugar. She braids the fingers of each hand behind my head, using her arms to shade us, just her and I in this small pocket of cool darkness. She uses her nose to brush against mine. This is the closest our faces have ever been. I can see one small wrinkle curling under her right eye. There's a light brown freckle on her left eyelid, visible only when she blinks.

"There's nothing wrong with us doing this," she says. "Life is meant to be lived."

"I live too much I think."

"Living is the key to wisdom. Wisdom is the key to everything."

My mind races, searching for a way to rationalize the situation. Part of me knows I've already stepped across a boundary my wife would certainly be both uncomfortable with and disturbed by. If I told her what Aunika and I discussed today, told her I let her put her hands on me, pull me in, create this little cove between our heads, it would be just as bad as if I told her we kissed. It would be. I think. I don't know anymore. I close my eyes, let the breeze settle on my cheeks. Her lips part. I can sense her getting closer. Heat. Sweat.

"Shit," I say. "I can't. I want to, but I just fucking can't." I put my hands behind my head finding her wrists, and slide them down to my waist.

She smiles tenderly, almost appreciating my self-control. She nods her head. "I understand." She gently removes herself from me, runs her fingers across my cheek, letting her thumb play with my lips. She inhales, and opens her mouth. Inside this breath, certain consonants and vowels wait to be deployed, words that could possibly change my mind, push me over the edge and into her legs. She could press her tongue to the roof of her mouth and against her teeth, manipulate the air between her vibrating vocal cords and say, "Phoenix made out with another woman the other night. And she does coke." I watch her mouth. She presses her lips together, inhales again, those words and sentences still caught in her throat, nods her head, closes her eyes, a wrestling match between upper and lower eyelid, right and wrong, causing her face to nearly twitch. She

197

opens her mouth one more time and says, "I'll always be here. Whenever you want me."

She picks up the wine, slips the bottle into her mouth and takes a few swigs. "I'm gonna get drunk," she says.

She makes her way to the side gate of the backyard, looking over her shoulder just before she leaves. "Please don't tell Phoenix about this. I'd hate for her to hate me."

"I won't."

"I'll call you about the bar shit. Don't freak out. Everything'll be cool."

The gate closes, I see her hand raise, waving back and forth, until it disappears.

I move directly for the bottle of bourbon and take a shot, wiping the burning spit from my lips. I look up to the sun. It's hot out here, hotter than it was several minutes ago. I need to cool off. Inside, I pull an ice cube from the freezer and drag it across the back of my neck. I check my phone, finding a text from Phoenix—*I love you. I hope you are having a beautiful day.* I drop the needle on The Gun Club. I sit down in the middle of the living room on the hardwood, roll over onto my back, and begin to cry. We all want what everyone else has. We glorify hopeless, impossible love. We call it fate, destiny, and we romanticize the moment true love is found, and everything else in the world becomes meaningless. True love is a single road leading to the same place every time.

I love you, I type into my phone. I press send.

I look up into the sky through the skylight, drawing shapes in my mind with the clouds speeding overhead. We are spinning in outer space. We are spinning on earth. We are spun. *Oh, Mother of Earth/ the wind is hot/ I tried my best, but I could not/ and my eyes fade from me/ in this open country.*

Fifteen Minute Blues

Once or twice a week, Phoenix and I see each other for only a few seconds in passing, and sometimes not at all. Today will be one of those days I don't see her. I don't have to be at work until seven, but decide to leave around three to make sure I don't see her. I can't see her today. I can't look her in the eye after what happened with Aunika. I need time to compartmentalize all of my emotions. I figure if she asks where I am when she gets home, I'll tell her Bulch needed help reorganizing the liquor cabinets and cleaning out the ice machine and I had to leave a couple hours early. I'll tell her Bulch wanted to talk to me about a few new cocktail ideas—he wants to do Cachaca with strawberry syrup, elderberry reduction, and Chilean vanilla limes—and an egg white. We'll call it the Titicaca Paw, or something like that.

What I don't know is Phoenix walked out the door of her office at 2:45 with her press release in the can. It wasn't her best writing, but it was adequate. Her boss signed off, she slipped out the door, her stomach still tight with pain. Taylor walked her to her car, his hand still resting on her spine, rubbing up and down. He opened the door for her, put his hand on her shoulder, and said, "I really hope you feel better. This place sucks without you."

She wanted to smile, but couldn't. Taylor had been a good friend today. It pays to have a young man infatuated with you, makes the loneliness and the fear fade a bit, allows your mind to absorb happiness, release serotonin. This young man is like a hit of a moderate-strain of weed—just enough to keep your mind off reality, but not enough to make you sex-crazed.

At 2:50 p.m., Phoenix breathes "Thank you" through her clenched teeth and slides into the driver's seat. She starts the car, and pulls out of the garage, watching Taylor's raised hand fade left to right in her rearview mirror.

She fiddles with a cd case, finding her new favorite band, The Growlers, the sounds of which are Southern California personified—the purple haze of beachy June mornings, hot sand and cool surf, violent peace, bare feet, tan butts, waves crashing on your head, the salt water surging through and between your sinuses, a grilled ahi taco with lime crema and a can of Tecate with salt and lemon after a cool summer night on acid—in short, these boys remind her of home. She lets her jaw unclench, rests her head on the headrest, lets the lyrics flow over her body like a big California wave. *Think back about the things you used to care about/ And now they're so insignificant/ Think how lame your fears seem now/ And how you might not get to live again.* Her stomach releases the stranglehold on itself, unraveling like old rope. This car, this music, the escape from the cubicle seems to be the antidote. She knows what it is. She can't do anything about it. Stress and anxiety are as much a part of her life as pissing in the morning, blinking, breathing. She pulls up to the stoplight, rolls down her windows and says to herself, "Someday, it's gonna end."

***

At 2:58, I open the front door, jump down the porch, and hop on my beat-to-shit beach cruiser. I'm not sure where I'll go for the next four hours, but have a hunch it'll be Stanbury, the bar down the road, with the cute bartender who wears rad old Levi's. I'll watch her sing Doors lyrics out loud to herself, and I'll pretend to be a famous painter, letting my fingers dangle in the air as if they're chasing butterflies, let my eyes interpret my surroundings, never saying a word, only nodding "yes" with my brilliant head and saying "thank you" when another beer is delivered by her tender fingers. That bartender will tell people about me someday, that I used to sit right in front of her and drink beer, and she thought I was a painter, but wasn't sure, and she never knew who I was until I died and the NY Times wrote an obituary about me—"Choose Your Own Adventure Erotica Author Dies in Tragic Surfing Accident High on Drugs on Abandoned Mexican Beach."

***

At 2:58, Phoenix begins a right turn, twisting her wrists around the steering wheel, pulling herself onto our street. If there were a hidden camera framed on her face, her expression would be one of pure delight, eyes wide, a smile—she's even begun singing along to the songs—she needs her husband, needs to be in his arms, needs to be home, or someplace that resembles it, and her husband is as close to home as she can get. She needs to tell him she knows what the stomachaches are from, that they're caused by stress and anxiety, that she's had them for years, and that, yes, she does believe she's being punished for the abortion, but she's sure she can make amends with God for what she did. She plans on galloping through the door, opening the bottle of Chardonnay in the fridge and telling me about volunteering at the soup kitchen downtown—giving back life instead of taking it away. She knows this subject is difficult for me, but she needs to say it out loud, to release whatever it is pressing against her chest. Then maybe later, she wants to make love, as long as her stomachache is gone. Lovemaking is relaxing. She needs to do it every day as part of her new way of life—and it doesn't need to be a whole production. She could just walk in the door and I could be waiting with a hard-on and she could pull up her skirt and we could be finished in three minutes, the time it takes to pull the cork out, have that first sip of wine.

As a matter of fact, "Fuck it," she thinks. She'll walk in the door, make love to me first, then go for the bottle of Chardonnay, then tell me everything on her mind. She'll tell me about California, how she carries guilt for wanting to move away from it, putting us in this position of unhappiness. She'll tell me about a way back there, job opportunities near San Jose, living in a tent on unmapped land if need be. She'll tell me my writing is worth a damn, that my Choose Your Own Adventure Erotica will pay our bills and mortgage, that the California Coastline will be our home forever, and big California Cabernets will drip from our chins, along with our smiles. Happiness—it's that simple.

As she approaches our home, looking at our covered porch, she sees a bicycle down the road, a blue-flake beach cruiser moving the opposite direction. She squints her eyes. "Is that Cassidy?" she says to herself. She checks the clock on the dashboard—2:59. "No way. Too early. I'm nuts." She pulls into the driveway, pushes her hand into her gut, feeling around her vital organs, searching for any residual pain. She checks both side mirrors and the rearview, sees her eyes, glazed but young, vibrant but tired, sexy but deathly—gazes over each shoulder, then gingerly pulls her underwear off, down her legs, around her heels, and tosses them into the backseat. She leans into the mirror in front of her, checking her lips, tapping the small swollen bags under her eyes. Age. Time. How old is she? Who cares? This is not the time to care. This is the time to love, live.

The car door whips open, the keys lock the door, the heels pound against the brick sidewalk, up the wooden stairs to the porch. The keys jam into the door, the knob twists, a leg pierces the threshold. A woman enters her home. "Babe?!" she calls out. She moves to the kitchen table, takes off her shoes, lifts up her hem, and bends over. "Babe!" she yells again.

Silence. She remains bent over on the kitchen table for a minute, maybe more, thinking perhaps Cassidy is outside or in the bathroom, or maybe he's writing with his headphones on, lost in prose. One minute. Eleven seconds. Twenty-eight more seconds. What are seconds made of? What's smaller than a second? Nanoseconds? Milliseconds? Nothingness. She pulls herself up off the table, drops her hem, and begins searching the house for her absent husband. He could be dead. She knows he thinks he's going to die young. But he's not so young anymore. He still listens to Nirvana. But that doesn't make him young—it makes him retarded.

"Babe?" she says as she opens each door. Out back, she sees a blanket, a bottle of bourbon, two glasses, an empty guacamole bowl, and a bag of tortilla chips. She grabs the chips, moves back into the kitchen. Her stomach sounds a loud, internal noise, like a child crying underneath a blanket. "Who was here?" she says out loud, but already knows the answer to the question. The only person who drinks bourbon this early in the day besides her husband is Aunika. Fucking Aunika. She opens the refrigerator door, prepared to do battle with that bottle of Chardonnay. She pulls out the celery, radishes, a few bottles of Kefir, Kombucha, nitrite and nitrate free smoked turkey, a six pack of Sierra Nevada—that Chardonnay isn't in there. She slides back outside, past the empty bottles in the yard, to the trashcans. She pops open the recycling bin and finds the empty bottle—God damn it would have been good—2008 Napa Valley. "Fucker," she says. Back inside, she rips her dress off, the zipper sticking for just a moment, then moves into the bathroom with her cellphone in hand, and starts the water for a bath. Naked, seated on the edge of the tub, her feet dangling in the rising water, she texts her husband, *Where are you?*

***

Clothed, on my bicycle, I feel the vibration of the phone in my back pocket. I carefully one-hand the handlebars, rub on my mustache, reach into my pocket and pull out my phone. I nearly run a stop sign, but am saved by the blast of a car horn. I see the driver's face through the windshield—sixty years old, a tie, receding hairline. He looks at me like I'm an alien with a death wish, eyes all twitchy. His blood pressure is sky high, 175 over 100. I could have died. He could have killed me. How many times have I been saved? Who's watching out for me? Are you? Is He? I stop, check the message. *Where are you?*

I assume she's at work. It's 3 p.m., and she's got that candy tampon deadline. But now I'm not so sure. I check my phone for missed calls, wondering if Phoenix is in the midst of some emergency, but find no one has called. She must be at home. She must have come home early. Shit. *I'm heading to work,* I text back.

I travel two more blocks.

***

She slides herself into the shallow bathwater. *Why are you going to work so early?*

***

Stop sign. I balance my bike as best I can, using my left thumb to type. *Bulch needs help reo]rganizing th liquir cabnet.* A right turn, an old man with his German Shepherd on the porch sucking on a cigarette. A police car talking to a young black man with a backpack.

***

The water level rises, covering her belly. She slides further down. *Don't text and ride.* Her body glides down the porcelain, closer to the faucet, lifts up her hips to meet the running water, climaxes forty-two seconds later with thick, rippling contractions. She lights candles in a silhouette around her body, and closes her eyes, exhaling everything inside of her.

***

I arrive at Stanbury, on the corner of Shady Lane and Shakedown, in the old railroad district that smells like antique typewriters. From the street the joint looks abandoned, and inside, it feels the same as it looks. As I enter, I find I'm the only soul there at 3:11 on a Tuesday. The bartender recognizes me, smiles warmly, turns The Doors down a bit.

"You can keep the volume up," I say.

"Cool," she says. She's reading Schopenhauer, a bottle of Basque cider next to her, a packet of Bubble Yum next to the bottle. Her jeans are ripped to shreds at the knees. Her boots are scuffed. Her tank top reads "Free Albertina Sisulu And All Of South Africa's Political Prisoners." She has a black heart tattooed on the inside of her bicep—I've never noticed it before. It seems strange. I sat right here in front of her countless times. She pushes her bangs out of her eyes. Her image says everything she wants to say to the world without saying it.

She sets her book down, on its face, open, page 111—she'll be getting back to it shortly—I never talk to her—I only watch, witness the words pass between her fingers, between her ears.

"Beer?" she asks.

"That'd be cool."

"IPA?"

"That's my flavor."

She shuffles her feet down the bar to the tap and pours, slides the glass down to me, and reclaims her position leaning on the counter next to the till. She waits for me to take a sip, keeping eye contact, then smiles and gets back to her book.

I never talk to her. I never talk to any bartender because I'm a bartender and I know how much I hate to talk to people, especially strangers, and especially strangers who are regulars who never talk. I'll never be that guy on the other side of the stick, blathering on about what life is or isn't, looking for a soul to dump everything on, then shove it all into that poor soul like a sharp Italian stiletto, as I get further and further wrecked, forgetting I ever said anything in the first place.

"I'm having a rough day," I say. I'm despicable. I should be thrown out of the union.

"Oh yeah?" she says. She keeps her face buried in Schopenhauer, licking her finger and turning the page.

I know it's best to say nothing more, to perhaps excuse myself and go to the restroom, but I need to talk. I can't speak to Bulch or Cherise about what happened between Aunika and I—they're too close to the situation. Cherise will definitely talk to Aunika about it, and Bulch will just say something like "Well sonny boy, looks like the roses finally hit winter." I'll have no idea what he means, but I'll love the way it rolls off his tongue, walk away just as confused as before with nothing gained.

"I'm married. And I think my best friend is in love with me."

The bartender dog-ears her page this time, and slides down the bar towards me with a smile on her face, like I'm speaking her language, like she's just heard the most epic sentence in the entire world.

"I was married once," she says.

"How old are you?"

"Twenty-eight."

"You look eighteen."

"Well, I'm not." She nods her head and takes a sip of her cider. "I was married to a guy and his best friend told me he was in love with me."

"What happened after that?"

"Shit. Things got crazy. After about three years of him expressing his love for me, we were all on vacation in the Bahamas and we got really wasted. My husband passed out in the hotel room, I hopped in the

Jacuzzi, his best friend followed me out, we hooked up, he cried, I cried. Then I got divorced."

I set my beer down. "Did you get divorced because you hooked up? And wait, what kind of hooking up? Just a kiss or what?"

"No, not just a kiss."

"I see."

"I don't want to go into details, but I think with a kiss, I might have been able to forgive myself—but maybe not. I'd never cheated before."

"I've only cheated once in my life, back in college, but I did it so I could get out of the relationship. You know, like to force myself to break up by feeling guilty all the time around her."

"Yeah well, the weird thing is, his best friend was the exact opposite of what I'm attracted to. I think it was just the danger or the novelty of it. But it ruined me in the end. I couldn't look my husband in the eye. I had to leave. And I never told him why. I was too fucking young to get married anyways. Small town Ohio type shit."

"I don't know. I love my wife. I love my best friend. Up until a few days ago I had no idea my best friend was interested in me, and now that she is, my brain's kind of switched gears with her. I look at her and I think all this time we could've been having sex *and* having a rad time."

"Yeah, that's what you think, but in reality once the sex kicks in, the rad times end."

"You mean like marriage?"

"How so?"

"Once the ceremony is over, so is the sex."

"That's just what boring people say. It's not true, unless you suck at life."

"I know. You're right. I'm pretty sure I don't suck at life. I for sure don't suck at life."

"My advice is to stay away from your best friend for awhile and let that mellow out. She'll feel embarrassed about what she said, and then it'll all pass and you can go back to hugging, but the hugs might mean more, which isn't such a bad thing."

"Yeah, a good, emotionally heavy hug feels good sometimes. Sparks ignite near the heart—the emotions can be palpable—gives you something warm—almost tangible."

"Ahh…so poetic."

"I write, I guess."

"Uh huh. I have friends who do that."

She rips a bottle of Old Crow out from the well and holds it up to me asking with her eyes if I'd care to imbibe. I'm already a bit tipsy from the heat and the wine and the bourbon and Aunika's side boob, and Aunika's breath, and Aunika in general. "Sure," I tell her.

She pours us each a shot, raises her glass and says, "To fucked up days and best friend's with crushes."

I take that drink with her. I take everything down with that swallow— all of today's events melt somewhere inside of me, turn into liquid, get locked in my gut, volatile like the earth's core. I miss my wife. I miss my life. I miss where I was eleven months ago, struggling in California with the memory of an abortion haunting me. Today, those things we ran away from seem more manageable than everything else does. We can work through these nightmares, but we can't run away from them. We are west. We are who we are and we need to accept our decisions.

I decide to take a mental inventory of things I've done that I feel particularly guilty about to this day:

1). In high school, a kid named Sean Kilian, skinny and ineffectual, was getting bullied during P.E. class. In the locker room, a few boys, all of whom were my friends, held him up by his ankles and repeatedly punched him in the gut. I didn't partake, but I also didn't stop it. I'll find him on Facebook tonight when I get home. I'll apologize—offer to buy him a drink next time I'm in L.A., if he still lives there.

2). In grammar school, I had forgotten my lunch. Eleven years old, I was trying desperately to be cool, even though I was relatively poor and my shoes weren't as cool as everyone else's. We were having a morning assembly in the auditorium. My mother entered with my lunch in hand, slipped in her high heels on the linoleum floor and completely ate shit. I pretended not to see her fall. A few boys with more self-confidence helped her up. I'll call her tomorrow and tell her I love her.

3). A few years ago, back in Los Angeles, I had a pretty decent bartending gig at the world's diviest bar. One of our bartenders, one who had all the good shifts even though she was terrible at her job, but nonetheless was the ex-wife of the owner's son, was fired for stealing money from the till. It wasn't her. It was the doorman. I didn't say anything and I got her shifts. I won't do anything about this scenario because the woman, after all, was a pill-popping sociopath that slept with just about every man who told her "I can take care of you, financially." But I'll let it roll off my shoulders now, forgive myself.

Sitting in this bar I come to realize for most of my life my indecision has been my biggest fault. Because I decide not to make a decision, to be indecisive, the lives of others have been affected. Some might point out the fact that indecision is inherently a decision—a decision not to decide—but to me, it isn't. Decisions are made when you do something for yourself, changes your own course in life, not others. I swear to myself from this point on I'll be the one making decisions. I won't say "I don't care" when my wife asks me what I want to eat for dinner. I'll say, "I want a burrito. I will settle for nothing less. And I would like one lengua taco as well, with the spicy green salsa and pickled carrots and plenty of jalapenos."

The bartender has done enough for me today as far as readjusting my soul. I'm a fucking amateur. Keep your mouth shut—every bartender knows that. "Thank you," I say. "For the shot."

"No worries."

She slides back over to her book, and turns The Doors up a bit— Light my Fire. She starts singing softly to herself, sucking on her cider, her neck twisting a bit to the beat.

I've still got a few hours to kill, but don't think I can manage to kill them in this bar alone with this bartender. I sip at my beer, telling myself if someone walks in the door in the next fifteen minutes, I'll stay for another. And then, fifteen minutes after that, I'll again rethink my next move. I pull my boots up to the bottom rung of the barstool and hunker down, waiting.

Minute Fifteen

She turns two pages in her Schopenhauer book. I scratch at my chin for an inordinate amount of time, even though my chin doesn't itch. I guess it makes it seem as if I'm deep, but it probably just makes me look unclean, simian, like I have bird mites.

Minute Fourteen

I get a text message from a number I don't recognize. It reads *Attack of the Crystal Meth Killer Bees was ahead of its time.* The words sound familiar, but the number isn't. I can't place it—where the hell is a 605 area code from? I'm pretty sure *Attack of the Crystal Meth Killer Bees* was a cultish B-movie from the mid 70's, but if it wasn't, it should be.

Minute Thirteen

I watch a dog take a shit outside the bar window. The owner looks around, leaves the dog shit on the sidewalk. The bartender says, "That is so fucking disrespectful."

Minute Twelve

I pass a few seconds tapping my fingers to the music against the bar. Light my Fire is still playing. The bartender starts singing at full volume, using Schopenhauer as a microphone.

Minute Eleven

Aunika grabs hold of my mind. She was so fucking close. I wonder how she masturbates. Does she roll over on her stomach, using the pressure of her hand? Or does she do it porno style, on her back? I'll go with "on her stomach"—it's more realistic, quicker, feels better.

Minute Ten

I get a minor erection, which I casually fold up into the waistband of my jeans. I push my tongue around my mouth. It feels dry and heavy. The bartender flips through two more pages in this minute, shaking her head in a satisfied manner, moving her lips with the words as she silently reads.

Minute Nine

Light my Fire hits its stride with the epic guitar/organ solo. She turns up the volume one more notch and looks over to me for approval and I give her a thumbs-up and a nod. I'm such a dork. Who does the thumbs-up anymore? I should bring back the "hang-loose" sign—it would seem ironic like short, neon yellow swim trunks and pink plastic sunglasses.

Minute Eight

I see Cherise pass by the window, but I can't flag her down because I've got one hand on a beer pressed up to my mouth and the other hand wrapped around a fistful of blistered peanuts. I drop the beer down to the bar and wave, but she's already passed. The bartender sees me wave, then looks out the window at nothing and no one, and looks back at me like I'm fucking crazy. "I saw a friend walk by," I say. She goes back to her book.

Minute Seven

I literally do absolutely nothing during this minute. I don't even have a thought. Nothing happens. It is perfect. Light my Fire ends.

Minute Six

Phoenix scrubs off the dead skin from underneath her ankle bones. Bulch changes a keg of beer. Cherise bumps into one of the regulars from

211

Bearclaw's on the sidewalk. She says "I'm late, I have to get going," even though she's early and just wants to have a couple drinks before our shift. A kid in Minnesota is born that will discover a *real* underwater pyramid in twenty-nine years. Archeologists will speculate this pyramid is proof of the lost city of Atlantis. Others will testify aliens from the middle of earth built it and launch spacecraft from it.

Minute Five

A man walks up to the door, stops for a moment, checks his watch, then continues down the road without setting foot inside. I'm a bit upset about his departure because my beer is getting dangerously low and I'd like to order another—but I made a decision to leave if in fifteen minutes no one shows up. I must stick to my decisions. I must make them and stand by them.

Minute Four

How the fuck did we land on the moon? It's fucking nuts. How do people make, like, automatic bowling alleys? Like, where do the parts come from? Is there a machine that makes the things that go in machines? Do you have to invent a machine to create an invention? I'm so happy I'm not an engineer. What an endless amount of shit you'd have to deal with. Questions with answers that reform as a question—an endless circle.

Minute Three

I can feel it in my body—no one is going to walk in the door. I take a quarter out of my pocket and spin it around, stopping it with my finger, upright, on its side.

Minute Two

I reach for my wallet, pulling out a ten-dollar bill. I wish I had a calico cat that went everywhere with me. I'd name it something cute like, Wilbur or Roscoe. Shit. Those are just street names back in my hometown.

Minute One

I say, "I think I'll settle up with you." She puts her book down and says, "Five dollars." I push the ten out in front of me. She takes it and returns with five singles. I leave three on the bar, and shove the other two in my pocket.

Minute Zero

I pull myself up out of my barstool. She raises a hand and says "Take it easy." Aunika opens a door somewhere. Phoenix dunks her head underwater, bubbles rise to the top, explode.

Library Blues

Cliff and Charlie wake up early, noon, Pacific Standard Time. About the time I'm leaving the bar to head to Bearclaw's, Cliff and Charlie are taking a shower. Cliff showers in the bathroom inside the loft and Charlie showers on the rooftop of his building, where he had a pipe shimmied up the exterior wall, pumping hot water from the building next door. It's illegal and the job is entirely against building code, but he had a junkie plumber friend rig it up in exchange for a bunny painting and a couple balloons. The painting got pawned a week later—seven more balloons were bought.

This rooftop shower is surrounded by four walls made of vintage umbrella fabric that Charlie stitched together himself. He especially likes the fourth wall—Hula girls from the 1950's—green grass skirts, red lipstick, pineapples in their hair, exaggerated hips, thick, curvaceous bodies—like something you'd see on the forearm of a sailor in 1945. Charlie spits water through his teeth at their faces periodically, aiming for their mouths, watching the water peel down their bronze breasts, drip back down, roll under his toes.

Charlie hates it when Cliff showers at the same time as him because this inevitably means when they're both done, they'll have to share the mirror in the bathroom while they shave, pop black-heads on their noses, and push pomade through their hair. They use their shoulders to battle for prime position in the glass, and most of the time, bruises appear as a result of the struggle. If there's anything Charlie doesn't want any longer, it's bruises. He's been clean of heroin for thirty-six hours and has been cutting the withdrawals with a steady diet of Ativan and beer, whiskey when the rattling in his bones gets to be too much. It's better to be an alcoholic than a heroin addict—he knows that for sure. The withdrawal from alcohol can be kicked in a week—heroin takes a lifetime, and even when that lifetime ends, it still hurts.

But the brothers' showering and primping habits are not what is of utmost importance today. Today is the day The Mustard Brothers apply for a trademark on both the name The Mustard Brothers and The Whiskey Jelly Donut. If all goes accordingly, if these forms they are to obtain from the US Trademark department are filled out correctly, no one in the United States will ever again be able to use the name The Mustard Brothers for a business, nor will they be able to sell something called "The Whiskey Jelly Donut." Cliff is proud of his Internet research that yielded this information—he calls this type of labor "stooge work." He believes the Whiskey Jelly Donut is something that could possibly capture the entire nations' heart—he sees himself, his brother, and their surrogate brother, Cassidy, on Good Morning America, spinning the heartwarming story of three friends, bonded together, trying to bring one of them back home with a simple, delicious, inebriating pastry.

Although the trademark process can be accomplished via an online application form, Cliff has made the decision to make a day of it, to act like a business, move with purpose down the sidewalk, enter the library, take advantage of the public computers, and afterwards, suck down the days work with a few cold ones at the local paisa bar, just like a real stooge.

Six minutes later, shoulders collide in front of the mirrored glass resulting in two bruises, pomade re-greases the hair, lotion soaks into the colors of tattoos, zippers of jeans buzz upwards. Charlie puts on his paint speckled boots. Cliff slides his "NOT IN MY PUSSY" button through his threadbare t-shirt, the one where if you yank the fabric down about an inch, his nipple will poke through a hole in the 50/50 cotton-polyester blend. He calls this type of shirt "a sexy shirt." He tops off his look with a battered and oiled brown suede vest, complete with a flask of whiskey in the front pocket.

They kick back out onto the sidewalk and into the visible heat of Los Angeles, waves of weather rippling with transparent vapor, a blazing snake tongue of humidity.

"I feel like the sidewalk is my home," Cliff says. "I feel like I could just walk up and down it all day, maybe drop my fine little ass on the curb and smoke a cigarette, think about a camel with a shit-eating grin sucking on a popsicle. Did you know Saudi Arabia imports camels from Australia? Australia sounds neat."

"I lived on a sidewalk for a summer in Vancouver. I was all fucked up on…"

"I know the story already."

"I'm not allowed back in Cana…"

"Charlie, Jesus Christ, I already know the fucking story! You need another sidewalk story, one with a beard and a hot dog or something people give a shit about."

In case you haven't heard the story, Charlie traveled north to Vancouver because he heard the art scene, chicks, and heroin were pretty rad, full of "ballsack righteousness"—a phrase popular to describe the vibe up there. But the ballsack righteousness is a heavy trip. As a result, he ran out of money, couldn't afford to paint, and never got laid. He lived on the sidewalk outside a cannabis café for three weeks, (several days short of a full summer as he insists), before being picked up for vagrancy and public intoxication. A blood test revealed heroin, cocaine, tetrahydrocannabinol, and alcohol coursing through his veins. He was deported, and told not to return for seven years. This was four years ago. Charlie feels proud about being banned from Canada. He's part of an elite group of thuggish artists who pray to the great stone. "Fuck

Canada," they say—"They don't let the cool people in."

"In three more years I'm going back and selling my paintings. I'm gonna have a party on that fuckin sidewalk. I'll swallow the city whole."

"And you'll get arrested again while your mouth is wrapped around the great throbbing white north cock as it spits into your esophagus."

"Whatever. I'll probably sell some paintings."

Cliff pulls a cigarette from the back pocket of his jeans, lights it, thinks for a moment, and says. "You know what? You might be right, old Charlie boy—your art might do well up there. I'll look into it."

Cliff and Charlie arrive at the library, all painted gray cinder block walls, an underfunded prison of literature, sliding through the glass door and between the metal detectors, stinking of sweat and volatile organic compounds. Charlie winks at the librarian—a middle-aged woman with a coffee stain on her beige blouse. She doesn't wear glasses and her hair is cut just below the ears. Cliff slides his hands along the spines of books as they pass through the Psychedelic Fiction section, before making a right turn and passing through the row labeled "California Authors with Perfect Mustaches and Drinking Problems."

"Steinbeck!" Charlie yells.

"Shhhhhh…." Cliff says. "We're in the goddamn library. We're Mustard Brothers. We've got to uphold a certain level of dignity in our community, for Christ sakes. The last thing we need is for people to be gossiping about the Mustard Brothers' blatant disrespect for volume regulations inside a library—it would be a marketing nightmare. They'll ask us about it on Good Morning America, and we'll have to come up with some smart reason for being so loud inside the fucking library. Can't you see what we're dealing with, Chuck? We're a social beacon of change. We're carrying a donut torch that has never been carried befo…"

"Shhhh…" a collective rustling of strange, faraway voices cruises through the cracks, penetrating the light between shelved books.

"Fuck! Now we're fucked. You see what happens?" Cliff says

rhetorically to himself and to his brother, who by now is several yards behind him, caught up in the middle section of *Tortilla Flat*.

"Well I've just about had it," Cliff says, then punches a fist into his hip and strikes a pose, letting his head fall back and his greasy hair cascade down in thick strands, exhaling through his lips with a motorboat ripple. From his vest pocket, he pulls a flask of whiskey and takes a pull. A bead of sweat sticks to the fibers of his goatee. He uses a finger to set it loose, watches the syrupy liquid fall to the thin gray carpet. "Everything is so fucking gray when it comes to the government," he says to the anonymous spines of books in the "Displaced Californians Who Write About How Much They Miss California" section.

Charlie starts a light jog with his hands out in front of him, catching up to his brother and pulling the flask from his hand. "I don't know man, is library government?"

"How'd you hear me?"

"You're fucking loud. Everyone can hear you."

"It's the Mustard Brothers, man. We've got to be more careful."

"Shhhhh," the strange voices respond.

"Shhhhhh!!!!" Cliff responds to the response.

"You're so fucking loud. It's like you talk with your belly instead of your neck."

"How else are you supposed to talk? And let's not forget, this belly talk is what sells your shitty little paintings."

"My shitty little paintings sell themselves, dickwad."

Cliff flicks Charlie's dick with his finger, making his brother wince with a sharp ounce of pain.

"Hey man. Fuck. Let's get to the computers," Charlie says and pulls on his brother's arm, but Cliff doesn't budge. "What's your problem today? You're being a fucking dick."

"I don't know. I just didn't have a good shower. I just don't feel clean, like there's mud under my tits. I feel like if I don't have a good shower, the day is kind of ruined. My mind isn't in it. I know I have to get over there to those computers and fill out that application but I just don't feel like touching the computer."

"Because it's dirty?"

"Of course because it's dirty! It's a filthy machine with the Cheeto stained hands of adolescent public school punks all over it. Just look at them. They're all Mexican punk goth freaks, and then the one white kid over there has a haircut like a campground host at Kern River. He looks like he hasn't had a decent shower in weeks. He probably kicks the neighborhood cat in the ribs and sucks on old pig bones, sleeps in Confederate flag pajamas."

"You need a drink."

"Of course I need a drink! This is high stress! This isn't the art world! This is the donut world! No one gives a shit about paintings, but donuts, holy shit, if you fuck that up, it's your ass!" Cliff pulls from his flask, his face filling with color, his lips widening with a smile around the neck of the container—he sees a security guard approaching. Lean, black—the guard even has a nightstick. Cliff sees him, but continues to pull. He crosses the aisle between "California Authors who Believe Rome is a Close Second to Los Angeles as the Best City in the World" and into another realm, "East Coast Writers who Work too Hard in Freezing Weather."

"I'm going to have to ask you boys to please leave," the security guard says.

"Why on earth do you need a billy-club at a library? How gnarly can things get around here?" Charlie asks.

"We have our reasons," the security guard responds.

"Give me one reason," Cliff says. "Just one fucking reason you need to bash the head in on a library stooge."

"I don't need to give you a reason."

"Yes, you do. I'm a citizen. I'm in the library. I'm a Mustard Brother. I formally request a reason."

"Sir, please leave. I don't want to deal with this any more than you do."

"I'll leave as soon as I get my hands on one of those computers."

"Sir, you need to leave now. We've had several complaints about your volu…."

"My volume!? Fuck this shit. I need to trademark Mustard Brothers." Cliff takes a step towards the security guard, towards the computers, and the security guard drops his hand down, stopping him by pressing his fist into his chest.

"Sir, you will not be using the computers. Please leave now, or I will be forced to remove you and call the police."

Charlie begins to laugh. It starts as a ripple of a giggle, then crescendos into a bellowing guffaw.

Cliff can't help himself either. A wide smile grows across his face, a smile so wide, if you saw it on the highway, a banner would be strung across it with the words "Wide Load" written upon it, a little red towel attached to a yardstick poking out from his teeth.

The security guard pulls out a walkie-talkie and says, "Dispatch, this is officer threezerosevenseven. I've got a situation on level one, Displaced Californians Who Write About How Much They Miss California section. Request backup."

"Oh fuck it," Cliff says. "You want a nip?" He pushes the flask in the security goon's face.

The security goon grips his wrist, twists it, removes the flask with his other hand.

Cliff strikes another pose, both hands on his hips, unamused by the shenanigans. "Ok man, cut the shit. Give it back."

"Sorry, sir."

"Sorry what?"

Charlie doesn't waste any more time. He knows that flask and the

Ativan in his pocket are his ticket out of the big heroin shake and the bottomless bruises pulsating within his joints. He pulls back his arm, and throws a solid straight right directly into the security goon's chin, dropping him to the floor.

Cliff grabs the flask, and the two brothers make a beeline for the door, boots thump thumping across the library. They hear the sounds of walkie -talkie static, radio voices, as they pass the librarian, escape outside. Once outside in the orange burn and gasoline garden, they assume a comfortable gait, a gait displaying both an intent to arrive somewhere, and a non-felonious harmony. This is not their first rodeo. Act natural. Cops pick up on unnatural activity.

"We have about a half hour before the cops come," Charlie says.

"I'd say closer to an hour—it's lunchtime."

Without acknowledgment or question, the brothers move, as if by instinct, towards the bar. They spend the first few minutes walking in relative silence, thinking of what it is that makes them outlaws, why the fiber of their being tells them to rebel even in the most non-rebellious atmospheres—for god sakes they were just in a library and didn't last five minutes inside.

"Is it us?" Cliff asks. "Or is it the world?"

"It's the world," Charlie says. "The world made us like this. We didn't make the world the way it is."

"Shit man, I was really looking forward to filling out that application. I was really looking forward to Mustard Brothers t-shirts," Cliff says, lighting another cigarette.

They turn the corner on Sunset Blvd., hit Portia Ave, dip into the cool darkness of their paisa bar, pull up a couple stools, drop their elbows on the wood, wipe the sweat from their brows. The Mars Volta coke dealer shoots pool, gives them a recognizable head nod, drops the eight ball in the corner pocket. "No blow today," Charlie says to himself. "Only Mustard Brothers."

"Two Tecates with lemons and salt," Cliff says to the barkeep.

The brothers' facial hair dips into the aluminum brew, sucking the citrus and salt back from the wild strands.

"This is more than just Mustard Brothers," Cliff says to his brother. "This is about bringing our other brother home." He takes another sip of his beer. "When I get home, I'm filling out that application on our own computer and we're bringing everything we love west. Nothing is gonna fucking stop me."

"To never stopping," Charlie says, raising his Tecate.

"To never stopping," Cliff says.

Getting Stopped Blues

Cliff is a thirty-two year old man. He knows his limits. He and Cassidy discussed his limits one day at the old bar in Los Angeles, the one Cassidy bartended at where Cliff was a regular, this paisa bar he's standing in right now. Cassidy was the only white bartender the paisa bar had ever hired, and it wasn't because Cassidy knew how to speak Spanish. In fact, Cassidy only knew a handful of phrases in Spanish before he started the job. "Me gusta beber jugo de pinocha." "Cerrado la porta." "Abre tus piernas." "Chingaderes, guey." "Puta madre." "Donde esta llello?" "Mochate, guey." He was hired because he owned a switchblade. It fell out of his pocket during the interview, popped open on the ground, it's neon blue tortoise shell handle spinning like an upside-down turtle. It was Cassidy and his hair and tight pants that turned this paisa bar into the hipster/vato den frequented by a large cross-section of conflicting cultures it has now become, a California border town inside an 1100 square foot box.

Cliff used to belly-up to Cassidy's 1960's psychedelic band anecdotes on a daily basis, listening intently to stories of White Lightning and The West Coast Pop Art Experimental Band, sucked into the narrative as if Cassidy had fronted all bands that had come before, thumping the great stone with long hair and drug boners. Cliff knew straight away the two of them were kindred spirits, both boys never shy to shovel key bumps of cocaine into their nostrils at all hours of the day, disrespecting all things deserving respect—fighting swine flu with whiskey, genital warts with rubbing alcohol, marriage with pornography, cops with middle fingers. They periodically pressed their bellies together, transferring energy between them in a ceremonious act Cliff and Cassidy believed had been introduced by the Sitsui Sanh tribes of Nauru. In the midst of summer sunsets, they rested their chins on each other's shoulders, eating lollipops underneath palm trees—crying or smiling, or simply taking breaths in, in, in, in, in, in, out. But, fuck, Cassidy isn't here any more and the palm trees only peel and cause tragedy, and the lollipops are bone dry.

Cliff is a thirty-two year old man who's been drinking for twenty-one years. After twenty-one years with only a handful of sober days peppered between the 1,092 weeks, it's safe to say he knows his physical limitations. At twelve, it was three Miller Lights. At sixteen, it was a pint of vodka. At twenty, it was a six-pack and six shots, one hit of weed from a bong or a full joint of schwag. At twenty-four, it was as much booze as his gullet could muscle, plus a gram of cocaine and a packet of cigarettes. At twenty-eight, it was the same gullet debauchery, plus a gram of cocaine, a packet of cigarettes, and two pills of opioid to fall asleep. At thirty it was seven beers, two Manhattans, a bump of coke, a hit of weed, and whatever downer he could get his dirty little tongue wrapped around. At thirty-two, it's five beers and as much marijuana as he can handle. Five beers and the world becomes tolerable. Five beers and he's able to wake up in the morning without his heart rattling his ribs, pounding and speeding like an errant freight-train desperate to burst out of his body. Five beers and he can say hello to a stranger in a pink button-down shirt and maybe even talk to them about something he doesn't care about, pressing syllables against his tongue, keeping his mind completely shut off from the nonsense, in line at the grocery store while purchasing more beer—maybe the cashier says something about the weather, and he agrees, never knowing or caring what the temperature is outside.

But today it's a flask of whiskey and his fourth Tecate. The Mars Volta cocaine dealer drops another eight ball, this time in the side pocket—still unbeaten after two hours. He looks back over his shoulder at the brothers, another nod. Whenever they're ready, they can lift off, spin like roman candles straight up into the sky, then come right back down, never look up again, burned out, a flickering reminder of what was once way up there.

"One more round," Cliff says to the bartender. One more round doesn't matter much now that he's gone over his limit. Five more rounds won't matter. Seventeen thousand shots and a Pacific Ocean of cheap Mexican beer and a moon made of lemon wedges won't make a difference. A hangover is a hangover. It will be dealt with.

Double Tecate's split open—lemons, salt. Beer bobsleds down esophagi. Charlie doodles a cowboy with a condom over his six-shooter on a paper napkin and Cliff excuses himself to use the restroom, slapping Mars Volta on the ass as he passes by. Mars Volta hands his cue stick to a homie in a pair of black sunglasses and follows Cliff behind the door. In the graffiti blasted stall, the two men converse in Spanglish over a toilet bowl of stale urine.

"Wassup, ese? You want cocaine? Crack? The heroin?"

"Co-ca-ina"

"Pura vida, holmes."

In the end, money is brought forth from the bowels of a deteriorated leather wallet, and a small plastic bag is passed from Mars Volta to Cliff. Cliff offers Mars Volta a snack—a tribute, a respectful gesture of social decency. They each dip the widest key of their key rings into the bag and inhale, smiling in agreement at the quality, the ease—no gasoline smell, minimum burn, pure numbness of the nasal cavities, and then, boom, an ecstatic blip in the heart rate, veins surging towards the big erect, fueled by the electricity of the great stone. Mars Volta pats Cliff on the back and Cliff pulls him in for a hug. "Gracias, mi hermano."

"Chingon."

Three in the afternoon high on coke and drunk on Tecate and shitty whiskey in a dark bathroom in a paisa bar in Echo Park, Los Angeles, CA with an up-and-coming painter brother, divorced from his one true love, on the brink of donut fame, covered in radddd tattoos, and a near-full packet of Camel cigarettes in his back pocket, plus a "Not in My Pussy" button attached to a beaten suede vest smelling of ancient California and wild patchouli—If Cliff could have told his sixteen-year-old-boy-self how totally bitchin his life would become, his sixteen-year-old-boy-self would have masturbated so many times in a row that he might have been hospitalized, his crooked mind warped for eternity, skin burned right off the shaft. If he coupled all this information with the prophecy of easy-to-access high-definition internet porn to his sixteen-year-old-boy-self, his sixteen-year-old-boy-self would have had a heart-attack, convulsing naked underneath the dial-up buzz of 1998.

This is life—this is two brothers, drunk, drugging, making donuts, going nowhere and everywhere simultaneously, the great march towards death or life—it's too difficult to define any longer. This is life, where the world is a blurred line between night and day, real and fake, where the sidewalk has a soul, where the street bounces underneath your boots. This is life, where this dark paisa bar means more to you than your mom. This is life where it doesn't matter because we all end up the same way, guey.

Cliff is life, where his legs won't stop twitching and his fourth Tecate has now become his seventh and his brother Charlie won't stop smacking the jukebox with his fist. This is life where the eses roll up on Charlie and say "Yo, you need to relax, homeboy." This is life where Charlie realizes he can't punch three eses in the face. This is life where Charlie tells the eses "It's all good, fellas. Just trying to get this Pearl Jam song on." This is life where Cliff overhears Charlie talking about Pearl Jam and says, "If you put fucking Pearl Jam on, I will join up with those eses and kick your little ass." This is life where the eses laugh and walk away adjusting their sag. "For real, bro," the eses say.

This is life. We all don't want to hear Pearl Jam in a bar in Los Angeles.

How many more beers before this day becomes as memorable as birth? The answer is two, which Cliff and Charlie deliver to their bloodstream with smiles.

"I really think I could just watch a raindrop fall from a cloud, all the way down, all day long. If I could stop a raindrop, in midair, and dissect it, I would." Cliff puts his hand in front of his body, then takes his other hand and touches it. "I'm still here," he says.

"I think a raindrop would be fun to dissect," Charlie responds. "A scalpel to the molecules? A bead cut into a thousand prisms of rainbow, reflecting, tiny microscopic crystals pulsi…"

"We get it," Cliff says. "Raindrops are beautiful. I already pointed that out. You always have to take it too god damn far."

"Too far is where the art comes from."

"Whatever. Let's blow this popsicle stand. We have applications to fill out. Mustard Brothers, brother."

Cliff pulls out his wallet to pay for the last round of drinks—he's in charge of finances for the brothers. His wallet feels light, not as heavy as before the drinks and the cocaine. As a matter of fact, his wallet is so light, it's empty. This wallet, if it could be dissected and placed under a microscope, would be made up of exactly one element—beef leather. There's no identification, no credit card, no debit card, no Rite-Aid card, no business card, no coin, no cash, and no condom.

Juan is a fair bartender, at least that's what Cliff thinks. He's polishing a soccer trophy behind the bar, one that reads—

El Rio de Los Jesus Rosas
Champions
Echo Park League
Adult Division
1986

Juan is a good man, in his late forties, with a gray goatee and hard eyes—every now and again he'll slide the brothers a shot of tequila down the bar and into their pulsing paws—they deserve it. Sometimes he challenges hipster douchebags in old-timey vests and bowties to an arm wrestling match, then throws them out of his bar when they lose.

"Hey Juan—got a bit of a problem."

"Que?"

"I'm outta cash."

"Chingaderas, guey. Go get some."

"It's all at my house."

"Go to the pinche ATM."

"Juan. Look at me. Do you think I have a bank account—with money in it?"

Juan takes a good long look at Cliff, letting his eyes move up and down across his face. Cliff certainly doesn't look like the kind of guy who has money in his bank account, nor does he look like a guy who even has a bank account. But what Juan doesn't know is that Cliff does have a bank account with money in it—more money than probably you and I. He just doesn't have an ATM card or a credit card, so the money just sits in there, rotting away like a dangerous felon behind bars.

"You look like a gay truck driver," Juan says.

Cliff takes a look at himself, brushes off a few pieces of lint stuck to his suede vest, spins a ten-thousand dollar grin. "Thank you, Juan."

"You pay me next time?" What Cliff can't see is Juan's left hand, which grips a small blunt metallic object, an object stained with the blood of the last patron who couldn't pay.

"I'll pay you double next time. I'll fucking pay double and tip you like a stripper."

Juan's hand releases from the blunt metallic object and nods his head. "Don't fuck with me, guero. I'll take your head off."

"Juan, I would never fuck with you! This bar means more to me than my mom!"

Cliff slides out of his stool and bows for Juan. He waves goodbye to Mars Volta, then steps outside where the sun streaks across the skyscrapers to the east, searing white rods of light reflecting off the windows and smog, too bright for the eyes.

"Nothing's gonna stop me," Cliff says then begins a sprint ahead of his brother, hauling ass like a hot rod, down the sidewalk, his boots bruising his heels, the fat of his cheeks slapping against his jaw, until, Wham!—the boot heel grabs an elevated crack in the concrete, and he face-plants into a tree, eyes roll back, body spins wild, a backwards tumble to the ground, cranium splitting on the curb's edge, lights-out, blood gushing from the wound, spilling underneath the tires of a nearby BMW, stopped.

Unconscious Blues

INT. PAISA BAR- DAY

Dark, divey. Worn Pesos stapled to the wall behind the stick, empty Tecate cans litter the joint. A cat cleans itself atop a barstool. An autographed copy of Herb Alpert's record "Whipped Cream and other Delights" sits proudly on a shelf above the bar. The sound of pool balls bouncing off each other tickles the ears in the distance. A candle next to a statuette of The Virgin burns, adding a sultry dim yellow to the room. CLIFF, 32, bar patron sits at the bar, staring nervously into an empty leather wallet—literally, there is nothing inside. JUAN, 49, the bartender, pulls at his handlebar mustache eyeing Cliff suspiciously.

                    CLIFF
          Hey Juan—got a bit of a problem.

                    JUAN
          Que?

                    CLIFF
I'm outta cash.

                    JUAN
Chingaderas, guey. Go get some.

                    CLIFF
It's all at my house.

                    JUAN
Go to the pinche ATM.

                    CLIFF
Juan. Look at me. Do you think I have a
bank account—with money in it?

Without warning, Juan pulls a blunt metallic
object from underneath the bar and crushes
Cliff's skull with it, blood squirting out just
above his left ear. Juan rips the empty wallet
from Cliff's hands, and shoves it into his
mouth, chewing.

                    JUAN
Fucking gringo.

Cliff's brother, CHARLIE, 31, spins into the
room with a wet paintbrush growing out from his
urethra, giggling maniacally. Charlie's arms
turn purple, then black, then peels from his
torso, falling to the ground where they morph
into rattlesnakes.

```
Cliff's teeth begin falling out, one by one,
until there is nothing left. He falls from his
barstool, staring up at the black painted
ceiling. The snakes attach themselves to his
neck.


                    CLIFF
        It's all over. They stopped me.

    CUT TO:
```

What God is Witnessing on Sunset Blvd in Los Angeles at 3:22 pm

From the sky looking down, He sees Cliff's collapsed body, halfway in the street, a crowd gathering around him, as Charlie slides to his knees next to his brother's unmoving body. Each onlooker frantically jams their thumbs and digits into iPhone screens, taking pictures, calling 911, updating Instagram. In a frustrated rage, Charlie punches the rear lights out of the BMW in front of him with his bare hands. Blood spills from Charlie's knuckles, mixing with the blood seeping from his brother's head. He pulls off his shirt and presses it into Cliff's skull. "Fuck," he says, then looks up to the sky. The blood won't stop. "Please God," Charlie says. "Fuck, man."

God untwists the top of an Oreo cookie, licks the cream, and continues watching.

Trash Blues

It's Tuesday and the drink specials at Bearclaw Murphy's are as follows:

$3 Goonheart IPA

$4 Yellow Sea Snakes

$5 Carney Barney Electric Cava

$6 Amazon Woman Double Vanilla Bean Bourbon

$40 Shots of Cherise's spit

Employees, however, always drink for free, and do so regularly without any questions asked—including Cherise's spit, which she has in the past liberally donated to her co-workers gullets.

On Tuesday, Bearclaw's opens at five p.m., just in time for fellow service industry associates to get their fix before the hell begins. At five, Cherise begins the shift, handling the handful of stooges that accidentally wander into this strange hole thinking it's a high-class joint with an extensive martini menu and deep wine list. At seven Cassidy comes on, and at eight, the place is always full, sweating, pulsing.

At 4 p.m., Cherise writes the drink specials in a hard-to-read scrawl on the chalkboard behind the bar. She has yet another bandage wrapped around her hand, another wound inflicted by the chainsaw she wields, a necessary risk and punishment for her passion—as she drags the chalk behind her wrist, she thinks to herself, "We all bleed one way or another for our art. This pain feels good. But I feel heavy today, like nothing good is happening. Like I'm stuck. I have to keep moving forward." She can sense Bulch's presence, his eyes and bones behind her, and somewhere inside she wishes his hands would come and take whatever it is pressing down on her chest off, throw it to the floor along with her top, dive right into her, take her $40 spit down his throat.

But Bulch's hands don't reach for Cherise. Instead, he sucks from his vanilla pipe, seated cross-legged on the bar, admiring Cherise's handwriting, the way the "b's" sort of trail off downward, towards the bottom of whatever it is they were once on top of. "An ancient sort of penmanship," he muses. His freshly polished boots surround him in the scent of turpentine. In the air, a rough-mix of Volcano the Spacemachine's latest single, "Part Time Astronaut," flitters and floats, rattling the windows and trinkets of the establishment. Bulch nods his head as the drum solo begins and nods his head again when it ends seven seconds later. "A drummer who understands the futility of a long solo is the paragon of profundity."

Out on the hot street, peaking through the glass garage door that is the entrance to Bearclaw Murphy's stands Aunika. She raps on the glass, the sound of her knuckles lost in the electric buzz reverberating off the walls inside. Harder she pounds until finally Cherise looks over her shoulder, finding her, her hair mussed and disheveled. Cherise holds up one finger, moves to the well, pours herself a shot of Cosmic Grizzly, and heads to the door, sliding it up a few feet to allow Aunika to duck down underneath and enter.

Bulch drops down from the bar and tips his greased safari hat to the stunning blonde. She's been on his mind lately and perhaps his mind manifests whatever it wants—Perhaps he has this power— after all, he wanted the world's best bar, and he owns it. He wanted a vial of banana oil for this Tuesday afternoon, and he received it. He wanted to reach the great stone at the top of Mt. Watusi, and did.

"What's up?" Cherise says.

"I need a drink," Aunika responds. Her eyes are red—she could have been crying, or perhaps she's already drunk, or perhaps it's only allergies—the pollen won't stop pouring down—yellow this time of year.

"Did something happen?" Cherise inquires.

"Yes."

"Come on in."

"How's my lovely donut farmer doing?" Bulch asks as Aunika approaches, straightening his quad-pocketed khaki shirt and sorting out the fine fibers of his mustache.

Aunika grins, slides her thin arms around Bulch's torso, and presses her cheek into his firm pectoral, resting it against the elephant tusk pen protruding from his breast pocket.

"I'm feeling a bit down and out," she mumbles into him.

"A bit blue? Down in the old snake pit? Well my love, I've got something just for you." From his lower left pocket, he pulls a vial of banana oil, untwists the top, and removes the dropper, dangling it above her head like mistletoe.

"No thanks," Aunika says. "Just booze for me." She unwinds herself from his embrace and draws a finger underneath her puffed eye.

"I've never seen anything like this," Bulch says under his breath. "A refusal of the banana oil, the great stone." Confused and nearly heart-broken, his eyebrows twist. "Perhaps she's not attracted to me."

He decides not to overanalyze the situation. He drops the banana oil into his mouth, then kicks his heels together and pulls out a barstool for Aunika, offering her a seat. "Lets have a drink and rap about your brain. What's sort of blues got you down? Lend old

Rangoon all your troubles and I'll return them gold."

Cherise pulls the bottle of Cosmic Grizzly and sets it down for Aunika to help herself. With her mangled hand, she gingerly cuts limes and lemons, squinting her eyes in pain each time the citric acid penetrates a breech in the gauze.

Aunika pours herself a drink and looks up around her. She isn't sure what she should divulge, if it might be better to just dwell in the bottle instead of her heart.

"I don't know," Aunika says. "Life's a bit more difficult than I wish it to be."

"Life is a bit more difficult than a hippopotamus hunt, but not much more," Bulch replies. "If you spin yourself around, you'll make yourself dizzy. It's hard to see that way." His hand reaches for her spine, a long finger sends a warm shiver straight down into her hips. "Is it work or love?" he asks.

"Both."

Cherise finishes slicing the limes and pulls herself up on the drop-in refrigerator behind her. "Fuck love and fuck work," she says. "The only thing worth anything in this world is yourself. Everyone and everything else is more trouble than anyone could possibly want." She delivers this sentence to Bulch, hoping for a response, one that might give her some glimpse of his possible affection for her. But Bulch's eyes are set on Aunika, where they remain.

"Only goatfuckers believe that," Bulch replies. "And a goatfucker doesn't know much about anything."

"Are you saying I'm a goatfucker?"

"My sweet, Cherise, how can I believe you believe what you just said? If anyone believes in love and work, it would be you. Your hands are carved up from the blades of a chainsaw, and that chainsaw is powered not by gasoline, but by the fuel of your heart."

Cherise opens her mouth, then closes it. Nothing to say—he's perfect. God damn, she loves those eyes—they see themselves, know everything, maybe even the exact coordinates of her body, where each imperfection slopes into perfection. That birthmark underneath her left breast on the ribs in the shape of Australia—he's been there, wrestled with a wallaby, pulled a python out, sucked on giant can of Fosters and pissed it out.

"Tell us about your love," Bulch says to Aunika.

"My love can't exist without dismantling something beautiful." She uses her hands to form a cube and then dissects the cube as if it were made of toothpicks.

Bulch nods his head. Not enough information to infer her possible love for him, nor for him to make a conjecture on where this love lies. "Can you be more specific?"

"No, unfortunately I can't because it involves people you both know and I don't want to fuck shit up more than I already have."

Bulch straightens his shoulders. At this point he's nearly positive Aunika's love troubles do not involve him. He'll turn his heart elsewhere, towards oiling his elephant gun in the office, or acquiring that photograph of Hemingway boxing with the natives of Zimbabwe—or even better, purchasing a sailboat and naming it "Radical Rangoon," shoving off to the Panama Canal, leaving it all behind, eating lobster and bananas, papayas the size of Cherise's breasts, climbing trees and yelling from the top of his lungs the poetry of Rainer Maria Rilke.

Cherise senses in Bulch a lack of interest towards her. She knows the only way to soothe her own soul is to approach Bulch, push him into a wall, plant her lips on his, press her hand somewhere, and hope for his hand to do the same—but this is an ill idea because it lacks both intelligence and patience.

Cherise has lacked patience since she was a child. She thinks her lack of patience results in such things as:

–the chainsaw wounds on her hands.

--the small drug and alcohol addiction she thinks will
someday go away, as if by magic, but never does.

--her inability to have orgasms from oral sex.

--why she hates French New Wave cinema.

--her inability to endure the chase for an unending love she
believes exists somewhere, perhaps right in front of her.

"This is boring," Cherise says and hops down. "I'm gonna take the recycling out." She drags a large blue barrel behind her and out the backdoor. Outside, she lights a cigarette and takes a seat on the ground in the alley, leaning against a chain link fence overgrown with vines. Maybe she'll call that Ansley fellow she met the other day— maybe she'll show him her new sculptures. Maybe she'll make love to him, then never speak to him again. Or maybe she'll fall in love with him and divorce him and never speak to him again. Or maybe she'll hop a sailboat, take it wherever the captain is headed, roll around in the sand somewhere, never speak again, only make love with her lips silent, surrounded by trees—the raw materials to create, hands bleeding into the sweet blue water.

Bulch can sense the uneasiness of Aunika's presence. This isn't a normal problem, and he can tell—he knows women—he could press his hand to her thigh and read everything inside of her, if she'd let him. He spins himself around in the barstool, hopping off on its second revolution, and slides behind the bar, creating the barrier that feels natural to him. This stick of wood, for the bartender, might as well be the Berlin Wall. He pushes his palms into the bin of ice, slides a few cubes into a glass, pours two fingers of gold rum into it, a bit of pineapple, a splash of orange, coconut rum, a dollop of red grenadine, floats dark rum on top, drops an orange peel in, rimming the glass with the bittersweet oil. "A cat always hunts for birds," he says. "A cat will always chase mice. A cat will kill a bird and a mouse for the owner it loves. In this same way, you should pursue your love as if it were a mouse or a bird, and then present it to this man… or woman."

"Is it wrong to love someone who can't technically be loved because he's loved by someone else?"

"No—It's not wrong to love someone who's already betrothed. It's only wrong to ignore love. Love doesn't always need to be physical—perhaps it would be enough for you to love this someone from a distance, keep this love inside of you, let it blossom when you wish, and cut the stem when you don't. Roses return every spring and bring with them the fragrance of love—they are resilient, and always beautiful."

Aunika nods her head in agreement. "Are you suggesting I have a relationship with my secret vision of this person?"

"Love is in the mind and heart. It's almost inconsequential whether or not that person is physically there. The mind can be more powerful than you think." He pulls his vial of banana oil from his vest pocket and rolls out a bead onto his tongue. "Dream of him, often, and you will not be so disappointed."

Bulch deftly wiggles a hand into his back pocket and removes a business card, sliding it across the bar to Aunika.

Hiroshima los Angeles de Sonnesson
Dream Guru
If you can think it, you can dream it!
777.111.1144

"Hiroshima's done wonders for my psyche, gathering my obsessions and making them accessible. One caveat, however—her

239

eyes are made of clouds—don't let that put you off."

Aunika examines the card, presses it into the front pocket of her jeans, wipes the sweat from her armpits and drops her chin on the bar. Bulch refills her glass of whiskey.

She looks up into his eyes and says, "I know something I shouldn't know that could possibly change everything. But maybe not. Fuck."

***

I decide to head over to Bearclaw's a bit early and grab a drink, keep the joints oiled and the brain full of beeswax. I exit Stanbury with my boots thumping heavy against the concrete, The Doors trailing off in the distance behind me—Morrison, you madman! I unlock my bicycle, hop on, and begin a comfortable ride towards my destination, my body light on the frame, feeling the bounce of my rubber tires as they glide across the cracks in the sidewalk. The streets are relatively quiet—it's Tuesday, the most dreadful day of days. The weekend is still too far away, the energy of Monday has sucked everyone dead. Tuesday is the South Pole of weekdays. It's lonely, empty, with nothing to offer aside from Cherise's $40 spit special.

I turn the corner and see a homeless man with a well-groomed beard, a purple ascot, and a German Shepherd puppy in his arms. He seems happy, but most likely isn't. He asks me for a nickel as I ride past, but I can't stop, and besides who the fuck has nickels anymore? Besides, I must get to the drink, I must put the drink in me, I must forget this strange day that should never have happened, I must put my life back together by tearing it apart and heading back out west—but it seems too insane to go back now that we are here. Or is it more insane to stay here? East West. Chocolate Vanilla. Life

Death. I suppose everything has its upside.

On this electric blue beach cruiser, I realize how many questions I don't have the answer to. For example, what happens to the recycling I drag out each night at Bearclaw's? What happens to those bottles? Is there a man in a lab-coat somewhere organizing each bottle, placing it in a pile that will somehow get sent back to the brewery or distillery of its origin? Or do they just crush all the plastic and glass together, send it to some kind of factory where they melt it all down and turn it into plastic and glass containers again? And what if there's, lets say, a tampon stuck inside one of these bottles? Who takes the tampon out? Is there a man somewhere whose duty it is to remove tampons and snot filled tissues and used condoms from empty beer bottles? I see hundreds of recycling bins all over the city and I become anxious because I know there's no possible way for all of these materials to actually be recycled—the toilet paper roll from the other night?—no fucking way is that getting reincarnated. All this trash everywhere! I'm swimming in it! That Malaysian Airlines plane went down and they can't find it because there's too much trash in the ocean and they can't differentiate between car parts, Chinese tennis shoes, and commercial jet pieces. All this damn garbage. And then, of course, the abortion—it hits me whenever I think of trash and I feel sick.

I'm a bit riled up, a bit antsy. My mind races. My wife tells me when I get drunk, I become loquacious. I talk during Woody Allen films because during Woody Allen films, I'm always drunk—they're just better that way, and I believe all of art is. And if life is art, then, well, let's have another.

I take the corner on my bicycle, blowing through a stop sign, nearly missing a skateboarder, who seems not to care, and actually waves at me with a smile, kick-flips over an empty beer can. I wave and smile back—"Sorry, brother!" My mind clears for a moment.

Up ahead, the glass garage door of Bearclaw's beckons to me. It's not often my place of employment beckons to me, but on this day, I'm glad I'm a bartender. As a bartender, I can drink. As a bartender, I can think. As a bartender, I can shrug everything off, remove myself, use the wood to separate me from the stooges, from the bozos, from the real world, from those who don't know and myself who doesn't know as well, but probably knows a bit more—I stand and you sit and you wait, and you look to me to make you feel good—but maybe I don't want to make you feel good and maybe I don't feel good, and maybe I never will. This stick of wood is the barrier between heart and brain, work and pleasure.

I can smell the vanilla smoke of Bulch's pipe as I lock my bike to the rack out front. I don't bother looking inside because it's Tuesday at 4:07 pm and I know who's inside. Inside is Rangoon and Cherise, drinking, twirling fingers around locks of hair or mustaches. Inside we can use each other's shoulders to support ourselves. Across the street, La Di Donuts is packed with patrons aglow in tattooery and strange cut-off shorts, neon sunglasses and, of course, interesting footwear. I can see the fresh face of the young blonde cashier crumbling under the pressure of delivering several donuts to customers in exchange for the correct currency, her blue eyes transforming into the lost spiral of the universe. As far as I can see, Aunika isn't there, not in the front of the shop—she's probably in the back, stuffing creamy animal livers or strange plant extracts into pastries, experimenting, maybe even drinking, side boobs peaking out from the edges of her apron, smearing salted peanut butter glazes on foie gras donuts.

I can see the garage door isn't all the way closed, so I wedge my hands underneath and use my legs to lift. The rattle of the door on its tracks makes my heart sing—a few more seconds and I'll be with my friends, my colleagues. I'll take a drink and I'll ask them about recycling—Bulch will tell me about the man-eating ferns he encountered in Southern Rhodesia and how he fought them with only an eel tooth attached to a crooked Singalong branch—my favorite tale. I'll tell them abstract things about love, how it can never be measured and how it can be infinite, can be sent towards a million people, or maybe just two, or perhaps, for some, only one, and still for others, only for themselves.

I take a step inside, shake the stars out of my hair, slip into the scene as if exiting the ocean covered in sea salt and sunshine, swiping the water from my eyelashes, the brine on the tip of my tongue.

Fuck, man. I see her.

"Long time no see." She shoots me a grin with only half her face. The bottle of Cosmic Grizzly in front of her tells me everything I need to know about how she's feeling at this moment. "Come sit with me." She uses her long fingers to rap against the barstool next to her.

Bulch eyes me, an eyebrow rising, pulling from his pipe. "I see," he says. "A real rattlesnake."

"Rattlesnake what?" Aunika replies.

"Don't let the rattlesnakes get ya," he says. He twists his body, stretching his neck out towards the sky. "I'll be in the office polishing the old elephant gun."

I know Bulch has an elephant gun, so the phrasing doesn't seem odd to me. Aunika on the other hand, doesn't know Bulch has an elephant gun, and misconstrues his statement as something obviously perverse. "Gross," she says. Bulch doesn't understand Aunika's sentiment, and crumples his eyebrows like an old newspaper. He uses his long legs to gather his banana bones and twirl towards the door, each step as delicate as the next, as if he were walking across windows in the middle of the sea.

The sun is behind me, the light creating a sort of halo around my head, dousing my face in shadows, cutting the contours of my cheeks, allowing the wavy tendrils of my hair to stray outward like rays of sun behind a lunar eclipse. Aunika sees this image in her dreams, or so she thinks she does. She's pretty sure she does, no, now that I'm walking towards her, she's sure of it. This has happened before. I have come towards her with the sun at my back, and next I will touch her waist and pull her head into mine.

I walk towards her, I sit on the barstool and I pull from the bottle of Cosmic Grizzly. This is not her dream. This is all real. This is all happening.

"I was riding my bicycle here and was wondering what happens to all our trash. What happens to all the recycling, the bottles with tampons stuck in them."

"It just gets sorted out."

"It's impossible to sort through all that trash. I don't believe it. We throw everything out and there's nowhere for it to go. We just leave it to someone else. We leave everything to someone else. Even my decisions aren't my decisions. They're based on someone else."

"If you didn't have someone else, what would your decisions be?"

"There wouldn't be any decisions. It would just be living."

"And what's living to you?"

"Not deciding. Being stoned."

Aunika places her hand on my forearm and rubs it. She exhales and pulls her attention away from me, towards the vacant space behind the bar. "I need you one way or the other," she says. "You don't have to decide. You just have to live. I'll let you live."

"When did this start?"

"What?"

I use my hands to gesture towards the space that no longer exists between us. "This."

"It started in first grade, when I was running in your grandparents backyard and skinned my knees on the deck and you went and got me one of your GI Joe band-aids."

"I remember that. It was my birthday."

"Was it?"

"I'm pretty sure."

"I don't think I ever thought about love and how it is a seed that can be planted at any point in life and grow into something you don't remember planting. I guess the bud didn't blossom until recently."

"Does that make me your dirt?"

"It makes you my soil. My very fertile soil."

***

A Quick Flashback to My Wedding Night

Phoenix and I dance our first dance, listening to the music, letting the lyrics of our song carry us and only us up and out into the starry sky.

Look at the face/the shape of the skull
Leave the road/follow the path.
It's midnight service at the Mutter Museum/and I'm glad,
lad that you're here.

As we turn, together, a unified couple under the mid-summer canopy of sycamore and oak of California, Aunika stands, alone, in a flowing crème dress, her bare shoulders bronzed from her recent travels to the Ping Islands, barefoot—hair partially dreaded from midnight excursions to the sea, a skinny dip with the jellyfish, drunk on rum cannonballs—sobbing. As Phoenix and I turn, I see my mother, my sister, both with tears in their eyes—but not sobbing. Their tears are tears of joy, a raindrop. Aunika's tears are tears of tragedy, a hurricane. It seems odd to me as I pull Phoenix in closer and we kiss and our guests applaud. Why is Aunika so upset?

I do a keg stand several minutes later, sucking Sierra Nevada from the tap, too drunk to make love later that night, throwing my fists into the dry perfect air, pulling at the starlight of the west and seeing my future up there somewhere in the black—it will all be perfect.

***

Back to Bearclaw's

"Why were you crying at my wedding?"

"Why do you think?"

"Because you were alone?"

Aunika chokes up a laugh. "Yes, I was alone."

"Are you lonely?"

"Yes, I'm lonely. That day was the day I realized I wouldn't be the only woman in your life, and that you would care about someone else more than me. You probably already felt that way, but it wasn't until then that I realized we would never be the same."

"I knew we wouldn't be the same as well, but I just thought we'd pretend like we were, get over the awkwardness, and somehow grow back towards each other. I was stoked when you and Phoenix got along and figured the three of us would become inseparable."

"Yeah, and I think that would've been fine, for awhile, which it was. But even then, it's just chasing a ghost down a black hole. You're married, you'll have kids, your life won't be my life, and my life won't be yours."

"Why didn't you ever tell me you were attracted to me?"

"Because I wasn't attracted in the traditional sense. I wanted a man like you, but there is no man like you, and eventually you realize you fucked up because the man you wanted was right there."

"But I'm not that rad of a guy. I drink in the morning. I have tattoos and gnarly long crazy hair and my feet are way too big so that when I wear tight pants I look like a fucking duck. I write shitty Choose Your Adventure erotica books and psychedelic poetry, bartend at Bearclaw Murphy's, and suffer from frequent chode rashes and major bouts of depression—plus I take drugs and have HPV."

"If you took that sentence and put it in a book, you'd sound rad."

I chuckle. "I don't know if HPV makes you rad."

"Everyone has HPV." She pulls at her hair, twists it around a finger and uses her fingers to dance across the bar towards nothing. "Fuck it," she says. "This is life, right?"

"It is life."

"And trash is trash."

"Some trash is more valuable than other trash."

"We all forget the trash, eventually."

***

Phoenix has been staring at herself in the mirror for thirty minutes in perfect silence, her hair wrapped up in a towel, her naked body drying in the heat of July. She meant to sit down in front of this mirror and apply lotion to herself—she had just shaved her legs and pubes and armpits in the bath. She usually feels better after shaving all her hair off, as if she's shed a layer of diseased skin and memories, bringing out something new, an instant spring season arriving on her body. But today, the disease remains attached to her.

Her anxiety is tangible again, a result of her inability to express her emotions and worries, her thoughts and hopes and dreams to her husband—He's gone. He works too much. We work too much. What can we do? What is there left in this world for us? It's filled with trash. Did you know the Malaysian Airlines flight went down and they couldn't find it because of all the trash in the ocean? Is my baby floating around there? Is that poor little fucking thing that was stuck inside of me that I unknowingly doused with booze and drugs for the first two months, somewhere in that junk, floating with a million other fetuses?

The pain shoots right up into her gut, continues, traveling as if by razor blade into her heart. She doubles over, using the hardwood floor as a punishment to her head, pounding and pounding until the pain on the bridge of her nose supersedes the pain in her stomach, and then it passes…passes…passes…passes…but will never go away. "I miss California," she says out loud to the mirror above her. "I fucking miss California! I fucking miss California! I fucking miss California!"

She needs a drink. We all need a drink. Everyone in this story needs a drink. She moves to Cassidy's office, pulls open his bottom drawer and finds the bottle of Rebel Yell he hides underneath the folders of the last five years of tax statements. She's known for years the bottle's been in there, but never wanted to admit it was and what it meant—her husband is an alcoholic with gnarly long crazy hair who writes psychedelic poetry and erotic Choose Your Own Adventure bullshit and bartends at Bearclaw Murphy's and gets to drink and flirt with Cherise and other hot chicks with interesting shades of lipstick that could to turn his dick into a rainbow, and she's stuck in the gray, sucking from the gray tits of fat rich men, chewing the gray from candy tampons, and watching shitty sweaters pass before her eyes like billboards for pea soup in the fog on the I-5 to San Francisco.

***

A Quick Thing About Pea Soup

No one who isn't from California will understand the above pea soup reference, but screw it. Did you write this book? Three words—Certified. Public. Accountant. I'll do it—I'm not fucking around. I'll tell you about his collection of Spongebob Squarepants boxers if you're not careful.

***

Phoenix sucks from the Rebel Yell. She says, "I'll find us an Airstream, we'll buy it and we'll move it to California and we'll buy a small piece of land and we'll live in the airstream, and we'll live, and we'll be happy, and we'll have kids—He promised we'd have kids—when we're ready—and that will be our life."

***

I pour a shot for myself and Aunika. I say, "Let's forget about the trash."

Aunika takes her shot, inhales deeply. "Your wife does blow and makes out with other women."

***

Charlie rides in the ambulance with his brother, bouncing up and down as the vehicle crosses a million potholes. He pulls the near empty flask from his brothers' pocket and takes a pull, the metallic neck striking his teeth with the turbulence. The paramedic says, "You can't drink in here, man. What the fuck are you doing?" Charlie raises his fist. "I fucking need it," he says. He rubs the dried blood from above his brother's eyelid.

***

Cherise finishes her cigarette, walks back into Bearclaw's and sees an expression on my face she's never seen before. It's as if my face has been rearranged in the mind of Salvador Dali. She slides behind the bar and pours herself a drink from the Cosmic Grizzly. "Where's Bulch?" she asks, but we don't respond—only thick air and breaths collide between us.

***

Bulch throws his newly polished boots up onto his desk, cracks open a heavy IPA and brings a small tape recorder to his mouth. "Rangoon, chapter four. The dunes were too difficult to cross at dawn. We hunkered down underneath a layer of mongoose thicket, weathering the east-born storm that would continue for several hours, before loading the raft with our belongings, and setting course south down the Warasong River, through Pin-swit Alligator country. We didn't know what we'd come home with, hopefully our legs, but that's about all we were hopeful for. I suppose there was nothing left to lose." He pulls out his elephant gun. It's loaded and could kill, well, an elephant.

Last Breath Blues

White Charlie doesn't remember much about his three years in Catholic school. He was expelled for painting a rabbit on the wall of the hallway, a full color, floppy-eared rodent chewing on the tits of the Virgin Mary. After he got caught, he pulled down his pants in front of Sister Dorothy and raised his middle finger to her face. At seven years old, Charlie was a hell-raiser outfitted in his father's cowboy boots, which he insisted on wearing every day even though they were several sizes too big for him. Even back then, Charlie viewed the world as a shootout—last man standing wins. Tonight, in the back of the ambulance as it makes a right turn off Sunset Blvd., the gross white lights of the hospital coming into vision, he realizes he may once again be the last man standing. Cliff is unconscious. Cliff's breathing is erratic. Cliff doesn't move, oblivious to the world around him, half-dead. Charlie presses his palms together and bows his head for a Hail Mary. Mary loves him—always has—she's gotten him out of several jams in the past. Like that one time he acted as a middleman and accidentally sold two pounds of oregano to a big-time weed dealer who then put a hit out on him—$10,000 for his head. It was Mary that week that allowed Charlie to broker a deal with the dealer for a gym bag of stolen firearms in exchange for his life. She works mysteriously, for sure.

Charlie's finished the flask without any more lip from the paramedic and his shaky hands have taken on a much needed calm in the face of chaos. The ambulance pulls into the ER, screeching to a halt in front of a team of trauma nurses. It's hard to repeat what everyone's saying as the back doors pop open and his brother is lifted up in the air, held up in the hands of strangers under the great California sky. Tongues rattle off a bevy of numbers, hurried speech where vowels can't catch up to consonants and vice versa. The scene passes before him like a deck of cards falling from the sky—there's no way to know what's what and who's who. That nurse talks like an Ace of Diamonds, and that doctor moves like a Jack of Hearts. Spades everywhere, clubs and hearts and blackness and redness encircling him, separating him from the gravity of the situation.

Charlie lets one leg dangle out the back of the ambulance and takes a deep look at his hand. Only a minute ago, it had been attached to his brother's limp knuckles, squeezing, pulsing, as if trying to pump the blood lost back into him. And now, his palm is empty, nothing else to pump into. The sky is a darkening blue with a few clouds, the sun is changing color—he thinks this city would look a lot cooler if it had a waterfall in the center of it. If there was a waterfall in the center of this city, he would pull off his dirty clothes stained with his brother's blood and wade deep into it, let the cool water rush down his face, soothe the bruises on his arms, cool the burning heels inside his boots. He'd say a prayer to the waterfall god of the city, drop a few wishing pennies into the surrounding pond, float on his back, and watch his brother spill down the waterfall and into his arms, smiling and splashing. "Not in my pussy!" Cliff would yell. Charlie would give him a big kiss just like Cliff used to give him when he was a baby. They'd never leave that waterfall in the center of the city. They'd be like an otter exhibit at Sea World, their bellies bobbing in the pool, beards beaded with sapphire, spitting water up into the air and cracking open beer bottles like clams.

But these are fantasies—not reality. There is no waterfall in Los

Angeles and Cliff isn't yelling "Not in my pussy!" As a matter of fact, Cliff isn't saying anything. Eyes clamped. It takes several seconds for Charlie to realize the paramedic has been saying something to him for the past minute or so, and judging by the young man's face, he isn't too happy. This young paramedic has a face like an Italian underwear model. His lips move, his eyebrows cross, his hands grab Charlie by the shoulders, pulling him out of the ambulance. Charlie pulls back his arm, ready to throw one more punch, but instead, gets kneed in the groin. He falls to the ground in pain, covering his balls with his hand. The ground is hot, singeing his elbows and forearms.

"Are you out of your fucking mind?" the paramedic yells at Charlie. Charlie looks up at the man as he hurriedly jumps back into the rear of the ambulance and watches as the vehicle burns rubber, speeding away like a bolt of lightning that was never there.

"Yes," he responds into the void.

A nurse rushes out to him with an icepack, dropping it onto his chest. "Get up," she says and rushes back towards the hospital.

"It's strange," Charlie thinks to himself, "that this place exists. How much blood do these people see every day? What does it matter?" He sees his own blood pull up out of his vein and then shoot back down almost every day. Blood. Beautiful. It thumps through us or pours out of us, or kills us when it picks up trash, clogging up arteries and killing cells. Trash is everywhere, Charlie thinks. He's trash, his blood is trash. If he were underneath the waterfall, people would just think it was trash bobbing around— they'd remove him, forget about him, and that would be the end. This can't be the end for his brother. His brother hasn't created enough yet to die. He must be remembered by something.

A homeless man shuffles down the sidewalk, sees Charlie in the road, and asks him for a dime.

"Get outta here," Charlie says.

The man asks one more time, "Hey man, gimmee a dime. I gotta eat."

"If Cliff dies, I'm gonna keep Mustard Brothers going. I'm gonna make him a fucking famous posthumous donut mogul. And then, I'll give you a goddamn dime."

"Who in the hell wants to eat a mustard donut? Forget about the dime, man. Shit. You're crazy as hell."

Charlie sees the nurse at the automatic doors waiting for him. "Get your pinche ass over here, gringo!" she yells. She's Mexican, or Peruvian, hard to tell, about thirty, with tattoos across her knuckles that read S L O W D O W N.

Charlie pulls himself up, keeping the icepack wedged into his crotch. He stumbles over to the nurse who looks in his eyes and says, "What's your blood type?"

"I don't know. Same as my brother's I think."

"We need your blood. We're low on O-Negative."

"Is he going to live?"

"Let's go, causa."

Charlie kind of digs this Mexican Peruvian nurse—eyebrows thick like Giant Silkworms, cheekbones high as Machu Picchu, skin dark as a brazil nut. If his brother lives, maybe he'll ask her out. She probably has access to the good shit, of which he'll need plenty of to get through this trauma. Fuckin-A, he's a junkie. Nurse Jackie is a junkie. Maybe all nurses are? That would be dope, pun intended.

***

The O-Negative Situation

How could a hospital run out of blood?

A car collision on the 101 freeway involving a semi-truck full of extra-sharp axes and three passenger cars (one of which was carrying seven teenagers, and another with a trunk full of fireworks that ignited and exploded), two pre-adolescent gunshot wounds from playing with their parents pistol, a gang-related double stabbing, a lawn mower mishap in which an entire set of toes were chopped off, a sprinkler accident which severed a main artery in a seven-year-old girl's thigh, two skateboarders trying to 50-50 fifty stairs and shattering a total of four ankle bones with two compound tibia fractures, a thief who tried to escape through a 7-Eleven window resulting in a million shards of glass piercing and wedging into his face and neck, a severed and eventually amputated leg from a scaffolding collapse/gas leak explosion at a Fox News construction site, and a vicious four-dog pitbull attack massacre on a three-year-old boy while blowing daffodils in his front yard occurred today on the Eastside of Los Angeles. Each of these victims were type O-negative and brought to the very hospital Cliff is currently unconscious and barely breathing in. How random is that?

***

Charlie takes a seat in a hospital bed adjacent to where his brother lies. The nurse asks him questions about his health, prying into his history. How many sexual partners have you had in the past year? How much trash travels through your veins? But all Charlie can think about is how long it takes for heroin to leave the system—minutes, days, numbers, equations—her words dropping on his head and crashing to the floor like a hail-storm made of glass. He replays each hour since the last time he shot up, realizing he can't be totally sure how long it's been—time ceases to exist right after the great stone kicks in, the world takes on properties of the surreal, rocks turn to water, eyes drift outward from the body like carpenter bees looking for wood to burrow into—he may have been three days in the desert chasing an eagle for all he knows. No, wait, it couldn't have been three days chasing that eagle—he was at the gallery for only a few hours, and then, he only shot up enough to take the edge off, enough to give him a syrupy grin and lazy eyes, enough to take the harsh edges off reality's contours, make it all just fade away a little.

The nurse rattles off questions, and Charlie answers them, but he's not sure what he's saying or who he's saying them to—instead, his mind continues to solve what seems like a never-ending math equation—"When was the last time I used?" The irony and the reality begin to set in—it's up to Charlie's blood to save his brother. But his blood is filthy—God only knows what lives inside of it— creatures with spikes, ex-girlfriends with pointed teeth, dicks shooting toxic come. He only shared needles with one person, an ex- girlfriend who's dead now. But she didn't die from HIV or Hepatitis, he's pretty sure about that. No, it was a car accident in Fresno. No one knows why she was in Fresno. No one cares about Fresno. As a matter of fact, was it a car wreck? Or suicide? He can't remember. Maybe this ex-girlfriend was the one who died in East Los Angeles after falling in the L.A. River drunk on horse and wine. Shit, how many ex-girlfriends have died? Three? No, two. No wait, three? The last one was definitely a suicide. Did she have a funeral? Was she cremated? Is she underground?

"Have you ever used intravenous drugs?" the nurse asks Charlie.

He smiles a grievous grin. "No. Never."

Even if he's still got a bit of the horse left in him, he's pretty sure his brother can handle it—might even thank him for it later. Cliff will wake up and say something like, "Man, it was all goin south and then that cool wave of H dropped in and kicked my ass back onto the planet."

"Bullshit," the nurse says, flicking a vein in his forearm. "But the hell with it, we gotta save him."

"I'm the only one with O-negative, eh?"

"How long has it been since you last used?"

"Two days, but it was just a taste."

"Lay off the drugs. Let this be a lesson to you."

The nurse rigs up, prepares her needles and bottles. It doesn't take long for her to find a vein—as a matter of fact, the veins on both of Charlie's arms pop out like an earthworm looking for the moon. She sticks the needle in and Charlie giggles saying, "It tickles."

The nurse rolls her eyes, shakes her head, pulls a pint from him, sends it over to the doc to transfuse into Cliff.

"As clean as it's gonna get," she says, dropping a hip for the MD.

The sound of blunt metallic medical instruments twangs down the hall. Cliff's heart-rate beeps in a slow, unnatural rhythm, barely there.

"I like your Reeboks," Charlie says, pointing at the nurse's all-white footwear, the brand name stitched in pink on the side. "Those are vintage, eh?"

"Yeah," she says. "Dug Reeboks since I was kid." She takes a long look at Charlie. He's an attractive man, with body odor like summer sand mixed with rosemary in the rain. She likes his beard, his big wandering blue eyes, his stature, elegant yet informal, like an unfinished sculpture. He has the look of a man who's seen it all, pulled everything out from within him and lets it all teeter-totter on the tip of his tongue. She places a hand on his broad shoulder, rubs deep down into the tissue. "We're gonna do all we can to save him. You're lucky—we got the best E.R. Doc on this shift. He's gonna be all right."

Charlie pulls his legs up onto the adjacent hospital bed, lies down, lets his bones elongate, then contract with his heart. He lets his arm dangle off the sides of the mattress, takes a deep breath, and closes his eyes. "He's gonna be all right," he says out loud, then drifts off into a somnambulist paradise where bunnies chew on perfect dandelions and grow bright red cardinal wings, fly straight up into the sun.

On the other side of the wall, behind a baby-blue curtain, the doctor plugs Charlie's blood into Cliff, tries to stabilize and assess the extent of the damage to the man's cranium. Charlie's crimson juice drifts into Cliff's vein, pushing upwards to the shoulder, drops off the cliff at his collarbone, a big heroiny waterfall dumping right down into his heart with the power of a thousand Niagara Falls. Cliff's eyes pop open, his lungs gasp for air. The medical staff jumps back. "He's back?" the doc says. Cliff's eyes close, his lungs shut down, his chest sucks back in, throat closes, skin turns blue. His heartbeat quits. One long high-pitched beep. Flat line. "Mierda," the nurse says.

Kissing Blues

My phone buzzes with either several text messages or several missed phone-calls—it doesn't matter. Inside Bearclaw's I feel warm, safe, but also tragic and helpless—nothing to grab hold of and no need to grab hold of anything. The first note of the Jerry Garcia Band record Cherise has just placed under the needle pings through the near-empty bar. I take a deep breath, noticing a stuffed boar's head I've never seen before just above the jukebox, dusty and dark in the shadows, eyes yellow and glassed over.

When my eyes swirl back around, I lock into Aunika's ocular vibes—pure turquoise, pure sunshine, pure evil, pure life, pure sex—I can't tell what's what anymore—those two stones in her face could be planets spinning away from everything, and maybe I can hop on board, twirl right out into space. She hasn't said a word since divulging what she saw at St. Claire's rainbow—that my wife is a possible drug addicted lesbian. Instead, she's been waiting for my reaction, gauging what her next move will be based upon the next sentence that comes out of my mouth.

"What do you mean? Is this like, a normal thing?"

"I don't know if it is or not—I just want you to know what I saw. As your friend, I think you should know."

I don't really know how to react to Aunika's revelation. Part of me feels upset about not knowing every detail about my wife, but part of me is relieved. Shit, I have a secret bottle of Rebel Yell in the bottom drawer of my desk underneath file folders of our old taxes Phoenix has no idea about. Plus, I dabble in the narcotic baggie every now and again, right here at Bearclaw's. I've seen Cherise's tits. I've done a line of coke off them with a grin the size of Saturn's rings. I'm pretty sure Phoenix wouldn't be too stoked on that if someone told her. I suppose of the two things I've just learned, I'm more upset about the make-out session with the other chick. Most men might say "That's so rad! Maybe she's into other chicks! You can totally pull a threesome!" But when you're married and you love someone, you don't want to hear about their tongue in someone else's mouth, no matter what gender they are or what your fantasies may be. Marriage is marriage—you belong to each other and to no one else.

I have to rationalize the events of this day in order to move forward. I take a moment to process all the information I've received in the last few hours. I come to a pretty obvious realization—Aunika is making a strong move towards disbanding my marriage. She is self -centered, myopic, crazed. Her telling me these alleged actions of my wife are a turn-off, born of evil and not born of love.

"I guess I need to talk to her then," I say. But inside I know I won't say anything. I'll let her do a thousand lines and kiss a thousand women. She's perfect and she deserves a kiss and a line for everything I put her through and everything she's endured. The blood and skin of our fetus has poured out of her. She writhes in pain on the bathroom floor. Holy shit. She was writhing around on the bathroom floor after The Rainbow. It was probably the cocaine—it's probably always been the cocaine, maybe an allergy, maybe the baby laxatives they cut it with.

When I begin to believe these stomachaches are simply a result of a bad reaction to subpar blow, a smile grows on my face, shocking Aunika. I can tell she's shocked because she shakes her head, disagreeing with herself and her decision to tell me everything she's told me today.

"I fucked up," she says, exhaling her boozy breath into my face.

"You didn't fuck up," I reassure her, but maybe she has. This friendship can no longer be the same. We've added pure Na sodium to the water; we've split the atomic nuclei. I have to be aware of her at all times now. I can't get drunk and pass out on her couch. I can't get drunk and be stuck in a dimly lit room alone with her. I can't be drunk and alone on an elevator in Rome with her. I can't be drunk in a midnight river near the coast of California during a summer heat wave in the light of a bonfire with her. I can't camp, hike, listen to Fiona Apple, watch Wes Anderson films, plant a garden, eat guacamole, or drunkenly dance to 60's psychedelic rock with her. I can't be drunk with her, period. I look at the beer in front of me, unable to remember when it got there. It could have appeared in front of me during birth or death, or perhaps somewhere in between, which is where I think I am. Where am I?

"Can we just forget everything and move forward. I haven't been myself for a while and I just needed someone to love, I think. And since I already love you, in more than just a physical way, you just seemed obvious," she says.

I take a swallow of my beer. I'm already drunk, so there's no escaping her. She softens her eyes and two tears in the shape of glass pyramids drop from each corner. I feel sorry for her. She's in love, or maybe she isn't—maybe she's just lonely. I pull her head into my neck and a river of tears runs straight out of her face and onto my skin, hot and wet like her tongue at The Rainbow.

"We can go back to the way we were before," I tell her. But we can't. The turn-off is quickly morphing into a turn-on with each breath that escapes her mouth and tickles my earlobe. This possible turn-on is further exacerbated by her left breast resting on my arm, pumping ever-so-slightly with each big, thumping heartbeat.

"I'm so sorry," she whimpers into me.

"It's cool," I say. "I mean, if it makes you feel any better, if I wasn't married and you told me this…"

"Don't say it."

"…we'd be naked in a river in California right now…" I don't know why I would say that. I'm not sure if it's true, or maybe I'm just telling myself it might not be true so I don't feel like an asshole. Or maybe this woman in front of me is the key to forgetting everything. She is the proverbial "blank slate," a place to start over, from the bottom up. Perhaps there's hope, perhaps this hope is something that the great gods of the…

She grabs my face, pulls me into her lips, separates my mouth with her tongue, pushes it inside, finds my tongue, wrestles it into submission. Fuck. This is a kiss. I am a man. There's no blood, no stomachache, no abortion. I pull my tongue out from underneath hers. I pause, think for a moment of Phoenix. It's already too far and maybe it's best to just let this kiss happen, then watch it disappear, treat it like trash, forget about it. I let my tongue find my way on top, and press hers down. She pushes her thighs to mine, pulling herself off her barstool, then drops onto my lap, straddling me. I let my palms push up her spine, wrap my hands around her hipbones, push my fingers underneath her shirt, touch her ribs, move further up. She grinds, she pushes into me as if trying to fuse us together. She drops a hand into my crotch and rubs. I pull her in further. I drop a hand down to the waistband of her jeans, tease the brass button for a moment.

And then we stop. We take a breath. We unwind from each other. I put my head in my hands. She says, "Now you're even."

She grabs her purse, leaves a twenty-dollar bill on the bar, walks her hand through my hair, and turns away, yanking up on the garage door and sliding out across the street to her donut shop. Gone—for now.

If you chase after Aunika, turn to the next page

If you let her go, turn to Page 269

Refrigerator Blues

I slide my beer away from me and watch her move across the street, holding up traffic with an elegant right hand extended. She opens the door of her donut shop and hugs a woman in a t-shirt with a Rubik's cube on it that reads "Can't figure me out."

It dawns on me that Cherise has been in the bar witnessing everything this entire time. For some reason, I just assumed she was somewhere else. She's been quiet, over there in the corner, but now, she has a grin on her face as wide as the Southern Pacific railroad.

"Holy shit that was hot," she says.

I don't worry about Cherise saying anything to Phoenix about this kiss because Cherise and I have that unspoken bond between us, the foundation of which can be summed up by this motto—"Never rat on a homie"—we will die for each other, we'll take each other's secrets to the grave. We'll wash glasses for each other when one of us has hands sliced to shreds and we'll give each other CPR if we ever OD on bathroom cocaine.

"That was kinda hot, for sure," I say. I stand up, grab the bottle of Cosmic Grizzly, take a pull. The world sort of sways in front of me, the lines blurring, the heat of the day bringing beads of sweat between my pectorals, dripping down, curving around my belly button and disintegrating in the fabric of my blue jeans.

I say "Fuck it," yank open the garage door, slide underneath it, cross the street, stop traffic with my hand and enter the donut shop.

A tangible sugar-sweet stickiness envelops my sweating body, massaging its way into me. A mass of bodies swell and push against the counter, throwing greenbacks in the blonde cashier's stressed-out face. The sound of loose change falling, the whistle of paper money sorting through fingers. Mouths open wide, cramming fluffy donuts into their hot holes, bellies splashing with sugar and salt, foie gras and butter pecan bacon cream.

I push past them all, ignore the twenty-year-old donut artist who says, "Hey man, you can't go back there," and find myself in the kitchen. I see Aunika bent over in the walk-in refrigerator, looking for something. She doesn't notice me. She pulls out a bottle of beer and pops it open with a large chef's knife hanging from the door.

"Hey," I say.

She jumps, turns around. "Hey," she says. She smiles. The sun has kissed her cheeks just enough to give them a rosy bronze, a bit of sweat. Her hair, disheveled, blonde, thick with the seafoam genes of the Pacific, twists in the light breeze created from the industrial sized refrigerator fan.

I take a step, and another, and another, until she's directly in front of me. I pull her waist into mine, press my mouth to hers, and between our teeth I can see our childhood slipping through the cracks, exchanging our skinned knees for French kisses, our merry-go-rounds for moisture and hard-ons. I lift her body up off the ground, let her legs wrap around my waist and slam her spine into the heavy metal door. She says "Uhh," with the thud. I drop a finger down to that button, the one only moments ago I had been teasing, but this time, I maneuver the brass through the hole in the denim and pull it open. I take another finger and unzip her, slowly, the jagged teeth rippling, letting the heat escape into my hand. I press my tongue to her ear, draw it down underneath her jaw, lick the salt down her neck.

She uses her own two long fingers to unzip my blue jeans, running her soft knuckles across the tip of my erection. She pulls off her tank top, exposing her breasts—perfect almonds, the nipples like petals of pink jasmine.

I let her legs drop from my waist, step back, remove my shirt, wipe the sweat up from the crease between my pectorals. We press back into each other, our moist skin connecting, sticking and pulling apart with each kiss. I move my hand between her legs, push her underwear to the side, let my fingertip dangle just above her, the heat pulsing—but I don't touch her. She smiles.

"Come on," she says. She wraps her fingers around my wrist and pulls with all her strength, but I don't let her win. I remain just out of reach, just enough to make her push her hips towards me, but I pull back.

"Fuck you," she says with a grin, then wraps a leg around me, pulls my body, my hand into her, and moves slowly against my fingers.

I move my head into her neck, let the whiskers of my mustache create goosebumps on her arms, then move down her body, kissing each rib, until I find my tongue wrapping across the sharpness of her hipbones. I use my thumbs to pull her jeans down an inch, then another, and yet another, until they are around her ankles. I kiss her thighs, lingering too long. She takes both of her hands and presses my forehead into her center.

"No," I say, pulling back. "I want to look at you."

I pick up one leg, then another, removing her jeans, tossing them into the corner of the refrigerator. Her underwear, lavender and yet transparent, reveals a piercing behind the fabric—a silver hoop through her clitoris.

She doesn't wait for me. She uses her own thumbs to shimmy out of the undergarment. She stretches out her arms, drops her head back, shaking out her hair. "Look at me," she says.

And I do. I look at every inch of her body, calculating the way her bones are constructed as if by an architect, each line in perfect correlation to the other, each imperfection, an inherent perfection— the three-inch scar above her knee; the right breast slightly larger than the left; a small belly, perfect, feminine. I look at her body, and I can see in each attribute a book I'm about to open, all the stories I'll explore with my mouth and my body and my soul.

I drop to my knees in front of her and let my tongue roll against the silver hoop, delicately toying with it, using my teeth to give a gentle tug. I can see the blood rush to the tip, sending waves of warmth through the ring. She raises a leg, drops it on my shoulder, drives her fingers into the thickness of my hair, lets her fingers play like dolphins in a wave.

There is a slow rhythm, a song of our psyches. We move in synch with the instruments of our body, until there's nothing left but one organism, fused together, vibrating in the great hum of the world.

We spin, we push. I use my tongue to dive and swim, come up for air, then back down again. Her ocean tide arrives, I lose myself in it, wander around in the deep blue, blind, only focused on rising back up, conquering her. I use my head to push further and further, taking her wrists in my hands, and pressing them against the cold metal door, pinning her.

She tells me "Stop, I don't want to come yet."

I refuse.

I push a little deeper with my tongue. Her leg begins a quiver at the ankle, moving towards her knee—I pull back. She exhales, "Fuck."

I push my lips together, blow a gentle wind across her sea, then set sail again, directly into the eye of the storm brewing. I rock, teeter, fall under, move north, then south, east, then west, west, west, the west is the best, until I feel the strength of her arms break free of mine, her fingers grip handfuls of my hair, slam my face into her while she wildly escapes this world, our memories, drips her love onto my tongue, her head pounding once, twice, three times against that door.

Her hands release, her leg drops. I stand before her. She wipes my lips with a finger. Behind us, the blonde cashier says, "Excuse me."

We pull each other into the refrigerator, close the door, find the beer, say nothing, seated in the cold, passing it between us. Our fingers interlock, squeeze, then fall apart, away, unlocked. There is nothing in front of us but a wall of cold air and a refrigerator door, and that's about as far as my eyes can see.

Tongue Blues

Nothing will ever be the same between Aunika and I. I'm back where I belong, behind the bar, pouring Bulch his customary Mai Tai, wondering about my tongue. My tongue has either created beauty or disassembled it, throughout my life. Words, sex, sentences—they're all the same inside my heart.

My tongue has damaged my wife. My tongue has told her I love her. My tongue asked me to marry her. My tongue gave her her first orgasm from oral sex. My tongue has been inside of Aunika. My tongue pushes booze into my face. My tongue should be ripped out and eaten as a taco from an East L.A. taco truck.

I read somewhere once a quote by Ernest Hemingway. He said, "A kiss is never a mistake, unless it's with death and the snow is falling too thick at the summit of your dreams."

It took my tongue to realize the summit of my dreams. I think for a moment about my actions and I can see now it isn't Aunika—she's lustful, not loving. No, the summit of my dreams was realized the day I married my wife.

Phoenix wore a dress we had saved months of my wadded-up tip money to purchase. We bought it from a gypsy woman who lived in a trailer overgrown with jasmine vines in a white-sand cove near Malibu and who had designed it herself—white lace with long bell shaped sleeves, the hem short enough to make me crazy as she walked through the piñon and sycamore and oak forest to join with me in eternal love. A wreath of dried purple and yellow flowers saturated her long brunette hair.

We passed a flask between us, along with the rings. We vowed "happiness eternal." We vowed to smile, to always be in the midst of an adventure. It took only two months to realize "happiness eternal" is impossible, but perpetual adventure is not. Since that day, adventures, good and bad, have consumed our life.

We've bled, we've kissed others, we've done drugs, we've kept secrets, we've pretended to sleep instead of having sex, we've moved east and prayed for the west, we've been broken down on Highway 1 in the rain outside Big Sur, we've seen rainbows in Santa Cruz, we've met Bulch, we've written books and eaten candy tampons. We've thrown chairs, glasses, parties, Frisbees in the sand dunes of Oregon, accusations of drunkenness and cruelty, trash into the street. We've had chode rashes, stomachaches, an abortion, depression, anxiety, foie gras for the first time.

We've slept through life, and we've been insomniacs. We've been naked, spiritually and physically, raised our palms up to the sky, prayed for winter to start, prayed for winter to end, prayed for the sake of praying. We've pushed through the gray of the world, the bozos of the world, the drunks of the world, the kooks of the world, the weight of the world, the garbage of the world, the unethical auto mechanics of the world. We've slept together, we've played together, we've smoked together, we've argued with each other, we've argued against others together, we've masturbated together. But perhaps, most importantly, we've made guacamole together.

Together.

This modern world isn't cut out for togetherness. I'm having these thoughts and in the meantime, seven people have arrived at the bar, waiting as a group for my tongue to say something, and for my arms to begin spinning wildly, booze flying through the air like a trapeze act of liquid molecules—pineapples and maraschino cherries, sprigs of mint and tarragon dropping like miniature bombs into colorful drinks with a cute, barely audible splash.

Cherise doesn't speak, focused on doing both of our jobs, understanding of my predicament. I notice now that each time she passes me, she rubs her hand across the small of my back— something my mother may have done at birth or death or somewhere in between—I can't remember anymore. She sucks at a glass of bourbon, swirls it around in her mouth, spits it into a shot glass—"Forty dollars," she says to the young man with purple hair and a Parquet Courts t-shirt. He gives her fifty, sucks the shot into his mouth thinking to himself, "I have her fluid in my gut now and any of her fluid is a fluid I want inside of me."

I wonder how much my spit would be worth right now, sticky with the natural liquid of Aunika—pure and hormonal, laced with only the finest pheromones. I could sell it to the highest bidder, two thousand? Three? We could get back west, riding on Aunika's wave, toes to the nose.

I fucked up. I know I have. Bulch knows it. He's looking at me with a suspicious gaze. I've perhaps fallen short of his expectations of me. Or perhaps I've surpassed them. I can't tell what kind of man Bulch is—The kind of man who has discreet affairs and loves his wife, or the kind of man who hates his wife and has discreet affairs? Or maybe he's the kind of man who believes everything is as easy to decipher as an elephant gun. He's just about done with that Mai-Tai, the pineapple wedge dripping with grenadine and deep black rum hanging halfway out his mouth. "You know, Cassidy, a pickle can't be a pickle without a little vinegar. In the end, it's just as satisfying as a cucumber."

I drop down behind the bar, out of sight. I'm drunk and whatever has just happened or is happening doesn't seem to be happening at all. It could be a dream. If I could convince myself this day is a dream, perhaps my brain would always treat it as such. I could forget about it, put it in the journal on my nightstand, never look back on it. I could say, "It was just a dream."

From underneath the bar where the errant bottle caps live I say, "Not everyone likes a pickle."

"That's the risk you take in life," Bulch responds. "But even I crave a pickle every now and again."

I'm never quite sure what Bulch is talking about. His Rangoonisms come from some other time, where pickles were sold on street corners and kids would tug at the hem of their mother's dress for one.

Down here, hiding from the elbows on the bar, I realize I am the generation of sadness, of miscommunication, of no communication, of instant gratification. I'm the last generation to use a push button phone, to use a "computer lab," to listen to cd's. I'm the last generation and it's all going to end—so whatever actions I do, don't mean a thing in the future. If we're all going to die, there's no need to torture myself. There's no need to dwell on the past, however close the past may be. The past is just that. I am drunk, so I can convince myself of anything. The drunk mind holds a small temperamental switch within it, one that can be flicked up or down, on or off. Up. On.

"Fuck it," I say. "I love Phoenix and I'm a fuck up and I can admit that, but I'm not a bad person. I know what I did was wrong."

I pop back up from underneath the bar, see the faces of fifty beautiful men and women smiling, here to forget life, or remember life, or make mistakes, here to use their tongues to get somewhere else, somewhere far away from where they think they are, or maybe to arrive back where they think they once were.

"Who needs a drink?" I ask the masses with my arms swirling

into the air. Bulch smiles, slides his pipe between his teeth, twists that bubblegum mustache. He's got a good goddamn bartender. "I have a soul!" I announce to everyone. "And sometimes, it fucks up."

Cherise spits the Grizzly Bear into a shot glass and slides it over to me, the thick one ounce cylinder stopping at the back of my hand. I take a look at the glass, roll it through my fingers, admiring the pureed froth of her saliva gathered at the top, the amber glow of the hooch in the tangerine sunset.

"Fucking drink it!" the Parquet Courts boy says, rattling his fingers against the bar in a drum solo lasting far too long.

I hold it up to my lips, throw the spit back into the crevices of my neck, hear the crackling of applause, feel Bulch's hand wrap around mine in a firm Rhodesian handshake, and my phone vibrate in my back pocket. "To the west, towards Phoenix!" I declare. My stomach burns. I reach into my pocket, and then my eyes flitter.

$5000 Blues

It would be borderline retarded to cross the great U S of A in a car without stopping at The Grand Canyon, El Canon Grande, Ongtupqa, Wi:ka'i:la, The Big Hole, Earth's Vagina—and Black Charlie knows this. He's gone out of his way, zig-zagged through the Midwest, spacing-out on the big flat, the lack, the endless sky of twirling air, tornado country, just to get out here where the west was won and the Colorado River was lost.

On the rock, boots dusted with red dirt, Charlie writes in his travel log:

To describe the Grand Canyon to someone who has never been here is nearly pointless. It's so vast, so uncomprehendingly beautiful, with it's pinks and oranges, burnt siennas and sunsets, blues and purples and glittered dust and prisms of antiquity, that it does no justice to see or hear the words. I will forever be small and humble in relation to this world—it is deeper than I can ever go, farther down, farther wide, expanding.

On the hood of his car at the very edge of the canyon, Charlie stares out into the vastness, looking southwest, the river below trailing off…somewhere—east—no, west. He reaches into his back pocket, removes a metal container with exactly two joints. He lights one of the joints, pulls in the smoke, aligns his spine with the axis of the earth, ankles bent at 70°, and exhales. The smoke mixes in with the dense sound of silence. He's got a new pair of black motorcycle boots he picked up in Denver at a thrift store—only fifteen bucks, tough leather, neoprene oil-resistant soles. He wears a new pair of tight black polyester Levi's he picked up at a thrift store in Santa Fe—a perfect crease down each leg. He smacks the dust off his knees with his new black Stetson hat—wide brimmed with a brown leather strap on top and a bright red cardinal feather stuck between. On his back, a faded black Wrangler western he nabbed in a discount bin outside a Goodwill in Pueblo—pearl buttons, beige tooling around the chest pockets.

Charlie isn't aware of how the colors of his apparel transformed from the Lion of Judah into the blackness of now—but I can tell you how it happened, why the Rasta became the outlaw.

After Charlie bailed out of Warren, OH, he purchased gasoline at a truck stop in Great Bend and ran into a young blonde girl, topless, cruising down the sidewalk in the sunshine with a bucket around her wrist. "Goo balls," she said in her dusty voice.

Not one to shy away from the great stone, Charlie approached the young blonde, slipped her a five dollar bill, held out his palm and received a kiss directly on his fate line.

"No gooball?" he said.

"Just your future," she replied.

"What's my future?"

"A kiss of fate. It's already happened."

She moved down the sidewalk for only a few more steps before being stopped by The Man, and led into the backseat of a squad car, her bucket of strange granola left behind on the small patch of dead roadside grass.

Charlie got his hands on that bucket, dropped it into the passenger seat, strapped it in with a seatbelt, and used his tongue to continually ingest the cannabis soaked edibles for seventeen hours straight until the Great American Night out his windshield became the Great Savage Angel, soaring and booming in with the big ionic bolt.

Now, The Great Savage Angel is no ordinary angel. It doesn't wear a white gown, it isn't accompanied by harp or harpsichord or tripsichord, nor does it have wings. No, this angel more closely resembles Waylon Jennings in a strung-out honky-tonk blur, brewed in whiskey, stinking of cheap midnight perfume and Tijuana crotch sweat, a strong, well groomed beard wrapped around a prominent jawbone. A furrowed and shadowed brow draws the eyes directly into the greased-up hairdo, swimming in the sea of slick black pomade. A cigarette dangles from chapped lips, and this voice, good Lord, makes the earth rattle, an earthquake with every breath, charged with the energy of the core, spitting everywhere.

The Great Savage Angel opened his mouth and said with a big deep rumble, "Black Charlie, you ain't a rainbow." And then... Boom!—A flash of purple light twisting time and space into the epic nothing, a tuft of smoke soft and feathered like a duck's ass, all that remained. The Great Savage Angel floated off into the night, howling like a wolf on a bullet to the moon. That's all Charlie remembers before he passed out. When he woke up, he was parked on the side of the road in the twilight of morning, naked, with the tail of a scorpion scratching at his window, crackling with electric light like a live wire.

Sometimes it doesn't take much for someone to change. Sometimes it takes only a couple pounds of hash-soaked gooballs and a visit from The Great Savage Angel, waking up naked on the side of a highway with an electric scorpion in your eyeball to get the mondo-metamorphosis in full swing. Rainbow—indeed Charlie is not. This life he brought upon himself is a far cry from the calculated earthly beauty of a multi-colored spectrum and more closely synched to the deep black emptiness of the far-off corners of the galaxy. If his life were to be presented as a tangible physical object, it would more closely resemble a black hole than a rainbow. The grime of city life, the weight of child support, a son who barely knows or cares for him, rampant unemployment, both silent and overt racism, income taxes, sales taxes, BPA laced water bottles, gargantuan holes in the ozone, trash fucking everywhere, rent rent rent going up up up, car payments on cars not worth a dime or a damn—the list goes on and on. Blackness. That is what Charlie is, has been, and always will be. It is what he is surrounded by.

There's something liberating about dressing all in black, sitting there on the edge of the Earth's vag, a few feet from the big deep plunge. There is a sense of permanence with black. Black is a color you can never cover up—it will always bleed through. Out here, under the sun, Charlie uses the faded black kerchief tied around his neck to wipe a bead of sweat stuck between the peaks of his upper lip. His lungs expand, contract—he is aware. Above, an eagle rides the dense wind, speaks to him with a needled squawk—"You are the river, dammed." When the great stone kicks in, blood rolling in reverse, and the nerves begin to twist, unraveling into the unknown, he pulls the black hacky-sack he purchased at a head shop in Durango, and tosses it up into the air, letting it fall to his chest, down to his hips, pop it out and up, grab with the ankle, back up into the air, to the forehead, shoulder, to the air, to the toes of his boots, let it all rest. Take a deep breath.

There's not much to do at the Grand Canyon, alone and stoned in the western sky. Hiking sounds like a drag in this heat and in these boots—plus both his socks have holes in the heel. A river-rafting excursion is too goddamn expensive and even if he could afford it he'd be stuck in the hole with several random stooges who may not know shit from Shinola—they could even be Republicans against campaign reform and a woman's right to choose—what's worse than that? Nothing—maybe unjust war or Texans not from Austin who aren't named Waylon or Willie or Hank. No, the only thing left to do here in Arizona is stare, let the silence take over, calm the nerves, slow time down enough to a point where you can actually see it passing, hear the ticking, feel the earth spin. Another toke from the joint, it doesn't matter how much time passes any longer—After the seventeen-hour gooball-binge, Charlie knows he can make it through anything, sleep anywhere, survive, wake up the next day and start over, press his foot down on the gas pedal. This entire journey is a fresh start. East to West—Manifest Destiny. Destiny will be manifested.

Human interaction is overrated, Charlie writes in his journal, dropping a heel to the steel bumper. He's having what he once considered irrational thoughts, wondering about the solitary man, the shapes earth objects take in the mind, the vice grip modernity has strangled his neurons with—televisions and plastics and pop music. But, fuck all that noise. That vice grip is loosening. Out here, only the sky holds you captive.

Have you ever thrown a party for yourself and been the only one to attend it? No. Neither has Charlie—his neighbors would have had him committed, his son never allowed to see him again, the vice grip contracting, cracked cement asylum walls and light green painted shower stalls and men jerking off with apple sauce dripping down their chins. So, out here, in the desert, a party will be thrown, alone, away from all the kooks and pennyfuckers, dickgrabbers and muffinsuckers. All Charlie needs is the six pack of hot beer from the trunk, a little electric guitar music, and the remnants of this joint to cut loose, carve his existence into the big universe like a bumblebee buzzing a figure-8 in midair.

He slides his torso through the window of his car, jams the keys into the ignition, turns the electric on, twists the radio dial until the electric guitar twang snaps through the canyon, reverberating like broken teeth. He pulls himself out of the car and digs his boot heels into the dirt, twisting his hips, shaking in the sun. He pops open his shirt, lets the heat lick his skin. He throws his neck side to side, shoves fists into the air, uses his lighter to pop the top off his boiling brew without missing a beat, lets the foam spill down his body, to the ground, stomping the froth into a fine mud.

This dance continues until the orange and the purple become the deep blue of an AZ night, until the joint is but a scrap of charred leaf burning into his fingertip. "Ouch," he says, then sticks his finger in his mouth, soothes the reddened tip. He pulls his finger out of his mouth and puts his hands into his pockets, his nails scraping against the scraps of paper left behind from 7-Eleven's across America. He pulls them out, inspecting them, taking care not to drop a single one, not to litter the great hole, not to spread the trash into the earth's vag.

A particularly great note to himself: *Don't tuck your dick between your legs in a nickel mine.*

He can't remember why he wrote that down on the back of a lottery scratcher, but nonetheless, there it is—words without meaning, existing regardless. That scratcher. Huh. Strange. He forgot all about it—Sevens and elevens back in Ohio. This scratcher is neat looking—pink and purple glittered paper, nine whiskey bottles in the center and a rifle on the left with six bullets. "Showdown," it's called, the letters written in the scrawl of a Tombstone saloon. "Shoot a bottle, win the prize."

He jams his hands into his pockets, searching for a coin, finds a dirty penny, Lincoln's face nearly worn completely from the metal. He scratches at the first bottle—"Miss." The second and third— "Miss Miss." Four and five and six. "Miss Miss Miss." Seven. "Hit." He holds the penny in his hand, sucking in the Great West, listening to the cricket legs scratching, his own scratching, the prize revealed underneath the edge of his penny—*$5000.*

"Holy shit."

A siren squawks in the distance, growing closer. A flash of red and blue light. A great mechanical voice sucked through the battery void. Charlie looks back into a floodlight, sees the cop car, waves his hands in the air. The black boots of The Man crush the dirt below, an ominous grind, an echo of power. One man smiles. The other frowns.

Fade to black.

80,000 Word Blues

I am so tired, so hungover, so full of shit. My bones ache. There's nothing to see out this window. These periods are following me everywhere. . .

. .

. .

. .

.

Cliff is Dead Blues

Text messages are hard to comprehend, seventy percent of the time. I've received text messages that read, *Holy shit, it finally happened,* and for that minute between my response of *What happened?* and the response to my response, the mind races. *Holy shit it finally happened,* can mean just about anything. It could mean, "Dude, I finally had that threesome!" or it could mean, "Dude, I finally had that threesome with my girlfriend and your wife!" Different meanings, altogether.

I've learned over time never to get too excited about a text message. *I'm dying,* never actually means *I'm dying.* And so, texts that read *Cliff is dead,* never actually mean *Cliff is dead.* As a matter of fact, whenever I receive a text from 2/3rds of the Mustard Brothers, I'm almost 100 percent sure it's the opposite meaning of whatever it is. I admit, staring at the words *Cliff is dead,* startles me for a moment. My eyes sort of open up and my breath sucks back down my throat before it can leave. But, shit, come on, it's Cliff and Charlie. They'll never die. Built to last. Those two boys can survive a car wreck with a semi-truck full of axes and a trunk full of fireworks. I take a moment to scroll through the other recent text messages sent from Cliff and/or Charlie.

The donkey mule rode the goat dick up the giraffes neck. Untrue.

I made cocaine popsicles to stick up Cliff's ass when he falls asleep tonight. Untrue.

WHISKEY JELLY BLUES

There's a bus bench with your face on it in Echo Park and I saw Sasha Grey squatting on it and taking a shit! Untrue

Did you know tonight is a blood moon? Untrue—Charlie was two days late on that.

I crossed the arrow with a moonbeam and sucked from the goddesses tits—oh and I got a bag of coke from a transvestite prostitute in exchange for a two second handjob. Hard to tell, but I'd still say Untrue.

I stare at that text message, stuck behind the bar, knowing I have to respond regardless of how ridiculous and false I believe it is. Whatever's happening with Cliff right now is bound to be awesome. *Cliff is dead.* He's probably just hungover, or his eyes have rolled back into his head again—exhaustion, booze, heat. It happens twice a year, by my estimation.

I respond with *What he do this time?*

I mix three drinks—

Yellow Sea Snake

¾ oz Yellow Chartreuse

2 oz Amazon Woman Double Vanilla Bean Bourbon

½ oz pineapple juice

½ oz house made Orange Peel Vodka

Cuba Libre, Bulch Style

2oz gold rum

1 oz house infused chocolate rum

Fill glass with cola

pineapple wedge, dipped in red grenadine

L.A. Margarita

2 oz blanco tequila

1 oz fresh lime and lemon juice

Justin J. Murphy

1 oz Triple Sec

½ oz simple syrup

mescal rinse

smoked salt rim

lime wedge

orange peel

I hand the three drinks to three different people. One of them wears an old cowboy hat, greasy locks, a shit-eating grin. He's twenty -five or so and says "Thank you, pardner," hands me a two dollar tip, clicks his spurs together and swings back into the action with an elbow out and a hip flying.

Another is a young woman who doesn't speak at all after ordering. Instead, she just smiles and sheepishly hands me a ten-dollar bill and walks away sucking on the straw down inside her Yellow Sea Snake. She has a cute butt in a pair of jeans that look like they've been yanked out of the trash.

The third is covered in tattoos—one above his eyebrow says "Pray for me." I won't pray for him because as far as I can tell, he's doin' all right. I probably should be praying for Cliff, but, as I said before, I'm nearly positive nothing is happening to him. He's probably rubbing his belly in the sun and stroking the hooch down from his moist beard into his mouth. He's probably smashing a cheap can of Mexican brew into his teeth and laughing. I remember that time down in La Fonda, Baja, just the three of us, on a surf trip. We headed south with our palms dangling out the window of my old VW Vanagon, the one I thought I would someday live in parked somewhere near a banana plant in Big Sur, way back before I met Phoenix and got married and moved east and stuck my tongue into Aunika. We ate fish tacos from a ramshackle shack on the side of the road on a cliff staring straight down into the edge of The West. Cliff ordered his tacos with "no cebollas"—he's positive to this day onions make him sick—maybe he accidentally ate a fucking onion and that's why he's dead? Yeah right. We kept going south with a bottle of tequila in each of our laps, paying off the federales to let us keep the trip going, until we hit La Fonda, squatted up in an abandoned gringo resort, let our feet dangle off the unfinished concrete, ran our hands against the rebar, staring at the sea with our arms and sweat. We ate fish ripped straight out from the sea and drank golden tequila out of used honey jars for days, praying to the sunset each night with a fat joint and a naked dip in the Pacific. We said, "Fuck it, lets just stay here forever," and we tried, but a week later we all wondered about never having sex again, packed up the VW, and headed back up to L.A. When we crossed the border, Cliff placed his hand on my knee and said, "I love you, brother." And entering back into the U.S. with these two outlaws made me feel alive, connected. We could go anywhere and do anything together, as long as we are together. We're not together anymore and maybe I have myself to blame for that. Maybe marriage and moving east is never a good idea, or maybe being unnaturally attached to another man is never a good idea, and maybe making decisions based on the wants and needs of others is never a good idea. Maybe we should all be doing exactly what we want to be doing, without regret, self-centered and unfettered. Or maybe love is transformative, can change shape, can travel back and forth across the country, can survive through an abortion, through childhood memories, through tongues, through beer, through whiskey jelly donuts, through death.

My phone buzzes again, but I'm in the middle of pouring a beer, so I can't quite reach it although I attempt to, using one hand to simultaneously hold the glass in midair and pull at the tap.

"Five dollars," I say to a guy who looks like a young Elvis, with quaffed hair and perfect pyramid sideburns. I dig his Misfits patch on the back of his black leather jacket.

I grab my phone from my back pocket. I don't like the tone of this new text. It says, definitively, without a grain of humor, with only pure, serious intention—*Call me.*

I motion over to Cherise, leaning over the bar dropping her whiskey soaked saliva into a shot glass and grabbing her forty dollars loot with a five dollar tip. She turns, as if in slow-motion, the rouge of her lipstick streaking across my vision, smiling in the dim yellow of the room. My heart moves from the center of my chest, upwards, choking me. What if Cliff is dead?

Bulch sits in a golden velour loveseat in the corner of the room, his dusty brown boots crossed over one another on the matching ottoman. His eyes are closed, taking in the music, the sounds of which I can't hear. Shit, dude, I can't hear. The only sound I hear is Cliff's voice raging through my ears, repeating over and over again in a hot breath, "Not in my pussy, not in my pussy, not in my pussy" which has absolutely no meaning to me whatsoever. If not in his pussy, then in whose pussy? Why am I hearing his voice? What's all this pussy business?

"Cherise," I say. She turns to me. Her smile turns from upward and pouty, to downward and deathly. It's the expression on my face that creates the rather stark metamorphosis of her physiognomy. It feels as if the blood has left my cheeks, only cold bones remain where warmth once was. My eyes feel heavy and my chest feels as if it were made of mud and a Sherman tank is parked on top of it. I think of my high blood pressure, how I should have taken those pills, Lisinopril, or at the very least, should have taken that aspirin today, or at the very very least, had come to work today with a pair of aspirin in my pocket just in case the heart attack happens.

I can have a heart attack, I know I can. You're never too young to have one. The nurse at the clinic when I was testing for genital warts told me so. She said, "I've seen men younger than you with your same high blood pressure die from heart attacks, have strokes and never be able to use the left side of their body again. And sex is hard—you have to almost train yourself to do it again. You should get checked out immediately." And I never did, because alcohol thins the blood and you can pump thin blood through anything, including motorcycle engines and the heaviest of all hearts.

I'm flexing my vocal chords into what should be the word "Cherise" coming out of my lips, but I can't hear it. I repeat her name, yelling it, tongue scratching at it, stretching my throat out as if it were dangling from a noose, watching as she moves towards me—still nothing. Her face continues to swirl, the redness of her lips like the pattern of a peppermint, until, holy shit, only the dim yellow light is reflected upon my vision, the eerie yellow sea snake taking hold of my mind, wrapped tight around, squeezing. My knees buckle, and I feel only for a fraction of a moment, the pain of the concrete below me against my eyebrow.

Rebel Yell Blues

She doesn't know her husband is unconscious on the concrete in a puddle of spilled beer behind the bar. She doesn't know her husband's best friend is dead in a sweat and blood-filled bed in a Los Angeles hospital. All Phoenix knows right now is the bottle of Rebel Yell in her hand. She understands her husband a bit more with each pull she takes from that bottle—it all makes sense now—this bottle erases bad memories as it loses volume. It's a mathematical equation. Rebel Yell+bad memories=nothing to remember. Shit, it works with good memories as well. Rebel Yell+good times=nothing to remember. Rebel Yell is like the space-time-continuum—it can be folded upon itself, time insignificant.

Rebel Yell can make you feel like a god. Rebel Yell can make the lion caged inside your chest lash out, break the chains, suck the marrow out of life. She removes her top and moves back in front of the mirror. Rebel Yell can make your body look magnificent. Those lines once so vibrant and self-criticized around her hips are now just hazy soft curves, delightful, like two scoops of vanilla ice cream in a humid bayou thunderstorm. Her breasts look the same as they did a decade ago, maybe a little smaller, which seems strange to her—one pound gained per year—they should be bigger. She runs a finger up and down her body, tickling herself to the point of a smile. But then, like a fistfight between six dickheads at a beach party, the full-on bummer hits—she sees the two lines of crows-feet underneath her right eye. Crows-feet didn't exist in California. She wonders if the stress and the gray and the cubicle and the artificial light and the endless winter have taken everything desirable away from her. She's sure it does. She can't write these press releases any longer. She can't stare at the computer like a zombie stooge, a lifeless kook, a boring wife with nothing to talk about aside from candy tampons and ironic sweaters. She can't stay indoors, she can't watch the rain fall from behind a window and wear thick jackets for months on end. She can't not see the sun and the moon, she can't be away from, shit, everything. It's all there, back home. The coastline, the sweet California coastline where the world just ends and the ocean sucks it all up, spits it back with each wave, sprays it onto your lips and sun-kissed cheeks, peach and purple salt under your tongue. What the fuck is she doing here?

Fuck everything and fuck it all. She spins herself out of the bedroom and into the living room, drops the needle on the record with a scratchy thud—Gun Club. She never liked Jeffrey Lee Pierce's voice—until now. Now, the Rebel Yell is kicking in and Jeffrey's voice is a rebel yell, shrieking like lightning if lightning had a voice. She can't believe what this whiskey can do to a day, to a psyche, to a body. It's a wonder drug. More and more, drinking and drunk, the stomachache disappearing, her eyes flittering, the pain of the booze burning down the throat locking up her subconscious, sending her into a trance. She takes off her pants, her underwear. She stands naked and lets the electric buzz roll up her bones, lift her off the ground, levitating up towards the skylight.

And were you ever thinking/ When she came home from work at night
And you kicked her into a coma/ While she was still alive

She drops back to the ground, her toes crammed into the planks below. She claws at her hair, shakes her neck side to side as if trying to rip herself from the jaws of an alligator, feels her breasts bouncing up and down, pounding against her rib cage, the fat of her buttocks slamming into one another.

She screams. She falls to her knees. She pounds her fists into the hardwood. She crawls to the record player with a spider-web of spit dangling from the side of her mouth and turns up the volume. She pushes her forehead to the wall and raises the bottle back up to her face, lets a little spill down her chin, between her breasts, collect inside her bellybutton where she takes a finger and drops it down into the hole, the hooch popping up and out, spraying like Old Faithful.

"I want guacamole," she says. But the avocados are gone and so is her husband. This is loneliness, battling the trash that keeps coming back, a can barrel that never gets picked up, a bottle never recycled, a toilet overflowing. The stomachache starts at her left ankle. She stares at her leg, terrified as if a tarantula vampire were crawling up it, feeling the sharp pain move slowly up her body, unlock her kneecap, slide under, pry through her pelvis, wedge itself into her gut—explode out like a switchblade through her. "Fuuuucccckkkkkk!" she yells.

She falls down to the floor, wrestling with herself in an unwinnable match. She takes three quick deep breaths, pulls the bottle back up to her chin. "I will win," she says. "I will win, I will beat this." More whiskey, more fists to the floor. It passes. She turns up the song. She says, "I don't want to do this anymore. I don't want to work in a cubicle. I want to write. I want to do something good for people. I need to make money and make people happy and I need to be myself again and I want it all." She rubs out the remainder of pain in her gut, presses her hands to her head, her palms sticky with sweat.

Her cell phone rings, but it's too damn far away to get to right now. Not right now. She could give two shits about whoever is calling. It rings and rings, and then it stops.

More volume, more volume. She doubles the volume of the record and the volume of alcohol in her blood. She wants to wake up and see nothing, hear nothing. She wants nothing, because nothing is the result of what she's doing. She slumps down onto her side, the faintness of that cell phone ring pinging through her eardrums as she closes her eyes, becomes nothing.

Arizona Blues

Everyone seems to be losing consciousness, but not Black Charlie, although, shit, he wishes he were sunk down in the big black right about now, that this heaping wad of bullshit was just a bad dream, just an hyper-inventive backdrop to the subconscious. But, shit, man, he shouldn't have left that drug bucket in his car, stewing and melting in the desert heat, reeking of cannabinoid stink. Hashish isn't looked upon too highly out in this part of the West, and most likely the oily substance they'll find wrapped around those gooballs will be just that—the sweet Moroccan stone. Marijuana possession, well, that's a felony too. And glass pipes?—well just sing your blues away, my boy, cuz you're gonna have to go inside for that as well. Shit, everything in Arizona is a goddamn felony—just like that movie, was it *Tombstone* or no, wait, older than that? Yeah, *Unforgiven*, that's it.

Charlie's like Morgan Freeman in *Unforgiven*, and not just because he's black—it's because he's sure they're gonna string him up, post-up his dead body inside the coffin at the city limits as a warning to those entering—"This is what happens when you trip out on the Grand Canyon, bozo." Wait. No. *Unforgiven* takes place in Wyoming. Thank God he's not in Wyoming. Maybe Arizona isn't so bad— maybe he'll live, get let off with a warning, The Man forcing him to throw his drugs and glass pipe down into the canyon, carried down the mighty Colorado to Lake Havasu where they'll find happy homes in the mouths, lips, and lungs of drunken college co-eds. "Shit," he thinks to himself, "I win five g's and I'll probably have to use it all on bail." Maybe everything happens for a reason. Maybe those five g's are for this moment, to keep him free, to pay the fine of being free, to keep freedom moving west. He tries to get into his back pocket, to make sure his lottery scratcher is safe, but he can't reach it. God damn handcuffs make shit hard to do with your hands—ahh, yes—this is why they were invented. They aren't just the novelty he used on that gnarly night eight years ago when his son was conceived and his ex-girlfriend's lips quivered with each plun...shit, there I go again.

Charlie stares into the front seat of the squad car, the computer screen displaying his name and age, a picture of his identification card from back east, his face—man, he looked younger three years ago.

Charles Kingsley
Hair: Black
Eyes: Black
Height: 6'3"
Weight: 185
Age: 711

Seven hundred eleven? What the hell? It's happening again. Is it the gooballs? Is this whole thing a hallucination? Has he even gone west yet? Is California just an acid trip and perhaps doesn't exist, like it's the end of the world and you just fall off when you get there and you land in the middle of some nightmare daydream, twirling around in the tumble-dry of psychedelic existence for eternity? He sees the shotgun, the radio, a cup of coffee stuck precariously between the steering wheel and dashboard, a picture of a brunette woman, aged mid thirties, the photograph from the early 1980's perhaps, creased around the edges, smeared with finger grease as if caressed for centuries. His hands throb behind him, but it's not so much the wrists that sting with the metallic burn of the tightened cuffs—no, actually the sting is in his shoulder blades. No one ever talks about how bad handcuffs can put the bull on your shoulders, stretching those muscles backwards with your wrists outfacing like dislocated duck feet, forcing your spine upwards unnaturally in an effort to keep from leaning back onto your hands. And then Charlie's lower back begins to tighten up from leaning forward off his wrists—he's got lumbar problems from years sitting in the plastic cubicle suck-throne as an insurance stooge. Damn, there's nothing left to do but lean back to provide relief to that bruised lumbar, so he shifts his weight down onto his palms, but then, just as soon as he presses the weight of his body against the seat, the blood stops flowing to his hands, sending a rushing tingle through his arms, his skin losing color underneath the metal. So up he must go, until his forehead is jammed against the little metal fence separating the criminal from the cop.

"Handcuffs are medieval."

"Keep it quiet," the cop says to him.

Charlie can't believe the goon can hear a word he's saying. All the radio static of fellow goons yelling street numbers and suspect descriptions seems to be taking up what was only a few minutes ago the sound of pure, distilled, natural silence.

He thinks, "There can be no peace in this world. Even when you're in the midst of it, there'll always be someone or something to ruin it."

"Hey man," Charlie says, "I have something important in my pocket. I just want to make sure it's still there."

"There's nothing in your pockets. It's all out there on the hood." His goon finger outstretches through the windshield towards a small pile of confiscated possessions.

Charlie pulls his head back, inspects the hood, sees his wallet, his keys, his sunglasses, a couple gas station receipts—but no lottery scratcher. "Say brother, I don't see it out there. Are you sure? Can you just check my back pocket and make sure it's not in there."

"Listen buddy, you can sort that out when you get processed."

"Processed? Like a chicken?"

"What's in the bucket in the front seat?"

"Granola." Charlie strains his fingers, pushing them out as far from his knuckles as they can reach, feeling the joints crack and scrape against his skin, struggling to get into his back pocket.

"Doesn't smell like granola."

His fingertips brush against the outer edge of his pocket, dip inside, cool. "I picked up a hitchhiker this morning. She had the bucket with her and left it in the car." Shoulders contort, an elongated crackle of tendons ripple downward like a twig across a xylophone through his body.

"Jesus Christ. It's always the same," the copper says out loud to himself. "Let me explain something to you." He pushes his eyes into the rearview mirror, his glare jabbing Charlie right between the pupils. "Lying to me is only gonna make it harder on yourself. You can tell me exactly what's in the bucket, or I can take it in and have it tested in the lab and waste all the taxpayer money and fuck around. But let me tell you something—There's no way out of this. The quicker we get you processed, the quicker we can get you to trial, and the quicker we can get you sentenced, and the quicker you can get out. Time is not your friend right now. You're going to want the seconds to pass as fast as possible. "

"I honestly don't know what's in the bucket." Charlie's index finger brushes the edge of the winning scratcher. Thank god. It's still there. He presses down against it, wedging the ticket between a fingernail and his ass. But the springs in the backseat squeak with each sudden movement under his body.

"What you doing back there?" The fuzz turns around, gives him a once over. "You feel like doing two years for possession and distribution? Because I can check a box and make it happen for you."

Charlie looks at him with those eyes, deep dead black, sending out the darkest of vibes, praying for a meteorite to fall from the sky right through the windshield, strike the pig's face with a lethal blow, ricochet off his skull, cut right through the handcuffs, set him free. He looks up to the heavens—no meteors, no savage angels. Two years for gooballs sounds a bit extreme and impossible to endure. This is the bad time—the time where the great stone wears off and reality starts to take bites out of his soul until all that's left is a stomach full of butterflies. A wind of panic blows through his arms, sending a numbing sensation right down to the bone, so cold he can't even tell if his limbs are still attached. His mouth, teeth—they move. "Of course I don't want to do two years. Holy shit, man, no way. Is that for real?"

"You've got a bag of marijuana and a pipe, and whatever's in the front seat of that car, which I'm assuming is made of some type of narcotic substance you intended to distribute."

"I'm not distributing. I'm not anything. I don't understand. I'm a good guy with a kid and I just wanted to get out of town and check out the canyon. What the hell, I, uh, shit, man. What's gonna happen to me?"

"Not sure."

"I can't go in, brother. I'm going west. I'm not doing anything bad. I'm not dealing, I'm not hurting anyone. I just wanted to check out the Canyon."

"Well, that may be. But I'm not the judge and jury. I'm the

enforcement of the law. If you cooperate, I can let the judge know you were cooperative. He might be a bit more lenient when it comes to sentencing."

"I don't want to go in. I can't go in."

"Listen, listen, listen. You need to get that out of your head. You're going in no matter what. How long you're in is entirely up to you. Now, what's the substance in the front seat of that car?"

"I don't know. I can't go in, man." Charlie pushes his fingers back down his back pocket, securing the ticket, the backseat creaking with each subtle movement.

The front door opens, the cop exits, the back door opens, the cop enters and slides his large frame into Charlie. He places his hand gingerly above Charlie's hips, around that strained lumbar, moves his fingers down like a lover in a rose covered bathtub, down down down and into his back pocket, pulling out the lottery ticket. He takes a quick glance —"Is this what you're so worried about?"

Charlie's heart rate climbs, rapidly moving up up up, through the roof, out into the sky, through the atmosphere and out into space, orbiting Mars at light-speed. His eyes twitch, breathing becomes heavy. He wrestles for a moment with the cuffs, stops when he realizes the futility of his actions.

"This seems like a pretty important little piece of paper."

"I'll trade you," Charlie says.

The cop takes a look at the ticket, still unable to comprehend its worth. "Trade me what for what?"

"That ticket's a winner. Five thousand bucks. You keep the ticket, and I'll dump all the pot and the bucket into the trash. I'll get rid of it, I'll get out of Arizona, I'll never come back. I'll say a million prayers for you. I'll write you letters for the rest of your life. I'll tell the world about peace. I'll help feed starving children in Kenya. I'll volunteer here, in Arizona, if you want me to."

The cop just smiles, lets those teeth shine, glimmer in the peach-skin light.

Most cops are honest cops who believe in their job and some of them even care about people. Most cops would never think twice about a bribe, might actually get offended by it. This might be one of those cops. Charlie's tactic seems a bit risky to him now. Now, it seems trading his ticket for freedom is a terrible idea. It seems as if by asking the cop to look the other way in exchange for money, he might be getting himself into more trouble. It seems as if this is yet another wrong choice in a life riddled with wrong choices, perhaps the worst choice altogether. Worse than not wearing a condom, handcuffing and knocking up his ex-girlfriend, marrying her and then divorcing her with only a note that read "I can't do it anymore" left on the nightstand on his way out of town. Charlie realizes this ill-thought-out choice almost immediately after the words escape his mouth. He presses his forehead back into the window. "Shit," he says under his breath.

"A bribe?" the cop questions. He takes a look at the lottery ticket, shakes his head. "Bribes don't work with me, or any other officer of the law. What do you think it is we do out here? We keep punk asses like you from spreading drugs across the country, from destroying the minds of my children, turning them into junkies, prostitutes, thieves. See, you don't get it. Drugs aren't something we can just look away from. They're here, and they're dangerous and they kill people." He takes a long pause, draws a deep breath, and pulls a key from his belt, unlocks the handcuffs. "Gooballs?" he asks.

"What?"

"The bucket in the front seat. Gooballs?"

"I'm honestly not sure what it is. Just some sticky stuff that tastes good, like chocolate and honey."

"Shit man, either you're green, or you're a liar. I used to love gooballs." The cop leans his head back, exhales through his teeth. "See, I used to be a pretty cool guy, I think. Don't know how I wound up here, out on the edge." He uses his finger to point out the window again. "I'm from Delaware," he says, then takes his finger and points in the other direction. "My mom passed when I was eleven. I started doing strange things like kicking the neighbor's cat in the ribs and wearing topsiders without socks. It's weird. The last thing I remember about my mom is that she killed my teddy-bear, Oliver. She stuck a knife through him, then pulled it out, covered in ketchup."

Charlie takes his hands out of the cuffs, leans back, rests his head. "I don't know where I'm from anymore."

"Five thousand bucks is a decent chunk of change," the cop says. He wraps his arm around Charlie's shoulder and pulls him in. "I used to be a pretty cool guy. Still not so cool with drugs though, not with drug dealers. I get it and I don't at the same time. We all need release." He opens up the back door, steps outside, kicks around at the dirt, looks out across the canyon into nothing, the black. "Come on out," he tells Charlie.

Charlie stands, moves like a tomcat hunting a parakeet towards the cop. "What's goin on?"

The cop unfastens the hinge around his pistol, a click-clack of the button, a squeak of the shiny black leather holster. Charlie takes a step back, processing the situation—he's going to get shot. Escape plan. He needs an escape plan. He could run, but he can't outrun the bullet and a cop car. He could make a beeline for his own car, grab his keys off the hood along the way, dodge the bullet, run the cop over, pop the lungs right out of the goon's body, never look back. Or shit, he could just run and jump off the edge, fall down into the great vag, die by his own hands, a rebel Rasta martyr.

The cop grips the handle of his piece. "You see, out here, things are a bit backwards."

Charlie takes a step forward, back to where he was only a second ago. He'll go for the car. It's his only chance to live. Everyone will understand him when he tells the story—he was just smoking a little dope at the canyon's edge and then this crooked cop tried to kill him and make it look like he was trying to flee. Shit. He's fucked. No one will believe that. He's black and on drugs in Arizona. Mexico isn't far. He can cash the scratcher at a gas station on his way out of town, head it down to Sonora, make it through the border before they've got a suspect.

The cop removes the gun, holds it at the end of his hand, thick index finger massaging nervous oils into the metal of the trigger.

Charlie's brain tells him to run, but his body can't make a move, his bones stuck between gears, jammed. He's lost in the desert in the midst of pure fear, frozen like a statue, the purple dust swirling around him. Killing a cop, running to Mexico, living his life in the shadows—that's not what he wants. No, now is a time for prayer. He closes his eyes, raises his palms up. "Please God, get me out of this." He hears the sound of footsteps, heels digging into the dirt, movement. His lips twitch, silent, putting together the words "Hail Mary, full of grace…" And then, the sound of air, silence, pure, perfect and crystalline, eyelids flitter, and hands fall. "The Lord is with thee…" He hits the ground, eyes still closed.

Captain California Blues

My eyes pop open, one at a time, first the left then the right. It takes a second for me to realize what I am—human. My body comes back to life as if it were a rebooted computer, each part flickering on with flashes of neon green, one at a time. Eyes, then hands, knees, feet, heart, then the pain in my eyebrow. Fuck, it hurts up there. Pressure chokes my ears into silence. A muffled hum. My ears reopen. My sense of hearing pierces my skull—the sound of scratchy voices, Bulch standing over me, pressing a blood-soaked bar towel into my face.

"Can you hear me?" he says. "Are you there, can you hear me?" His voice sounds rushed, startled. Over his shoulder, Cherise is on her cell phone, staring at me, her eyes crushed underneath the weight of worry. She says into the phone, "He's awake now, his eyes are moving." She says, "Hold on a sec, let me check." She grabs Bulch's arm and asks him, "Is he breathing regularly?"

Bulch puts his hand up to my mouth, feels the air escaping my lungs across the hair on his knuckles. "Yes," he says. "He's got the wind." He winks and raises his glass to me, taking a pull, sucking the grenadine from his Hawaiian pineapple wedge, licking his wet lips. "I think he might have had a touch of the old barroom fever." He says these words, but I don't hear them. My hearing goes in and out, jumbled electric notes crashing against each other. I hear only white noise, the sound of a television station with no response, the sound of crumpling paper if paper were made of thunder. Just below the static, a ringing rattles my eardrums, and just below the ringing in my eardrums, the buzz of electricity, like a guitar amplifier that's just been switched on and Keith Richards is all geeked-up on a mad heroin craze adjusting the knobs in a Mediterranean chateau in 1972 while watching German porn.

Bulch pulls the towel from my face, dunks it into the sanitizer rinse in the sink, wrings it out, and pushes it back into my eyebrow. I look down at my arms—covered in blood, the hairs peaking up through the red mess. I feel a bit queasy. I haven't seen this much blood since the abortion. I think about that terrible afternoon, the suspense brewing between my wife and I after she swallowed the second termination pill. We waited, lying together on the bed, watching television, as if we had just eaten acid, waiting for it to kick in, wondering what would happen, where we would go, what the future would look like afterwards. And then, she was doubled over in pain, crying, and as I carried her to the bathroom to put her in the tub to ease the contractions, the blood poured out of her, all over my hands, a hot ooze, dripping down her and onto me, onto the floor, into the carpet, across the tiles, into the water, down the drain, onto the toilet seat, down the pipes, into the ocean, the Pacific, the end, nowhere else to go.

I don't want to get up, and even if I wanted to, it seems impossible. My body feels as if it's been outlined in cement. I wonder about what's happening to me. I wonder how I got down here, under the bar. Why am I lying here? Why am I bleeding? Why is Bulch so concerned?

My memory is hazy. I know only one thing right now—I want my wife. I want her to bleed in my arms. I want to hold her and I want to be held. I want to feel her little belly against mine in bed after the toilet has been flushed. I want to feel her weight, the weight she's carried with her since that day, that bathroom, that pill. I want to feel that weight in my chest, to take the weight off her, and place it directly on myself, and I want to tell her about this weight—I want her to know I know about that weight. I want her to know that just because I never talk about the abortion, I carry it with me all the same. I saw that little bubble of skin and bones, I saw it swirl down, I saw it carried away. I saw her on the bathroom floor, scared, wondering if something had gone wrong, wondering why so much blood came out of her and hoping she had enough blood still within her to stay alive herself. I want to tell her how sorry I am for being a bartender and a Choose Your Own Adventure erotica author. I want to apologize for not being a lawyer, or a doctor, or a certified public accountant with good table manners—if I had been one of those things, maybe we would have kept that child, maybe he'd be about a year old right now, maybe we'd be happy, maybe we wouldn't. Maybe we would have made a mistake. Maybe maybe maybe everything.

"Hey Captain California , can you hear me?" Bulch says, one more time.

I nod my head. "Yeah, I read you, Rangoon." I reach up to his mustache, twirl the edges of his hairs between my fingers. "She had an abortion," I say, "And it was my fault."

Bulch doesn't know what I'm talking about. He says over his shoulder to Cherise, "I think his head's a bit out of sorts. We'd better keep him down here for a few more minutes—make sure the elevator's working in the brain hotel."

It feels good to admit things, to say them out loud, to get everything off your chest. I say, "I've got genital warts."

Bulch replies, "Who doesn't in the French Congo?"

I say "I stole a bottle of rum from the bar last week."

"None of us would get anywhere without stealing something

from someone else."

I say, "I made guacamole with Aunika."

"Sometimes we make guacamole with other people. But it's who we love to make guacamole with that matters."

I drag my hands across Bulch's chest, wrap my arms around his neck, pull myself up. "Is Cliff dead?"

"I'm not quite sure who Cliff is," Bulch says.

"Am I working?"

"You were."

"Am I still in the east?"

"This is indeed the east, unless you're in London, in which case this would be the west."

"If I keep going east, will I eventually get west?"

"In theory, yes, but it be a sight easier to just head west."

"Can mistakes be corrected?"

"Always."

It stinks of beer down here. I see my pant legs soaked. I hope I didn't piss myself. "I need a drink," I say.

Cherise shakes her head, "No way."

Bulch pulls a canteen from his belt loop, untwists the aluminum top, holds my head in one hand, glides the canister to my lips. He leans down, presses his mouth into my ear. "It's rum."

The sweet burn of the Demerera hits the back of my throat, ignites my heart, brings a smile to my face. The blood continues to trickle down my cheek.

"Thin blood," Bulch says. "But it's not a big wound. Maybe a stitch or two."

"No stitches," I say. "No health insurance."

"Do we need an ambulance?" Cherise asks.

"No," Bulch replies. "This boy's got a two-by-four for a heart and a chupacabra for a liver. Plus, his head's just about right. Everyone

needs a good thumping by the hands of God every now and again."
He looks to Cherise and says, "Gimmee a hand, will you, love?"

Cherise hangs up her cell phone, squats down next to Bulch and
for a moment their eyes meet, and for a moment I think I see
something magnetic. She leans into him and he leans back. He
smiles, and then, as if watching a sunrise, Cherise's eyes lose
whatever weight was upon them, open up, sparkle like a new day.
They both slide their arms underneath my armpits.

"One, two, three, up!"

And here I am, on my own two feet, my arms covered in blood
again, alive, on earth, with friends holding me up, a round of
applause from the inebriated masses of the full bar. I raise my hands
in triumph, see the blood, the trash of myself, and I let it all drip
down into the beer-soaked floor, out, gone. I've got to get rid of
guilt. I've got to give more love. I've got to get us back west, or turn
this east into west, keep moving until I come back around again. But
what about Cliff? I've triumphed. Has he? Have I had a heart attack?
I push my hands to my chest—no pain. Just that damn eyebrow.
Cherise grabs a Band-Aid from the first aid kit and presses it to my
face. Then she grabs another, and another, until the blood finally
stops dripping down my cheek. "Jesus, I cut myself with a chainsaw
every other day and I've never bled like this. Too bad you can't
donate it."

"I'm O-negative," I tell her. "But there's probably some drugs in
there. Doubt they'd dig too much on it."

I take a moment to think about the term "self-centered." My
mother used to tell me I was "self-centered" when I was young. I
like to think as a result of her criticism I made a conscious effort to
never again be called "self-centered." But now, here, with my hand
pulling down on a beer tap, a glass raised to my face, a smile, the
relief of having not died, reality starting to creep back into my skull, I

realize, maybe I am. Cliff might be dead, but I'm glad I'm not. Is it wrong to cherish a personal victory when someone else is failing? Is that self-centered? Am I supposed to never be happy again knowing kids in China are making Nikes, their little hands bleeding with a thousand needle pricks, their faces worn from days on end without sunshine or leisure, without sleep and teddy-bears and Cap'n Crunch cereal? I will allow myself this one beer, this one minute of freedom without guilt, and then I'll call Charlie, get to the bottom of the mysterious text. He's not dead, I know he's not. And then, I'll finish my shift, go home, tell my wife everything, move forward, east or west—either way, we'll end up in the same place.

How Many Dead or Alive Blues

It's that goddamn electric tailed scorpion again, crackling with the fire of a thousand Greek Gods, sparking and igniting against a flint rock at the base of Black Charlie's chin. It's this sound, the electric buzz, like a dentist's drill on a molar, the hum vibrating across the jawbone, into the brain stem—it's the chainsaw whip of that scorpion's tail that peels one eye open, then the next. Charlie's mouth is filled with the red dust of the Big Hole. He spits it out, feels the cool air of the desert night against his cheeks.

He feels a hand grab him by the collar, yank him up and roll him over onto his back. In the twilight of the desert, a few million stars popping out through the blackened blue, he sees the face of the goon. The panic comes again, ice up his spine. He springs up and falls backwards in a tumble, then crawls, scrambling away. Where does it hurt? His chest. It throbs. No time to check for bullet wounds. This is survival. Got to make it to the main highway, call for help, pray the judge believes his story. But Charlie doesn't get far. His knee buckles, and then he feels the strong grip of trigger fingers wrap around his ankle.

"What are you doing?" The cop says.

But Charlie can't tell what's what and who's who. How long has he been unconscious? The last thing he saw was a tiny black speck travel through the sky. He's dead, he must be, and this is hell. Hell is where dead-beat bum-daddies wind up, condemned, sentenced to relive the most horrific event of their life over and over again, eternally terrified.

Charlie can't respond to the goon's question. He pushes his fingernails into the dirt as the cop drags him backwards, towards the squad car, leaving trails in the dust.

This is torture. He's been shot, been maimed, been sodomized— it all happened during the blackness. He can feel his asshole throbbing, his tongue bruised. "Please," he says. "Let me go."

"I did let you go," the cop says. "And look what happened." The cop drops Charlie's ankle to the ground and Charlie rolls over onto his back. His strength has left him, his will to survive is shrinking. He must confront this masochist, and if he must kill him, then so be it.

"What happened?" he says, catching his breath, tightening his fists in front of him.

"You're free, man. You just passed out. Fell straight on your head."

Charlie scans the perimeter of the space. He's positive it's another setup. The paranoia has gotten to him—too many gooballs, too many joints, too many people out there, too many child support payments, too many cities, shit—it's all expanding, and they're all coming for him. Who else is out here in the desert, waiting for him with an elephant gun, ready to dismantle his skull? "Hey man, I don't want any more trouble."

"There's no trouble," the goon responds.

"No trouble?"

"No. I threw my pistol into the canyon. I can't do this any longer. Had a wife—she's gone. She told me I was a dick, that I'd changed, that I lost sight of everything that was once sacred to me—which was her. This job isn't good for the soul. I don't do enough good, and when I do, no one cares. I always wanted to be a painter. I'm pretty good at portraits." The goon moves over to the squad car, removes a polaroid camera, points it at Charlie. "Freeze," he says, then shoots.

Charlie pulls himself onto his feet, looks the goon over once, twice, a third time. His gun is missing. It could be the truth. Still, he hears sounds in the nearby brush—is that a flicker of light? Is that the sound of a hammer being cocked?

No. It isn't. I know, because I saw it all happen. And if life could be replayed during our unconscious states, Charlie's would have looked like this:

The cop unholsters his gun, takes a long drag from the surplus of desert air, takes the weapon in his hand, and flings it into the Grand Canyon, swallowed whole. And then, Charlie's face hits the ground. For five or ten seconds, the cop tries to resuscitate him, gently toeing him in the ribs with his leather boots, and finally flicking his eyelids with his pinky finger until Charlie's eyeballs begin to twitch. Charlie's lucky the cop's attempts at awakening him ended there. The next step was to shove ice cubes up his ass.

"I think I'm a pretty good guy," the cop says out loud. "Everyone deserves a second chance. My second chance got me out here, to you. You see, I was out on a call a few hours ago, near a real shitty trailer park—a big hangout for the tweekers on account of the rather large meth lab located in the center of it. And there was a girl there, dead, about twelve years old. She had been raped and left to die a few miles outside the park. No one knew who she was. No one could identify her. There were turkey vultures, moving in on her, and I shot at em, unloaded a few rounds, and I just got so choked up and mad, I had to come out here, try and get some peace and quiet, and so when I saw you out here, drugging, I think something inside of me snapped, but then almost simultaneously came back into focus, and now that focus has lead me in the right direction. I'm no cop. I'm a guy who likes gooballs and the smell of pinon. I like Cap'n

Crunch cereal on top of strawberry soft serve ice cream. I like watching baseball in the summer."

"Far out."

"I give you a second chance and maybe you give me one. Maybe you tell me I'm a good guy, a decent man, who's filled with compassion. Maybe that gun down there in the hole turns into something else—the final piece to a beaver dam, and maybe that beaver is happy."

"Are there beavers in Arizona?"

"I don't know."

"You think whoever killed that girl deserves a second chance?"

"They deserve a second chance in hell."

"I'm Charlie."

"My name is Jack Straw, and I've been out in the great beyond for too long," the goon says. "Can I have a gooball, please?"

Charlie squints his eyes, unsure of what kind of trip the goon might be heading out on. But he doesn't have much of a choice here. He's got to let the goon do as he wishes until he's sure they're equals. "Help yourself."

Jack Straw heads over to the bucket in the front seat of Charlie's car, and Charlie scans his surroundings, paying close attention to any movement in the brush. He's still not sure what to make of Jack Straw. He's got a nice enough face, solid, but with a sweetness around the cheeks and under the eyes—a face that's seen tears. But still, this man is a cop—he hasn't formally resigned, and so, is still active in the field of duty—a rogue perhaps, like Colonel Kurtz in *Apocalypse Now*, but an officer, nonetheless. He won't be comfortable until that fuzz swallows that gooball, takes a trip to the Great Stone, lets his eyeballs turn to *Twilight Zone* spirals, howls at the moon.

When Jack Straw gets to Charlie's car, he asks "You want one too?"

Now Charlie is getting suspicious. As far as he can see, one of three things can happen.

The first—he and Jack Straw trip out on the Grand Canyon together, become best of friends, maybe even head west together tearing ass down highways and through dusty ghost towns—he could be a valuable asset out here on the road—an ex-cop on his side, pointing out all the speed traps, divulging the best pickup lines he's used on speeding young women, flashing his badge to get out of tickets.

The second—they both take gooballs, Jack Straw turns out to be a complete sadomasochist, handcuffs him, dumps gasoline over him, lights a match, and throws him over the edge. Maybe he even cuts off his dick first while serenading him with Bette Midler's "Wind Beneath My Wings."

The third—neither of them eat gooballs and Jack Straw turns out to be a complete bore who only talks about old high-school football games, and reminisces the best crew-cuts he's ever received, or talks about radioactive gravel or the gross domestic product of Lithuania like a character out of a Jonathan Franzen novel.

"I don't mean to be skeptical, brother, but ingesting drugs with a cop sounds like a setup, or at the very least, the worst trip ever."

Jack Straw laughs. "No shit. I would hate to get all gooballed with most of my dickhead colleagues. But man, I spent two years in Hawaii after my mother passed—I took drugs and stared at the sea, took more drugs and drank more booze, until there was nothing left to use to kill my sadness. I guess I'm one of those people who can't handle death. It seems unnatural. I got straight, became a cop to keep me from doing any of those things again, to force myself to deal with the sadness—but the sadness is infinite. I mean shit—that stuff today—she was twelve years old, man. And so, fuck it. God brought us gooballs and hash and dope to cope." He reaches into the bucket in the front seat, pulls out a massive chunk of the sticky granola, rolls it into a ball in the palm of his hand, takes a huge bite out of it. "Fuck it," he says. "I want it all to go away." He pulls himself up onto the hood of Charlie's car, leans back against the windshield, the sound of radio static requesting backup seeping like schizophrenic helium out from the squad car. "Go ahead and unplug that goddamn radio."

No communication. No way out. Only the canyon. The Big Black Hole.

Charlie heads over to the cruiser, yanks out the cord, grabs a hunk of cannabinoid granola, and gets on top of that hood with Jack Straw. "You're a good man," he says, then takes a bite.

Jack Straw takes a deep inhale. "Thanks, brother."

Charlie settles back into the windshield, wraps his dreads up behind his head and uses the thick tendrils as a pillow. He takes in the panorama—black all around him—black like gold. Golden donuts—he can almost smell 'em now. He kisses his lottery scratcher, raises it up to the moon. "It's a beautiful night for a little Whiskey Jelly."

Hiroshima Blues

The atmosphere of the industrial sized fridge at La Di Donuts isn't cutting it for Aunika. She's been sitting Indian style inside the steel walls for about fifteen minutes, the skin of her arms now cold to the touch, legs covered in goosebumps, her breath visible with each long drawn exhale. She needs the cold to cool off, her body still buzzing with the heat of Cassidy's tongue. Up above her, she sees the herbs—mint, tarragon, rosemary, thyme, purple guru, elephant razor—she can almost smell them through the big plastic bags they're stuffed into. Elephant razor—a tall grass three feet in length, the scent like a sunset made of strawberry—the taste, a sweetness that envelops the tongue. She reaches into her pocket, searching for something, anything, it doesn't matter—there's nothing left in front of her. She only wants to take her mind off of what has happened. Is she a homewrecker? She's been called a lot of things in her day, some of them true and some of them false—but never a homewrecker. She's not a homewrecker. A homewrecker intentionally puts themselves between a family for personal gain, not for love, not to fulfill the sanctity of the most human of emotions.

Love is what got her in the refrigerator, and love is what will get her out of the refrigerator. Love will tell her what to do, if she could only find where it is down inside of her, give birth to it, and ask it a question: "Love, what do I do now?"

If love could answer, it would tell her to forever love Cassidy, but to also love Phoenix, and to love everyone else around her. Love is respect. Love loves love. Love is circular and therefore her love of Cassidy will someday come back around and kiss her heart, pump it full, send a big juicy bubble of strawberry blood up her neck, out to the tip of her tongue. She'll taste that love. She'll know it'll always be there, and she knows it already is. But for some, love is not enough. Her hands are still in her pockets and she feels the edges of a business card wedged between her hips. She's forgotten about this business card, the one Bulch gave her only an hour ago. It could be the whiskey, the wine, the beer, the booze, the tongue, love.

The business card: Hiroshima de Los Angeles Sonnesson— Dream Guru.

Aunika's no square—in fact, she's a real boss hoss. Taking advice from a man named Bulch who worships the Great Stone and rides it toes-to-the-nose in the form of the banana oil trip is a good idea. *"If you can dream it, You can live it."*

Aunika swings open the large refrigerator door, letting herself out. She sees the young cashier drinking a beer and reading *L'Etrange* with a half-eaten elephant razor donut in front of her. "It's my break," the young cashier says. She swipes her blonde bangs from her forehead and takes another bite. "Hot," she says and winks.

"I'll be back," Aunika replies. It's a cryptic message. Back when? Who knows—maybe never, and at this moment, that'd be all right.

She slides out the kitchen and through the throngs of hungry donut patrons, each of them attempting to stop her, to congratulate her on her success, to bend her ear about which flavor is next—Tart Cherry Chocolate Mousse? Someone heard there might be a purple guru donut? Is that true? Purple guru doesn't grow in these parts. Where can you find it? Hydroponic? A secret strain that can withstand the humidity?

She keeps her lips pursed, tight, so that the blood retracts from them, keeps them white around the edges. She slides out the door, feels her boots hitting the concrete. She heads west towards Hiroshima.

The streets are uninteresting when you're in a hurry. For instance, she doesn't even notice the topless girl passing her by with a bucket dangling from her arm whispering, "Gooballs" into her ear like a kiss of wind. This girl wears a spectacular skirt, long, to her ankles, made of bluebird feathers, flattened wine cork, and emerald green Sierra Nevada bottle caps, all in the pattern of ocean waves, interlocked, moving with each step. On any ordinary day, Aunika would have stopped the young woman whose brunette hair reaches her tailbone, and without even noticing her supple exposed breasts, would have asked, "Where did you get that skirt? It's remarkable."

And the young woman with glass blue eyes would have said, "Out there," and used her neck to point in a direction impossible to decipher. And the young woman would have dropped her slender fingers, each one with a bell attached, into the bucket, pulled out a gooball, and dropped it into Aunika's hand, kissing her forehead like a mother, and using one of her barefeet to shove her in the ass down the road in the opposite direction. This would have been a great day for Aunika with a gooball in her hand. She would have chewed it, tripped out on all the shoes slapping the concrete. She would have stopped at the park, rolled in the grass, thought about a new donut flavor—Whiskey Jelly. Has she heard of that before? It's in her subconscious. God damn, a whiskey jelly donut is a great idea.

But no, instead she pounds those boot heels against the concrete, past the topless gooball peddler, sucked into the city, drowning in concrete, without whiskey jelly on her mind.

To her right, a man screams at a parking meter, but she doesn't hear him. She doesn't even see him pull a machete from the backseat of his car and attack the coin machine with several heavy blows, glass shattering and sparks flying.

To her left, a young woman throws a middle finger into the window of a Bank of America, screaming, "You ruined my life!" and runs away, raising her finger higher up to the sky—Aunika doesn't see any of it.

In front of her, it might as well be only a white canvas—she doesn't even see herself walking towards her, the hands of her spirit-clone outstretched as if waiting to receive something. She just flies past herself, past her own blue eyes and a tank-top made of pure marijuana leaves stitched together with inchworm silk fortified with Ethiopian Gravity Beeswax—unmeltable and impenetrable. God damn, that tank top is a conversation piece—is it even legal?

Time passes like all time passes like time is passing right now. These streets are just physical expressions of time, moving forward or backwards, to the future or back to the future. Even right now is the future, and when you return, well, that's the future too. There is no turning back, and so, when she arrives at Hiroshima's small space—a 1920's cottage painted lavender with a big bay window and a Dutch-door with a hummingbird feeder above—she decides it's time to continue forward, to pursue her love in any way possible. This love, this love could kill, this love could give birth, this love could lick her eyeballs, splash across her belly, create sunshine in the deepest gray of winter. She could carry this love with her, hold it like a child in her arms, push it into a water bottle and spray it on everyone at a hot music festival in the desert.

She twists the doorknob and enters Hiroshima—the place is a disaster—of antiquity. Every inch of wall space is covered in images—The western wall is an 8 x 15 foot shrine to the King himself. Elvis lives in here. Jumpsuit Elvis. Tight jeans Elvis. Military Elvis. Thai Elvis. Elvis on safari—is that Bulch? Elvis at the Taj. Elvis waterskiing on the backs of dolphins.

Aunika loves walls. This wall calls to her. It calls to her in such a way, that she doesn't even notice the woman seated on the cushions in the bay window holding a furry black cat on her lap, dragging from an evenly rolled joint. She walks straight past this woman—can't even see her, just like everyone on the sidewalk before—to the wall, raises her fingers up, draws them against Elvis' crotch. She's entranced, lost in the sea of Elvis—black and white Elvis, color Elvis, Hawaiian Elvis, Lithuanian Elvis with piles of radioactive gravel in his arms.

"You can tell a lot about a person by what wall they're drawn to," the woman with the cat says. The origin of her accent is undetectable—a cross between Sweden and Barbados. "I'm Hiroshima."

Aunika turns her face over her shoulder. She internalizes the rest of the room, deciphering each wall. The south is dedicated to Miles Davis—Miles on fire, Miles in the sun, Miles on the sidewalk, Miles on stage, miles and miles of Miles.

The east—Antarctica. Visions of nothingness, serenity, pure white, ice-breakers, a lone scientist wrapped in fur carrying a Norwegian flag, snow shoes made of East Antarctic walrus tusk.

The north—Molotov Cocktails. Men and women throwing flaming bottles through storefronts, at tanks, at themselves, into the sky, into cars, lighting them, flinging them, staring at them, making them. Some of them are Bosnian, some of them Ukranian, some of them Amerikan.

"I'm Aunika." Aunika looks over Hiroshima—a tall woman, legs extending out from her hips like the towers of the Golden Gate bridge. Her face is bronze, cheeks sparkle with perfect, subtle perspiration, her hair—black as night. But her eyes, what are those eyes? Aunika moves closer, looking into them. Blue? No, white? Fuck, are they clouds? They are made of clouds and they are made of sky and with each passing moment, they move with the wind of her soul, and this can't be possible, but it is what it is.

"Come sit with me," Hiroshima says.

Aunika smiles, feels relaxed in those eyes, can picture a giraffe in them, no, wait, it looks more like a clipper ship. She moves languidly towards the woman, takes a seat at the foot of the bay window, leans her back against it, and feels the cool hands of Hiroshima move across her scalp.

"Tell me what it is? Love?"

"Yes, love."

"Love with a man that loves another?"

"Yes."

"Love with a man who loves another who loves you as well?"

"I think."

Those hands, so perfect, so cool. This voice, so perfect, so cool—like a light rain near the ocean. Aunika's eyes close, her breath loosens from within, and she exhales an exhale that carries with it the heaviness of a million lost lives, the weight of a shipwreck.

"Dreams can be transferred," Hiroshima says. "Dreams are transference. We can live inside our dreams. We can see the parallel."

Hiroshima moves her thumb down Aunika's scalp, presses it into the center of her forehead, massages it, loosens the chakra blockage.

"Tell me about him."

"He is perfect."

"Nothing is perfect."

"Some things are."

Hiroshima smiles and pulls from the joint, extinguishing it on the windowsill. "If that is what you believe, then so it shall be."

Please Come Home Blues

I've finished my beer, I've celebrated my victory over death. I've died and come back to life. I've fainted, and been helped up. I've confessed my sins, I've been absolved by Bulch, I've felt remorse, I've cried.

I move gingerly off my barstool, rubbing the itchy Band-Aids above my eyebrow, and head outside for some fresh air, but the air doesn't feel so fresh—it's humid this time of year, sucking-in feels like drowning in a tepid bathtub. My hair curls up into spirals, my eyelids sag with moisture, my scalp drips with sweat, carving down the valleys of my tendrils, soaking the back of my neck. At least the moon is out this evening. Most nights, the moon is masked by the clouds born of the Atlantic, the haze of the eastern seaboard, the ocean melting a few miles away. I can see that moon, the same one that soon will be shining out west in the still desert air. I don't want to make this phone call because knowing Cliff is dead would ruin part of myself, would send me down deep into the bottle, put my tongue in places I don't want it to go, drive me to the brink of insanity, force me to question the existence of God and what the point of life is. I'd sit on the sidewalk and rub trash all over my face. I'd punch a parking meter, swallow a gooball if there was one, throw a brick through a window. I'd walk towards myself with my hands outstretched and ignore me, give myself the finger, tell myself to fuck off. I'd have to sit down and write something trite in an attempt to capture everything that a lifetime is—nothing—only time, a blip in history, an eyelash in space.

I know he's not dead, and I know I'll make this phone call and feel stupid for ever believing something serious was happening with a couple stooges like Cliff and Charlie. It's probably all part of an elaborate plan to get me to spread cream cheese across an armpit, or announce to a group of strangers I have no penis or something else ridiculous, non-sequitur and humiliating, and at the same time, virtuosic.

I pull my phone from my back pocket, find Charlie's number, and press the little green button. It rings. It rings again. A woman passes me, topless, with a plastic bucket in her hand. She whispers "Gooballs," in my ear and I immediately remember this woman from St. Claire's Rainbow. The gooball woman who made my wife crazed, who loosened her brain enough to suck on another woman's tongue and snort the great white stone up her nose. I want this gooball woman to tell me about her tits. I want this gooball woman to be a ghost I can wave my hand through, leaving only vapor behind. I want this life to be the exact opposite of life. Maybe this gooball woman will kiss my neck and I'll turn into a rose, a fragrance as sweet as honeysuckle in a sugar pond.

I say, "I'll take one."

She rolls one up into a perfect sphere, and presses it into my palm. She says, "You've got holes in your future."

My eyes twitch, hot coals burn out from under my shoulder blades, raging into my fingertips. "Holes in my future" sounds terrifying. Holes have been causing me problems all day, and perhaps holes have been giving me the jam-up since the day I was born. Holes are made of mouths and mouths are made of holes. Vaginas are made of holes, assholes are made of holes, ears are made of holes, donuts are made of holes, and my future is made of holes. Can

I stick my tongue in my future? Can I taste what will come of me? Can I twirl my future around my tongue like a halo?

I ask, "What are the holes? Which ones?" and the gooball woman just smiles and nods her head.

"You know which holes and you know what holes." She shuffles down the street, raising her arm above her head and letting her wrist dangle in the air, pirouetting between passersby.

God damn, what is her skirt made of? An ocean? Are those bottle caps? Bluebird feathers? Exquisite. Aunika would love it. So would Phoenix.

The fourth and fifth telephone rings come and go like last breaths, until it is only the sound of Charlie's recorded molasses voice. "It's Charlie, I'm out chasing bunnies." Beep.

"Hey Charlie, it's Cassidy, I'm a bit freaked out right now. Some topless gooball peddler just told me I have holes in my futu...."

Call waiting kicks in. Beep Beep. I look at my phone and see Charlie's name written in digital scrawl across the screen. I press the green button and Charlie's voice is there, somewhere.

"He's dead," he says. His voice isn't covered in molasses. His voice sounds like sandpaper left out in the desert, stepped on by brittle camel toes, sucked up in the dry wind, dropped back down on a hot rock. There's barely enough lubrication in his throat to form the words, to cough them out. He attempts another sentence, but it sounds like a man choking to death on a dry chicken bone.

I hear the word, "head," and that's about it. Maybe he said "blood," and "everywhere," but that's speculation. Is it possible to faint twice in twenty minutes? Yes, it is. My knees buckle, but my heart kicks in, pushing blood out as fast as it can—this is survival. I catch myself before the blood stops pumping up to my brain, take a deep breath, bend down to my knees and drop my head to the sidewalk. The blood feels good rushing back into my cranium, a warm surge tickling the nerves fluttering behind my ears. Breathing is good. I take a deep inhale, sucking in the wet air, letting my lungs fill with water, drown a bit, dunk my head underneath, come back up—I'm swimming. I'm waterskiing on the backs of dolphins.

"He's not dead," I say into the phone. I say this because I still don't believe Cliff is dead. Cliff doesn't die. In my life, I die. Everyone comes to my funeral and gets drunk and talks about all the ridiculous shit I've done in my life—that time I smoked cocaine with Cliff in my car in Hollywood before getting thrown out of the Burlesque show for unzipping my jeans and pissing on the bar…that other time I had sex in my friend's closet next to a stuffed Elmo doll, wrapped up in vintage t-shirts…and still, that other time I threw water-balloons filled with shaving cream at a bunch of junior high school kids when I was wasted on a Tuesday afternoon, yelling "Your future is uncertain!" And what about the switchblade story? That shit was crazy, when I pulled it out and the dude ran and then lightning struck, nailing him right between the eyes, and he convulsed in the parking lot with his head whipping back and forth against the parking pylon! And that time that kook smashed my car cuz I 86'd him from the bar and I broke his nose and I'm pretty sure his blood turned green on the asphalt, and then he got arrested and spent three weeks in jail and I had my friend trump up the estimate on the damage to my car so I could sue him for more money. And that time I tripped on mushrooms and everyone looked like a pirate and so I thought I was one too and I walked around the bar using one hand as an eye patch and talked to everyone as if I were a pirate and everyone was like "what is wrong with this asshole," and kept frowning in my direction so I went home and swallowed a bunch of pills and fell asleep and woke up with that rad lesbian in my bed who ended up vacuuming my dirty floor and putting away my clothes for me because I was too hungover and serotonin deprived to do anything positive with my life that day and she told me "You are beautiful. Why are you so destructive?" And who can forget the night we bribed the tattoo artists with hot pastrami sandwiches with extra mustard to open up the shop down the lane and blast spacemachines on our wrists? And fucking Bangkok? Are you kidding me? I bought a twelve-year-old prostitute and fed her dinner and let her relax for an hour so that she wouldn't have to bang that disgusting fat bald British man, and then her "Madame" told me it was "inevitable," that I didn't "have enough money in the world to save her from her fate," and yanked her back inside the café to bang the fat bald British man, and I spilled noodle soup on my lap and cried for hours as monsoon season began.

"He's not dead."

"He's dead."

"No, Charlie. No, Charlie."

"Cassidy, please come home."

I sit down on the sidewalk, push my hands into the dirt and scum collected on the earth, collect the trash at my sides, and rub it across my face. I eat the gooball, stand, smash the parking meter in front of me with my hands, blood flying from my knuckles, glass shattering, and then, I begin looking for a brick and a window. Charlie's voice cracks, moistening with tears, trailing off in the digital distance hanging from the end of my arm—"Cassidy, please come home."

I lick the blood from my knuckles and take a look at myself in the window. I look like a shipwreck off the coast of Tierra del Fuego, my bones floating out to Antarctica, never returning.

Something Good Must Be Happening in the World Blues

It would be myopic to say the only world that exists is this one right in front of you—mine. It would be "self centered" to only tell my story, to tell you about the death and the abortion, the east and the west, when there is still the north and the south, life and birth, you.

Today in the city of Majuro, Marshall Islands, a woman from Oregon accepted a professorship at Micronesia Community College, where she'll begin work teaching upper level English to a population deprived of resources, both natural and financial, a population plagued by the effects of global warming, decimated by floods and typhoons, sea garbage, and post WWII nuclear testing. This woman will mentor a young woman named Kuji, who will form a union of Pacific Islanders dedicated to preserving the environment—her first act as the first president of this union, five years from now, will be to replace diesel and gasoline fuels with coconut oil in all vehicles on Micronesia. And, man, will it smell good there.

In Greenland, just outside Sisimiut in the Davis Strait, a young Inuit hunting for seals will find an anomaly in the water surrounding his kayak. He'll take a temperature measurement, find the small whirlpool on his starboard side he's stumbled upon is actually 100 degrees Celsius, boiling, and yet the water immediately surrounding this whirlpool is only 0.7—nearly freezing. This discovery will have a major impact on our future, but to tell you how would be frustrating because I can't comprehend the theory, mathematically or scientifically. To put it in my own words, it means "there is a miniscule galaxy somewhere in the ocean near Greenland," and "this miniscule galaxy is parallel to our own, unraveling and twisting at the same rate." Screw underwater pyramids, this shit is way radder. Far out.

And if that isn't enough, here's something good happening right in front of you:

The certified public accountant got laid tonight. He may have even fallen in love. He told her his name, Wayne Kramer, and she told him hers, Bernardine Dohrn. He brushed his teeth, side to side, top to bottom, spit out the toothpaste, and kissed her long in his bed, the numbers removed from his mind for eleven minutes, until, wham, they came crawling back on their curves and edges—but it didn't matter—his neck was caressed by the hands of another as other's tax problems seeped out of his pores and nothing could break his spirit. His teeth were immaculate, flossed by her pubic hair. He made a great breakfast in the morning in a stunning pair of Spongebob Squarepants boxer shorts.

And if you want even more, here's something else right in front of you:

Bulch and Cherise are behind the bar, smiling, laughing, touching arms and smalls of backs with soft fingertips, bodies brushing up against each other as they pass behind one another to pour whiskey and spit, intentionally touching even though there's enough room to get by without contact. Their clothes interact, the dust jumping from Bulch's safari pockets, landing on Cherise's strawberries, fabric intertwined, eroding, disintegrating between them, until in only a few hours, perhaps there will be nothing left to separate them but skin. He notices her breasts, perfect, her hips, round like the strawberries she wears. And she notices that mustache, prays for that mustache, closes her eyes and licks her lips for that mustache. And those bar patrons, well they see the love growing between them, the bond forming, and they throw money at them as if it were made of trash, landing on the bar, stuffed into the copper-plated tip jar.

They play with each other, joke, smile, high-five, take shots, dance, pull each other in, rattle their tongues in French—"De tes yeux, je veux puiser mon amour et sentis mon coeur pres de votre dans une ile de Polynesie."

And this room, dimly lit with only the ancient yellow electricity of Congolese light-bulbs, the flicker of oil lanterns twisting gently in the summer breeze, the scent of old metal and elephant-gun powder, savannah boots and rhinoceros tusks, shadows dancing in the candlelight against a backdrop of Hemingway's Kilimanjaro—this room is enough to create love as if it were creating a galaxy, as if it were made up of a boiling whirlpool in the midst of a frigid sea—it is, will, and can be the center of the universe if only for a few minutes, those minutes where Bulch looks into Cherise's eyes as she exchanges her bourbon spit for forty dollars and says, "My God, you are the sun, on fire, bright and the reason for life."

Jelly Hole Blues

Black Charlie, foot down to the ground, pedal to the metal, flooring it, cutting loose, hauling ass, redlining, burning-rubber, screams through the simmering Mojave desert, tongue thick with whipped and dehydrated saliva, thirsty for life and blood, eyes filled with dust, thinking of her underwear, the underwear he used to see every morning, crumpled next to the shower by the handcuffs, used, dirty, trash. He used to pick up that underwear, smell it before brushing his teeth and heading off to adjust insurance, tied up to the neck in responsibility, numbers, the problems, the regulations, that top collar button—god damn did it dig into his throat. He'd keep that scent with him all day long, think of her, black eyes, black hair, black nails, the mother of his child spitting and purring in his arms during the good times, the times before he left, the times when he was home— "I'm only doing this until something else comes along—then, we'll find that perfect spot—maybe Spain—Grenada, eat sardines straight from the ocean, paella off your belly."

He'd eat an apple for breakfast, sniff the skin, all the way down to its core. He'd dream of war on his way to work, picture himself with a sword or a spear or an arrow, piercing the hearts of his enemies, born to sit on a golden throne, born to win, or born to lose, and his history would unfold before him as he traveled down those roads, turned into the parking lot, the guillotine dropping on his neck as he moved through the door and arrived at his cubicle. It wasn't the life of a king. And neither is this life, now, speeding through the desert on gooball residue with an ex-cop at his side—he's an assassin—an assassin of life, of donuts, of holes, of lottery scratchers.

It's the morning and California is within him. The air, solid, stiff, unmoving, doesn't cling—it's strange—not like the east where it hangs around your neck, makes you feel like you're in the midst of a mid-stroke aneurysm. In fact, the air seems to disappear as he shifts gears, moves into sixth, presses his forehead forward, his greasy skin nearly kissing the windshield. The air just parts like her legs, lets him in, allows him west. The sand is out there, rocks ripped apart by the sun and wind, just like his heart, just like his skin, just like the black.

"Whiskey jelly!" Jack Straw yells out the window. He's digging the cruise, 101 mph through the blistering heat, his black cop shirt unbuttoned, chest hair twisting outward towards the sun. He's cut those black slacks into shorts, rides them mid-thigh, sockless, sweating feet stuck inside his untied shitkickers. That badge? It's stuck somewhere in the dirt near the Grand Vag—a child will find it someday, along with the squad car, rusted, a monument or a carcass of what he once was—his molten shell, his rattlesnake skin—left forgotten—the metamorphosis of robot bozo to human.

"From cop to donut mogul," he says. "Hot damn."

Charlie digs on Jack Straw. The great gooball trip worked out all right, with the both of them watching the sun come up with their feet dangling over the edge, talking about praying mantises and how they look like aliens—so they obviously are, and are plotting a takeover—the evolution of Memphis blues musicians and how each one of them has a star shaped birthmark underneath their right elbow and how they all use their thumb to clasp down on the E string for a B chord, how there are so many swans in the river in Zurich, whatever river that is, and those swans all say the same thing—"Ba-gock." Oh and Charlie met a Danish girl once who taught him a drinking game she learned in New Zealand and it was called "Ba-gock," and that's a total fucking mindblower, especially because Jack Straw met a Kiwi girl once who taught him a drinking game she learned in Denmark called "Cock-bag."

Those two gooballed boys even held hands for seven minutes, experimenting with Homoerotic Energy Anatomy Transference— HEAT—Jack Straw read about it in National Geographic, a wise man in Gujarat developed it. In the end, they both decided it was beneficial for men to hold hands. Their bodies felt rejuvenated— they both reported an elevation in libido—also, ancient memories of past lives came racing in, unrolling before their eyes like 16mm reels. East Indians—those motherfuckers know everything about energy. They can walk on nails and fire, swallow swords, live through diseases we can't even imagine where warts the size of Portobello mushrooms pop up across their eyelids, wade knee-deep in trash, dead bodies, filth, piping hot aloo gobi, all without flinching—they can tell history without knowing it. Maybe we can too? "Fuck yes," Charlie says.

And Charlie wants this car to go faster. He wants to break the sound barrier. He wants to pass another car and he wants that driver to think to himself, "Holy shit, was that a rocket ship? A spear of lightning? A laser? God?"

This is history—each moment passing becomes a page in a textbook.

"When do we hit L.A.?" Jack Straw asks Charlie, adjusting his seat, laying back, pulling off a shoe and dropping his foot out the window.

"Not sure," Charlie says. "Three or four hours maybe."

"Three or four hours," Jack Straw repeats, raising a tightly rolled J to his lips and burning it up. "Three or four hours and we grab a bottle of whiskey and we make donuts. I know my donuts. My cop friends know donuts. Not a better idea in the whole wide world than getting your ex-cop gooball buddy to start a donut business with ya. Just you wait and see—these donuts will change the world. I know my donuts, I know my fucking donuts."

"I hear ya." Charlie grabs hold of that joint, exhales across the California border, that invisible line where marijuana suddenly becomes legal and the air is heavier with wild dreams born and blown from those back east.

"I had a donut once in Jericho—great town. The hole was massive in that pastry, biggest hole I've ever seen, I could fit myself into it, maybe fall right through, disappear—and the flake—holy shit, you've never seen a flake like this on a donut. Donuts are usually dense, sticky under that glaze—No, the Jericho donut was flaky like a croissant, or an onion ring or something. I asked the man—he had one eye—how he made the dough so flaky. You know what he told me? He told me he used butter churned by the hermits of the Hanging Garden. Did you even know there were hermits there?"

"Butter churned by the hermits of the Hanging Gardens?"

"That's right."

"What makes it so special?"

"They got pink belly cows there."

"Pink cows?"

"Well, they aren't pink—just their bellies. The milk is denser, contains more sugar."

"Is that right?"

"It is."

"Can we get it?"

"I'll make a call. See what I can find."

"Where the hell is Jericho, anyways?"

"Can't remember. I was living in Hawaii at the time, and like I said I was a bit fucked up on account of my mama's passing. But I'm pretty sure it wasn't on any of the islands. I went a lot of places back then—caves, lagoons, coves, dreams. But this place was different. Built into sandrock, dusted in sunset, paved with gold."

"You think you can replicate that flake from the Jericho donut?"

"I doubt I can replicate it, but I could tell you if it's as good. My lips'll never forget that flake."

"Fair enough. We've got time to experiment."

Charlie smiles. He's got five thousand bucks to start his donut business, and with a little help from his pal Cassidy back east, maybe he can find the right people out here in California to bring those whiskey jelly donuts to fruition. He knows the whiskey jelly donuts aren't his idea—and for this he's prepared to offer Cassidy a partnership, or at the very least, a decent monetary sum for the whole shebang, although he'd prefer the former. Working on something alone, with only Jack Straw, a relatively new acquaintance who still can't be completely trusted—for shit sakes, he just threw a pistol into the Grand Canyon, dropped his PD badge in a pile of red dirt, and left an $50,000 police cruiser with a ripped out radio teetering on the edge of a massive cliff. No, it's probably a bit more logical to bring in a friend, one not too close, but one that's not too far either. Heavy friendships can ruin business, just like they ruin bands—Lennon McCartney, Marley Tosh. You have to go with instinct. All of Charlie's instincts tell him Cassidy is a good man, a man who loves his wife, a man who brings him beer in the middle of the night and appreciates his hacky-sack skills, dreads, and colors. Cassidy is a man of his word, and his word is "whiskey jelly"—well, two words. And without those two words, Charlie would just be sailing west without a spyglass, staring off into the horizon without a clear vision of the future. This desert might seem miserable, desperate, deathly, uninspiring. But in reality, this desert is only the final barrier between him and the Pacific—he heard her waters are cool, tingle the skin, harden the soul, bring Bluefin tuna and steelhead trout across its currents, sacrifice the algae to the old King Crab. Down in that deep black water, light disappears and only the shivering unknown survives. Deep down inside Charlie is the shivering unknown, waiting to be discovered, pulled up with a net, fileted, eaten raw, drawn into the warmth of a human soul.

"We're on our way," Charlie says. "Towards the big hole."

"The two of us and one big hole."

"Three of us."

"Three who?"

"My boy Cassidy. If I'm the donut and you're the hole, he'd be the jelly."

"There's no holes in jelly donuts."

"There isn't yet."

Jack Straw nods his head. He's only hitchhiked on this rainbow ride and if it lands in a pot of gold, well then great, and if it lands in a pile of shit, well, it's nothing a hot shower can't fix. But fuck it, a whiskey jelly donut with a hole? This is a revolution.

Shampoo Blues

A quick bit of advice from Bulch to a bar patron who's just stepped knee deep in a pile of bullshit—"There's nothing in this world a hot shower can't fix, as long as there's whiskey in the shampoo bottle."

This House Ain't a Home Blues

If I had any idea how I got on this train, I'd be a fucking genius. The blood on my knuckles seems strange to me. I feel no pain in my hands, and yet, blood continues to pour out from them, dripping down my wrists and dropping down onto the floor. Unbeknownst to me, one of the Band-Aids over my eyebrow has come loose, dangling from the side of my face. It's still relatively early—about midnight, and so the train has quite a few travelers on board with me. They stare at me in semi-horror, wondering who I've killed and why, secretly texting about me on their phones, and some of them not-so-secretly taking pictures—just in case the police need to know where this maniac landed.

Landing. Shit. I'm flying pretty high on the gooball right now and landing seems like it'd be a feat of certain disaster, overshoot the runway, burn in an icy sea. Cliff is dead. Cliff is dead. Cliff is dead. I'll never feel his belly against mine again. I'll never hear his irreverent drunken voice squeal like a kid running down the hallway on his last day of school, out the door, into the June sun, middle fingers raised up to the sky again. I'll never suck his saliva from the bottleneck of a warm High Life, press my face into his thick, hairy chest, drop my nose down to his Colombian key bump, smile, laugh, kick, dance to the MC5, fall to my knees in tears, kill a parking meter, drink too much during the day, write a socialist manifesto, get fired from a decent paying job for selling marijuana to teenagers, conspire against the government, make fun of Charlie's heroin problem, roll a joint and rack lines on a Boz Scaggs record, jump off a helicopter and land on a speeding freight train with him ever again.

I think back on the past few minutes or hours or days but I'm easily distracted because the gooball is shining through, and so, instead of thinking about my discretions and indiscretions, I focus on the young Indian in the corner of my train car, unzipping and zipping up the zipper on his jeans. It's as if he's just discovered the zipper for the first time. The fact that he has a feather tucked into the leather headband around his head seems inconsequential to me—that's how stoned I am. Also, he's got a great pair of Minnetonka moccasins on—the knee-highs, I can tell. But, now I'm starting to think—looking at him a bit harder, shirtless, brown skin, the feather, the headband, the peculiar zipper action—that maybe those aren't Minnetonka's after all. No, upon further inspection, they seem handmade—maybe wild buffalo skin—can't be sure. Where's Bulch when you need him?

This young Indian continues playing with that zipper, zip up, zip down, until finally everyone's attention refocuses on him. No one cares about my blood any more. I'm just a normal midnight freak—but this young Indian—he's out there on the freak scale, teetering on eleven.

If any man is like myself he's probably thinking one thing—is this young Indian wearing underwear? Judging by his outfit, I'd say he's a pretty traditional young Indian. Maybe there's a loincloth underneath there, or maybe he's got the jeans over his buckskin chaps. But I doubt it—Indians are practical and it's fucking hot out tonight. Hoka hey. It's a good night to die. I can feel the sweat between my legs, under my arms, under my chin, on the back of my neck, the tendrils of my lank hair moistened.

I watch this young Indian zip, zip, zip. Up and down. Up and down. This is what life is. We go up and we go down. We take drugs to get up, and we take drugs to get down. We get up in the morning, and we lay down at night. We pull a drink up to our face, and then we fall down on our face. We are born from nothing and grow up, and then are buried into nothing, down in the ground.

This zipper is the key to understanding—it is the physical embodiment of yin and yang—right here in front of me. This is what Basho was talking about. I think it's Basho. Who the fuck knows? I stare at the young Indian's crotch. I see Cliff in it. He yanks up and then down, up once more and down again, and then a high pitched squeal—"Awwiiiiieeeeieieiieiiwwiiwiieieieieie!" I can't tell if the young Indian is shouting his war cry, or if something far worse has happened. I see a few men in neckties rush to his side, looking at the bloody mess mangled in that zipper. The young Indian tries desperately to pull his balls out from the teeth of the zipper, but the men in neckties tell him not to. The young Indian disagrees, takes a deep breath, and pulls the skin from the teeth like ripping a Band-Aid off a beard. The result is exactly what you'd think it'd be—blood. There's so much blood pouring out of this young Indian's scrotum that's it's beginning to make me ill. The gooball trip is always far out.

I'm not sure what the next stop is, but it doesn't matter. I can't be in this train car any longer. The temperature has risen with the bloody genital panic—it must be over a hundred degrees in here. The train stops, I stand, I walk out the door, up the stairs, through the turnstile, and out into the night. I'm out near The Docks—shoes everywhere—are those avocado skins?

I can't figure out why I was even on the train. I rode my bicycle to work. I should have just gotten back on my bicycle and headed home—It must be something subconscious—Cliff has died, and so I got on something that would take me somewhere unknown—I was riding the wave with Cliff, heading out to anywhere—it doesn't matter. I'm surrounded by metaphors—the zipper was life and the train is pure death. We take a ride to a place we've never been, and maybe we arrive or maybe we don't. Maybe we end up at The Docks, or maybe we end up in The West. Shit, some of us might end up in The East, or even worse, The Deep South, spiraling all the way down.

"Cassidy?"

I look up from the avocado skins placed in front of me and see St. Claire. I'm at first more shocked he knew my name than I am to see him casually trolling the streets in a pair of avocado skin boots without a vast entourage in his wake. I've never seen him outside of a Rainbow party, and so I assume I'll see the reflections of rainbows when I look into his eyes, but I don't. They're brown and look sad even though his face pushes up as if he were pleased to see me. He's got brown suede pants on, tight, accentuating the obvious bulge and leftward lean of his cock. These suede pants are so tight I can see the circular outline of his head where it attaches to the shaft—thick, bulbous—on par for a man who struts around town in avocado skins and makes magic happen in the sky of all women.

"Quoi de neuf? " St. Claire asks.

I don't speak French. And so, this conversation seems like it will be problematic before it even has a chance to start. "Huh?"

"Ca va?"

I shake my head. "I don't speak French."

"Parlez vous Francais? No?"

"No parlez vous."

"Hmmph. Je viens d'avoir une idée. Whisky et beignets, ensemble. Puis-je parler a ton amie, Aunika, de ça?"

"I have no idea what you're saying."

"Ok. Bon nuit."

"Sure."

St. Claire tips his hat to me, lets his structured tendrils of hair fall down with it, and continues down the road. He's shirtless, with a peach ascot tied around his neck. His outfit would be strange anywhere else, but not The Docks.

I look up at the moon and think of Cliff. He could be up there already—I'm not sure how long it takes to get to the moon after someone dies, but if it's anything like Star Trek, I'm sure the pure power of raw energy can blast a soul up there in no time at all. I think about why we believe we go to the moon when we die—aside from the obvious—Jesus told us we do in the Third Testament. But even so, it seems like human energy should be transferred somewhere positive, kinetic, essential—like the sun. The moon isn't the sun—it isn't glowing, on fire, burning through the universe. The moon creates nothing but a gravitational pull, fairy tales—affects tides and moods. Moods. Has my mood been affected by the ones who've died before me for the entirety of my life? Have these assholes been fucking with me this entire time, making me feel depressed when I should feel happy? The body is made of seventy percent water—just like earth. I take a moment to make a decision, to answer a question. The answer is "no." I've been unhappy because of my decisions—it's no one else's fault but my own.

Cliff is up there, I know it, giggling at me as I wander through the streets of The Docks towards the subway station headed back the way I came, searching for a way home in the deep black death night. He's up there with a tub of cream cheese, waiting for me and my armpits, waiting to spread it across, throw an eleven pound salmon into the cheesy crevice, take a picture, frame it, show everyone— even Mother Theresa and Abe Lincoln, popes and Roman emperors. I wonder who he's friends with up there on the moon? I wonder if time passes the same as it does up there than it does down here?

He'd make friends with everyone within a minute, I bet, his arm draped across a bottle and the other around Marilyn Monroe, spinning wild tales and anecdotes of his relatively short life—that one about sleeping with the cilantro farmer's daughter in San Felipe, and how he spent the next three days pulling the leaves and stems out from between his teeth and under his tongue even though he never ate any—if you catch my drift—and everyone will laugh and the wind will catch Marilyn's hem and pull it up over her ass and she'll just let it ride high, pressing her rouge lips to Cliff's cheek and petting his belly, the smoke from that cigarette twisting up into the grease of his hair, blue ribbons of vapor dissolving in the moonlight.

If I had any idea how I got on this train, I'd be a fucking genius. I can't remember the walk from The Docks back down to the subway, paying my fare, finding this stained bubblegum seat on this screaming train car. My knuckles aren't bleeding as badly—now just feel sour. I don't seem so freakish at, shit, what time is it? 1:15 a.m. At 1:15 a.m. most of the people on the train are bleeding somewhere—either from knuckles and lips, livers and spleens, or hearts and brains. Tired faces, eyes mired in loss, marked by lines, clothes hanging like chains, boots that refuse to be picked up and put back down again.

I watch the stops pass through the greasy window, reading each street name carved into the emerald tiles of the subway walls, golden letters shimmering in the dim—Love St., West Shakedown, Bobcat Jesus, NE Easy. I always wanted to live off Bobcat Jesus—oak-lined streets, Victorian homes with covered porches and mandatory weekend wine-and-cheese garden parties for all inhabitants—otherwise you pay a fine—a bottle of wine to each neighbor on the block. The roses grow big and red, the sweet scent penetrating the wood and walls of each house—less traffic, more money, less stress, more radness, less hair, more hair, less kooks, more bozos. I'm no bozo, but I don't mind living around them and their loafers and their pink neckties—Shit, hombre, I can carve a pocket for myself out of just about anything—that much I'm sure of and always have been. I'll carve a little spot out for Cliff and I, and Phoenix too, someday, in the mountains of the moon. We'll have a little table made of moonrock and a small lantern to play cards by, drinking the juice and sliding in and out of each other's infinite time tornado.

When I reach my stop I get off, slap my boot heels to the street, head west one block, south two. When I get to the door, I pull the keys from my belt loop, take a deep breath, think about life, realize I'm not here, nowhere, nothing, never have been, never will be. I don't want Cliff to be dead. I don't want my kid to be dead, moontrash. I'm praying to you, author, change it all, make it all come back, reverse time, send me back West, give me what I need to survive. I slide my key into the keyhole, waiting to see what's inside.

L.A. Blues

At first glance, Los Angeles is a paradise of tight-jeaned women, slender men with ironic 1980's florescent sunglasses, lipstick, tans, cafés, yoga studios, signs pointing towards the Pacific Coast Highway where the ocean coldly pulls back and whips the coastline with three foot overhead waves. The freeways are stacked one atop the other, street exits fly by every half mile or so, each turnoff a different neighborhood, something new, mysterious—Spanish style villas or mid century stucco apartment homes, mansions with butlers or gangs with guns—down through The Valley, homes that look like mausoleums erected by the Persians, bringing home to their new home, stand out in the midst of what was once 1950's tract housing, homes where milk and the *Los Angeles Times* used to be delivered to the doorstep, now an unrealistic, yet harmonious blending of several opposite cultures.

It takes the dense traffic to expose Los Angeles for what it truly is—a dust bowl without water, trees choking on smog, semi-green leaves of palm trees and white oak covered in the remnant soot of struggling overheated automobiles. Cars everywhere, unmoving dry heat, exhaust in your lungs, suck it all in. It's the opposite of the east. These trees can't survive—wouldn't even be here if it weren't for the Colorado River, Hoover Dam, all the unnatural disasters of the Mulholland water era.

Los Angeles is a filthy oasis in the middle of a wasteland near an ocean, and nothing more. It was erected out of nothing and someday, will pass again into nothing. It's a zipper town—up and down, up and down. The real estate rises, and the real estate collapses. The junkies on Sunset rise, and the junkies on Sunset collapse. Actors rise to fame, then fall into obscurity. Bands rise up to the stage, lose all their money, drop down into nothing, become checkout baggers at grocery stores, reunite ten years later for one last mini-tour, but it's too late and no one cares.

Charlie and Jack Straw are stuck in traffic on The 101. They haven't moved in seventeen minutes, and have done a quarter mile in the past thirty. They have time to take in this city—the gang graffiti, the taste of exhaust, and holy shit, there are a ton of Mexicans here. Literally, they outnumber the two men ten to one.

"We should get us some real Mexican food," Charlie says.

"You've never had real Mexican food?" Jack Straw asks.

"I have, but I bet they do it better here."

"L.A. and San Diego have the best, man. We need to get you some carne asada fries."

"Carne asada fries don't sound too authentic."

"There's no such thing as authenticity any more. Mexican food can be whatever it wants to be, just like humans."

The boys are heading West, towards the ocean. It's always everyone's first destination when they reach L.A., aside from Hollywood. Millions of people come to the city of angels every year to see a celebrity, eat a sandwich at a sidewalk café, and touch that ocean filled with the polluted runoff of urban sprawl, the water an opaque green, colored by decaying bodies, shit, and motor oil, salty, cold, reeking.

"What's the plan?" Jack Straw asks his partner.

Charlie pulls a crumpled piece of paper from the pocket of his black polyesters, holds it up in the sun. "Cassidy told me to give his friend, Cliff, a call when we got out here. He said he'd let us crash for a few days, he'd show us around."

"Does he live by the beach?"

"Maybe. The beach is probably close to everyone."

Cliff doesn't live near the beach—didn't live near the beach. Didn't. Huh. It sounds weird to refer to Cliff in the past tense. He "didn't" live near the beach. He never "did" anything he didn't want to do. He "was" always fucked up, and his smile "was" rad—like a llama at a country time garage party.

Cliff lived on the east side—the side where the rawness of life is tangible, visually apparent. Immigrants sell melon with chili pepper, boiled corn dipped in mayonnaise, margarine, and cotija cheese, hot tamales, fresh oranges, stuffed animals, socks, fake leather wallets, bootleg DVD's, right out on the street, pushing their carts up and down for hours on end, looking for a little extra loot to send home to the rest of the family struggling down south in Tijuana, Tecate, Mexicali, Nogales.

From a distance, if you separate the warmth and hot chicks from the equation, Los Angeles is a complete waste of time. It's not hard to see the struggle in everyone's eyes, especially when you're traveling two miles per hour next to millions of them, four hours a day. Those eyes don't see much beauty—at least not any more. They're here because they have to be. If they aren't, then they're here because they're rich, and being rich in Los Angeles is like being rich nowhere else. The world is handed to you. You become someone, even if only in your mind. You purchase season tickets to Lakers games. You buy thousand dollar lunches at secret clubs at Disneyland. You take limousines to the premieres of Johnny Depp movies, eat caviar at the after party, fuck a model, male or female, later that night. Anything is possible in this city, even if you're a dickwad.

Charlie and Jack Straw are here to realize that goal. They want to be a pair of dickwads sitting next to Jack Nicholson at Staples center watching Kyle Kuzma dunk on Lebron. They want to fuck Megan Fox in an infinity pool on a cliff in Malibu and videotape it. They want a Maserati that does 185. They want to live in a tree-lined canyon next to Joni Mitchell and John Mayer, become the percussionists on his next tour, get drunk and make fun of him with Fiona Apple backstage. Who wouldn't?

But the donut mega-company still needs to be formed, and, unbeknownst to the both of them, White Charlie and his brother Cliff have already cracked the code and taken hold of the market. You know, for a heroin junkie and spaced-out artist, White Charlie is pretty smart. When his brother flat-lined, red-lined, whiskey-lined, coke-lined, horse-lined and wound up dead, his first thought was to preserve the legacy of The Mustard Brothers.

Cliff was and has always been the catalyst behind everyone's vision. He took his brother from shitty art galleries in Echo Park, and put him in upscale galleries in Santa Monica. He took his brother's bunny paintings from kitsch to high art. And he was about to take whiskey jelly donuts from a novelty to a billion dollar movement. It was time for White Charlie to step up, put down the needle and paintbrush, pick up the computer, and immortalize his brother. And so, in those strange gray minutes passing after his brother was pronounced dead from a massive head wound on Sunset Blvd., Charlie filled out the trademark and patent applications, sent them to the bureaucracy, sat down in a chair next to his brother's body, and cried into his dead armpit.

The traffic isn't moving for Black Charlie and Jack Straw. The freeway sign reads "HWY 1, 3." At their current rate, they'll reach the beach in about two and half hours. "Fuck this," Charlie says. "Traffic sucks, it's ruining my soul, I can feel it." He drops his head down to the steering wheel, rolls the electric windows up, and twists the air conditioner knob to the right, the fans cranking—but the cold air isn't coming out—only hot stagnant smog blasting into their faces.

"Don't think the AC is working," Jack Straw points out.

"No shit."

Charlie pulls his head up from the steering wheel, expecting the car in front of him to be a thousand feet ahead—it's not. Still there, brake lights engaged, the sun reflecting off the steel bumper directly into his retinas.

"Let's call your buddy's buddy," Jack Straw says. "We've got plenty of time to check out the Pacific—maybe we'll live right on top of it, all the whiskey jelly donut boys, bronze chested and gooballing in the water, waterskiing on the backs of dolphins."

Charlie pulls his phone from his back pocket, lifts his foot up to the dashboard, pulls the lever on his driver's seat, drops back into a reclined position. He dials the number written on the crumpled piece of paper. Rings twice, three times. "Not answering," he says.

"Of course he's not answering. Who the fuck answers random phone numbers on the first call?"

Charlie hangs up. Dials the number again. Rings twice. Three times. Four—a languid, molasses voice, "Hello?"

Charlie pops up in his seat. "Oh, hey, is this Cliff?"

"Who is this?"

"My name is Charlie. I'm a friend of Cassidy's."

"Is this a fucking joke?"

"Excuse me?"

"Why would someone do this?"

"Do what?"

"Charlie?"

"Yes."

"Your name is Charlie and you're a friend of Cassidy's and you're looking for Cliff?"

"Yeah."

"Fuck you, you rabbit fucker."

CALL ENDED

"What happened?" Jack Straw inquires.

"I have no idea, but whoever it was hates the shit out of Cassidy. They just said 'Fuck you' to me and hung up after I told him I knew him. He called me a 'rabbit fucker.'"

The car in front of Charlie crawls ahead three feet, but Charlie doesn't press his foot to the gas. Instead, he engages the parking brake, lets his burning heel cool off the pedal, massages his strained eyeballs. "We're gonna have to do it ourselves," he says. He takes a deep breath, removes his sock, rubs his pedal foot. "Fuck it." He pops the parking brake, throws his blinker on, inches his front fender into the lane next to him, moving towards the exit. "Let's get off this freeway, grab a donut, drink some whiskey, and see what we're up against."

Gold Tooth Blues

It would be both a literary and social faux pas to discuss what happened during Aunika's dream session with Hiroshima. I think describing dreams are best left to a maximum two-sentence synopsis—*Aunika dreamt of her body, naked, by a pool in the sunshine overlooking the Pacific. Cassidy came to her, lied by her side, placed his hand on her hip, and slid his soft fingers across those bones, through the valleys of her ribs, upward to her chin, where he delicately pulled her face to his, and kissed her.*

The rest can be left to erotic authors, "Fifty Shades of The West." Legs wrap around each other, sweat and fluid flowing through holes, nails carving into skin, blood and love and semen exploding like big pink fireworks across bellies and breasts, yada yada…

For four straight hours, Hiroshima guided Aunika through her visualization, drawing her long fingernails across the woman's forehead, massaging out her desires, four straight hours where Aunika could picture the life she coveted, four straight hours where she could sit across from the man she loves, staring at him, watching each movement with the same anticipation of watching a bullfight. And then, her eyes open, looking straight into Hiroshima's, watching the clouds pass, turn sky blue, as she says, "Thank you."

"You're welcome," Hiroshima replies. "Did you live what you wanted to live?"

"I did," Aunika says. She pulls herself up off the floor, sees the wall of The King across from her, Elvis with a gold tooth chopping off the head of a rattlesnake with a shining silver axe. "The King," she mutters.

"The King is an interesting character—so many people try to be him, and we, if only for a moment, squint our eyes and pretend he's real. 'Real' is something that exists in our minds—anything we want can be real." Hiroshima pulls the extinguished joint from the windowsill and relights it, a long slow drag deep down into her lungs, an exhale like a delicate summer breeze. "Care to join me?" she asks.

"I dig what you're saying about The King, and I dig dreaming, controlling those dreams, pretending it's real. But The King never waterskied on the backs of dolphins and doesn't have a gold tooth, and so, I never made love to Cassidy by a pool overlooking the Pacific Ocean."

"You just need to reframe your subconscious. You can live there, if you want, changing the shapes of the world as you walk through it."

"I'd prefer it if he just loved me, here, on earth, where the shapes remain the same—the donuts still have holes in them, and they're made out of circles."

"You can do as you wish—this is your life, not mine. But remember, donuts are made of circles, just as life is. Each circle connects on a different plane, and each decision we've ever made circles around the next."

"I'll leave the circles for donuts." Aunika stands, shakes the woman's hand, and walks out the door, dropping her hip in the moonlight.

A moment later, the door crashes open. "Hey!" Hiroshima thunders.

Aunika turns, finding the woman standing unamused with a hand on her hip. "That'll be eighty dollars."

Aunika turns around, pulls out five twenties, and hands the

woman the money. "Thanks. Keep the rest." She takes four steps away, into the night.

These streets are darker now. It must be after midnight. The streets still creak with the subtle bending of bodies, the sidewalks still move, forward and backward. She has a decision to make—which direction should she go? To the west, Cassidy's house. To the east, the donut shop.

She takes a step forward, crosses the street, puts her hand in her purse, grips onto her little canister of mace, just in case, and begins the fifteen minute walk towards the future.

After midnight, the freaks and the junkies come out. Tonight, they seem peaceful to her—comforting instead of threatening. They huddle in groups on corners, smoking cigarettes and asking for change as she passes, and they are content in their own misery, not concerned with anyone else's. Perhaps she could learn something from these junkies and freaks—she could become content with her own misery. No—she can't. She's rarely been content with anything—she's always been striving for something more. Most of the time these goals were seemingly unattainable, insurmountable, but nonetheless, she beat the odds, attained victory. No one believed in her donut shop, no one had the foresight to see donuts would become the trend that hit a big wide vein in this generation, that donuts would become more fascinating to the mid-twenties through late-thirties demographic than craft cocktails and microbrew beer, authentic Vietnamese cuisine and crispy sweetbreads. She wonders if attaining Cassidy will quench her thirst for life, will satiate whatever it is that boils in her belly, forces her to chase dreams at the expense of the dreams of everyone else. Maybe he'll settle her down. Maybe he'll change her forever.

She doesn't care if he will or won't. She's taken the step forward, she's headed west, and when she gets to that door, she'll knock on it, she'll see Phoenix, and she'll tell her everything. She'll be the honest woman, she won't be a homewrecker, she'll be a noble human, lay it all on the line, see where she lands—but either way, she'll feel better about herself, she'll feel better about Cassidy's tongue, and she'll feel better she has another card to play, one last dire move to pry her best friend away from his wife and into her arms, make love by that swimming pool, overlooking the Pacific.

Guacamole Blues

I twist my key into the doorknob, wrap my fingers around the brass—I expect, author, when I step inside, this home will somehow have been transported, transformed. I've prayed to you and I know you will answer these prayers. When I open the door, this home will be a comfortable cedar cabin in Big Sur, and this story will be about a loving couple with a beautiful son, who stare at and philosophize the ocean and drink crystal glasses filled with big California Cabernet's in the Jacuzzi on a redwood veranda each evening, listening to the waves crash against the cliff below, holding hands in the natural moonlight, reciting poetry in French.

I close my eyes, waiting for the big reveal, feel the light of inside kiss my eyelids, slowly swing open the door, and see Phoenix passed out, naked on the floor, the stink of whiskey and sweat, tears and pain, heavy in the room. On the ground, next to her, my secret bottle of Rebel Yell. I immediately start thinking of excuses for why I have a secret bottle of Rebel Yell in my desk drawer, wonder if the discovery of the Rebel Yell is the reason why she's passed out on the floor naked, if this discovery was too much for her, that she realized her husband has a colorful drinking problem, uses it to repress the sadness of the past year, the loneliness of the East, out here without a family, with a homewrecking childhood friend, and a dead best friend. I see her lying there, the needle on the record player itching with emptiness with each revolution that passes. Dead air.

I take a few steps, careful not to wake her, cringing with each creak of my weight against the floorboards. I grab the blanket from the couch and drop to my knees next to her, covering her naked body. "I put my tongue..." I say. I take a moment to stare at her mouth. This mouth is perfect. This mouth has told me a million times it loves me. This mouth has been everywhere on my body, has claimed territory, has bitten, licked, kissed, whispered, spoken, and breathed onto and into every inch of me. This mouth has penetrated me in ways that can never be described. I am guilty, I know, but what good is releasing guilt if it poisons the heart of someone else? "I put my tongue in Aunika," I say. I can't figure out why I phrase it this way. It seems like stating where my tongue has been is a more accurate description of what has happened today, a more graphic description, carries with it most of the guilt within me, but also sounds detached—sex and kisses are more than just a tongue—those words denote an emotional connection—but my tongue, it's only a body part—it swallows birds and bacon, booze and bad burritos.

Phoenix stirs, a small catlike grin widening on her face. She takes a breath in, her chest heaving upwards, then her chest falls back down. I gently run my fingertips across her eyelids, tickling her eyelashes.

Her eyes open like a velvet curtain in a dark Parisian playhouse. "What are you doing home?" she whispers to me in a somnambulist purr. She rubs her eyes, refocuses on me, and says "Holy shit, what happened to your face?" She reaches out and reattaches the dangling Band-Aid back to my skin. "Oh my God, are you ok?"

"I'm sorry," I say.

"For what?"

"Everything."

"What's everything?"

"Cliff is dead."

Her face skips the normal process of computing emotionally disturbing information. Her face becomes pure, perfect pain instantaneously. Her eyes well with tears the size of boulders. She pulls herself up, rolls to her knees, drops her head to the floor, and begins to sob.

I drop the side of my face to her spine, grip onto her, and let it out, crying like a waterfall, the tears sliding down the curve of her back, and I rub that curve with my hands, massaging the perpetually tightened muscles wrapped around the bone.

She rocks back and forth in my arms, trying to catch her breath, air choking in and out through her lips. Strange. I never realized how much Phoenix cared for Cliff. Cliff and her spoke and were friendly, but to call them true friends would be a stretch. Perhaps when I lose something, so does she. "Everything dies," she says. "And we have to live through it."

I wipe the tears from my cheeks, drop Phoenix from my arms, pick up the needle, drop it down on the Gun Club.

He's dead on the lawn/ of the house that he owned/ what will they say about him?

"I'm sorry," I say again. "I'm sorry we threw everything out like trash, let it all slip down the drain. I'm sorry we came here, that we ran away from everything. And now, you're right, everything dies, and we have to live through it."

She spreads out facedown on the ground. She lets her fingers crawl out from her body like a spider towards the bottle of Rebel Yell. She rolls it towards her face, arches her spine backwards, licks up a nip from the neck, tightens the cap back on it, and rolls it behind her to me. I pick up the bottle, take a big swallow—Rebel Yell—It's what I need. I take the largest inhale I've taken in years and with everything down inside of me, I scream. I scream so that the hairs on my arm vibrate. I scream into the skylights above, through the glass and into the night, reverberating through the neighborhood. I scream as the seconds pass into time, the rumble from my belly regurgitating everything sick inside of me, expelling the trash littered throughout my soul. I scream to let God know I am here. I scream to Cliff—can you hear me, fucker? And then she pushes herself up to her elbows, and she screams. She pulls everything from her womb, everything still stuck down inside of her, the remnants of what once made a home there, and lets it out her mouth. We scream together, in unison, in perfect harmony, until we're both out of breath, and all that is left is an electric guitar solo carving itself into the air.

I let my body collapse next to hers, on my back, stretch my vertebrae, our chests thumping, up and down, up and down. Strange what our lives have become—so far away from California, and yet still on the floor, screaming in pain. Nothing has changed. Nothing ever changes. You can move east, redecorate, but you can't change yourself, what you feel, who you are. There's no way to escape the past or the future. We are contained within a prison of ourselves and so, we must make our prisons homes, and our homes must be livable, enjoyable, happy. And happiness, joy, and life, come from love. I love this woman, and so, I will never tell her about Aunika. I will never degrade her in that way again. I will only love her, I will sleep with a hand always touching her leg so she knows I will always be there. I will deal with my indiscretion, place the blame on myself and no one else. I am responsible for my actions, and I will accept them and cope with them and when I have compartmentalized my actions, locked them away somewhere deep, and dark, I will never think of them again. I will not help Aunika with her bar, I will not share a bottle of wine with her, I will not compliment her on her tank tops and eyeshadow—No. Never again. I will distance myself from her completely. And if Phoenix asks why Aunika and I had a fallout, I will tell her "Because I realize who I am and what is important to me and she isn't. And I think she's self centered." And I will forgive myself. I have to forgive myself. Someday I will forgive myself. For everything.

"What are we doing here?" I say. "I've only wanted one thing in my life, and that was to love you on a mountain near an ocean. That shouldn't be so hard. We could buy an Airstream, gut it, make it a home, park it somewhere in California under a canopy of sky and Redwood. I could write outside underneath the trees, shake my hair at the summertime bees, listen to the buzz of rattlesnakes in the distance. You could drink wine, play the guitar, let your hair grow as long as you like, all the way down to your ankles, and we could kiss, constantly. And there would be no one left but us—and we could change everything, turn the time in our minds backwards."

I raise my hand, drop it gently upon her head, and twirl my fingers through her hair. I transfer all of the love I can hold within myself to the tips of my fingers and press them into her scalp, stimulating the blood vessels of her mind.

She looks at me with the weight of some unknown problem, teardrop eyes sparkling like a glittery constellation in a unicorn universe. She pulls her chin off the wood, licks her lips. "Did you make guacamole today?"

I open my mouth, push my tongue to my teeth, but before I can answer the question, I hear the slow drawn out sounds of boot heels, one by one, thump…thump…thump, up our wooden stairs outside, an eerie pause, and then the meticulous, heavy rap of knuckles against the door.

Dead in Debt Blues

It's been twenty-seven hours since Cliff was pronounced dead, dried blood matting the hair at the base of his head, lips cold. Charlie is outside, removed from his brother, boots to the street headed in a direction he's unsure of, but going towards nonetheless. He's back down on Sunset Blvd, in the heat, covered in smog and sweat, the sound of traffic, burning brakes squeaking in the waves of heat he glides through. He sees a palm tree, a single frond bowing outwards to him, begging to be ripped off, thrown into the street, causing a mother and her baby to careen into a semi-truck filled with gasoline, spark, ignite, light the whole goddamn city on fire. Charlie can't go home—the only reason to go there is to check the mail, see if the certificate has come claiming him as the sole king of whiskey jelly donuts and The Mustard Brothers franchise. No way in hell can the state of California put anything together that fast—that new law ruined everything—a required background check for all would-be donut moguls. It seems that place out east, La Di Donuts, sparked huge consumer interest in the pastry, and whenever there's huge consumer interest in something, the government finds a way to better "regulate" it and make money off it. Fuck man, you need a background check for donuts and guns. Someday soon, there'll be dealers on the corner, selling donuts with cocaine glaze and sprinkles of marijuana leaves out the trunk of their car. No, home will only remind him of Cliff and he can't think of Cliff right now. If he did, he would only be able to stand paralyzed, in the middle of the street, weeping. If he thinks of Cliff, he'll want to kill himself, he'll want to find a balloon, push the H into his arm, retreat into the eternal blackness. If he thinks of Cliff, life becomes pointless, not worth living. Gotta keep moving.

Charlie has an internal compass he's been unaware of since birth. When he was eleven, he woke up in a dense Redwood forest outside Redding, CA. No one knew how he got there. It was as if he'd been teleported. He hiked his way through the bush, munching wild berries and chewing twigs for two days until he found his way out, dropped his thumb across the highway, and wound up back in Los Angeles. There were theories—all the Golden State newspapers covered the story. Some say his mother finally had it with him, drove him up north, and dropped him in the forest—he's always been a bit of a maverick. Others speculated alien abduction and experimentation, and still others said he had strange brain waves that may have caused epileptic type seizures, loss of memory, huge synapse gaps filled with black holes dotted through his mind. He might have gotten up to Redding the same way he got back to L.A. And as the author I can tell you exactly what happened—but first the certified public accountant has something to say: "Don't forget, tax season begins January first—it's not just a new year—it's a new 'tax' year!"

Charlie has an internal compass as well as an internal mechanism which generates constant forward movement—he's like a toy racecar with undying batteries and without a remote control. He got up into that forest because his body wanted to, and he came back from that forest for the same reason. Charlie isn't someone you worry about. Charlie is someone who will survive the nuclear war, live with the cockroaches, paint bunnies in the black soot that remains.

Charlie's internal compass drives him west, and before he knows it, he's in front of the paisa bar, the scent of mildewed beer and cigarette butts leaking out the building, stinging his nostrils. Cliff would want this. Cliff would want his brother to get as liquored up as possible, put Pearl Jam on the jukebox, take one on the jaw from the Eddie Vedder hating vatos, buy a bag of coke, roll around on the sidewalk like trash, tumble all the way home and then rinse it all off in the rooftop shower, watch it fall down the drain. Cliff would want Charlie to keep painting his portraits—Cliff getting fucked by a bunny in his armpit; Cliff growing bunny ears from his saggy pectorals while sucking on a giant rainbow-swirl lollipop; Cliff zip-lining pantless through a burning bunny forest. Cliff, even while dead, is a pretty funny guy and appreciates odd, self-deprecating humor. In fact, if he could speak right now from beyond the grave about the circumstances of his death he'd say, "That was a hell of a 'trip,'" and he'd do a drum roll with his tongue and cymbal crash with his mouth.

Standing in front of that big black door, Charlie lets his teeth show for the first time since the hospital stooges told him his brother was dead. He tells himself, "No H today. Cliff wouldn't want that. I got to respect him and I have to live. I have to be his Mustard Brother. I have to keep my O-negative clean, have to cram that boozy pastry down Amerika's throat for the sake of him. It's up to me."

He opens the door, takes a step inside, one paint-speckled cowboy boot landing in total darkness. His eyes need to adjust to the black, the stark contrast between outside and inside, within and without. As he stands, blind, inhaling, wanting only to wrap his hands around the ice-cold aluminum of a Tecate and swallow all the shit back down, he hears, "Hey, guero, you and your hermano owe me money."

And when he opens his eyes he sees only Juan, the bartender, holding a baseball bat, standing before him. A shootout. "Oh shit."

Juan pulls back the bat, rests it on his shoulder, sizes up Charlie's head, ready to knock it out of the ballpark. Charlie throws his hands in front of him, falling backwards into the door. "Wait wait wait!" he says. "He's dead!"

"Who's dead?"

"My brother. My hermano. My hermano is dead. Muerto. Mi hermano es muerto."

Juan steadies the bat, eyeing Charlie suspiciously, unwilling to relent. There ain't too many bozos in this story and Juan isn't one either. He knows Charlie and his brother, knows they're drunks and junkies—he's seen 'em march into the bathroom with Mars Volta and he knows what's happening in there, matter of fact, he's got a hand in it—Mars Volta gives him ten percent of whatever he sells inside the bar. No, Juan's no bozo and he knows gringo drug addicts can't be trusted.

"How'd he die?"

"Yesterday, after we left here. He tripped and hit his head on the sidewalk, that's it. He died."

"Dios mio, guey! You better come up with somethin' better than that."

Charlie looks down, sees his hands, still spotted and stained with his brothers blood. He raises them up to Juan, the thick coagulated liquid stuck underneath his fingernails, pale fingertips tattooed red.

Juan takes Charlie's hands in his own, inspects them, nods his head, then shakes it. "Let me get you a cerveza, mijo."

Charlie bellies up to the bar, lets his elbows fall to the dinged and dented, cigarette burned wood. He lets his greasy hair down, falling across his cheekbones, building a fortress for his face to hide behind. His skin is hot to the touch, almost red. He takes a deep breath, sucking in the cold air-conditioned air. He thinks about planets, how his body is a planet, its own ecosystem of polluted continents, his blood like the Pacific, poisoned with toxins and plastics swirling around his kidneys, islands of trash the size of Texas floating through him, clogging everything up, killing whatever sunken life is down there, sucking the marrow from his brain.

"You got the money he owes?" Juan asks. Juan is no bozo. Juan knows money makes the world go round, and just because you're dead doesn't mean debt disappears. It gets passed on to kin, and Charlie is kin, and unless you've got a great certified public accountant, you're screwed.

Charlie pulls out his wallet—nothing inside but an old receipt from a gas station popsicle, the backside drawn in black ink corner to corner of a bunny circling in a ballot for Fidel Castro in an election dated "November 22, 1963." There's not much to say to Juan but the truth. "I got nothing. I am nothing. Cliff is nothing."

Juan pulls the baseball bat back up from behind the bar, raises it to his shoulder and spits on the ground. "No money, no good, holmes." He pulls back on his shoulder, brings that baseball bat as far back as he can, his eyes focused on his target. He lets his fingers tighten, knuckles turn white.

Charlie bows his head, takes a sip of his Tecate. "I don't give a fuck."

Juan grins, "All right then." He takes a step in, sizes up Charlie's head.

"Tranquilo, guey!"

Juan turns his head—Mars Volta. The handsome drug dealer with the curly black bangs drops a hundred dollar bill on the bar, sliding it towards Juan. "For whatever he owes and whatever he wants."

Juan grabs the bill, stuffs it into his pocket. "You have good luck, guero." He turns around, drops the bat, forgetting, and begins folding a pile of bar towels into a neat stack.

Charlie sucks down the rest of his Tecate in one irreverent slug, letting the brew fall down his chin, drip down into a puddle before him. "I wouldn't call it luck."

"Maybe God loves you then."

"God is an evil bunny who took my brother from me."

"God ain't a bunny. He's The King."

"Give me a double shot of Don Julio, chilled, with a lime. And one more for my friend."

Mars Volta nods his head, "Thanks, ese," and takes a seat next to Charlie. He reaches down into the back pocket of his jeans and removes a cocktail napkin, the words "Mustard Brothers, home of the Original Whiskey Jelly Donut," written across it in Cliff's unsteady scrawl. He slides the napkin to Charlie and lets his hands rest on the bar in front of him. "Tell me about these whiskey jelly donuts."

Knockout Blues

I'm still on the floor with Phoenix, although now, we're both on our knees, staring at the door, listening intently to the heavy knuckle rap against the wood. These knocks aren't the knocks of a friend—no, they are the knocks of The Man, someone with a reason to get inside, to get to the bottom, to sort something that needs sorting out.

"I bet it's the fuzz," I whisper to Phoenix. "All the screaming." We wipe the tears from our eyes, and our breaths shorten up. "I hate dealing with cops when I'm drunk."

"You're drunk?" Phoenix says.

Ordinarily I would lie in this situation, tell her I had a few beers after I heard about Cliff, but I'm not drunk, because being a drunk husband is a drag to a wife—she has to think about all the times you may have been drunk but told her you weren't, and the next time her friends ask her about her husband, she'll have to lie through her teeth and say, "He's doing great—he's working on a big idea for his next book—Choose Your Own Adventure erotica," and the whole time she'll be thinking "Holy shit, he keeps a bottle of Rebel Yell in his bottom right desk drawer and comes home from work drunk." But tonight, something is different—the truth needs to be told. "Yeah, I'm drunk. It's been a long, strange day."

"So am I," she replies. "Drunk, for sure."

I put my arm around Phoenix and kiss her temple, move my lips up to her forehead—she's hot, maybe a fever.

I pull myself up off the floor and tiptoe to the front door, careful not to make a sound. The knocking continues, every few seconds, the pounding. Phoenix stands, pulls on a pair of jeans and covers her breasts with her arms. "Who is it?" she asks.

I turn around and put my finger to my lips, telling her to be quiet. Shit, it's after midnight. No one randomly knocks on doors after midnight except cops. I take a few deep breaths, try to focus, try to suck the bloodshot from my eyes, send positive cool waves of water across them. I rub the dried blood from my bandages, thinking to myself "Shit, this isn't gonna look good to a cop. Screaming, bloody, my wife half naked behind me." I put my hand to the doorknob, twist, and open the door one or two inches. I peek my head around the door into those two inches and I see Aunika, standing in her tank top and boots. Her face turns from an expression of determination to one of astonishment.

"What are you doing here? Aren't you supposed to be at work?" she says.

I answer her questions with a question of my own. "I'm not at work. What are *you* doing here?"

She throws her hand into her mouth and begins chomping on a fingernail, turns around and looks behind her. Behind her. Everything that has happened is behind her, somewhere, lost in that never-ending donut circle of life, twisting out and away.

She turns back around and sees me in front of her. I don't open the door for her. I think about why she's here, at my home, expecting me to be at work, only wanting to see Phoenix. I put it all together, realize her motives, and I can't believe she would do something like this—this is teetering on the verge of psychosis, a low blow, backhanded shit.

"Are you here to talk to my wife about today?" I ask.

She chews on that fingernail a bit harder, takes a deep breath in, and a tear forms in her eye.

"Who is it?" Phoenix asks.

I have to tell her who it is. I can't just shut the door on Aunika's face. Why would I do that to my best friend? I should be overjoyed to see her, should be inviting her in to suck from the bottle, let it drip across her chin and onto the floor, roll around on the couch, eat popcorn and watch Star Trek.

Aunika. She still hasn't asked about my face. She's too involved in herself to see anything else. At that moment, her tears suck back into her eyeballs and she grabs my chin. "What happened to you?" She puts a thumb to the wound and rubs across it. I wince.

"Did Phoenix do this to you? Did you tell her?"

I take hold of Aunika's wrist and pull it from my face. "No. Phoenix didn't do anything."

"Babe, who is it?" Phoenix asks again.

I turn around. "It's Aunika."

Phoenix makes a face like "What the fuck does she want at this hour. How ridiculously peculiar." Her eyebrows smush together. "Are you gonna let her in or what?"

I turn back to Aunika, shaking my head. "My friend Cliff died," I tell her. "And then I passed out behind the bar and hit my head."

"I'm sorry," she says.

I open the door for Aunika, and as she steps through, I see everything in front of me—these two women and myself, a bottle of Rebel Yell, an avocado-less refrigerator.

"Hi," Aunika says to Phoenix. "I uh…" She pauses and pushes her hand into her forehead, pressing the perspiration back into her hair. She sees it all in front of her as well—What her next sentence could mean to the three of us. And if I could get inside of her brain, I bet I could tell you what she's seeing. But I can't. There's too many brains to get inside of right now, and I'd like to focus on my own. My own thumps on each side with each heartbeat. My own sees myself alone, without either woman, paying rent on a house in a place I don't want to be, wondering if someday I can find a job as a tree trimmer up in Redwood country—maybe I could smuggle weed from Humboldt County down to Los Angeles for extra dough, become the host at a campsite, selling firewood to tourists and helping them erect their tents.

Aunika repeats herself. "I uh…" She pulls her head up and sees Phoenix before her, the bottle of Rebel Yell at her feet, bleary-eyed and worn out. This woman is in the way. This woman is in the way of her happiness. Aunika starts silently weeping.

Phoenix stands, lets her arms down from her breasts, and approaches Aunika, pulling her into her neck. "Is it Cesar? Do you miss him?"

Aunika doesn't nod her head yes and she doesn't nod her nead no. She simply cries into my wife's neck, sucking in enough air to either lie, or tell the truth. I can't tell.

I shut the door and walk over to the fridge, praying for one last beer. If my life is about to shakedown this way, I at least want to never remember it. I want to black it out, wake up alone, move on as if I'd just been reborn.

I see these two women embracing and I think to myself, "Shit man, this is what I thought it would be like. These two women, friends, caring for each other, and me, enjoying the love of my wife and the love of my best friend." But perhaps this is too much to ask for. Perhaps we're all attracted to each other, or perhaps we're all secretly jealous of each other. Maybe I wish I had become a lawyer and could afford vacations to the Bahamas, or maybe I wish I had never been born and been thrown out like trash, washed out to sea, never learned love and hate or pain and pleasure—just a piece of the void, deteriorating, broken down into the smallest forgotten molecule.

"It's okay," Phoenix whispers to Aunika. The fact that they're embracing starts to make me feel even more disgusting than I already do. If Phoenix knew Aunika's true motives, if she knew what had happened earlier today, she'd be shoving a fist into the woman's teeth, throwing her ass out of our house, before pulling the butcher knife from the magnet on the wall and chasing me down the street with it.

Aunika wipes her tears on Phoenix's skin, pulls herself from the embrace. "I have to tell you something," she says.

I find that beer and I pop the top off with a cigarette lighter, take a big slug, waiting for the blackness, waiting to be thrown out to sea.

"I am in love with your husband," she begins.

I take another slug of beer. Phoenix turns around and looks at me. My face is without blood. I know this because it's all rushing down my legs, and my knees are feeling like they're about to buckle for a third time today.

"What does that mean?" Phoenix asks. She looks at me and says, "Are you in love with Aunika?"

"No, he's not," Aunika replies. "He's not in love with me."

"I asked him, not you."

"Trust me, he's not."

"How do you know?"

"Because today I told him exactly what I'm telling you, and he isn't."

I'm a man. I'm a man. What would a man do in this situation? I finish the beer, open the fridge, pull out one more, pop the top. I take a deep breath. A real man confronts obstacles, fights through pain, fixes problems, tells the truth, no matter what. I say, "Something happened between us today and, uh….fuck…shit. I feel like…man…I think both of us regre….”

“No,” Aunika interrupts. “Nothing happened between us today. It only happened between me and myself and all the other parts of my fucked up self.”

“What are you two talking about?” Phoenix starts backing away from us, towards the door, her face filling with blood, eyes beginning to crumble. “What happened between you two?”

“I came on to Cassidy, I kissed him. That was it.”

“You kissed her?” Phoenix asks me.

I look to Aunika and she shakes her head. She mouths the word “no,” to me. I look down at the ground, then back up into my wife’s eyes. “I kissed her.”

Those three words nearly ruin Phoenix—I can tell because she grips her stomach immediately and begins to dry heave, retching, guttural belches slicing through the silent air. “Youuuhhhggggckk.” She puts her fist up to her mouth cramming whatever wants to come out back down.

Aunika runs over to help Phoenix, but Phoenix shoves her out of the way.

“He didn’t kiss me. I kissed him. He didn’t have a choice.”

Phoenix drops her hands to her knees, stops retching for just a moment to scream “Bullshit he didn’t have a choice! We all have a choice!”

“Well, he didn’t!” Aunika yells. “I came onto him, I forced myself on him! And I need to tell you the truth!”

“She didn’t force herself on me,” I say. “She told me she loved me, I couldn’t believe it, and then it happened, and I regret it and we both regret it, but it happened.”

Phoenix falls backwards onto the couch, puts her head in her hands. “I can’t believe this.”

Aunika drops down on her knees in front of Phoenix. “Don’t

367

listen to him," she says. "I put him in an awkward position and he did everything he could to deny me."

"My stomach," Phoenix says.

I set my beer down and move over to her. "Are you okay?" I place my hand on her belly and she rips it off.

"Don't touch me. Neither one of you touch me."

I take my hand from her. "I'm sorry." I am sorry. I am guilty. I've ruined everything in both of our lives. Who am I? What kind of a man am I? I am a man. I am only a man, me. And the man I am runs from responsibility and puts himself in precarious situations, not just with his best friend, but with all things. A bartender who writes Choose Your Own Adventure erotica? How fucking stupid is that? How can that man ever support a woman, one who loves him and goes to a job in a cubicle every day to write about candy tampons? One who has stomachaches so severe she can barely function, one who has stomachaches because I can't handle responsibility? I drink all day and dance to the Gun Club with a chode rash. "I don't love Aunika," I say. "I only love you, and I've always known that."

"No you haven't always known that—if you had we wouldn't be sitting here right now doing this. This isn't happening. This can't be happening."

This isn't a story where the man gets away with what he's done. I can tell it won't be, no matter how bad I want it to be. I want to stay with Phoenix right here in this house. I don't want to leave. I don't want to wander the streets all night, replaying all the shit that went down today and how easily it could have been avoided if I hadn't told Aunika anything, if I had stayed relatively sober and thought about the repercussions of my words, of my drinking. I hate Aunika right now. She is not a good person. I want to throw the blame somewhere else—it's only natural. I don't want to take responsibility for my actions, but I already have, and if I had been doing this my whole life, I probably wouldn't be in this situation to begin with. I'd probably be back out west with a kid and a decent job, drinking wine and dealing with life like everyone else does—maybe every six months we get to get away for a couple days, go camping on the beach, go to Disneyland. But I've always been larger than life. A 4.0 in high school wasn't good enough—it had to be a 4.3. And having a decent job wasn't good enough—I had to be a writer. And having a perfect wife wasn't good enough—I had to taste Aunika. And getting away for a couple days to camp isn't good enough—I have to island hop in the Caribbean, go to Euro Disney.

I don't have to leave because Phoenix decides to leave instead. She stands up, doesn't say a word, and heads into the bedroom. I look at Aunika. She drops down to her knees and rolls onto her back, begins sobbing. I stand, turn my back to Aunika, and walk into the bedroom where I find Phoenix tossing clothes and underwear into a suitcase. "Please don't go," I say. "You can't go." I cry. I squeeze a few words out through my clenched jaw, my pathetic tears. "I'm so fucked up, it isn't my fault. I just fucked up, that's it. She was in front of me, and she pushed, and I don't know what happened."

"Shut the fuck up," Phoenix says. "Everything is your fault and you know it is. I'm going back home."

I can feel a panic attack about to blow through my body like a tornado, starting at my feet. I sit down on the ground and watch her pack. I wish I had something to say, but there isn't anything I can say that will change her mind. Phoenix isn't that kind of woman. She expects certain things from me, and I haven't met those expectations—she's leaving, and she should.

"I'm not a bad person," I say. "I've tried so hard to make everything perfect."

"There's no such thing as perfection!" she yells at me. She pulls a shoe from her closet and throws it at my face, hitting me between the eyes. "There's no such thing as a perfect life! I've done everything for you! You think I wanted to have a fucking abortion? You fucking sociopathic asshole! You think this is what I want from life? To have a drunk bartender idiot husband who makes out with his best friend?! I hate you. I fucking hate you!"

I crawl on my knees towards her. I grab hold of her knees and press my cheeks to her skin. "Please please please, I'm sorry, I didn't do it, let's just reverse time, I never should have said anything."

"So you could just lie to me the rest of our lives and pretend it didn't happen? Let me tell you something—It is happening. This right here, is happening." She points at her suitcase. "I'm not a dumb little housewife who puts up with bullshit. I live in a fucking cubicle. I write about fucking tampons." She throws a few more items in the suitcase, punching the fabric down with her fists.

I pull myself back from her. I think about what to do next, what card do I have up my sleeve? What manipulation can I possibly create to make her stay, to move forward, to see only the future and not the past. I find that card, and I pull it out, desperate. "I know about you and the woman at the party. I know you made out with another woman and I know you do coke. Let's just call everything even." Even. Ha! The words sound ridiculous coming out of my mouth.

Phoenix stops what she's doing. Her face goes white. "This is what our life has become?" she says. "Our life has become getting even?"

I don't want our life to become getting even. I want our life to be getting awesome. But there's no way around it—this is my one last shot at keeping this together. "Aunika told me. She saw you in the elevator at the Rainbow. And you were never going to tell me. But I knew, and I didn't care, because I love you and I think a kiss doesn't mean shit."

"This woman wasn't my best friend."

"It's the same thing—a kiss is a kiss." I think about earlier today. Was it just a kiss? Or did something more happen between us? How guilty should I feel? Are we really even? Who is making these decisions? Sometimes it doesn't feel like I'm the one making them.

Phoenix closes her suitcase. "Maybe a kiss is just a kiss, but either way, it's not healthy to be living like this. We're a few notches away from a healthy relationship at this point. And you know what else? I knew she had a thing for you—they always do. She was crying at our wedding." She rolls the suitcase into the living room where she finds Aunika blocking the front door, arms crossed.

"You can't leave," Aunika says. "You have some lies we should get out in the open, too. You can't just make him feel like he's the only person who's done anything wrong. I know about you, and your drugs, and that other woman. I know you don't have sex any more, I know about your so-called 'stomachaches'—he's a man and you don't treat him right. You don't give him what he needs."

I can't believe what I'm hearing. I can't believe anything. "Aunika. Please shut up."

"I won't shut up—she needs to know she's ruining you."

Phoenix turns to me—"I can't believe you tell her about our private life. That's our life, not hers. Those things are between us. Private. What's wrong with you?"

"Nothing's wrong with me, I just needed to vent, and she was there—I didn't see this coming. I wasn't complaining, I was venting.

Don't tell me you've never vented about me to someone else. I know you have. I can see it in their faces when they ask about when we're having kids."

"I've never said anything bad about you. Never."

Aunika raises her finger to Phoenix. "You need to take responsibility for this too. It's not just his fault or my fault—I see how you treat him, and I can see he's unsatisfied, and you're not a fucking saint."

I yank at the collar of my shirt. "Aunika! Please shut up!"

"It's her fault, just as much as it is yours! It wasn't just your decision, it was hers too! The abortion, the coke, the other woman, your sex life…that's up to her too!"

Phoenix releases her hand from the suitcase. "I will fucking punch you in the face."

Aunika pulls back her shoulders, lifts her head, squints her eyes. "No you won't."

I step between them, "No one's punching anyone in the face," I say.

"I'm punching someone in the face," Phoenix responds.

Aunika throws me out of her way, raises her arms, "Punch me in the face then!"

Phoenix tightens her fists, pulls back the hammer, and plants a right hook directly on Aunika's chin, dropping the woman like a sack of rocks. Her eyes roll back in her head, reaching unconsciousness before she even hits the ground. In that second, my heart thumps twice, two big irregular heartbeats that can't be healthy. I don't know what to do, how to react. If I run to Aunika, it will seem as if I care for her, but shit, I do, regardless of how much I hate her right now—she just got knocked out. Phoenix turns to me, a look of bewilderment on her face, then takes three steps back, surveying the woman's limp body in front of her. "Oh my god," she says. "I killed her."

I run over to Aunika, press my fingers into her neck, searching for a pulse, somewhere, anywhere—can't find anything. I frantically twist my fingers around her neck, press as hard as I can—where's the pulse? Fucking shit, where's the pulse. My God, my wife is a killer. Two dead friends in two days. I press harder. My wife is a killer, and I'm an accessory. This is murder. This is the end of life, this is the end of everything. As I drop my chin, a chill taking over my body, two small twitches pulse out of Aunika's skin and into my fingertips. I turn around, take a deep breath. "She's still here, holy shit."

"What am I doing?" Phoenix says. "I write about candy tampons. I have chronic stomachaches because of stress. I just punched someone in the face! I hide drugs from you, I hide kissing women from you, I hide how I feel from you, all because I love you. But that isn't love. None of that is love. This isn't love."

"It's all part of love! All of this is part of love—you said this isn't a perfect world, there's no such thing as perfection—here it is, right here in front of you, imperfection." I stand up, try to pull her into me, but she just pushes back. I stand in front of her, take a breath in. "Stay with me. We can work through this. I love you. This was a mistake, just one mistake and I don't know—shit, it's love and it's a mistake. We both made one mistake. One mistake shouldn't end it."

"It's not just one mistake," she says. "And you know it isn't just one mistake. We made one big mistake together, and now we're making a million smaller mistakes together as a result of the one big mistake."

I can tell by the way she shakes her neck from side to side she's erasing the knockout punch from her immediate memory—Aunika deserved it. She regains her composure, grabs her suitcase, pushes Aunika away from the door with her foot, and walks out.

I hear her car ignite, her wheels peel out down the street, into the darkness. Aunika's eyes open, find me in front of her. She tries to pull herself up off the ground, but can't. She reaches out her hand to me, those sky blue nails and long fingers twisting in mid-air, still searching for something to take hold of. I take one last look at her and I walk away.

Don't Get Wasted in Python Country Blues

It's morning of the third day of Cliff's death. The sound of traffic rouses Charlie from his sleep outside the paisa bar, between the bushes filled with dirty syringes and broken beer bottles, used condoms, and cigarette butts, candy wrappers and plastic grocery bags, loser lottery tickets, rotten fruit and dead rats. These bushes have been through hell, out back of the paisa bar in the darkness—a forgotten amusement park for the drunken, each night, filled with scum, more trash building up around their stems, the bottom leaves trying to keep their heads up out of the excrement like the souls in a chapter out of Dante's *Inferno*. And wrapped around this stem, down in the fifth circle of hell, lies one more piece of shit. Charlie opens his eyes, one by one, in the already sweltering heat of a Los Angeles morning—88 degrees at 7 a.m. Charlie doesn't remember much of what happened last night, after Mars Volta inquired about whiskey jelly donuts, slid the paper napkin with his dead brother's scrawl across the bar to him. All he knows, lying there, in the garbage behind the bar, is that his ribs hurt—they're uncomfortable, bruised. He wonders if Juan got at him after all, laid that baseball bat into his chest, took whatever his bar tab was out of his skin—how many rounds could he have bought? He spreads his sandpaper tongue across his teeth, making sure they're all still there—not one missing. He pushes his hands into his head, feeling around for bumps, bruises, cuts, scrapes—nothing. How did he get back here behind the bar, outside the fence? He looks up, finds a crude hole in the chain link, freshly cut, razor sharp points. That would explain the scrapes on his arms, and the terrible state the edge of his switchblade is in. But what about these ribs? What happened to them? He pulls himself up onto his elbows, looks down, and finds a roll of $100's folded in half, wrapped tight with a rubber band—there must be at least five grand sitting there on top of a dried orange peel and near a slimy caterpillar, by the yellowed condom.

What will take Charlie several minutes to piece together, I can tell you in a few short sentences, unless you're a glutton for punishment—"Sighs and blinking eyes, scratching of the head, and unsubtle crotch adjustments, spitting and saying 'What the hell?' to himself"—you get the picture. Charlie underneath this bush is about as exciting as that Certified Public Accountant, who, by the way, found a penny on the sidewalk just outside his office this morning and put it in his pocket. No, I think I'll just "cut to the chase," let you in on the most recent history of our friend Charlie.

Currently, at this moment, Charlie is not wanted for burglary, assault, or any other crime which might have brought the man a rather massive roll of hundred dollar bills. In fact, last night, inside the paisa bar sitting next to Mars Volta, he quite eloquently laid out the idea behind Mustard Brothers donuts, drew up the business plan on a few cocktail napkins, and sold the idea to his potential partner. Mars Volta is no bozo either. Mars Volta runs a successful drug operation out of a dark paisa bar in the corner of Echo Park and owns a modest, yet fashionable three bedroom Spanish villa up in the hills of Silver Lake—he understands supply and demand—he's got a swimming pool that didn't buy itself. He also understands the benefit of having a range of products in the market—some better than others, some better than the other ones. He always has three types of cocaine on him—the pura vida—the most expensive—the stepped on gasoline smelling bullshit—the least expensive—and the stepped on gasoline smelling bullshit that he sells for more than it's worth to douchebags he doesn't dig—mostly pink polo-shirt wearing kooks. And so, Mars Volta patiently considered Charlie's pitch and thought to himself—"Shit, a donut filled with whiskey jelly? That sounds pretty good." Mars Volta asked Charlie how much he'd need to get Mustard Brothers started and Charlie said "Five thousand." Mars Volta took Charlie into the bathroom, offered him up a big snort, saying, "No more H for you holmes, you got my money now, ese. I expect you to make me more of it. I want a Jacuzzi next to my pool." And Charlie nodded his head, "Okay." The two men shook hands, exchanged money, and parted ways for the remainder of the night. Charlie, flying high from the pura vida, drank ten more bottles of beer on Mars Volta's tab, stumbled out the back door, cut a hole in the chain link fence, and passed out in the filthy bushes behind the bar.

And here he is now, staring perplexed at the roll of dough in front of him, when, wham! his memory comes back to him and everything I just explained races through his mind like a freight train on fire.

But all this brain activity is making him feel dizzy—he's got to deal with that hangover, and this one is brutal, a rogue wave, a fucking tsunami, an earthquake with a tsunami with a nuclear energy power plant meltdown, radioactive migrating tuna. He begins counting the drinks—when he gets to eleven, he gives up, realizes his day is gonna be rough without hitting the bottle first thing, something to balance out the nausea, joint pain, anxiety, sugar crash, paranoia.

He wipes the dirt off his cowboy boots, and brings himself up onto his feet, using the thick stem of the slimy bush to help keep him steady. He crawls back through the chain link fence, opens up the back door and sees Juan behind the bar with three middle-aged men in front of him sucking on Tecates, their ranchero hats slunk down low above their heads—seven a.m.—goddamn—the alcoholic shift.

"Whaddya say, Juan?" Charlie bellows from the darkness.

"Where the hell you come from, guero?"

"Out back, man."

Charlie saunters in, boot heels echoing behind him, and takes a seat at the bar. "Still got any money left on that tab?"

Juan sizes up Charlie one more time. He had a feeling this crazy gringo might come back looking for the fifty dollars he left on the bar last night—Juan would be a pendejo loco to think Charlie would leave a fifty dollar tip. "Yeah, you got, uh, like thirty left on that tab."

"Gimmee a Tecate, with a lemon, and a little salt—and make sure it's cold—and bring me another one, set it down right here beside me, for my brother—he'd appreciate it."

Juan turns slowly to the drop-in cooler, pulls the ice cold cans out like twins from the womb. "Pinche guero," he says and snaps the tops with his dirty fingernail. "Crazy."

***

While we're on the subject of Charlies waking up and starting their day, lets head back over to the west side of town where Black

Charlie and Jack Straw are just waking up themselves.

Inside Charlie's car, sweating like bullets, the sun magnified through the windshield burning into their skin, Charlie and Jack Straw awaken in a Dunkin Donuts parking lot, a bottle of Early Times whiskey between them and the remnants of a bakers dozen of glazed, chocolate, orange, bear claw, and raspberry jelly donuts littered across their clothes like cholesterol confetti.

Assessing the situation, sucking the sticky sweet from his fingers, Charlie turns to Jack Straw and asks, "What the fuck happened?"

What will take Charlie and Jack Straw several minutes to figure out, I can tell you in just a few sentences, unless you're a glutton for punishment, in which case…fuck it, you get it by now.

After pulling off the freeway, stuck in traffic on their way to the beach, Charlie and Jack Straw found a liquor store, purchased a bottle of Early Times whiskey, turned a few corners, found a Dunkin Donuts, and bought the said "bakers dozen." Eager to experiment with whiskey and donuts, catch the trip, they headed into the dark recessed corner of the parking lot and began drinking and eating until both the donuts and the whiskey were gone, finito, donzo. In the beginning, notes were taken with diligence, but as the evening wore on, the notes became completely illegible, reading in dripping black ink, "Whiky inna dose anthenna got put the creem inhha." Eventually, the two would-be donut moguls passed out in the car, arm in arm, with half donuts drooping out of their mouths. About an hour after unconsciousness, an LAPD cruiser pulled into the donut shop, two young crew cuts looking for some bright coffee and a sugary snack. But out there, in the corner of the parking lot by the massive trash bins, that car caught their eye—dark, unmoving, suspicious to say the least. The two officers approached the vehicle with caution, took a look inside, and tapped on the window with the butt of their flashlights. No response. A few more taps. Nothing. These two bozos must have passed out after some type of donut hole sodomy. They decided the best thing to do was let the two passed out homos sleep it off, decided these two fags were of no threat to society, not worth the paperwork—shit, they're in West Hollywood, the old WeHo, gay Disneyland, after all—and if two dudes want to screw donuts and each other in a car in a parking lot, well then, cool. They each took a selfie on their smart phones, buzz-cut heads smiling between two passed out morons, and then they went on their way, seventeen minutes later busting a kid trying to break into cars with a screwdriver and slim-jim a few blocks down. These boys are lucky—ordinarily a black guy passed out in the streets of Los Angeles leads to much more trouble than a tap on the window and a selfie posted on Instagram. But, like I said before, there is such a thing as good cops, just like there is such a thing as bad people. With everything in life, the law of yin-yang is emperor—the zipper goes up and the zipper goes down—gravity on all levels—east, west, horizontal, vertical.

And now, back inside the car at seven a.m. in the blistering heat, Charlie and Jack Straw are rummaging through the remains of last night, searching for clues, trying to piece together a seemingly infinite puzzle. "Whiky inna dose anthenna got put the creem inh? What the hell does that mean?" Charlie asks.

"Let me see," Jack Straw replies. "Oh shit, I think we thought of making whiskey cream donuts?"

"Whiskey cream—sounds fucking nasty."

"It could be good."

"No way. No whiskey cream."

"What about Irish cream? Hot and sweet with a little salt?"

Charlie nods his head. "That could work. Lots of Irish cops out there in the world too, right?"

"Not in L.A. Only back east, Scorsese films."

"Whatever."

Charlie fires up the ignition, presses his foot down on the gas, pulls out into traffic. "Lets find us a space to open up. Something dope. With brick. And a rooftop garden. It's donut time."

***

The rule is three beers, minimum. Three beers to cure a hangover. White Charlie learned this trick from the Guru of Skid Row—a cross-eyed homeless man who gave life advice outside the bars in shitty parts of town—and it was always valuable advice. The three beer rule has never failed Charlie in all his years of boozing. That's why he's gotten the first two Tecates out of the way in about five minutes, and now, on his third, he's taking his time, feeling the muscles relax, expand, his mind regaining focus, his hangover becoming sobriety, and right after he finishes that third beer, sobriety hangs a sharp right turn and barrels down the deep dark road towards inebriation—sweet inebriation, glorious wondrous inebriation, the world slowing down to a manageable speed. Once he turns the corner, he'll head home, cry a thousand more tears, take a shower, let it soak in, let it burrow into his guts, and then he'll commemorate his brother forever, spin his paintbrush, create the Mustard Brothers logo, head out into space, East Neptune Los Angeles, and find that spot to open up—maybe that Dunkin Donuts down the street that just went out of business, the one that got robbed six months ago, nearly burned to the ground by that group of drug addicted teenage squatters. He can drop the five thousand in cash right into the palm of the building owner, sell a few bunny paintings, get some flour, whiskey, oil, sugar, pectin, and build the empire, straight up into the sky.

Eight more ounces to go, and the empire begins.

No one bothers to turn when the front door opens—the light is too goddamn bright to look at—they might as well be on the surface of the sun. No, the front door creaks open, the light breaks the black, and the door retreats along with the light. Now, only the sound of boots against the dirty linoleum, one by one, each foot in front of the other, a slow, deliberate gait, one that demands attention, a gait with the rhythm of an Namibian orchestra, a gait so powerful, Charlie, the always searching artist, must turn around to witness the thumping for himself. And when he turns around, takes in those footsteps, he spins right off his barstool and drops to the ground. Wham! All the weight on his tailbone. And when Juan sees Charlie on the ground with a look of terror on his face, eyes turning bloodshot, he too turns to the rhythmic gait-maker, and sees—holy shit, no way, guey!—Cliff, standing with a hand on his hip and a bandage across his head, right eyelid cocked and heavy.

"Pinche puto! You said he was dead, holmes!" Juan yells at Charlie, throwing a dirty bar rag at the young man's face.

Charlie places his hands over his heart, a heaviness crushing down on his chest—is it a heart attack or a panic attack? Limbs go numb. Left forearm starts tingling. Veins pop out of his neck. It doesn't matter—some type of attack is taking over Charlie's body, causing him to shake, freeze, die. "He's dead," he says. "Cliff is dead."

But Cliff is right here. Right now. "You're one whacked-out fucking stooge," Cliff says to his brother.

"They told me you were dead. I cried into your dead armpit, and it smelled like death. It was death. Death was there."

Cliff shuffles his boot heels, rearranges his feet, sucks on his teeth. "Yeah, dickbag, I remember you crying into my dead armpit, but I was too wasted on the drugs to tell you to get the fuck out of my armpit. And you know, since we're talking about armpits, I find it borderline insane that the first place you decided to bury yourself into my dead body was my armpit. My neck, I can see, it's luxurious and bold. But have you ever smelled my armpits? Why you would want to subject yourself to something so vile, peppery, sweaty, and hairy is far beyond my comprehension. It's masochistic. My armpit fluids could probably burn the paint off a car."

Juan's had about enough of these shenanigans. It's time to flex. "You gringos trying to pull something on me?" He asks, swiping a finger across his mustache. He grips that baseball bat with his bearlike hands, the knuckles swollen from years of fractures, fistfights, beer bottles. It doesn't matter that both of the brother's tabs are cleared and everything is cool—The problem is Juan doesn't like being lied to. Lying is disrespectful, and disrespect gets you in a hell of a lot of trouble on the Eastside of town.

Cliff pulls a cigarette from the pocket of his vest, slides it between his lips, throws fire at it, sucks, takes a second to think about a panda bear, the one at the zoo when he was a kid with a banana in its hand, exhales with a finger scratching at his sweating, bandaged forehead. "Juan, look. My brother is a total idiot—we both know this. He paints bunnies. He's a bunny painter. He was so far out in left field that he had no idea I'd survived that far-out trip and was alive and breathing in the ER. Now, in his defense, I did flatline for a little bit—apparently my brother's blood is filled with trash and it nearly killed me—and we all know what trash that is. He freaked out, screamed something about a Tyrannosaurus Rex chasing a fucking rainbow, thought I died, pushed his head into my armpit, and took off out the door like a full-on kook. I woke up this morning and was like, 'what the hell happened to Charlie?'—I didn't have a ride outta there, and they wanted me to stay because I guess I fucked my shit up pretty good, but I split anyways. I figured this douchenozzle would be here being a moron. As for myself, I have a pretty gnarly concussion. I have been concussed. I am concussing. My head hurts."

"Cliff, you're dead. Stop acting alive. Stop talking." Charlie rises to his feet and squeezes his skull with the palms of his hands, trying to force himself to comprehend. "I don't understand. How can you be dead and alive? What kinda trip am I on? Did I shoot too much?"

The paisas seated at the bar take a sip of their beers, push the brim of their cowboy hats up, take a peak at the dead brother, the zombie—suddenly this morning has become intriguing, worth their interest, worth their eyes.

"Ok, you jerk, I'll stop acting alive and stop talking," Cliff says, sliding onto a barstool. "Hey Juan, let me grab a beer."

Juan isn't sure what to make of these whacky havachos any longer, and standing behind the bar gripping that baseball bat, he decides he doesn't care any more. They're weirdos. That's an undisputed fact. But they buy a lot of beer and cocaine, and this is the Land of the Free, Home of the Brave. This is where opportunity lives. This is where money is made and money is God, and if money is God, well then, Juan is greater than God, Juan controls the universe. He opens that drop-in cooler, pulls out a Tecate, and slides it to Cliff.

"Good man," Cliff says, then drops a fifty-dollar bill on the bar. "Keep it," he says to Juan.

"You wanna tip me forty eight dollars?" Juan asks.

"I told you when you helped me with that tab the other day, before I took that barbaric and bloody tumble, that I'd tip you like a stripper. Now pop a button on that little western shirt you got going on there and give me something to bite into." Cliff gnashes at Juan with his teeth, growling like a baby tiger.

Juan nods his head. Cliff is a man of his word. A man of his word goes a long way on the Eastside of town. "Pinche hoto," he says, then cracks a mini-smile and gets back to work, fidgeting with the antennas on the television behind the bar.

Charlie still doesn't know what to make of the scene in front of him—it's like a Fellini film, disjointed, surreal—and no one cares about the scene aside from him. Cliff and Juan have moved on. But Charlie, no, he still doesn't believe it's Cliff right there in front of him, back from the dead, living breathing. He pushes a finger into Cliffs arm, watches the blood pull back, the sponginess of his fat and skin and muscle—it feels real—but then again, who knows what real is anymore—maybe his memory isn't quite correct about last night. Maybe that money is stolen. Maybe he hit that H too hard and this is what purgatory looks like. Maybe he's dead and stuck in this paisa bar for eternity, with his loudmouthed brother by his side to breathe sarcastic and condescending comments into his ear every second of the undying day.

He plops himself down onto the stool next to Cliff and takes a sip of his beer. This beer tastes real. He puts his elbows down on the bar. This bar feels real. Shit. This is a total mindfucker. He knows now what has happened. He's figured it out. He grips onto those bruised ribs, winces, and then with a full and comprehending noggin, he cracks a smile of wisdom. "I get it," he says. "I'm the one who's dead."

Juan just looks at him and shakes his head. "Yeah, I think you are, ese…at least your brain is."

And Cliff just sips on his beer and says with his casual drunken drawl, "Hey, dingleberry, wake up! You're not dead. You're just in Los Angeles."

And Charlie just drops his chin and says, "I'm dead and I know it." He pulls the wad of hundreds from his pocket and rolls it out on the bar, in plain sight of the paisas, a wad of loot big enough to get stabbed for in any part of town—but the paisas just drop their cowboy hats over their eyebrows and pull those ice cold cans up to their faces—the gringos aren't interesting anymore—they're loco en la cabeza. Fucking nuts. Out of their minds. What a waste. Plus, they work for the Mars Volta now.

"What's all this?" Cliff asks pointing at the wad of cash.

"Mars Volta," Charlie replies.

Cliff looks around, searching over his shoulder. "Did you kill him? Where is he?"

Charlie raps his knuckles on the bar. "He's a Mustard Brother now."

Cliff chuckles to himself, takes a big pull from his can. "Mars Volta? Mustard Brother?"

"Yeah."

"Well then," Cliff says, pulling up an arm, dropping it across his brother's back, and pulling him into a tight brotherly hug. "We'd better get started. Mars Volta, our brother Cassidy, and this concussed earth are all counting on us."

Charlie lets his shoulder fall, nestle into his big brother's body, lets those rackety bones take rest in the muscle and fat, feels the warmth cut into his marrow, absorb the love. And then, one big tear forms in the corner of his eyeball and drops to the floor with a gentle aqueous ping. "I love you, brother," he says.

And Cliff lets one big goopy tear form in the corner of his eyeball before swiping it away with this dirty thumb and flicking it over his shoulder. "I love you too, brother," he says. "But you gotta get off that horse."

Charlie drops his chin to the bar, eyeing the condensation dripping down from his deep orange can. "I've already got one foot off."

Cliff orders another round for the two boys—"Dos mas Tecates, por favor."

Charlie takes one last pull from that third beer, hangover defeated, sobriety in the driver's seat, inebriation up ahead, clarity. "Someone better get in touch with Cassidy and tell him you're not dead."

Cliff shakes his head side to side, pushes up his eyebrows with the palms of his hands. "Jesus Christ," he says. "You're such a fuck-up." He whips out his cellular phone, pushes his fingers into the digital keypad, presses send, a message out into the air, floating its way east. *Don't get wasted in python country.*

East or West Blues

It is morning in the east, 93 degrees, 98% humidity, scattered thunderstorms throughout the day. In a single bed inside a small motel room just west of town, Phoenix opens her eyes, takes a deep breath in. She didn't make it far last night, the weight of her decision to leave clinging to her eyelids, pulling them down on the highway out of town. Maybe decisions to leave husbands, to end marriages, shouldn't be made after a bottle of Rebel Yell, the death of a friend, and the intrusion of an insane woman. Maybe Cassidy isn't as guilty as she thought, and maybe she herself is guiltier than she believes. Maybe a kiss is just a kiss. Maybe she needed to flee in order to get back. What is it they say in those AA meetings? You have to hit rock bottom before you can start the climb back up. This is her rock bottom—alone in a shitty motel room just outside the town she can't stand to be in—her husband, the only person who understands what her past is and what her future is becoming, alone with another woman in her house. Or maybe he kicked that bitch out—if he's a good man. If not, well then, this decision, this motel room, is the right one.

This motel room is as depressing as a starving African child with flies on his eyelids. If she could take a snapshot from the ceiling, staring directly down, it would show a woman, in bed, naked, alone, sweating profusely under her arms and across her cheeks because the air conditioner blew-out last night. It would show several alien stains strewn across the mildew scented comforter, the carpet worn where thousands of short term visitors have walked back and forth, from front door to bed, and from bed to bathroom. This motel is not befitting of Phoenix. Ordinarily, she wouldn't be caught dead inside it. But it was on the side of the road last night, bright neon flashing lights, sending out a big beaming message, a message she could fully understand—"Vacancy."

And vacancy is what she now possesses. She is vacant of love, vacant of a child, vacant of a husband, vacant of herself. "Rock bottom," she whispers to herself, shifting between the sheets. "This is rock bottom." A picture of a flower on the wall gives her a small amount of comfort—at least there are still flowers in this world— roses that have lost their fragrance, but still, are beautiful to look at. This is a positive thought, and a positive thought is a step out of the vacancy, out of the bottom, a thought that can move her back up, start the climb. But the human brain is a strange beast. It rationalizes, it craves balance, that zipper, up and down, and so with the beauty of a rose floating through her mind she begins to think about those tongues—Cassidy and Aunika's. She imagines them twisting between each other, his hands around her waist, speaking perfect poetic musings about her hipbones, the poetry he once used to recite with his fingertips against her body. She closes her eyes and she can witness it all, their mouths touching, their tongues sliding in and out, and his erection—that penis she once used to playfully grab on her way from the door to the bed, from the bed to the bathroom. And what about bathrooms? What kind of horrible things have the walls of bathrooms across the world seen? Abortions, overdoses, East Bangkok Buffalo Parasite Diarrhea, stabbings, shootings, beatings—it's all happening in bathrooms.

Bathrooms are public. Nearly every place on earth has a bathroom, but not every place has a kitchen. Kitchens have seen far less tragedy. Kitchens are Shangri-la in comparison to a bathroom. And to the bathroom Phoenix must go. She's been holding her pee in since she fell asleep, not wanting to enter that vile place where everything terrible began, the place that sent her out east, the place that sucked everything out of her.

With inordinate reluctance, she pulls herself up out of bed and walks that heavy walk to the toilet, places a few pieces of toilet paper across the dingy yellowed seat, and drops her haunches down. She reaches out to the faucet, turns the water on, splashes it across her face. It isn't just her soul that stings today—it's her joints and head as well. The Rebel Yell is unforgiving on the body. Rebel Yell is for professionals, not amateurs. Rebel Yell is for Cassidy. Rebel Yell is exactly what it is.

She wipes, flushes. She turns the shower on—only brown water. She waits thirty seconds for the rusty pipes to finish cleansing themselves, but they don't. She turns the shower off. She pulls on her underwear, her jeans, a t-shirt, socks, shoes. This is the decision. This is the morning of a new day. Does she head back east, or keep going, west, driving across the country, heading back home?

She pulls her suitcase up to her chest, stands and heads towards the door, one foot in front of the other.

***

It is morning, east of a small motel outside of town, in a home with lost and vacant roses in the front yard, and I am a man, alone, in bed, staring out the window. I've never had a pet pooch before, because I think dogs are like children, and children are a lot of work.

Dogs need attention, need to be told when to shit, need to be fed, loved, taken places. Dogs need their masters to survive, to thrive, to grow, to be happy. But dogs aren't as smart as humans, and they never will be. Dogs think when their master runs to the grocery store they're never coming back. And so, staring out the window, I understand now that I've sunken so low, I've hit rock bottom, and I've become a dog. She's not coming home. She's gone to the grocery store. All there is to do now is stare out that window, wait for the sound of her car pulling into the driveway, run to the door, pull her in, kiss her, chase her to the kitchen, wait impatiently for a big bowl of guacamole.

I told myself last night I wouldn't sleep. I'd punish my actions by never sleeping again, replaying the sight of Phoenix walking out the door over and over, torturing myself. I listened from the bedroom the sound of Aunika weeping for a few hours before hearing the front door close for a second time that night around 4 am when she let herself out. She said, "I'm sorry," as she walked past my bedroom window, just loud enough for me to hear, and the sorrow in her voice truly made me disturbed. She isn't to blame, and neither is Phoenix. I am to blame for being a man who's been avoiding responsibility for decades. Women—they are responsible. They see their future and they move towards it. Men see their future and still head off down another path, wanting to explore, and when the exploration comes to an end, unfulfilled, they head back towards that other path, the one they left, and walk down it again, if they can. Women are perfect straight lines and men are non-sequitur zig-zags that take too goddamn long to get where they need to go.

Ah, screw it. Men are men and women are women. No one is perfect.

All of my instincts tell me to get up out of bed, grab a beer from the fridge, and get busy suppressing any emotions bubbling up inside me. Cliff is dead. Phoenix is gone. It's time to start dealing with it, and all of the greatest artists in the world have dealt with disappointment in the same way—numbness. And when it became too hard to numb, that's when the art was created. I think perhaps these double tragedies will make me write a better sentence someday, a sentence that says something perfect and beautiful, how bathrooms have seen so much shit, literally and figuratively, and how kitchens are safe, beautiful spaces that feed bellies and keep wine for rich lips. If when I die, I could come back as a room, I'd be a kitchen. I'd watch two lovers make guacamole, open a bottle of wine, kiss over a plate of pesto pasta, the garlic reeking between their breaths, and them just laughing about it, pulling pieces of basil from each other's teeth. I'd watch them do the dishes together, one scrubbing, the other drying, talking about Wes Anderson or Woody Allen, Hermann Hesse and Kurt Vonnegut. I'd watch them bathe a child in the sink, or give a dog a bone from their leftovers. Kitchens are where creation takes place. Bathrooms are the destruction, the final frontier of all the trash we hold inside of ourselves.

I walk into the kitchen and open the fridge. I grab a beer, thinking to myself "I shouldn't drink this early, it gets you into trouble," but people don't change. I pop the top off and get busy ridding myself of this hangover, the most epic hangover yet, with death and divorce looming above like the thunderstorm coming this way. It's getting darker outside the window, the ominous black moving in. Today is a good day for rain. You don't have to be happy when it's raining. Rain is perfect for death and divorce, and if I could, I'd just pack my bags and head up to Seattle for the remainder of summer, watch it rain every day, listen to Nirvana and Elliot Smith for weeks on end until I hit a new rock bottom I didn't know existed, then start my descent south, to the great Golden State, hopefully pick up the pieces, eat an artichoke. But men are stubborn, and moving to Seattle to wallow in depression sounds terrible. No, I think I'll stay right here and wait for Phoenix to return, and if she never does, then she can have the West, and I'll punish myself in the east. I'll never go back. I'll never stare at the perfection of Big Sur again, I'll never eat a fish taco in San Diego, I'll never have a beer in Santa Cruz, and I'll never drive up PCH again, teetering on the edge of the ocean all the way to the Redwoods, with a backpack and a tent, a flask of rum and a big bag of weed. I'll never see the beautiful Pacific, the end, the place where humanity finally had to stop migrating, searching. I'll never be Californian again.

The sky cracks and the windows rattle. A few moments later, rain dumps down on the roof of my house and it sounds like a machine gun. I head into the bedroom and pull on a pair of pants, head back over to the record player, drop the needle on the Gun Club, turn it up loud.

I've gone down the river of sadness/ I've gone down the river
of pain
In the dark under the wires/ I hear them call my name

I lie down on the middle of the floor and take inventory of my life, and as soon as I do, I begin to cry. I pour my guts out along with the sky, and then, as I listen to my heaving lungs rattle like the thunder, hear my tears splashing to the ground along with the rain, I realize something—I am my own world, my own planet, my own earth, with seasons and disasters, beauty and hell, wars and peace, love and hate. I close my eyes, let everything out, let my arm dangle in the air, twist the volume knob up higher so that now, there is no sound at all, only my silent tears, raging out from my eyes, rivers of tears carving canyons into my face. I look out the window and then back to myself. There's nowhere to go. I am my own West. I am the last place on earth. I'm done searching.

***

Phoenix's stomach feels as if there's a hot knife twisting through it as she turns the corner onto her street. Her house is just up ahead, and inside is either a broken down husband, or a two-timing motherfucker with his dick draped around another woman. About a block away, she pulls to the side of the road—she doesn't want Cassidy to hear her car, to run out to her like a dog. She wants to surprise him, catch him with his pants down, solidify her decision to leave, because, as far as she can see, if Aunika stayed with him last night, then it's truly over—There's no turning back.

She sits in her car on the side of the road and watches as the sky turns near black, and then, wham, thunder strikes, lightning ripping down from the heavens, striking a tree in front of her, igniting it, a small flame rising up, melting the green leaves, and then, rain like she's never seen before—it sounds like, shit, what does it sound like? A machine gun. This rain sounds like a machine gun with bullets the size of candied psychedelic jawbreakers, pounding into the ground, raindrops so large the small tree fire in front of her is extinguished and smoldering in only thirty seconds.

Are thunderstorms a good or bad omen? She doesn't know any more.

Out here in the east, good things happen when thunderstorms hit, and bad things happen when thunderstorms hit. It doesn't matter. She can make this thunderstorm good or bad—ominous or fortuitous—she realizes this now. And she realizes this thunderstorm is a metaphor. She is her own world—she controls her own decisions. She can forgive and forget, accept her actions and his reactions. Or she can turn the key back on, make a U-turn and ride that thunderhead all the way West, back home to the Redwoods and PCH and Big Sur, have a beer in Santa Cruz, a fish taco in San Diego, become Californian again. And he can have the East—The Atlantic, the flatness, the mosquitoes, the humidity, the sockless loafers, the women who watch golf. He can have Bearclaw Murphy's and his Choose Your Own Adventure erotica—his bullshit job and his bullshit idea.

She drops her head to the steering wheel, takes a breath in, and lets the tears drop out of her like boulders. She is the west. She is the last place on earth. She's done searching. She opens her car door, takes a step outside, drenched in only a few moments, and begins her sopping wet walk home.

***

The music is so loud now I can barely think. My thoughts—Cliff's death, this divorce—are crumbling under the all-out sonic assault. I think to myself, "I can keep this up forever. I can wear headphones and turn up the volume so loud, I can make myself go deaf. I could drown everything out, let it sink to the bottom, and never search for it again.

I writhe around on the ground, pull back my elbows, and pound my fists into the wood, and then I push myself up onto my feet, and I dance like a maniac, twisting my head and throwing my body around like a Category-5 tornado—stand back—I could annihilate everything in my path.

If the music wasn't so goddamn loud, I'd probably hear the

footsteps walking up the stairs outside, thump thumping on the porch. I'd probably hear the loud knock at the door, and I'd probably hear a woman's voice yell "Cassidy" at the top of her lungs, and the sound of the doorknob jiggling. But I don't. I twist around with my eyes closed, going dizzy, going blind. And if my eyes weren't closed, I'd probably see a woman move around to the side of the house, peaking in the window, waving her hand trying to get my attention. But I don't.

All I can think of is that rain coming down outside. The rain is here to cleanse. This thunderstorm is here to save me, to make me whole again, to wash away my sins. This thunderstorm is a bathroom in heaven, ready to carry all the trash inside of me out to sea. I run to the fridge, I grab a beer, I twist the top off, and I march towards the back door, and when I get to it, I pause, I force myself to smile, and I twist the doorknob.

"Cassidy," I hear a voice say. And this time, the voice doesn't startle me, doesn't cause me to fall to the ground, tumble backwards. In front of me, perfect, soaking wet, stands my West. "Phoenix," I say.

She stands before me, arms at her side, vulnerable, pulls her shoulders back, wipes the tears or the rain or the sweat or all three from her cheeks, and says, deeply, confidently, with her eyes burning down, "Was it just a kiss?"

I draw a thumb up to my eye, wipe away a tear, or a raindrop, or a bead of sweat or all three and open my mouth just enough to answer.

If it was just a kiss, turn to Page 403.
If it wasn't just a kiss, go to the next page.

The West is The Best Blues

She stands there in front of me with eyes like a homeless kitten, looking up at me, praying for the right words to come out of my mouth. She wants me to say, "It was just a kiss," then she wants to climb into my arms, push herself into me, fuse our bodies together, lie down in bed, make popcorn, watch the new Star Trek movie, the rain pouring down outside, cleansing this house, giving the roses what they need to survive.

But you and I both know it wasn't just a kiss. I followed Aunika into that donut shop, closed the refrigerator door behind us, and I dropped to my knees, pushed my head between her, put my tongue inside. And the only witnesses, aside from the two of us inside that refrigerator, were bags of herbs, elephant razor grass, medallions of foie gras. In times like these, the saying "What they don't know won't hurt them," seems altogether too true. I could lie to her. I could say, "It was just a kiss, nothing more, and I was drunk, and she forced herself on me, and I resisted at first, but she kept pushing, and she told me she loved me, and I felt sorry for her, and everything happened so goddamn fast." I could use my tongue to lie about my tongue.

But this is life. This is adulthood. And if my grandfather were here to tell me what to do, he might say "Lie to her and never do it again. Be true to her, and take care of her from here on out. Give her a child, build a family, work hard, save money for retirement, and teach your son to play ball." Or he might say, "A kiss is just as bad as a tongue somewhere else. You're a Catholic for God sakes." Or he might say, "It's no big deal. Men are men, and we all have urges, attractions. It's nothing a good bottle of bourbon can't cure." But he's not here and I can't decide what kind of a man he was. All I know right now is what kind of a man I am. I am a man that went down on my best friend in a walk-in refrigerator while my wife was at work writing about candy tampons. And that kind of man doesn't sound like a good man—in fact, that man sounds like a scumsucker—a real bottomfeeder. So the question is: Why would I want to lie to Phoenix about who I am? Why would I want to go through the rest of my life carrying a burden? I'm the kind of man who avoids responsibility, and the responsibility of lying to my wife for eternity doesn't sound appealing. I have this beer in my hand, and if I finish it right now, belch out the bubbles, pull my shoulders back against my spine, straighten my neck, broaden my chin, clench the jaw muscles, I might be able to gather up the courage, eek out the truth, and leave the decision up to her. If she wants to stay with me, go on with the ruse, I'll promise nothing like this will ever happen again, and then, I know it, she'll never trust me, and this marriage will become like going to work—a burden, a job, a place I don't want to be, but have to arrive at each morning, nonetheless. Or she'll pull back that hammer of hers and punch me in the face, drop me like a sack of potatoes, kick me out of the way, walk out the door into the gray, and this marriage will go down the toilet, out to sea, joining everything else I've destroyed.

"Was it just a kiss?" she asks again. She crosses her arms. She looks tired.

I take the rest of my beer in three loud gulps, look her in those big brown eyes, pull my shoulders back against my spine, straighten my neck, broaden my chin, feel my heartbeat triple—the attack is coming, but I'm not sure where from—inside or outside.

My phone buzzes in my back pocket, startles me, elevates the blood pressure, keeps the heart racing. Figures. This is the most intense moment of my life and I'm getting a text message. It could be from Charlie. It could be something about Cliff, that his funeral is next week, and I'll have to book a flight on a credit card, and I'll have to see our friends, and Phoenix will go as well and we'll have to explain at my best friend's funeral why we're no longer married. People will say, "Cassidy is a sociopathic dickhead," and I'll have to sheepishly agree with them, cower in the corner and drink whiskey until they all just blur out and away, become the out-of-focus edges of my reality. The lie. The lie. The Gun Club. The music blasts out at me from the background…

Things just fall to pieces/ when I sit and watch the door
I can never get to you/ any more and more and more

I reach for my back pocket, pull out the cell phone, and she looks at me like I'm crazy, like I have no consideration for her heart. She already knows the answer to her question because I can't answer. My God, it's taken this long just to say one word. But it will only take one word, a lie, to make things straight again, to get her back inside this house. "It could be something about Cliff," I tell her. But she doesn't let me look. Instead, she grabs my wrist. "Cliff is dead and we're alive," she says. "Was it just a kiss?"

Deep breath. Death. It surrounds me, in all its metaphorical and tragic beauty—like Antarctica or the moon. I'll remember this moment for the rest of my life, carry it with me forever like genital warts. This portrait—my beautiful wife, dripping clothes hanging from her fragile bones, framed in the doorway, underneath the picture of Jerry Garcia at Woodstock, the wooden blinds to her left, open, the rain falling like sheets of aluminum foil—goddamn that's a lot of rain—and to her right, the photograph of us kissing in the rain at Waimea Canyon, by the river filled with rainbow trout, near the waterfall. And behind her, in the yard, an empty bottle of bourbon, a backyard of gardenia and a brick pathway leading to the trashcans around the side—an empty bowl of guacamole filled with rain. And I see my hands—there's more hair on my knuckles now than there was when I was sixteen. I was once sixteen, with a muscle car and a smile, the taste of beer and a teenage girl on my gums. I'm not young anymore, and my decisions take on a weight I've never known—Atlas lifting earth—beer and women taste like mistakes. The lines on my hands are deep from years of dumping dirty glasses into sanitizer rinse, cuts and scrapes and scars from the sharp edges of cocktail shakers—a life built and falling apart in a bar. And to my left, the bathroom, the clawfoot tub she would soak in and call for me, and when I came running, she would tell me to "unzip your pants, sit on the ledge," and she'd give me a blowjob because she could see I needed one, she could see it in my eyes—my writing wasn't going so good, and Bulch wanted me to empty out the drop-in cooler to clean out some broken glass before my shift and there was a ton of mold and Cherise is giving me shit again about her chainsaw cuts and how I didn't slice the limes the way she likes 'em sliced. And when Phoenix would finish sucking and spitting, and I was relaxed and smiling, she'd splash around in the bubbles, dunk her face underneath and tell me to open a bottle of wine and find us a place to vacation, the perfect place for us when we had enough money to vacate—a place where we could stare at the sea and drink mojitos, never lift a finger, make love all day, take naps, watch as pink and turquoise fish swim up and tickle our ankles in the sapphire water. I look at her now, and I only remember the good things, even as she rubs her belly, presses against it, wincing every few seconds in pain. The suspense is literally going to kill her. My suspense is killing her. I am killing her and myself. I grab hold of her hands. I take them into mine, push my lips onto her hairless knuckles, her wrinkle-free fingers.

"Was it just a kiss," I repeat to her. And then, I do what needs to be done. I yank the Band-Aid off with one short rip. "No."

This is the climactic moment of my life, the moment where what I say changes everything and everything changes again after it. And this climactic moment of my life is not at all how I thought it would turn out. I feel like collapsing, and yet, I feel free. She doesn't cry harder, she doesn't try to pull her hands from mine, she doesn't pull back her arm and throw a punch. Instead, she pulls herself into me, hugs me as hard as she can, pushes her head into my neck, takes a big inhale, presses her nose to my chest and sucks in with her nostrils. "You smell so good," she says. She pulls back, drops her hands from mine, rubs a finger across my lips and says, "Goodbye. Forever."

This is the moment I'll always remember. This is the photograph that will haunt me for the rest of my life—she turns the corner, moves across the frame of the doorway, and disappears in the rain, moving forward, away. The neon red lights flash in my head—VACANCY.

"I love you, Phoenix." The words roll out into thin air, and with her, vanish, vacant, without a home.

I look at my cell phone—a text from Cliff. *Don't get wasted in python country.*

He's alive, I think. I'm alive, I think. I close the door, I close the rain, I close myself, I close my earth. She'll be the West. I'll be The East. The west is the best. This is the end, beautiful friend.

THE END

Just a Kiss Blues

She stands there in front of me with eyes like a helpless kitten, looking up at me, praying for the right words to come out of my mouth. She wants me to say, "It was just a kiss," then she wants to climb into my arms, push herself into me, fuse our bodies together, lie down in bed, make popcorn, watch the new Star Trek movie, the rain pouring down outside, cleansing this house, giving the roses what they need to survive, bringing a sweetness to life seldom known.

"Was it just a kiss?" I repeat to her.

And she nods her head, sticks her thumb into her mouth and begins chewing on her fingernail. "Yeah, was it just a kiss?"

I open my mouth, and all I want to do is turn back time, lie, blame everything on Aunika, pretend I have no idea about Phoenix's cocaine and her own homoerotic kiss, never go to St. Claire's Rainbow party, never know Cliff is lying dead somewhere in Los Angeles, his limp body growing cold, lifeless—no more text messages. But that isn't life, no matter how incredible this life seems to be. There is no "going back," only forward. Going forward means taking responsibility for my actions, being honest, working through what is bound to be a confusing and awkward several months, building up trust between us again. Goddamn, if I could turn back time, I'd wear a condom, and if I could turn back time even further I may not have even asked Phoenix on a date to that used bookstore—right now, at this moment, it would seem better to be alone, lonely, solo, without anyone to lean my head and heart against than to have lived through all the beautiful and tragic moments we've shared. But that isn't life either. The zipper up and the zipper down. Beauty and tragedy are part of life, part of a relationship, what makes them last, what makes them worth writing about, worth reading about, worth seeing a film about, worth waking up in the morning for.

Phoenix looks over my shoulder, lets her eyes scan the house behind me. "Is she still here?"

My answer takes too long and now her suspicions are growing. I should have just said, "Yes" a few seconds ago, but my mind is racing, busy regretting, replaying, reworking, redoing. And now, Phoenix is convinced Aunika is somewhere in the house dressed only in my Guns N' Roses t-shirt, her long legs propped up on a chair, a heaping bowl of guacamole in her lap, a bottle of cool bourbon by her side, smiling, victorious.

"No. Of course she's not here."

"When did she leave?"

"Last night. After you knocked her out."

She's done chewing on her thumbnail. She pushes her index finger into her teeth and begins gnawing. "So?" She says.

I take a deep breath in, and as I open my mouth, I flash to those moments we've had in this house—it isn't so bad here, if you dissect it, extract the good, separate it from the bad. It's not the west, the west is the best, but the east—it's tolerable when you have love. Love can make any place on earth better, if not the best. Love can make the east become west, and can make the west, well I suppose it would simply make it "the west." I take a deep look at her—I want to remember this moment for the rest of my life—implant it in my mind like a photograph in a frame. Phoenix stands before me, sopping wet, her clothes clinging to her perfect curves, those hipbones, Cabo San Lucas, Cape Mendocino—my God, she is beautiful, perfect. Why would I ever want anyone else? But I'm a man. I have instincts, but all of my instincts are generally incorrect—Choose Your Own Adventure erotica—I might as well put my head down, clench my teeth, accept my bartending future, dunk my hands day after day in that sanitizer rinse, get home at sunrise, watch my eyes and my health, my hope and my smiles go down the drain along with the beer foam. But what about whiskey jelly donuts? And Mustard Brothers? Cliff is dead—no more Mustard Brothers. Charlie is a junkie with a successful art career. At least the Mustard Brothers wasn't a bad idea. Maybe not all of my instincts are wrong, but most of them are—and it's all because I was created as a beast with a penis, the insatiable urge to make love, to conquer the world, even when I don't feel like doing either.

I look at my wife. Wife. I think of that word, place it as if it were a red neon sign flashing before me—W I F E W I F E W I F E—if my grandfather were here, he'd probably tell me to stop grab-assing and get on with it—fix what I broke between us, pull her into my waist and plant the biggest Humphrey Bogart kiss she's ever known right on her lips, massage her heart, order-in some food, make a pair of martinis and celebrate the future, not dwell on the past. He had regrets—we all do. None of us are perfect. We all have secrets, we all carry little ideas and events around with us that we'll never tell anyone, we lock them away. These secrets shouldn't be out in the open—For instance, would I tell my wife I take off my wedding ring when I masturbate to internet porn because if I leave it on, it makes me feel like she's watching? No way. That sounds crazy. It is crazy. I might be crazy, ready to be committed, on the brink, one foot dangling over the cliff. Cliff. All it took was a trip. How many trips have I been on? Far too many. And the gooball from last night is making me feel woozy—or maybe it's the contusion on my head. I take a sip of my beer and I smile, not big, a small, affectionate smile.

"Phoenix, I love you. It was just a kiss. And I regret it more than anything I've ever regretted in my life, more than, you know, uh…."

"More than what?"

"More than the abortion. We can't run away from that and we can't run away from this. But I love you, and if I had any idea Aunika felt that way about me, I would never have put myself in that position in the first place—I would have held her at arm's length for the rest of my life."

Phoenix nods her head, crosses her arms. "I'm sorry," she says.

"For what?"

"For kissing another woman, for lying to you about taking drugs, for not telling you how miserable I am here, for being at work so much, for the stomachaches…"

"You can't control the stomachaches."

"We barely have sex anymore."

"Let's start having more."

She looks down at the ground, takes a step back, away from me, and turns around. Something's wrong. The smile didn't work. Neither did the honesty. I've lost her. I can feel it. She just wanted to know the truth, to hear it from me without Aunika in the room, look into my eyes, and make a decision based on her immediate reaction—listen to her heart. But it doesn't make any difference—I know it. She knows we can't continue, that the next several months will hinge on regaining trust, on me proving to her no other woman could ever come between us, and her proving to me that kissing another woman when she's drunk and high isn't a big deal. But I've already forgiven her—it happens—we're all drunk and high, aren't we? That woman she kissed wasn't her best friend, and even if it was, it'd probably be better than a stranger—girls always kiss their best friends. They start young, practicing on each other. They stand naked in front of each other and talk about their jobs, men, kids, other women, other men, who they voted for, what they would be doing if they weren't married, what they would be doing if they were married, what life is all about, Ethiopian politics, how much they drank last night. They take showers in front of each other and help each other pull on jeans and zip up dresses. They show each other bumps inside their vaginas, ask their friend to look, use the magnifying glass, make sure it isn't herpes or genital warts. Women are comfortable with each other, and men are uncomfortable with everyone—that's why booze was invented, and why war exists, why we created guns and bombs instead of tropical birds that spit Hawaiian Punch into our mouths and rest on our bellies.

I watch as she takes one more step away, out into the rain, drops her head back. I want to take a step forward, grab her by the waist, raise her up above my head, carry her into the house, turn on Star Trek, roll around in a pool of guacamole with her, eat that tortilla chip right off her collarbone, smile with her. I take that step, feeling my phone vibrate in my back pocket, startling me. I'm not sure if I should take a look, pull it out at this very delicate moment, this moment that could define my life, this moment that could leave me stranded in the east, while Phoenix takes the west and with the west, my heart as well. But it could be Charlie—it could be about the funeral arrangements. Jesus. Cliff is dead. How can all this be happening at once? I don't have any emotional vacancy left. I'm filled to the brim, at capacity, no room at the inn. I take that step, deciding to leave the phone in my pocket, to pursue my wife instead, to straighten out my life. Cliff is dead. But Phoenix is still alive.

"Babe," I say. And she turns. And I take another step, and one more, until I'm standing in the rain with her. I am soaking. I am cleansed. I look up to the sky, see the clouds roaring past in thick dark procession, heading east, out to sea, where they'll disappear, vaporize, recycle themselves. "I want to be recycled," I say, and Phoenix looks quizzically at me. "I want to start over. I want us to go back. I want to take three steps back right now, the both of us, into that house, sell all our shit, and take three thousand miles back, and wind up in California. I want to pull up all our trash from inside of us, reform it, and release it back out into the universe, kick it out."

Her eyes well up. She nods her head. I take my hands, I place one on Cabo and the other on Cape Mendocino, and I pull her into me, kiss her with all of my body, toes to head. My tongue slides back into its home, that warm familiar place that has said everything I've ever wanted to hear and still long to hear. And when this kiss is done, she presses herself into my neck, inhales, and says, "Goodbye."

She pulls herself out of my arms, takes those steps forward, turns the corner. I drop my head back, catch the rain in my mouth. "I love you," I say. "I love you!" I scream. But there's no response. I let myself drop into the grass, right next to that empty bowl of guacamole, the empty bottle of bourbon, the empty everything. I pull the cell phone out my back pocket, read the text message— *Don't get wasted in python country.* My heart loosens itself from my chest, a few pounds lifted off of it. Cliff is alive. But I'm not.

YouTube Sensation Blues

It's official: Volcano the Spacemachine's set last night at the Gooseberry Festival in Eugene, Oregon has become legendary, one of the most epic rock and roll performances of all time, larger than Hendrix at Monterey Pop, bigger than The Doors first gig at the Whiskey-A-Go-Go—primarily because of their seventy-two minute version of their new hit, "Whiskey Jelly Blues." Seventy-two minutes of pure rock and roll, electric blues mayhem. Seventy-two minutes in which couples copulated, fornicated, ripped off their clothes, dropped themselves into tall grass, splashed around in the moonlight, ran down into the mighty Williamette, swam, dove, drank, stoned, picked themselves back up, and still had another thirty-three minutes to go, shaking off the river in the summer night. There was a quote that did a pretty decent job of summing up the experience in the *Oregon Herald* this morning from Rocket Dickinson, 26, of Bend, OR. He said, "This was the moment where life and death met in my mind, formed one great union, shook hands, and created me, born again. I have no fear, only love. A love of rock and roll, and a love for whiskey jelly."

Several YouTube videos have been popping up all over the interweb of the band's iconoclastic rendition of their instant classic. Specifically, there is one video, recorded from the soundboard and in HD which shows the band performing, with ominous, yet delicate lavender light pouring off their shoulders, steam rising from the stage as if their boot heels were made of flaming charcoal, singeing the floorboards, branding this moment in eternity. For seventy-two minutes, James Lord James, lead singer, threw himself around the stage like a possessed shaman, swirling and twirling, bleeding and sweating, creating an atmosphere unto himself—and the fans did the same, dancing between each other, spreading their skins and sweat until all tension, all hatred, all hang-ups, all inhibition had been thrown from their souls and all that was left was a pure perfect white light riding up the spine.

442,011 hits in less than twenty-four hours—an internet sensation. Barry Pearl knows he has a hit. Barry's the only producer The Spacemachine works with, on account of his superb sense of hearing, delicate fingertips, and excellent fashion in drugs. Barry's having that 7" vinyl pressed right now, available for pre-order through the Volcano The Spacemachine website. Over 15,000 units already sold. The comment boards across the Spacemachine website all say the same thing—"Best Spacemachine song ever," and "I can't live another moment without whiskey jelly." And the vinyl—wow—deep purple, with swirls of cream expanding out from the center—spins around the turntable like a psychedelic lollipop.

This is a phenomenon. The band knows it. Bulch knows it. Bulch keeps up on the times. Bulch reads the paper, scans the hip blogs, listens to the right mouths, and when he hears something he likes, he pounces on it like a Pink Tongued Ivoire Tiger. Lounging in his office, naked in his Murphy bed underneath the stuffed grizzly bear head, Cherise at his side applying her cherry red lipstick in the oil lantern light, he realizes "whiskey jelly" and all its possible permutations has struck a vein in this generation, hit a nerve, become the thought bubble attached to a collective consciousness.

But what does one do with whiskey jelly? How does one turn a profit? Spread it on toast? An English muffin? No. Too predictable. Pancakes perhaps? Something sweet. He'll think on it later, after he gives Cherise that massage he promised her last night. He slides his hand underneath the sheets and strokes Cherise's bottom. "Whiskey jelly is a hit," he tells her.

And Cherise smiles. "You're great with names. You're always a step ahead of the trend. You're a trendsetter."

"What do you think I can do with whiskey jelly? What does the world want from whiskey jelly?"

"Shots?"

"Whiskey jelly shots. Hmm." Bulch pulls his pipe from the nightstand, lights it, leans over to the record player—Barry had a 7" shipped to him this morning for immediate listening—He trusts Bulch's ear, wants to make sure the levels are correct, the trip is perfect. And that slide guitar kicks in, and then the kick drum, and wham! Bulch smiles, throws Cherise onto her belly, digs his hands into her shoulder blades as she purrs like a bobcat. "Hell of a night," he says, the smoke twisting through his mustache. "So much can happen in a night. You can catch a tiger, or be eaten by one. And either way, the next day, life will never be the same."

"You caught me last night," Cherise replies, growling like a tiger.

"And life has changed." He continues with his massage, the pipe smoke spreading out across her back, kissing the canyons of ribs, tickling behind the ear, and then, slides off her skin, soaking into the sheets. "Whiskey jelly," Bulch replies. "I said goddamn."

But Bulch isn't the only one hip to the Spacemachine's new hit single—it's all over Buzzfeed and NME—even made the cover of *Hott Doggs Rock and Roll Racket*—that's an international rag. And beyond that, Alice Cooper just tweeted about it, and so did Gary

Clark Jr. and Rihanna. And wait, Kim Kardashian just mentioned it on her twitter feed—"Whiskey Jelly morning #Spacemachine #Lovinlife #Blessed," trending, with a picture of Kanye feeding her orange marmalade from a gold spoon with a diamond encrusted bottle of Makers Mark in her hand. Shit, man, this song is gonna take over the world, be the theme to the next Olympics, lip sung at the Super Bowl by Taylor Swift, quoted by president B. Sanders in the State of the Union. Even the Greeks and the Turks and the Afghanis might dig it—the Japanese already have it playing on the big screen in downtown Tokyo, already created a best-selling hand roll—The Spacemachine—smelt egg jelly, rice, shrimp tempura, wrapped in papaya skin, shot of whiskey on the side. At least none of these kooks have figured out how to put the two together and stuff it into a donut.

And deep in the eastside of Los Angeles, lost and wandering, Black Charlie and Jack Straw drive aimlessly through the streets, checking out vacant buildings, old donut shops, none the wiser.

And deep in the paisa bar on the Eastside of Los Angeles, White Charlie and Cliff sit at the bar, sucking on their brews, embracing every few seconds, glad to be alive and drinking, sitting on their whiskey jelly patent—still pending, but in progress nonetheless.

And deep in the East, I hear Phoenix's car pass by the house, turn the corner, and fade into the distance. I'm now on my back, wrapped in blades of cool grass, showered in rain. I dial Cliff's number on my cell phone. I need to hear his voice, to know he's alive and that Charlie didn't just get wasted on the H, hit top gear on the great stone, and fall into some strange fourth dimensional state where he entered Cliff's dead body and became him, texting friends from the other side.

The phone rings. The phone engages. A breath. "The elegant

eagle couldn't find a pair of shoes appropriate for the bar-mitzvah."

I hear it, I know it. This is Cliff's voice. This is Cliff's brain.

"Holy shit," I say. I cry. I cry hard. I cry like this thunderstorm. If someone were lower than I, underneath me, these tears would bruise them.

"My brother is an idiot."

"You're alive." I suck in the air. I get another chance. I can choose my own adventure. I can change the outcome. I know I can.

"I'm alive, but I took a pretty gnarly tumble. I should probably still be in the hospital, but Charlie completely lost it and I could see he was gonna do something retarded, so I bailed."

"I don't have words right now. Fuck, man, I almost lost it. When I heard you died last night, I fainted behind the bar and knocked myself out on the concrete. I was bleeding everywhere. I spread trash on my face and ate gooballs and wound up on the subway watching an Indian play with his zipper."

"Yeah, well, blame it on the dumbass here."

I hear the phone pass hands, a loud Mexican in the background yelling, "It's four dollars, ese!" "All right, all right," I hear Cliff reply in the faded distance.

"Hey Cass,"—Charlie's voice has returned to that molasses drawl. "Sorry about last night—I really thought he was dead. I'm a fucking wreck. I heard the beep, you know, the long beeeeeep. And he was dead, man. I saw the green line on the thing attached to him."

"Lay off the H, brother."

"Yeah."

"Tell him about what you did," Cliff shouts at the phone.

"Right now?" he replies

"Yeah, now," Cliff says. "When else, dickwad?"

"What's up?" I inquire.

"Well, I got a little bent out of shape thinking Cliff was dead, so I went down and first thing I did was get a patent for Mustard Brothers—so that's all taken care of."

"Rad."

"But then I got pretty drunk and stoned and so, uh, well, we have a new partner—a new Mustard Brother."

"Who is he?"

"Mars Volta."

"Holy shit. The band?"

"No, he's a drug dealer, here, at the bar we go to. He sells coke. He's a pretty neat guy and he looks really cool. That's why we call him Mars Volta—cuz he looks like the singer and he's got great tight pants."

"We have a drug dealer for a partner? Like a cartel, or what?"

"Yeah. Insane right? But totally cool. Gives us street cred. And protection. We're thinking about opening up around here, you know, eastside."

Cliff grabs the phone from Charlie. "He's a total dumbass, but the dude gave us five grand in cash to get started. So sell your shit, grab your wife, and get your ass out here."

I look up into the rain, falling into my eyeballs, and I try not to close my eyelids—I want to feel the drops bruise my eyes, I want to feel the pain, because that pain is taking my mind away from Phoenix pulling away and vanishing from my life. "Phoenix just left me. She's heading back west, and I can't be there. She gets the west. I take the east. I fucked up."

There is silence on the other end. It's the first time I've ever heard Cliff be silent, stunned, with nothing to say. I check my phone to make sure we're still connected—we are. I wait three seconds.

One. Two. Three. "Hello?"

"Wow," Cliff says. "What'd you do? It wasn't the cream cheese in the armpit, was it? I can fix that."

"It's me and Aunika and I don't know, man."

"That hot blonde chick you grew up with?"

"Yeah, I fucked up, but Phoenix did too, and I think she just wants to get away from me. Just a kiss, nothing more, but she's running. And Aunika told me she loves me and you know, it's weird."

"Can't run away."

"I know."

"You guys already tried that. Nowhere else to go. You've pushed yourselves to the edges of the continent away from my belly and my sassiness."

"We've pushed ourselves further than the edges of the continent—we've created impossible scenarios in the universe."

"This is no good. This is Mustard Brothers. This is fucking Mustard Brothers, man."

And then, dead air. The phone call ends. I press Cliff's number again, and it goes directly to his voicemail—"The mailbox of the person you are trying to reach is full."

"Fuck!" I pull myself up off the grass and head into the front yard. Maybe Phoenix came back around, circled the block for dramatic effect, wanted to see if I'd chase after her. But her car is gone. The streets are flooding, water rising. The sky gets darker. One of the housewives next door pulls up in her car, pulls her child from the backseat, runs through the rain towards the cover of her porch, turns around, sees me—her expression changes when she does. The connection between mother and child—the glee of the storm, the feeling of safety and love, motherhood, that little glimmer in the eye, the knowledge of life, the wisdom of parenting—that expression shifts, her lips drop, her eyelids clench. I look like the opposite of what she holds in her arms, the complete antithesis of hope. She raises her free hand with her child on her hip and waves. I wave back, drop my head. I see those roses. They stand proud in the rain. It's strange. I can smell them now.

Waylon Blues

This joint is on the corner of Sunset and Elysian. This joint is on the eastside of the west coast. This joint has a broken window, a rat problem, smells like piss. This joint has a resident bum living in it that no one knows is living in it. This joint is made of brick walls, but the storefront is all glass, four chevrons, two facing north and two facing west. This joint has a massive deep fryer, a counter, a display case built in, a kitchen in back, a walk-in fridge the bum has been using as a bedroom. This joint was once a Dunkin Donuts, owned by P.J. Rhodes, an ex-guitar player, son of Bernard Rhodes, creator and manager of The Clash, but this joint got robbed ten too many times and now, here it is, covered in rotting drywall and dirt, empty beer cans and dust, the detritus of a big city accumulating within it. There's a few booths by the windows, crimson vinyl, tuck and roll, and it's said that in the one closest to the front door, Joe Strummer ate his first donut. Joe walked in, his first trip to L.A., and he sat down and he ordered a jelly donut and he said something about the palm trees. No one's sure what kind of jelly donut he ate, but if one had to guess, it'd be raspberry. Joe Strummer was notorious for his raspberry addiction—he brought them with him wherever he went on tour—at least that's what this real estate agent is saying. "Joe loved raspberries…And kung-fu movies," says Penelope Bartlett, Agent to the Stars.

Black Charlie and Jack Straw had just about given up on their search early-on this morning, the hangover and the traffic and the heat and the vastness of Los Angeles too much for them to handle. They saw her name on a bus stop bench—"Penelope Bartlett—Agent to the Stars." A photograph, tight portrait, her smiling face, the hills and palm trees in the background. She seemed as good as any one else. It took one phone call and then two hours later, Charlie and Jack arrived at this old Dunkin Dump, the site of punk rock pastry history. Penelope is exactly how you'd picture a real estate agent who claims to hob-knob with the stars. Those breasts aren't real. The blonde hair isn't real. And that red power suit isn't from Barney's. The gold wristwatch isn't from Tiffany's, the diamond engagement ring isn't a diamond nor is it an engagement ring. The fresh twenty-seven year-old face on the bus stop bench is actually closer to fifty. The car isn't a Mercedes—It's a Ford. This old abandoned Dunkin Donuts isn't the next Four Seasons property. And the Eastside is not the Westside.

"Joe Strummer, eh?" Charlie asks, taking it all in. "Don't know if that makes up for the fact that this place sucks ass and needs a complete redo."

"You could put a little gold plaque right here on the edge of the table that says 'Joe Strummer's first donut.' Punk rock's a pretty big thing in Los Angeles." Penelope is a hell of a saleswoman—earns over eighty grand a year, pays her bills, has a condo in the hills, heads out to Palm Springs to tan and drink martinis every three months, stays at that little hotel she's been going to for years, the one with the piano bar attached, the one with the good rib eye—and every now and again, she gets lucky with a man half her age. She's non-committal—too rad to settle down.

Jack Straw walks the perimeter of the space, checking the

construction, examining design, scribbling numbers down in a small notepad. "What's the crime like in this part of town?" he asks.

Penelope knows what's up. Questions like these are easy to handle. "A bit higher than average. However, there's a police station one point three miles away, so I'd say this area is relatively safe."

"They say some of the most dangerous parts of a city are the areas directly adjacent to a police station."

Penelope nods her head. "I've heard that. But just look at this mid-century window design."

Neither Charlie nor Jack Straw have any idea what she's talking about, but, nonetheless, "mid century window design" sounds pretty neat. Did Frank Lloyd Wright come up with that? Was mid century window design a major architectural movement in the, uh, mid century? Who knows? Penelope can sell anything.

"Yes, this part of Los Angeles is thriving once again. In the twenties, this part of town was where all the action was. Where all the stars met to dine and drink. Just south of here, West Adams— well Bogart lived there."

"West Adams?"

"Uh huh. This neighborhood is up and coming. The hipsters have arrived. Cheap rent, close to the freeway, Spanish style villas and Craftsman homes—it's just a matter of time before Echo Park, and further east—even East L.A.—become the new hot spot. I heard Gwyneth is looking for a home just up the road, now that she's single."

Jack Straw bends his ear and neck. "Gwyneth Paltrow?"

"Yeah. She's a wonderful young woman. Very generous."

"You know Gwyneth Paltrow?" Jack Straw asks. He puts his pen behind his ear, tucks his notepad into his pocket.

"I've lunched with her a million times. Great gal. Bought a condo from me seven years ago when she was shooting a film in

Downtown." Penelope leans in to Jack Straw's ear. "She's a great tipper. Loves the little guy. Supports local business wherever she goes."

"You hear that?" Jack Straw says. "Gwyneth eating a whiskey jelly donut?"

"Whiskey jelly donut?" Penelope replies. "What's this about a whiskey jelly donut? Is that what you boys are thinking of doing?"

Charlie's face would be bright red if you could see it. But his skin is a perfect deep chocolate brown, and so, he can play himself off as cool. "No," he says.

"Because that's a novel idea," Penelope replies.

"Nope. No whiskey jelly donuts. Just the regular ones, but, you know, made with organic ingredients and fair trade cocoa and flour and all that jazz."

"Huh," she says. "Well, to each their own. But I think you boys might be overlooking a great opportunity with the whiskey jel...."

"How much is this joint?"

"The owner wants only six hundred thousand for the entire property, parking lot, all twenty-five hundred square feet and all the equipment inside. But he's also willing to lease the space for forty-five hundred a month. It's a steal either way."

"Jesus Christ," Charlie replies.

"Ten thousand dollar deposit and we can get started right now—build your organic donut business. You won't find a better deal in L.A. You can trust me on that. Unless you want to be in The Valley."

"What's The Valley?" Jack Straw asks.

"It's a pretty big area over the hill where the sort of 'real' Los Angelenos live. And real Los Angelenos aren't the best and don't have the most money. Out here, kids come from Ohio and god knows where else, Minneapolis and St. Louis, and have mom and dad's money to spend. Actors. All of 'em. And a few musicians. But artisan donuts are hip right now with that demographic, and this area *is* that demographic."

Neither Charlie nor Jack trust Penelope as far as they can throw her. But there's something about her. It could be the fact that her shade of red lipstick matches her power suit precisely—and something like that, attention to detail, says a lot about a person. Do you know how hard it is to match shades of red? It speaks volumes about her reputation. And then her phone rings.

"Hold on a moment," she says to Charlie and Jack.

She sneaks away to the corner of the beat-down donut shop, kicks some loose gravel out of the way with her high heels—holy shit—her shoes match her dress and her lipstick perfectly. Perfection. Penelope thrives on it.

Charlie and Jack take this opportunity to discuss the proposition before them. Jack says, "Forty-five hundred a month sounds like a lot."

"It's L.A."

"We gotta sell a shit ton of donuts."

"The donuts will sell themselves."

"We don't have ten grand."

"We need a partner."

"You boys gonna take the place?" Penelope says, covering the speaker on her phone. "Because I got another pair of boys interested."

$10,000 Blues

Cliff and Charlie don't wait to hear what the real estate agent has to say about the joint—they don't trust anything they can't see with their own two eyes—plus, it took them two hours just to find her number in the back pages of the *LA Weekly*, right next to the prostitutes and Thai massage parlor advertisements. And besides all that, it's in Echo Park, on the corner of Sunset and Elysian—walking distance to both their house and the bar. And this neighborhood is up-and coming—they've seen the Midwesterners with stars in their eyes pushing in, putting up flags of Missouri outside their houses, driving their parents' old Mercedes's around town, on their way to an audition or a gig. Shit, they've even seen one or two of them stumble right into this bar, asking for a cocktail menu. Fucking stooges. Bozos. Kooks. But goddamn, they'd probably love a donut, one filled and burning with sweet whiskey. This is the demographic they need to survive, to start the empire, to take over the bellies and brains of an entire generation.

The brothers slam their beers, the froth spilling down their chins, dripping onto the ground. "Hey Juan, mi hermano, call us a taxi will ya?" Cliff says, slamming his Tecate can on the bar and crushing it with his bear-sized fist.

"We can walk," Charlie says.

"No way. My head is killing me. It's like it's made out of a semi-truck and the semi-truck is falling off a cliff and then it hits the ground, and I'm inside the semi-truck and I'm also the semi-truck itself. I feel weak, like I'm gonna puke and bleed everywhere. My pancreas hurts. Not to mention I almost died two days ago."

Charlie nods his head. "Yeah, you're right."

Juan doesn't call the boys a cab. Juan just stares at Cliff and tugs on his mustache. "Call you a cab? What do I look like to you? Your bitch?"

"Juan. You are not my bitch. Now you know that. You are my bartender, and you love me, and you love us, and we tip you better than the paisas, and we dance to the polka music, we dig the technobanda, the caballito—hell, remember two years ago we got you that sweet Mi Banda El Mexicano t-shirt, with all the dudes on the front of it with their green, red, and white suits on, and they weren't wearing shirts underneath their jackets? Who goes out of their way like that for you? No one." Cliff takes a lap in his barstool, twirling. Juan grabs the phone behind him.

"Juan, you're the best! You're like a box of raisins in a He-Man lunchbox next to a homemade tuna fish sandwich!"

The brothers step back outside, into the morning light. Hot today. It's gonna get up to 101 in the Valley, 92 in Hollywood. Fire danger, high. Air quality, poor. Waves, 3 feet. 84° at the beaches.

The taxi arrives and the boys fold themselves into the backseat. Cliff pulls the flask from his pocket and passes it to his brother, and the cabby takes a look in his rearview mirror—he's Pakistani—you can tell from the turban and the miniature flag of Pakistan on the dashboard. The cabby pulls his eyes from the mirror, nods his head at them—it's illegal to pound whiskey in the backseat of cabs in L.A., but who wants to fuck with these two dudes this early in the morning?

The brothers stare out the window, paying closer attention to their surroundings than they ever have. This is their business. This is something to care about. It means more to Cliff than bunnies, but it means less to Charlie than bunnies. But Cliff means more to Charlie than bunnies, so Charlie feels like the bunnies and the donuts are equal. He'll paint bunnies and he'll mess around with donuts. The neighborhood hasn't quite hit gentrification yet—it's obvious because of the trash twisting through the streets, climbing up palm trees, getting trapped in the fronds, sailing through the air, plastic grocery bags—weren't those supposed to be illegal in L.A. now? No one cares. Plastic is cheap.

"I think we should send all of our donuts out in little brown paper bags, like the kind you wrap around forties," Cliff says, scratching his dirty fingers at his bandage. "And you know what? I think we should sell the whiskey jelly separately—like how Noah's Bagels sells their shmear in the refrigerator."

"I dig that. Then, like, the people who aren't into donuts, like the girls who do yoga and shit, can eat the whiskey jelly on English muffins, or gluten free toast or whatever."

"Yeah. Fur sure. It'd be the healthy way to get fucked up at breakfast, before yoga."

"Whiskey jelly?" the cabby says.

"Transformers or Gobots?" Cliff retorts.

"What is?" The cabby replies.

"You seem more like a Gobots person."

And the conversation ends. If anyone knows how to end a conversation, it's Cliff. How else do you think he's gotten his brother so far in the art world? All those bozos in the galleries have a question for him. But questions are best answered with another question. And when they don't have an answer to Cliff's question, it just sounds like they're the idiots, not Charlie, not Cliff, and not the bunnies. e.g.—

GALLERY STOOGE

Why bunnies?

CLIFF

Have you ever eaten an entire
jumbo bucket of popcorn while
watching shemale porn?

How can anyone respond to that? Aside from saying "yes," or "no," and then stepping back a few feet, turning the other way.

But the truth is, there is no answer to art, and Cliff knows that—keeps it in his back pocket at all times.

So, from now on, this cabby will think he's more of a Gobots person than a Transformers guy, whatever that means. He flicks his Pakistani flag with his fingers, watches it dance.

The ride is short. There's not much else to do. They pass by that antique shop again—that damn Eames recliner still hasn't been sold. If Cliff could only get his hands on it, it'd be a revelation in relaxation. He can see himself now, a whiskey jelly donut in one hand, the New York Times in the other, his feet kicked up on the leather ottoman, some buxom beauty tying his shoes for him—He can't figure out why he fantasizes about getting his shoes tied. But, whatever, that's what's in his brain. "I'm gonna get that Eames chair, as soon as Mustard Brothers goes public."

"You know what going public means?"

"Not really, but whenever we get like an extra six hundred bucks, it's mine."

One left turn onto Elysian, and the cabby pulls over. "Seven dollars," he says.

"Gobots, man," Cliff says. He tips the man three bones, slides out the backseat, feels his boot heels strike the concrete, turns his head up into the sun, sticks out his tongue, refocuses, and sees the space before him, one black dude and a guy who looks like a cop standing out front, a wall of windows in the shape of a giant chevron. A man sells elotes from a small pushcart on the corner and Cliff immediately moves towards him. "Hungry?" he asks his brother and his brother rubs his belly.

"Nope," Charlie responds.

"Dope sick?"

"A little."

"Keep drinking, dickhead."

"Uno, por favor," Cliff says to the elote man—he's got strong eyes, chapped hands. He's been boiling corn for decades it seems, rubbing mayonnaise, cotija cheese, chili powder, margarine, and crema all over that stalk for an eternity, no end, just rows and rows of corn and fixings. "Not a bad life," Cliff thinks to himself. He drops the two dollars on the cart and throws an extra buck in the tip jar. "Extra mayonnaise, please," he says.

And the man nods his head. "Si."

Forty-two seconds later, Cliff's got breakfast in his hand and is approaching the front door of the possible Mustard Brothers Donut Shop, mayonnaise melting off the cob and seeping into his deep goatee. He stops when he arrives at the brother and the honky and says, "What's going on, fellas?"

Black Charlie adjusts his black shirt, stretches out his neck. "Just checking out the space."

Cliff nods his head, agreeing with him. "Cool windows," he says. "Mid century. Frank did some designs up in the hills not too far away from here in Silver Lake or Los Feliz, I can't remember—a bunch of kooks live over that way now and the houses are about a billion dollars. But whatever. Echo Park is cool. What you plan on doing here?" He takes a big boy bite from his corn, wipes the mayo off his lips with the back of his hand, slides his hand into his back pocket.

Black Charlie takes a glance at Jack Straw. "It's a donut shop."

Cliff glances at White Charlie who lights a cigarette, spits. "So donuts then?"

And Black Charlie nods his head, "Yeah, I guess."

"Well, you boys mind if we squeeze by you and head inside?"

And Black Charlie and Jack Straw part, and Cliff and White Charlie move through the door, kicking around the loose gravel and rat shit.

"Cliff, Charlie?" Penelope Bartlett, realtor to the stars, slides out from behind the donut counter and into view.

"Holy shit," Charlie says. "She matches."

"You know how hard it is to match shades of red," Cliff says to Penelope.

"Thank you for noticing."

Cliff pulls the L.A. Weekly out his back pocket, compares Penelope's backpage photograph with the person standing before him. "You're pretty hot, Penelope."

"Thanks, again," she says. She smiles. She's got these boys. They're playing tough with her, complimenting her, trying to butter her up. But she knows better. She's been in this business long enough to know when a man is trying to get the upper hand. "You have wonderful boots," she says to Charlie. "Are you a painter?"

"Sometimes. Other times I'm a drug addict."

Penelope strikes a pose, squints her eyes, shakes her head a second, as if trying to figure out if what she just heard *is* what she just heard. There's something about these boys. Something wrong with them. But, whatever, a commission is a commission. "Shall I show you around?"

"How much is it?" Cliff says.

"It's got incredible potential," Penelope replies, and begins walking towards the kitchen, her high heels clapping against the linoleum. "The equipment comes along with the…"

The boys don't follow. Charlie drags from his cig. "Per month," Cliff interrupts.

Cliff pulls out his flask. One more nip. Business shit sucks serotonin from the brain.

"Great parking, and these mid-century windo…."

"I mean like, is it less than five grand?"

Penelope stops, turns. Drops her hand to her hip. "Are you serious about this space."

"How much!" Charlie yells.

"Five thousand a month!" she yells back. "Ten thousand deposit! Six hundred to buy!"

"Fuck," Charlie responds.

"But it's a rad spot," Cliff says. "A dude sells elotes out front. And across the street is that dollar store that has those rad silver mylar balloons that last forever. I like having one of those around. They make me feel happy."

"It's an up-and-coming area," Penelope says.

"Who're the stooges outside?" Cliff asks her.

"Potential tenants."

"They got the loot?"

Penelope hesitates, twists the rolled gold necklace around her neck.

"They don't have the loot," Cliff says to Charlie.

"I never said that," Penelope responds.

"Where they from?" Charlie asks.

"Back east, I think."

"You know their names?"

"I'm not a liberty to give you that information."

"Anything cheaper in the area?"

"Honestly, no. I mean, you might be able to find a space that's much smaller, without a kitchen, but it's gonna cost you. And you'll need permits, the whole nine yards. Lots of restaurants have been popping up over here—people are swooping in on the properties, and a lot of the owners have been selling off the kitchen equipment—so it's kind of slim pickins. If you want to head more east, like East L.A., we could probably find something more in your price range, but to be honest, I don't think a couple of white boys making donuts in East L.A. is gonna go over very well."

Charlie takes a drag. "Think Cass has any dough?"

"I think Cass is fucked right now. I think he's gonna throw himself off a dock or jump in front of a subway train before he drops cash on this little venture. But he's the mastermind, he's the Mustard Brother. It's his idea. We gotta make it happen for him. And we gotta get Phoenix back in the mix, and we gotta get em back to L.A." He walks over to the front door, pops it open. "Hey," he says to Black Charlie and Jack Straw. "What's your deal? Are you gonna get the place or what?"

Black Charlie drops his head to the side. "What if I told you we had an idea and we needed an investor?"

Cliff drops his head to the side and says, "What if I told you we had an idea and we needed an investor?"

"Don't say shit," Charlie says. "Maybe we can get more loot from Mars Volta."

"The band?" Black Charlie asks.

"Are you a cop?" White Charlie asks Jack Straw.

"We don't want any more Mars Volta involved in this," Cliff says. "We'll be running guns out the back door. We'll have gnarly gun running eses everywhere, drive-bys and we'll have to learn a bunch of gang signs."

"Lets call Cassidy," White Charlie says. "I think this dude's a cop."

"I'm not a cop," Jack Straw responds.

"Cassidy?" Black Charlie says.

"You look like a cop," Charlie says.

"What about Cassidy?" Cliff asks.

"Rare name."

"Yeah, it's our other investor."

"I used to be a cop," Jack Straw says.

"Don't worry about him—he takes drugs and shit," Black Charlie responds.

"Still…" White Charlie says. "Don't like cops."

"Is this Cassidy married?" Black Charlie asks.

"Was, is, separated. I don't know, some shit went down with his wife and some other chick that owns a donut shop out east. He's a rad guy who writes stories and has like, long hair, and takes drugs every now and again," Cliff answers.

Black Charlie smiles. He has a feeling—both good and bad—separated? Those two are in love—Phoenix and Cassidy are perfect. "Is he married to a girl named Phoenix?"

And then, something rips through White Charlie's brain, the most electricity his cranium has seen in years, a lightning storm in deep space. "What's your name?"

"Charlie," Black Charlie says.

"Holy shit, man. Did you call me two days ago?"

"Is your name Charlie?"

"Yeah, I'm Cassidy's friend."

"Crazy," Jack Straw says.

And there is a moment of pure Los Angeles desert heat, a stillness, a calm. Clarity.

"What's next?" Jack Straw says.

"Whiskey jelly donuts?" Black Charlie says and pulls out his lottery ticket.

"Whiskey jelly donuts?" White Charlie responds and pulls out his wad of cash.

Cliff sticks his fingers in his mouth, whistles loud, pierces right through those F.L.W. windows. He drops his boot heel down, crushes it into the sidewalk, inhales that sweet hot dry air. "I said God damn." This is it, man—Odysseus reaching Ithaca. He swings the front door open. "Hey Penelope, lets sign some fucking papers."

Eleven Times a Day Blues

It's been exactly one week since Phoenix walked out on me, vanished from my life in the rain. I've been calling her eleven times a day, never leaving a message, but calling just the same, to let her now I'm still here, still waiting. I text her *I love you,* every morning and night at 11:22. 11 is my lucky number—22 is hers. Every day or night when one of us would catch the clock reading 11:22, we'd say to the other, "it's our time." Our time. Now just "my time," "her time." Those little things are what I miss most about her. I wonder about her stomachaches—I'm worried about her. Where is she? Is she sleeping in a bus depot, bent over in agony, people staring at her like she's crazy? Or is she staying with another man? Some other man wearing an ironic sweater that rubs her spine and tells her she deserves better and all of a sudden her stomachaches disappear and she sees something she didn't see in me? I bought avocados the other day, for guacamole, just in case...

I haven't checked my email in days, and I've asked for some time off work, some time to think. Bulch said, "It's a bad idea to let the brain soak in a muddy river all day," but he granted me time off anyways. He and Cherise come by every day and ask how I'm doing on their way to or from work. Last night they arrived at 4:30 a.m., knocked on the door, and stumbled arm in arm into my living room with a bottle of Cosmic Grizzly under each of their arms. They are together—it took one week for them to fall in love, play with each other's buttons on their shirts. She places her head on his chest and he lets his long fingers cruise up and down her body. She's even started smoking her own pipe and has taken on a few of his Rangoonisms—"Cass, love is like an alligator stuck inside a python— it swallows you whole and you can never get out—you can only pray the python swallows another alligator." She said this last night, in the heat, outside on the porch-swing while Bulch and I passed the bottle back and forth. The roses out front close up their petals at night—I didn't think roses did that. I never noticed. Maybe they're a different kind of rose? Wikipedia says only Rappahanock Penny Roses do that, but they don't grow in my part of the country. Regardless, their scent carries through my windows now, wraps me up—once forgotten, that scent now always a reminder of that day.

One week. It's three in the afternoon. I check my emails, I need to reconnect somehow, see what's happening with the world. I log in to my Hotmail account, look around the room—what am I gonna do with all this shit? I don't need it any more. I don't need this house any more. I can't afford this house any more. Maybe I can—if I live off Top Ramen and PBR. Never spend a dime on groceries or an old pair of boots or going out to bars. I can do that—I've done it before—Before Phoenix, when I was depressed and writing poetry on an old typewriter, holed up, lost, without purpose, in an apartment in Echo Park—I still smoked back then. Phoenix opened me up and gave me hope, changed my writing, told me my ideas sucked or were rad. We were symbiotic. We were in love, but sometimes love isn't enough when you're dealing with pain. Pain is powerful, more powerful than love. And if you can't get over it, then you can't let love in. Pain dams the river of love. That's what happened to us, but we'll always love each other—I know that. It's undeniable. We were made for each other. But maybe we were made for each other for only a certain amount of time. Maybe she's grown and now thinks lawyers and certified public accountants are interesting, *Iron Man 3* is a good movie. I check those emails, bills, Facebook notifications, and then, there it is—an overdraft protection notice from Wells Fargo. I click on the email, and it tells me money has been automatically transferred from my savings account to my checking account in the amount of $516.00. I go to the Wells Fargo website, type in my password, check my latest activity and see the plane ticket to Los Angeles, American Airlines, purchased five days ago, $387.00. I scroll down, seeing the next group of charges—Ghost Sea Tavern--$33.12 Il Capriccio--$68.72—shit. Those were our two favorite spots in L.A. Who'd she go there with? Is she alone? Tapatio #2—our favorite burrito joint, just down the street from her parents house. At least I know now she's staying with them. Three more transactions at Tapatio #2—she must be going there daily. Is she thinking of me when she goes to these places? Is she trying to swallow the memories? To relive the past? Is she using a burrito as a substitute for me?

I call her for the second time today. It rings and rings and then her voicemail engages. I hang up.

I stand and head into our bedroom. I see her side of the bed—untouched. I've been sleeping with her pillow, using it as my substitute for her—a substitute that is completely unfulfilling, but helps me get to bed, nonetheless. Sleeping alone is a strange feeling now. That pillow keeps me safe. I pull the sheets over my head and double check all the locks on the doors in the house. Strange that Phoenix felt like protection, made me feel like nothing bad could happen to me with her there—even though she weighed about 100 lbs. I wonder if she felt the same about me? Nah, she's way tougher. She's had to fall asleep alone since we started living together—I've been at the bar drinking afterhours and she's been taking a bath, getting into bed naked, closing her eyes, and falling asleep alone.

She's independent. She doesn't need me to feel safe.

Maybe it's in my subconscious, everything I've ever done. Maybe the stomachaches don't affect her as much as they do me. Those stomachaches made me feel unsafe, like she could vanish at any moment, die right there in front of me, and then, my own life would cease to exist. These stomachaches drove me away from her out of fear—I can't stand the feeling of not being able to solve a problem—helplessness. It stems from the abortion. Watching her writhe around on the ground—there was nothing I could do. There's nothing I can do. I don't want any pain, or problems, or stress. I just want everything to be perfect—smiles, a clothesline on a California river, a bottle of wine, no job, just poetry and my girl splashing around, catching tiny purple fish in her hands. I crumble under imperfection, I crumble under stress, I crumbled when she needed me most. I am self-centered. I am a terrible husband. But she's still out there.

I've got over three hundred unread emails and my voicemail box is full. I haven't answered the phone for anyone in a week, missing calls from Cliff, Charlie, Black Charlie, and an unknown number with an Arizona area code. These people call me constantly, but what's the point? Mustard Brothers? Fuck it. She gets the West. That's my punishment. I'll bartend until I die behind the stick, too old to pull the tap handle down, and I'll collapse just like I did a few days ago, push my hands to my chest, and this time it *will* be a heart attack. And there'll be a memorial service and people whose names I never will have remembered will attend and say some shit about a conversation I had with them one night while I was drunk. What a pathetic existence.

I hear a knock at the door, and I head over. I'm in the same pair of jeans I've been wearing since she left and I've slept in them every night because they're the last thing that touched her. If I think hard enough, I can smell her on them. She left a pair of dirty underwear in the laundry basket too. Sometimes I put them on her pillow and cram them into my face when I fall asleep at night. Don't call me crazy. This is my life.

I open the door and I see Bulch twisting his mustache, a twenty-two ounce bottle of brew in his hand. "Thought you might need this—get you across the river of rattlesnakes."

I take the twenty-two from his hand and nod my head. "Thanks, brother."

"May I come in?" he says.

"Sure."

He takes a look around the house. It's messy, but not the cliché "My wife just left me" messy. There's a few empty beer cans and whiskey bottles on the kitchen counter, and an empty frozen burrito wrapper on the coffee table. The bed isn't made. But other than that, it's quite nice. Except for the floor. Phoenix used to mop those hardwoods every week. She hated if her feet turned black when she walked across them. She was a good mopper, a hard mopper, and she listened to Neil Young and Crazy Horse when she did it, a joint dangling from her mouth, every Sunday morning starting at 10 am, even if I had worked the night before. She didn't care. I'd wake up to Neil's voice and open up the bedroom door and she'd smile and wave, yell "good morning" over the blasting of Neil's electric guitar. I'd smile and head to the bathroom for a piss, come back out, find a beer, kiss her on the cheek and take a seat on the couch, just watching her. She looked beautiful with her hair up, unshowered, in a ripped up t-shirt and a pair of underwear—perfect. I could have sold videos of her mopping to a million men for fifty bucks apiece, her hips swaying to the music, the holes in her t-shirt exposing her breasts every few seconds.

"Place doesn't look too bad," Bulch says. "You get any sleep?"

"Couple hours."

"Have you seen that mind-bender seventy-two minute Spacemachine Whiskey Jelly Blues performance yet?"

"How'd they come up with the name to that song?"

"I named it. It was an epiphany."

"I said that out loud one day to you."

"These ideas are all out there in the universe," Bulch says. "Who cares about whiskey jelly anyways?"

I shrug. "No one. It's lame."

Bulch nods his head. "Hear from Phoenix?"

"No, but I know she's in L.A.—saw some shit on the Wells Fargo account."

"Ahhh...reminds me of my first marriage to Maya Von Strohem—The Lord of Withington's daughter. A wise man, Paris Truman, a great safari man, once told me, 'Always have your own secret account—it'll save you a lot of headaches.' I always had a little something on the side for myself, no one would know about, just in case the shit hit the fan, and I needed to split. She never knew about my trip to Monaco—thought I was still in the bush doing Piranha research."

"I'm overdrawn because of it."

"Need some cash?" He pulls a wad of money from the front pocket of his safari shirt, peeling off $100's.

I push my hands in front of myself. "No," I say. "She deserves to spend our money and I deserve to pay for it, let her do whatever she wants."

Bulch straightens the gold cravat tied around his neck. "Self loathing is like swimming in quicksand—it gets you nowhere. Your life, be it here, or in the afterlife, must go on."

"Have you seen Aunika?" I ask him.

"She's been over at the donut shop. She hasn't come by though. She smiles when I see her and she's had some interesting shades of lipstick lately."

I shake my head. "She gets to go on."

He drops a vial of banana oil down on the coffee table and says, "In case you need to relax, the organic way." He rolls his tongue at me and heads back to the door, spinning on his boot heels, and tips his hat. "Good day, sir," he says, then back pedals out the door, down the steps, and into the street, moving as if by wind, down the damp lane.

I open the twenty-two ounce beer, head back over to the computer. I scroll down my inbox, looking for anything important, and find an email from Black Charlie, the subject reading, *Hey, where the fuck are you!?*

I click on the email and read.

We've been trying to contact you for days. I ran into your friends Cliff and Charlie out here in LA. We've found a spot to open up Mustard Brothers—it's like some Frank loyd right shit with cool windows, but there's a bum living in the refrigerator that we had to deal with and he was a bit nasty—pulled a knife on cliff, but then cliff pulled a switchblade on him and he ran! It was like that scene in crocodile dundee. There's a new brother, by the way, his name is jack straw and he used to be a cop. We put a deposit down. We couldn't wait to hear back from ya so we rented the space. Joe Strummer had his firs tever donut here! The three of us have been cleaning the shit out of it—Charlie's been busy working on some bunny paintings incorporating donuts and whiskey jelly which are weird, but I guess people dig em. And the drug dealer everyone calls Mars Volta has been kicking down some extra loot for utensils and equipment—he's a swell ese. You hear about this whiskey jelly blues song from Spacemachine? Strange shit man. Hit us back.

Charlie

Los Angeles. Where all my brothers are. Where my wife is. I look out the window. I see the housewife sitting on her porch. I see the roses. The sky turns from gray to blue to gray in thirty seconds, and then begins to rain. I drop the needle down on the Gun Club, take a big swig. I'm overdrawn. I am over drawn. What am I going to do with all this stuff?

Electric Fox Bite Blues

Volcano the Spacemachine

@
The Electric Fox Bite

21221 Hyacinth House Ave.
East Docks

10 pm

$21
$25 at door

Tonight

Whiskey Jelly Blues, brothers and sisters

Lupita Screams Blues

What am I going to do with all this stuff? I have no answer. Even if I wanted to head out west, back home to the Golden State, this task is insurmountable. I need to sell it all, including the stolen mid-century credenza we bought off that Mexican dude in the middle of the night. I need to stay here until it's all gone, out of my life, never heard from again. And if I stay, well, then all this stuff is just a bad reminder of what once was. This couch—my god, this couch. How could I ever make love to someone else on it ever again, knowing we touched, loved, kissed, 69'd, naked, on it, night after night during the good days. How can I rest easy knowing down between these cushions lies an errant popcorn kernel, leftover from a rainy-day *Twilight Zone* marathon? How can I sit down to a frozen enchilada knowing on the other side of the cushion is a come stain we could never get out? How can I take a seat, clip my toenails knowing our skin and sweat is soaked into the fibers, part of it now, made of us?

This is too much to handle—It's not possible to deal with—still too fresh to think about. No, it's time to keep pushing it down into the depths with another bottle of beer. I lie on the ground, put my feet up on the come-stained couch, swallow, swallow, swallow, until life becomes a blur and the Gun Club makes sense to me. My phone buzzes, over there on the kitchen counter. Ordinarily I would ignore it, let it pass into oblivion—but it could be her. I scramble across the floor on my hands and knees, reach up, and pull it down—it's a text from Cherise. *The Spacemachine plays tonight—we gotta go see if they shred as hard as they did in Eugene. No excuses. Bulch and I are gonna pick you up at seven, pre-party, shots bitch.*

"Stoney must be working alone tonight," I think to myself. I could probably bartend with him—it would get me out of being social. Plus, I could use the loot. He'll play some psych records and throw the sand from his pockets onto my forehead, baptize me, remind me of the West. No. Bad idea. No west. No baptism. I don't want to see or talk to anyone that reminds me of the west. I don't need an excuse to not be social—my wife left me—that's good enough. *Can't make it,* I reply to Cherise.

I look at my jeans, the same ones for a week, getting worn in the knees from all the crawling around I've been doing—standing seems disrespectful to myself—I need to slither around like a snake underneath the foot of The Virgin. I take a look at my jeans—gross, stinking. These jeans are the first thing I see in the morning, right next to my mattress, on the floor, the first thing I reach for, after the bottle on the nightstand.

Not an option, Cherise responds.

I think about it for a while, pulling at my earlobes, listening to the words of Jeffrey Lee Pierce.

Well, the docks they went on strike again/ It's you they don't want to see
They said they'd rather get high/ Than hear Lupita scream

Lupita. Who's Lupita? She's Lupita. We're all Lupita. I don't want Lupita to scream. No screaming. Cherise will scream at me if I don't go to the show, if when they swing by to pick me up at seven I pretend I'm not home. She'll walk the perimeter of my house shouting profanity and pounding on the windows for an hour until I can't take it any longer and I'll have to open up, let them in, take a shower, rub patchouli on my stinking jeans, pass the bottle between us and head down to the show. It's not worth it. It's a waste of time for all of us. I might as well accept my fate—there's no choice. The choice has been made for me. No, I've decided to change. I'll make my own decisions. I can control what's happening to me. I text her back. *Cool. See ya in a bit.*

I stretch my eyes towards the clock—It's only four p.m. That gives me a few hours to clean up, take a shower, eat a tortilla or whatever I can find in the kitchen—maybe some chicken noodle soup. Chicken noodle soup is always good for a broken body, a broken soul, a broken heart. Chicken noodle soup has been healing people for a century, longer than aspirin, longer than Ativan and Percocet, morphine and Norco, but still not as long as booze. Booze has been erasing pain since the Stone Age. Jesus gave his people wine and the people, they began worshiping him, made him a God. I take a sip from my beer, each ounce that drizzles down my throat removing the hangover of yesterday and the day before and the day before that. Beer and wine and whiskey will kill you in the end, I know, but this isn't the end. I'm not yet ready for the end. I haven't concluded anything. I have come to no conclusion—we're all still moving forward, even if forward feels more like backward, and backward feels more like nothing. I dial her number again, listen to it ring, ring, ring. No answer. Call number five. Six more phone calls to go before I reach my quota. I have to remember to call her periodically during The Spacemachine show, make sure I get to eleven.

In the shower, I take her razor, the one she used to shave her legs and vagina and armpits, and I press the blade into my palm, let a little blood out, mixing with her dead skin cells. I don't lather myself, I don't wash my hair, I don't masturbate. I don't do anything but stare at that goddamn razor. I take it, and I put it in my mouth like a popsicle. I carefully twist it around with my tongue, lightly dragging it against the blade, and then I spit out a little blood, watch it swirl down the drain, out to sea with everything else I've thrown away. I sit down and I drag that razor across a knuckle, removing the hair, and then I take it, and I begin trimming my pubes with it, pulling the hairs up, and slicing them in half. I love this razor. I'll take this razor with me to bed tonight, put it on the nightstand, so in the morning, it's the first thing I see—that light blue plastic handle with the mismatched purple razor head.

I spend nearly an hour in the shower, sitting, with the razor in my hand, until the hot water turns to lukewarm, and the lukewarm turns to cold. I close my eyes, and let the cold water pound into my face, my heart racing, my body waking up, and when I open my eyes, the world isn't as blurry as it was an hour ago. Cold water is the cure for any good hangover, for any good drunk, for anything that requires sobriety. If only I could eat piping hot chicken noodle soup in a cold shower, there would be no stopping me—I'd be invincible.

I turn the water off, dry myself, push some junk into my hair, use her razor to shave around my mustache, pop a few zits on my nose, then take that razor with me into the bedroom, place it on the nightstand on its side, so that it looks as if it's on it's elbow watching me, just like she used to do when we had a day off together and she was lying next to me, waiting for me to wake up—I could feel her eyes even in my sleep. I lie down on the bed, let my naked skin tighten as it dries and then I close my eyes. I need sleep. I don't deserve sleep, but as I said before, I don't want this to be the end. I know that now. And if I don't sleep, the end will come too soon, and then all there will be left is a certified public accountant working on new tax documents for a donut shop in Echo Park. How could I do that to you? To anyone? I'm not cruel. I'm not a dick. I'm a good guy that makes mistakes. And then, my eyes twitch, my breathing slows, and sweet sleep takes hold, my head gliding down a perfect peaceful waterfall…

I hear the screaming in the back of my mind, somewhere in my subconscious—it must be a dream. It's a woman's voice, peppered with shrieks of obscenities. I hear the windows rattle, I feel the house move as if a tornado were attempting to rip it from the foundation. I open one eye, then the other, lose my breath, wake up with a gasp. Lupita is screaming. Where am I. What time is it? I see outside the bedroom window only darkness, darkness all around me, and then, out of the darkness, a face in the moonlight. My heart drops right down into my thighs.

"Hey fucker! It's 8 o'clock! Open the door!" I let my eyes focus, see the cherry red lipstick—it's Cherise. And just over her shoulder I can make out that slender tall frame—Rangoon—grinning, twisting a knot of tobacco into his pipe. Cherise is slamming her fists into the window and I know if I don't get up, move right now, those muscular chainsaw wielding hands are gonna end up right through the glass. I jump out of bed, unconcerned by my nakedness, in some kind of fight-or-flight panic, and run towards the front door. I unlock it, swing it open, cover my junk with my hands, and scamper back towards my bedroom, hearing the subtle laughter follow behind me. "You have a pretty nice ass," Cherise says.

"Thanks," I say. It's a nice compliment for a man. I pull on my dirty jeans, rub patchouli oil over them, pull on a tattered white t-shirt that reads "Keep on Truckin." I see that razorblade on the nightstand staring at me. I see a little red on her pillow. I check my mouth, rub my fingers across the dried blood stuck to the corners of my lips.

I hear the sound of bottles twisting open and for some reason, at this moment, I don't want to drink. I've slept, I feel like my organs have healed inside. I check my face in the full length mirror—my cheeks are bronze, not red. Even my heart seems to be sitting correctly inside of me, not trying to escape, not trying to quit. It thumps with subtlety, with grace, with peace, not with tragedy and pain, stress and sugar and uncertainty. It seems as if whatever grip was knotted around my heart has released itself, and my heart, out of thanks, has come back to me. It feels as if all the trash that's been passing through it for the past year has somehow been purged—I look over at her pillow—more blood than I thought. It looks like a dying cat dragged its body across it. It all came out of my mouth, from my tongue, my tongue that's constantly ruining everything— not anymore. That bad blood is out, and now, my tongue will only speak the truth, it will follow my brand new heart.

I step out of my bedroom and I smile wide. The epiphany has hit me—life is life. You keep on living because there's only one alternative to life and I don't dig that alternative.

Bulch takes a pull from his Cosmic Grizzly bottle and dangles it out from his arm. "Here you go pal, take the edge off."

I look at that bottle and all of my instincts tell me to grab it, get it down my throat, feel the numbness, head to the show, remember only half of it, but remember it fondly the next day. My instincts suck. I shake my head, "No, brother. I need to straighten up a bit."

Bulch nods his head, and gives me a grin and a shrug—I can't tell what kind of grin and shrug it is, just like most reactions with Bulch—it could mean, "Finally, old boy, you've come to your senses," or it could mean "You wouldn't know what to do if a goatfucker threw a donkey through your window."

I head over to the couch and take a seat, see a half-smoked joint in the ashtray in front of me, and light it up. This is what Phoenix would do. She'd get nice and stoned, smile, get fuzzy and warm inside—people don't make stupid mistakes when they're stoned— the reckless courage isn't there—only heavy bliss, the need to keep things in order, or on a superb stone, the need to make things better—never destroy, only create. That's what true stoners are—lovers, believers, pacifists. Drunks are selfish, only looking for something to give their heart a tug and a thrill at the expense of everyone around them.

"Not drinking any more?" Cherise asks. "You're gonna suck to work with."

I pull from my joint and shake my head, "I'm not saying I'll never drink again—shit, I've been drinking all day. Just don't feel like it right now. I'm having a moment of clarity."

Bulch takes a seat next to me, crosses his legs, plays with his suspenders. "Clarity is a good thing in the bush," he says. "But fighting a Giant Yama Yama Bullfrog without a bottle in your hand can be dangerous."

"Why's that?"

Bulch chuckles, "Because the skin of a Giant Yama Yama Bullfrog is semi-permeable—pour a little hooch on it and it winds up on its back. You don't want to feel the riptide of its poisonous thorns through your blood—trust me—I've seen the eyes of my Dutch expedition partner, Jan Cremer, nearly pop out of his skull. I had to keep 'em inside his grape with my thumbs."

My brain is too goddamn fuzzed out right now to interpret Bulch's Rangoonisms. I light a candle and Cherise calls a taxi.

The taxi ride is uneventful, spent in relative silence as Bulch and Cherise pass the bottle between them, furiously necking when the bottle isn't at their lips, fingers crawling into dark places. I remember kissing in the back seat of taxis, remember feeling her tits—it's a strange feeling, knowing the cabby is checking it all out in the rearview mirror, knowing someone is watching, and right here, next to these two, I can feel the heat jumping off them. It is electric. It is tangible. And if you've never experienced love, then you can never understand a thunderstorm. All the power of the world can be felt between two people, all the elements of a perfect storm—but don't take my word for it—go out and fall in love, braid tongues drunk on Cosmic Grizzly in the back seat of a taxi with eyes on you on the way to a rock and roll show, and tell me I'm wrong.

I look out the window, watch the streets pass by—Peace, Love, NE Easy—people with great shoes, or no shoes, smoking or not smoking, laughing or crying—it's all out there—every tangible thing in the world—but not her.

As we roll up to the Electric Fox Bite it looks like the Rolling Stones are in town. A swarm of hipness surrounds the venue, high-fives are being exchanged at an alarming rate, and each one of this rag-tag gang of misanthropes seems to be pulling a flask out of their socks or back pockets, armpits, and waistbands, passing them around. The Spacemachine following is eccentric to say the least—the fringe of society living on their last dime, teetering on the edge of the pirate plank, not worried about being thrown over—in fact, this crew, out the window as we park, is without a care—life or death, all the same, feed them to the sharks. The cops cruise by every few seconds, eyeballs out the window, and they see the mayhem, the booze, the smoke, the rumble of inebriation, the hidden conversations and the semi-suave drug deals that look more suspicious than usual, and they just roll past—who wants to get into it with this group of dirty messes? Nah, if the shit hits the fan, then the billy clubs can come out. Until then, best to let these filthy beasts put their own heads into the ground, bury themselves.

We slide through the crowd, tied to Bulch's slender frame as he slithers his way through the bending bodies and arrives at the will-call window. He doesn't say a word, just winks at the young woman behind the glass, and she passes him three tickets. We head towards security, and Bulch once again stands silent before the men in the bright yellow jackets, takes a pull from his Cosmic Grizzly right in front of them, and they nod their heads, let us pass through—shit, I was worried they'd find that joint in my pocket—but sometimes I forget Bulch can do anything at any time wherever he wants, and when you're with him, that means you as well.

Inside the venue I first notice the chandeliers, champagne sparkles—pretty cool—way cooler than I can describe—like something out of a haunted mansion on acid—little spots of light swirling, twinkling across the walls and ceiling. It's dark inside, almost too dark. But I like it. I feel good within it. No one can see me, I can't see them—the perfect light for being social or anti-social—everyone wins inside this place, this palace, this planet.

We bunch up at the front of the stage—still half a bottle left, cradled between Bulch's long arms. I can feel the sweat of strangers rubbing up against my arms, slimy, dripping, spreading across my skin. No one knows when The Spacemachine is actually going to play—there's no opener, so everyone pushes and shoves, vying for the best view. But right now, there is no view, nothing to see—only a deep crimson velvet curtain strewn across the stage.

The voices surround me, loud, crushing to the eardrums, words that carry no meaning, a thousand people babbling at the same time, a cacophony of bullshit. I can make out the conversation directly behind me—"They ain't playing tonight man. I heard they got arrested, some shit about riots in Oregon." And another conversation to my right—"They pissed on some teenage girl—they're in the klink." And yet another—"They were running around the city naked on drugs—they're too big now—I want to fuck you!"

The volume inside The Electric Fox Bite is enough to make you go crazy, especially when you're smoking Phoenix's stash—Jesus Christ this shit could numb an elephant, could make Jim Morrison write about a lizard king, make Keith Moon drive a car into a swimming pool. I start rubbing my palms, the sweat bunching up into tiny puddles within them. The panic is coming. My eyes flicker, my head spins—I forgot to eat today. Shit. I let my shoulders down, try to take a deep breath, but only inhale the thick moisture of a thousand sweating bodies, 100% human humidity. I close my eyes, ready to fall. I feel two cool fingers touch each of my eyelids, pulling them up. Cherise grabs my hand, looks into my eyes, and says, "It's all going to be fine." She pulls my head into her neck, and then I feel Bulch's strong fingers wrap around my skull and press. I feel his mustache against my cheek, and I feel his kiss on my jaw. The three of us embrace, pull each other tight together, like a ball of rubber bands, and then, one amplifier, then the next, flickers on with an electric buzz. The crowd erupts. The Spacemachine is here. They've made it. The rumors circulating were incorrect. They weren't arrested earlier today for public nudity, urinating on young women, and inciting riots at a Co-op on the campus of U of O.

The electric buzz rolls through my veins and I can feel it—what's it called? The electric wilderness. It's what we are, it's where we live.

The curtains unfold before us, and then there, up above, The Spacemachine, torn apart, haggard. The lead singer, James, spits his beer into the crowd, his wad landing on the face of the girl in front of me, and she pushes her finger into it, shoves the brewed spit into her mouth and screams at the top of her lungs. The crowd comes together. From the great beyond, somewhere in the back, a chant begins. "Whis-key Jell-y. Whis-key Jell-y." And by the time it reaches the stage everyone is chanting, crazed, "Whis-key Jell-y! Whis-key Jell -y!"

The Spacemachine knows what's up. James leans into the microphone, then pulls back, grabs the bottle of beer at his feet, drinks it down in one gulp, motions towards the side of the stage for another, and another is delivered, and he takes only a sip from that one. He presses his face back into the mic, and whispers, "Double whiskey jelly blues." And then the eruption happens. Each instrument thumps in at the same time like the crash of a rocket into a nuclear power plant.

The noise emanating from the stage is so heavy, so thick, so visceral and horny, so fucked up and rad, that it feels almost as if there's someone on my back, like I'm carrying another body, like I almost can't stand up any longer. The guitar lines are so razor sharp it feels like a tongue is licking up the back of my neck, the kick drum so hard it feels like teeth are gnawing at my earlobe, so much so that I have to turn my head around to make sure I'm not tripping, not losing it, not about to blow my mental load, and that's when I see her face, feel her hands, feel the heat of her thighs, smell the booze of her breath, see those blue eyes, feel that blonde hair dangling down my face—Aunika. She wraps her hands around my neck, starts to choke me, licks my neck again, whispers in my ear, "I don't fucking care anymore. Take me home."

I put my hands underneath her ass, holding her up, for fear if I don't she'll take us both down and we'll be trampled by crazed Spacemachine fans. "Take me home," she repeats. "I won't wait for double whiskey jelly."

I pull my eyes back up towards the stage, watch James light a bottle rocket, fire it off into the crowd, bring my eyes back down, see Bulch's hand up Cherise's dress, nearly lifting her off the ground. This is life. Life is life.

If you take Aunika home, turn to the next page.

If you refuse Aunika and stay for the Double Whiskey Jelly Blues, turn to page 459.

Up and Down My Spine Blues

She's on my back again, her eyes painted orange with bright green swirls, like a parrot flying through the sky, a cool Caribbean sunset behind its outstretched wings—in fact, that's exactly what they are— her eyelids are literally painted with two parrots soaring through a perfect sunset. And her eyes replicate that sunset, that parrot, the blue center absorbing the colors, takes me on vacation, puts me right down on the beach at the shores of her tropical heart. Maybe Aunika is a vacation from everything, maybe our friendship has always been a vacation—she was always the one I turned to for advice, to vent, to cry, to understand—and she never turned me away, was always there to listen to me, put a hand on my spine, relax me. Like that time, when we were kids, and I fell off the orange tree in my grandparents backyard and fractured my skull—she was there, and she held my head in her tiny little hands and called for help, and she wiped away the tears, looking at me with the love of a mother—she said "It's okay, Cass. It's okay," and then my breathing slowed and I could see then, in those eyes, that I would be fine, I would stand up, I would live, I would crawl up that orange tree again someday. And I believed her then and I believe her now. Maybe my head has always been in her hands, has always been cradled by her love, and maybe I was the idiot who didn't understand it—not the other way around. All these years, it should have been us, me with my fractured mind, and her with her perfect beauty, compassion, those eyes I soak myself in, bathe within.

I've got her wedged up on my back—we won't fall, my muscles are tight—marijuana strength. The bass line rips through us—I can feel the heat surging out from between her thighs, crawling up my body, beads of sweat breaking on my skin—just like at St. Claire's Rainbow—I can feel the vibration of her ribcage, her breasts swimming against my shoulders. History repeats itself. And when history repeats itself, you have a chance to change history. What will my history be? How will I rewrite it?

I use all of my strength to spin her around, never letting her touch the ground, until her legs are wrapped around my torso, and her face is directly in front of mine. I've never seen Aunika vulnerable. She only wears emotions on her face when something is purely tragic or something is purely beautiful. Here, now, her eyes produce two diamond shaped tears, stuck in the corners, waiting to drop.

I feel something rattle in my back pocket, a strange synthetic vibration—my phone. Shit. It's my turn to make a decision, change history, move forward into the unknown. I hold her in my arms, lifting her up gradually, until finally, the rattling in my back pocket stops. "I'll take you home," I say. I inch my head forward, James's bottle-rockets whizzing past our ears, exploding into the crowd. Her hands take my head, cradle my fractured skull, hold everything inside, keep everything together, and then, we kiss. We kiss without worry. We kiss without guilt. We kiss as lovers kiss. We kiss as if we have never kissed before. We kiss in front of everyone. We kiss for the world. We kiss for love.

I let her legs fall, let her feet touch the ground, and I see Bulch and Cherise, bottle raised, a toast to the four of us sorting through all the trash and finding each other. Aunika takes the bottle, pulls from it, and holds it up to my lips, pours it down my throat for me, and I feel that familiar burn, but this time it's a different type of burn—not the burn of suppression, of stomachaches, of cubicles, of financial instability, but the burn of letting it all go, rock and roll, irresponsibility—drinking for adventure, not out of necessity, grief, hell. This place, the east, isn't so bad if you let yourself be there, if you let yourself live there, if you let go of The West. I have to let go of The West. And as our fingers intertwine, as I take that first step through the tidal wave of bodies, backwards towards the door, pulling her behind me, I can feel the Redwoods disappear, the cold of the Pacific leave my veins, the dry hot wind exit my lungs, and in their place, oak, The Atlantic, snow, hot chicken noodle soup in an ice cold shower. And as we enter the taxi, I can feel the gridlocked traffic of the 101 and the 405 release from my gut, from my heels, my hands pull off the steering wheel, and I let myself take me where I want to go. We're in the backseat, we're embracing, we braid our tongues on our way out of a rock and roll show and into something else—it could be anything—uncertainty and destruction, or something more incredible, more visceral, something even Bulch hasn't seen or could describe.

"Where you headed?" the cabby asks.

I pull my face from Aunika's, her tongue licking up my cheek. "Home," I say.

He looks at me like I'm crazy. "Home?"

"East," I tell him.

He flips on the meter, presses down on the gas, and looks in his rearview mirror, watches the two of us, my hands heading up Aunika's thigh, our cheeks filling with blood.

We don't stop pressing into each other until we arrive at my house. I pay the driver, take a look at that front porch—it looks different somehow, quiet, lonely. I see the roses, the buds open even though it's night, but the fragrance is gone, no ribbon of red whipping out from the petals wrapping up my soul with sweetness. I take her hand, pull her up the stairs, unlock the door, move inside, flip on the light switch. Shit. All this stuff is still here. The couch, the bed, the wine glasses, the records, her books, her underwear, her razor, the blood all over her pillow. I need to erase it all, take a big paintbrush and paint over it. This stuff, all of this stuff, can be painted over, can be reused, can be remade, can hold new memories like an old canvas. I take Aunika to the couch, I pull her dress over her head, I pull down her underwear and I put my tongue back inside. We make love. We stare. We explore. We touch where we want to touch. She holds my head in her hands. She looks me in the eye. She says, "It's gonna be okay, Cass," and I'm immediately transported to childhood, all the emotions of a thirty year friendship coming to a head as we push and twist, never stopping, reversing time, dragging all those years out from behind us and putting them right in front, every moment, our future built out of the past. And when we're finished, there's nothing left, nothing but the two of us suspended in night, alone.

We take deep breaths, remain silent for a minute or so. We look around the room, understand our new environment, internalize the barrier we have breached—we've made love to each other. The world is different, minds have been altered, bodies have crossed into each other, have become one. We will forever be joined in some way, mentally, physically.

"You've always been way ahead of me," I tell her. "One step ahead."

She pulls herself up, reverses our bodies. "When I was twelve, I wrote you a love letter for your birthday."

"I never got it."

"I tore it up. I thought, even at twelve, that life was supposed to be filled with new experiences, a constant revolution, or an eternal renaissance. No need to hang on to anything—move forward, release, move on, discover. But that isn't life. Life is built on belief, on past experiences, not new ones. I would have traded a thousand nights in Ibiza for this one with you."

I pull the hair out of my face, take a breath, consider my words. "I have nothing to trade." I point my palms in the direction of all my stuff. "This isn't living. I haven't been living."

"Trade your life and all this shit for a thousand nights in Ibiza with me then."

Her words seem ridiculous, but looking at her, seeing myself in the blue of her eyes, I can see she isn't lying—her aim is true. We can trade everything, spend a thousand nights in Ibiza together, we can live on a dairy farm in Bretagne, we can stand naked on a cliff in Spain. We. "We" used to mean something else. "We" is something I'm not sure I can ever be again. "We" has been destroyed and recreated with one decision. "I've never respected the idea that life was infinite, everything possible. To me it's always been a journey to some sort of defined end, but when I get to the end, it just keeps moving further and further away. I thought Phoenix was my end, the East was my end, and when I got there, I still had to keep going. And now, I realize, it's not about the end, it's about a continuous beginning, an infinite amount of outcomes, where even the end, isn't the end."

"I'll begin every day with you, and, if, somehow, we come to an end, then I'll begin again with you."

I pull the joint from my pocket, light it up, pass it to her, stand, turn on Star Trek reruns. She says, "Uhura has great style," and I run my finger across her lips.

"I'm gonna open a bottle of wine," I tell her. I head to the bedroom, pull Phoenix's underwear and the blood-stained pillow case off her pillow, grab the razor from the nightstand, head back to the kitchen, and drop it all in the trash—I have come full circle, everything back into the trash. I open that bottle of wine, I see the avocados I bought in anticipation of Phoenix's homecoming, I pull one out, hold it up in the palm of my hand and I say, "Guacamole?"

Aunika falls back on the couch, and says, "I love your guacamole."

I slice into that avocado, chop up the cilantro, the lime, the jalapenos, throw in the salt and pepper, and I whip it all together, and throw it in the trash. "I'll never eat a good burrito again." I move over to the record player, drop the needle.

I had this girl breath/ Up and down my spine
But, that was a river ago/ I knew you'd come in time

"Cassidy?" she says.

"Yeah?"

"Will you come work with me, be my partner?"

I think about my Mustard Brothers, how they're all out there, in the west, about to take over the world, create a culinary revolution, bury La Di Donuts and drive Aunika out of business, and how with one sentence I could start my own revolution here, take my idea and run with it, Aunika and I knee deep in whiskey jelly.

"Yeah, I'll be your partner."

She smiles, lets herself relax. "You always have good ideas."

"Sometimes."

"Got any right now?"

I shake my head. "Nope."

"Something'll come to you." She hums a tune, letting her fingers tap against her belly, "Whiskey jelly blues," she sings softly to herself. Her head tilts to the side and her hair follows. Everything softens around us, the light, the world, our existence. I bring the guacamole over to her and place it on the coffee table. She reaches out her hand and we interlock fingers, then release.

I text Cliff, *The East is a Beast, and the west is the whiskey jelly. Keep the Mustard Brothers alive, for me.*

I push myself into the couch. I can feel Phoenix here, somewhere, and my stomach growls. I take a deep breath—forward, the only way left, no turning back. I press my fingers into Aunika's thigh and she stares into my eyes, long, too long for friends. We drink our wine. We'll move forward. We'll get to Ibiza, we'll get wherever we want to be, we'll trade it all in and hope for something greater in return. We close our eyes. We sleep. We dream. We. In the morning, elephant razor donuts and a beer, start it all over. God damn. Whiskey jelly blues.

THE END

Sea Air Tortilla Blues

She's on my back again, her eyes painted orange with bright green swirls, like a parrot flying through the sky, a cool Caribbean sunset behind its outstretched wings—in fact, that's exactly what they are—her eyelids are literally painted with two parrots soaring through a perfect sunset. And her eyes replicate that sunset, that parrot, the blue center absorbing the colors, takes me on vacation, puts me right down on the beach at the shores of her tropical heart. Maybe Aunika is a vacation from everything, maybe our friendship has always been a vacation—she was always the one I turned to for advice, to vent, to cry, to understand—and she never turned me away, was always there to listen to me, put a hand on my spine, relax me. Like that time, when we were kids, and I fell off the orange tree in my grandparents backyard and fractured my skull—she was there, and she held my head in her tiny little hands and called for help, and she wiped away the tears, looking at me with the love of a mother—she said "It's okay, Cass. It's okay," and then my breathing slowed and I could see then, in those eyes, that I would be fine, I would stand up, I would live, I would crawl up that orange tree again someday. And I believed her then and I believe her now. Maybe my head has always been in her hands, has always been cradled by her love, and maybe I was the idiot who didn't understand it—not the other way around. All these years, it should have been us, me with my fractured mind, and her with her perfect beauty, compassion, those eyes I soak myself in, bathe within.

I've got her wedged up on my back—we won't fall, my muscles are tight—marijuana strength. The bass line rips through us—I can feel the heat surging out from between her thighs, crawling up my body, beads of sweat breaking on my skin—just like at St. Claire's Rainbow—I can feel the vibration of her ribcage, her breasts swimming against my shoulders. History repeats itself. And when history repeats itself, you have a chance to change history. What will my history be? How will I rewrite it?

I use all of my strength to spin her around, never letting her touch the ground, until her legs are wrapped around my torso, and her face is directly in front of mine. I've never seen Aunika vulnerable. She only wears emotions on her face when something is purely tragic or something is purely beautiful. Here, now, her eyes produce two diamond shaped tears, stuck in the corners, waiting to drop.

I feel something rattle in my back pocket, a strange synthetic vibration—my phone. Shit. It's my turn to make a decision, change history, move forward into the unknown. The rattling continues, twice, three times…"I'm sorry," I say, "Hold on a sec." I drop her legs from my waist, let her feet hit the floor, reach into my pocket, read the name on my phone—"Phoenix."

"Holy shit," I say. I look up to Aunika, see her eyes fold—she knows who it is, knows what's about to happen. She sees now her timing has always been just a bit off—if she had leapt on my back, slid her tongue up my neck and wrapped her legs around my waist seven seconds ago, this phone call may not have been answered. We may have kissed, we may have shared the bottle with Bulch and Cherise, toasted to love. I might have led her out through the human tidal wave of the Electric Fox Bite, into a cab, pressed myself into her, led her up the stairs of my home, opened the door, made love on the couch, turned on Star Trek reruns, gotten stoned, made guacamole. We might have become donut partners, woken up in the morning with whiskey jelly donuts on our minds. Seven seconds. That's all it takes to change an entire life.

She looks at me, turns her head away. "Damn," she says. "It's her."

I nod my head. "I can't take you home." I run my hand across her cheek, pull it back, take one last look, and bolt towards the door, pushing my way through the gyrating Spacemachine fans, slamming my thumb into the "answer" button on my phone. "Phoenix!" I yell over the noise.

"Hello?" she says back. "Hello hello?"

"Phoenix! Hold on a sec!"

I push and scrape through the sea of body odor and ripped up shirts, beer splashing across my face, down my neck, cigarettes singeing my arms, until finally I'm out the door, on the sidewalk, out of breath in the eastern night.

"Phoenix," I say, sucking in air.

"Where are you?"

"I love you."

There is one pure, heart wrenching, long pause. Time stops, freezes. I take a look at the building behind me, the windows rattling, the heat emanating off of it. The cops roll past once again, take a long look at me, flash their teeth, keep moving. "I love you," I repeat. "I want to come home. I want to eat burritos with you. I want to make whiskey jelly donuts with you. I want to watch you in the sunshine, I want to watch you in the ocean, I want to touch you in the western sky. And I'll never fuck up again. I'll give you everything you want. I'll reverse the trash, I'll pull everything back up from the drain, from the toilet, put it back inside of you. I can do it all. I can do it with you."

"Then come here and do it," she says. "And we'll forget about the past. We'll build our life on new experiences, not old."

"Fuck the old," I say. "Only new. That's what life's all about. The past is gone—fucking meaningless."

"Come to me, right now."

I look around the city. I see the people. I always see the people first, their feet, up to their chins, never my surroundings. The people are what make the city—not the sculptures of angels on the cement stairwell of the Victorian building across the street, not the brick sidewalk I'm standing on. We are people living in ruin, we are people living for each other. We are the city, we are the east and we are the west and some of us belong to one or the other. What do I have here without Phoenix? I'm nowhere. I belong to nothing. I'm Midwestern at best.

"I'll do it. I'm gonna buy a ticket right now."

"What about all our shit?"

"Fuck it all. We don't need any of it."

"Can't just leave it in the house."

"Bulch'll sell it for us. He'll understand. We'll give him fifty percent or some shit."

Another pause. The sound of chewing. "Know what I'm doing right now?" she asks.

"What?"

"Eating a Tapatio burrito."

"God I would kill for one of those right now."

"I've had one every single day since I got back. I think I've been using the burrito as a substitute to you—it definitely tastes better.

"Not as good as you though."

"That goes without saying."

"I want to go back to the way it was before. I want to go back to the canyon, struggle, but at least have the eucalyptus and the giant oak, and the stars. I want to hear the waves crash, I want to watch the fog roll through the canyon at four o'clock, I want to drink too many beers at Ghost Sea Tavern, I want to walk home from the bar with you, up Fernwood Pacific, sweating and laughing, up that winding road to our overpriced rental."

"I want you to make fish tacos for me, real fish tacos, cuz fish tacos don't taste the same out there. Need the Pacific air surrounding the taco. That's what the real tortilla's made of—Pacific air."

I smile and the will-call girl looks at me and she smiles too because smiling is contagious, and then I look around myself and see the few Spacemachine fans without tickets, stuck outside, unable to witness the double Whiskey Jelly Blues, and they're all smiling, screaming wild anecdotes at each other, passing a bottle and a laugh between them. This is life. Life is worthless without a smile, without a bottle, without a laugh. A smile is worth a thousand dollars, ten thousand dollars, a hundred thousand dollars, one million. I haven't noticed smiles lately, only frowns, only the negative—never smelled those roses. Right now, I'm the richest man in the world, swimming in gold coins, barely able to lift my head above the precious weight. This generation, my generation, isn't so bad. We've got tight pants and mental problems, confusion and republicans, wars and democrats, but we move forward, we move we move we move, because we're bursting at the seems here in America, nowhere else to go, pressed to the edges of our continent, and so, the only place left is within ourselves, within each other. We are all the new Wild West. Lewis and Clark row down the rivers of our veins. Billy the Kid rides off into the sunset of our eyes.

"Lets forgive ourselves," I say to the night, and my generation nods their heads. "I'm hanging up. I'm buying a ticket on my phone. I'm coming home as soon as I can. Next flight. Don't care how much it costs."

"I love you," she says. "I love you, and I forgive you, and I forgive myself."

"I love you," I respond. "And I forgive myself."

We hang up. I've made the decision. I've rewritten my history. I find Southwest Airlines on my Smartphone, I purchase my "Gotta Get Away" ticket—flight leaves at 6 am. Six hours to kill. I can't find a taxi on my side of the street. They all seem to be going the other way, the opposite direction—an omen? Or a boon? To my right, a block away, I see a cab at a stoplight, light on, in service. No hesitation. I dart into the intersection without looking left. I see the flying headlights when it's too late. My breath stops, I throw my hands in front of me. My feet plant as if I've become part of the asphalt. I can't run. A deer in headlights. Funny, in that millimoment, that's what I think. That's what my death thought is. Not Phoenix, not Aunika, not Choose Your Own Adventure erotica, not swimming in the Mediterranean, or a tall glass of beer. "A deer in headlights." Pathetic. Unpoetic. I'll change it. "A deer in headlights" is about as good as what a certified public accountant would think. I think to myself, "How many moments have I wasted in my life?" and in that moment, I see everything I could be doing— standing naked on a cliff in Spain, living on a dairy farm in Bretagne, spending a thousand nights in Ibiza. I hear the screeching of the breaks, hear my voice shriek into the night, trail off into the distance until it all goes black with silence, stillness.

Shit. That was close. I open my eyes, see the car an inch from my legs. I raise my hand and say "Sorry," then gingerly saunter, cautiously, carefully across the street, hailing the taxi as I do. He stops for me. I hop in the backseat, alone.

"Where you headed?" the cabby asks.

"Home," I say.

He looks at me like I'm crazy.

"West," I say.

He slams his foot to the pedal, starts the meter, pulls into traffic. He's Afghani. You can tell by the little flag of Afghanistan attached to his dashboard. He says, "The west is the best," in a perfect Jim Morrison drugged-out croon, and I laugh.

"Damn, that was perfect!" I say.

"I love Jim Morrison," he says. "The lizard king." He sticks his tongue out, twisting the volume knob up on his radio.

If you give this man a ride/ Sweet memory will die

I watch the city pass through the windows just as I did an hour ago, but now, it seems different, filled with faces, possibility, life, energy. The east is just the east and the west is just the west. You can live here or there if you give up who you are and where you're from, become reborn, wash it all off, throw it down the drain, pull it all back up when you need to. You can live anywhere. We can live anywhere. I can live anywhere. Neon signs flash through the window, sparkle across my skin, turning it from pink to red to blue.

When we arrive at my house the cabby sings, "This is the end, beautiful friend."

I pay him an extra ten dollars, for The Doors. "Thanks, Lizard King." I stand out on the sidewalk, take a good long look at my house, the front porch. It looks different somehow—inviting. I see the roses, the buds open even though it's night, and the fragrance is stronger than it was a few days ago, spreading out, painting the night—I can almost see the ribbon of red whipping out from the petals. I take the steps up to the front door two at a time, twist the doorknob, flip on the light switch, run to the fridge, pop open a beer in celebration, not depression, not hell, not worry. I drink it down, drop the needle on the record player, tear off my shirt, dance my way into the bedroom, remove the underwear and the bloody pillowcase from the pillow, grab the razor from the nightstand, head back into the kitchen, throw it in the trash. We've come full circle— I'm going home. I toss a few pairs of jeans and a few shirts into a suitcase, I zip it up, I dance my way through the living room to the bathroom where I grab my own razor, some shaving cream, some hair junk, dance back out into the living room, drop it into the suitcase. I open the refrigerator door, find the avocados I bought the other day in anticipation of Phoenix's return, raise one up to the sky, say "I sacrifice this avocado to you, oh God of Guacamole, for the generous blessing you have bestowed upon me," then slice into it, grab the cilantro, jalapenos, onions, salt, and pepper, whip it all together, open a bottle of wine, dump it all into bowls and glasses, slide into the couch and turn on Star Trek reruns, watching Uhura shake across the screen with her untouchable fashion sense—that miniskirt and her glow-in-the-dark neon green hoop earrings—until I can barely stand it any longer, close my eyes, fall asleep...

The alarm goes off at four a.m. I open my eyes. I've got seven missed calls. Four from Bulch, three from Cherise. I call a taxi company, tell them I need to be at the airport at five and they tell me they'll be here in fifteen minutes. I look around the room. What can I take? What do I need? I walk over to the record player, grab my Gun Club record, push it back into its sleeve and slide it into my suitcase. That's it. All of my life can be contained within this suitcase, that record, that woman.

In the taxi, I send a text to Bulch and Cherise—*Don't let the yam-yam bite you back. Keep the goatfuckers at arms-length and the rattlesnakes on the other side of the river.*

Three minutes later, I send a text to Cliff—*The double dragon thought he was too fat for a bikini. I'll see you in six hours.*

Cliff, drunk, with his arm around his brother inside their loft, drawing up the blueprints for the Mustard Brothers shop with a bottle at their side, only grins, pours them both a shot of hooch. "The Mustard Brothers ride," he says. "Now where do you think the waterslide should go?" And Charlie just giggles.

I could tell you all about the six-hour flight back to Los Angeles, how I drank four tiny bottles of vodka and sat next to an ex-boxer whose teeth chattered the entire time, but I'd rather take this time and tie up some loose ends...

Bulch and Cherise got wasted at the Spacemachine show, rolling banana oil down their tongues, went home, fell asleep in the bathtub, woke up, and decided in one year, they would get married, in a ceremony, at the original site of the Woodstock celebration. After a few hours of research, piecing together what happened to Yasgur's farm, they realized that wasn't such a hip idea—at least the Woodstock part. They're not hippies—somewhere in between. Bulch said, "How about Rangoon?" And Cherise just smiled.

"Are there snakes?"

"There're snakes everywhere, my love. The trick is to let em pass without getting bitten."

Aunika—she's beautiful. Her outfits are incredible. How many poems could be written about her eyes? About her lips? About her hair and hips? Aunika pushed herself through the crowd right behind me after I left her at the Spacemachine show, followed me all the way out, watched me through the window, talking on my phone, ran out the door when I was almost killed by a car, then waved at me, unnoticed, as I pulled away in the taxi cab. She took three deep breaths, began crying, walked home, took a shower, and went to bed. She thought to herself, "I'll dream. And that will be my life. And someday, maybe, my dream will become real." In the morning, she pulled herself up and threw herself headlong into the donut business—whiskey jelly donuts? Huh. It's possible.

And what about that certified public accountant? Well, he's doing just fine—finished up the last of his clients who filed for an extension just this afternoon and spent the entire rest of the day cleaning his bathroom and ordering a couple cases of wine from California, before looking on eBay for used suits in his size.

***

Los Angeles. The end of the west. Nine a.m. She stands there in a dress made of synthetic orange peels. In her hand, a burrito, wrapped in tinfoil, grease from the carne asada dripping from the bottom. And behind her, Cliff and Charlie, tattered leather boots, worn and salted Stetson hats, a "Not in My Pussy" button attached to a well oiled brown suede vest, both shirtless, sweating, stand with a brown bag at the end of an outstretched arm. I walk out, as if in slow motion, into the dry heat, taste the gasoline and smog on my tongue, feel the cool of the Pacific Ocean rise into my heart, the heat of the Santa Ana winds fill my lungs, the traffic of The 405 and The 101 forge into my gut. I arrive at her, again, like the first time I met her. I drop my suitcase, I press my tongue into her, feeling the wounds of yesterday disappear underneath her saliva, run my hands up her thigh, and squeeze.

"I love you."

"I love you."

"I love you."

"I love you."

"I love you."

"I love you."

This is home. This is whiskey jelly donuts. This is Mustard Brothers. We love each other. We are all brothers, brothers and sisters.

THE END

CPSIA information can be obtained
at www.ICGtesting.com
Printed in the USA
FSHW02n0815080918
52046FS